SPAWN OF CHAOS

She saw his eyes first. They were like banked fires burnt almost to embers, hot and crimson and searing. The eyes smiled at her, laughed at her, and the full, sensual mouth below the hook of a nose smiled too.

Ygorla didn't shrink back. She remained motionless, knowing with a blend of instinct and learning what manner of creature this was.

"Why should Chaos have decided to send one of its demons to visit me?"

For a moment, her visitor's expression registered surprise. Then he laughed, a quiet laugh many mortals would have found chilling. He raised her hand to his full lips and kissed it. When he spoke again, his voice was a sibilant whisper that thrust a spike of ice and fire through her heart.

"I have waited fourteen years to make myself known to you, Ygorla. *For you are my daughter. . . .*"

Please be sure to ask your bookseller for the Bantam Spectra Books you have missed:

The Death Gate Cycle by Margaret Weis
    and Tracy Hickman
Dragon Wing
Elven Star

The Darksword Trilogy by Margaret Weis
    and Tracy Hickman
Forging the Darksword
Doom of the Darksword
Triumph of the Darksword

The Riftwar Saga by Raymond E. Feist
Magician: Apprentice
Magician: Master
Silverthorn
A Darkness at Sethanon
Prince of the Blood

Philip Jose Farmer's The Dungeon
Book 1: *The Black Tower* by Richard Lupoff
Book 2: *The Dark Abyss* by Bruce Coville
Book 3: *The Valley of Thunder* by Charles de Lint
Book 4: *The Lake of Fire* by Robin Bailey
Book 5: *The Hidden City* by Charles de Lint
Book 6: *The Final Battle* by Richard Lupoff

Rose of the Prophet by Margaret Weis
    and Tracy Hickman
The Will of the Wanderer
The Paladin of Night
The Prophet of Akhran

The Books of the Kingdoms by Angus Wells
The Wrath of Ashar
The Usurper
The Way Beneath

The Chaos Gate Trilogy
Book I

THE DECEIVER

Louise Cooper

BANTAM BOOKS

NEW YORK · TORONTO · LONDON · SYDNEY · AUCKLAND

For Jane Johnson
with thanks for so much help,
enthusiasm and friendship

THE DECEIVER
A Bantam Spectra Book / January 1991

ISBN 0-553-28821-0

Bantam Books are published by Bantam Books, a division of
Bantam Doubleday Dell Publishing Group, Inc. Its trademark,
consisting of the words "Bantam Books" and the portrayal of a
rooster, is Registered in U.S. Patent and Trademark Office and in
other countries. Marca Registrada. Bantam Books, 666 Fifth
Avenue, New York, New York 10103.

PRINTED IN THE UNITED STATES OF AMERICA

RAD   0 9 8 7 6 5 4 3 2 1

THE DECEIVER

1

Physician Carnon Imbro didn't normally take kindly to being roused from his bed in the small hours between first and second moonset. But the nature of this particular summons, and the fact that it was brought by Chiro Piadar Lin in person, overrode more selfish considerations, and Carnon shook himself fully awake, stopped only to belt a loose robe over his night garments against the autumnal cold, and hastily followed Chiro toward the castle's north wing.

They hurried through the maze of passages, darkened and empty at this hour. Chiro's face was set and grim in its frame of curling brown hair, and as they started down a flight of stairs, Carnon said quietly, "Have you woken anyone else?"

"No. I thought it would be more prudent to consult you rather than alert the other adepts." A quick, pallid smile. "I'm sorry, Carnon. It's a hazard of your calling."

Carnon grunted acknowledgment. "You haven't yet told me exactly what happened."

"He came into my room; half an hour ago, maybe a little more. I woke, and saw him standing at the foot of my bed—gods, I thought for a moment that something had come for my soul! And he looked strange, Carnon. I barely recognized him; that was why I was so shocked."

"Strange?" Carnon queried.

Chiro shrugged. "It's hard to put it into words; or at least, into words that don't make a nonsense of logic."

"You forget," Carnon said dryly, "that as well as a physician, I'm also a fifth-rank adept. Like you, I don't necessarily look for logic in my dealings with the world."

1

"Yes, of course . . . forgive me." Chiro relaxed a little, yet there was still a peculiarly hunted look in his eyes. "But truly, Carnon, this was downright bizarre."

"Tell me."

"Well . . . you're familiar with the portrait that hangs in the gallery above the dining hall? The one painted just a few years after the Change?"

"I know it well."

"The man in that same portrait was standing in my room."

The physician looked at him sharply. "You're sure you weren't dreaming?"

"I'm certain of it. It was Keridil—but Keridil as he was more than fifty years ago. I know how easily the eye can be deceived, especially in moonlight: but it wasn't an illusion. I *know* it wasn't."

Carnon was silent for a few moments. Chiro Piadar Lin, of all men, wasn't given to fancy or delusion; he was sober and practical almost to the point of stolidity, and if he said a thing was so, it was so. The vision, then, had been a true one, and to Carnon its implications were clear. This was the first sure sign that the soul of Keridil Toln, who for sixty years had ruled as High Initiate of the elite caste of sorcerers known as the Circle, was beginning to break free of mortal constraints in preparation for its last journey. Though they had all known that this time must come, nonetheless the knowledge sent a chill shaft, like the thrust of iron, through the physician's heart.

He said: "What happened then?"

Chiro shrugged. "He just looked at me—you know that peculiar intensity his looks have sometimes; as though he's seeing some extra dimension that the rest of us are blind to. I asked him if anything was amiss, if I could help him—"

"You still saw him as a younger man?"

"No. That phenomenon lasted only for a moment. I asked if I could help, and he said, 'Chiro, I'm going to the Marble Hall now.' "

"Just that?"

"Just that." Chiro glanced about him. "He didn't need

to say any more, Carnon. He knew I was aware of what he was trying to do."

"And you didn't try to dissuade him?"

"No, I didn't." Chiro stopped walking and turned to look keenly at the other man. "It's a personal quest, Carnon, and one that he's been trying to resolve for half a century. However much his mind may have deteriorated now, he was once a very formidable sorcerer. Who can say that the gods won't see fit to grant him what he seeks, now that his life's almost over?" He started forward again. "Besides, he's still the High Initiate. I haven't the authority to stop him, even if I wanted to."

"True enough." Carnon accepted the point. "But that makes me wonder just *why* he should choose to apprise you of what he meant to do in the first place."

Chiro frowned. "Me in particular, do you mean?"

"Well, anyone, if truth be told. After all, there's little enough logic in the idea of waking a colleague in the dead of night for such a seemingly valueless reason." Carnon looked obliquely at his companion, then smiled a little grimly. "I know what you're thinking and I also know you won't voice it, so I'll voice it for you: logic isn't Keridil's strong point these days, though it grieves me to say it. But really, Chiro, I think you're as aware as I am of why it was you, and no other, whom he chose to seek out tonight."

Chiro hunched his shoulders. "No, Carnon. I don't accept that."

"Like it or not, you'll *have* to face it and accept it before much longer. You know that Keridil's view accords with that of all the higher adepts—"

"The final decision will rest with the Circle Council, not—"

"And with Keridil, and the Matriarch, and the High Margrave. There's no need to tell me what I know as well as you do. But it's virtually a foregone conclusion, and there's no point in your trying to deny it. You're a sixth-rank adept, the highest grade but one; you're due to undergo the initiation trials for seventh rank, and there's little doubt that you'll pass. You're a skilled sorcerer and a superb diplomat. In short, you're the best man among us all. And Keridil wants you to become High Initiate when he s—no, don't give me that pained look, old friend; it's a fact, and we all have to face it—when he's dead. So if you wonder why he, in his poor confused mind, chose you in preference to anyone else to be the confidant of his secrets, you have your answer."

Chiro didn't reply. His face had set as rigid as mortar, as it so often did when he was faced with something that disconcerted him, and Carnon sighed inwardly. Chiro Piadar Lin's greatest defect, he thought, was a stubborn inability to acknowledge his own virtues, even to himself. It was a paradoxical trait, and one that Carnon, who was above all a pragmatist, didn't envy.

But as a pragmatist, he knew that to press Chiro on the subject would do more harm than good. He'd accept the facts in time: he'd have to. Until then, better to let the subject lie. They both had more immediate matters to concern them.

He said, "Well, whatever Keridil's reasons for doing what he did, you were wise to alert me. We'd best find him without any more delay."

The two men emerged into the castle courtyard and began to cross toward a colonnaded walkway that flanked the north wall. The court was a vast, silent well of intense shadow, dwarfing the feeble glow of Chiro's lantern; the ancient black walls seemed to crowd in on them, and the smaller of the two moons, almost at the full, glared down like a chilly, disembodied eye. Hunching his shoulders against the bite of the light but sly wind, Carnon glanced up at the vast, dim bulk of a titanic spire, the northernmost of four set at the castle's cardinal points. No lights glowed there, but he glimpsed—or imagined he glimpsed; he couldn't be certain—a peculiar shimmer in the air at the spire's summit, as though some unearthly energy had briefly flickered into life. He looked away and would have thought no more of it: but suddenly Chiro stopped and a faint frown crossed his face.

"Chiro?"

The adept raised a hand. He seemed to be listening, though Carnon could hear only the rustle of wind in the vines that rambled over the castle walls and, in the distance, the ever-present murmur of the sea. But then, after a few more seconds, he too heard, or rather felt it. A vibration, faint but increasing, that seemed to emanate from the flags beneath his feet as the ancient stones picked up and transmitted it through his bones.

Chiro was looking at the sky, and quickly the physician did likewise. The moon was taking on a ghostly halo of dark and slightly unhealthy colors, and its orb had begun to distort as though its light were being refracted and twisted out of true. Then Carnon saw that something was shifting against the sky's pewter-dark background, dimming the stars, tingeing the night with disturbing hues that seemed to hover on the edge of the visible spectrum. The vibration was gaining strength, almost audible now as a far-off, shivering moan, and Carnon gripped Chiro's arm in consternation.

"Gods, Chiro, how long has it been?"

"Two years. Maybe more. I'd almost forgotten what they were like . . ."

"It couldn't be a regular storm?"

"No." Long experience had taught Chiro that there was not and never could be a comparison between any natural storm and the aeon-old phenomenon now marching toward them out of the north. The oldest and most emphatic manifestation of Chaos-driven power; the voice, some said, of the gods themselves.

"No," he repeated. "Be in no doubt of it, Carnon. There's a Warp coming."

Sixty years ago, before the Change, the massive, supernatural storms known as Warps had been the scourge of the world. In an age ruled solely by the seven gods of Order, Warps had been the only surviving manifestation of Chaos whose overlords somehow maintained that one foothold against all the efforts of Order's human servants to eradicate it. Since the titanic and cataclysmic battle which saw the overthrow of Order's rule, the triumphant return of the Chaos gods and finally the establishment of a new equilibrium between the eternally warring forces, terror of the Warps had lessened; for where the lords of Chaos had once been feared and reviled, now they were worshiped together with their counterparts in the realm of Order. And no one—except, Carnon reminded himself grimly, for the last few remaining survivors of that past age, whose numbers diminished with every passing year— could now remember how the world had been before.

Yet despite his knowledge and experience, which told him he had nothing to fear, something akin to an ancestral memory awoke within him as the first herald of the Warp hummed in his marrow, and glancing uneasily at Chiro, he saw that the other man felt a similar disquiet. Warps had become a rarity in recent decades: the gods had been true to their promise and no longer flaunted their power in the mortal world without good reason. This didn't fit with the established pattern, and Carnon didn't like it.

He said very quietly, "Why now, Chiro? Why now, after so long?"

Chiro gave him an uneasy look. Overhead a flicker of brilliant crimson light suddenly slashed across the heavens, silent yet shocking enough to make Carnon start as it momentarily lit his companion's face. Far, far away the vibrating rumble was beginning to shape into a sound redolent of howling, tortured voices.

"I don't know," the adept said tensely. "But it occurs to me that perhaps someone has called out and Chaos has answered."

Bands of dim color were forming in the sky, turning slowly but steadily like the spokes of some vast, ghostly wheel whose axis lay far below the northern horizon. Another flash, blue-green and sickly, hurled the courtyard into stark relief and a network of silver striations crackled sharply across the night. The physician's fingers, still holding Chiro's arm, tightened with an involuntary reflex.

"You think Keridil may have—"

"Called on Chaos? I doubt it, my friend. Not Keridil of all men. But if he *is* trying to perform a rite, who can say what might choose to respond to his summons?" His eyes narrowed as he looked toward the walkway. "I think we should waste no more time."

They quickened their pace, reaching the colonnades in a few strides and hastening under the shelter of the arches. At the far end of the walk a small and apparently insignificant door had been set into the wall; approaching, they saw that it stood part open, and ducked inside. Spiral stairs led down; the flight was worn with age and Chiro swore as he almost missed his footing in the uncertain lantern-light. Here, with the castle's bones surrounding them, sound was muffled but vibration carried strongly, and the gathering strength of the Warp could be felt as a near-physical presence.

"There'll be some sleepless souls in the castle tonight," Carnon observed, trying to mask his own unease with an attempt at levity.

Chiro glanced back at him but said nothing. Conscious of his disapproval, the physician fell silent again, and they continued on until at last they reached the foot of the stairs and another arched door. Beyond this lay the castle's library, darkened and silent, its air heavy with the familiar and faintly claustrophobic smell of leather and dust and old parchment. Walking carefully to avoid colliding with one of the reading tables, Chiro picked his way across the floor to where in a cobwebbed corner a third door, black as the surrounding stone and all but petrified with age, led off the library and into a narrow but oddly symmetrical passage. On the threshold Chiro paused for a moment to splay his fingers in a quick, reflexive gesture that conveyed respect to all fourteen of the gods, then led the way through.

Immediately the corridor began to slope perceptibly downward. A glimmer of grayish light relieved the darkness, gaining in strength and making the lantern unnecessary. Chiro blew out the flame and they continued on, until the light brightened into phosphorescent brilliance and the last door, their destination, came into view ahead of them.

As far as Carnon was aware, no one had ever known the nature of the metal from which the door to the Marble Hall had been made. Harder even than gemstone, yet peculiarly warm to the touch, it shone softly, steadily, casting long shadows behind them as they stood before it. A simple but effective lock was the door's only adornment; the key was entrusted to the High Initiate alone, but even before the door swung open at Chiro's experimental touch, Carnon had guessed that the key wouldn't be needed tonight. Keridil must have known they would come—why else would he have alerted Chiro to his intentions? For the sake of a trusted witness, or perhaps for the sake of comfort, he didn't want to be entirely alone in what he was attempting to do.

The door swung back on noiseless hinges and Carnon exhaled a soft, involuntary breath as the Marble Hall was revealed. No matter how many times he'd entered this place since his initiation into the Circle, the awe he felt for it never had been and never could be diminished by familiarity. This was the Circle's innermost sanctum, the heart of their stronghold, the greatest wellspring of their power. The hands which had built it in a long-lost epoch had not been entirely human; the dimensions it contained reached beyond mortal ability to comprehend. It was the place of the deepest worship, barred to all but the initiated and now used only for the highest and most solemn rituals.

The hall was filled with slowly pulsing light, a mist of pastel colors that shimmered like reflections on still water. Slim stone pillars were set here and there into the mosaic floor, their crowns obscured by the mist, and the farther reaches were lost in the haze. The oldest and most fragmented records in the library contained oblique hints that the hall didn't entirely comply with the known laws of time and space, and Carnon sensed a vastness around him that seemed to defy physical limitations.

He glanced at Chiro. "Should we go in?" His voice was a whisper.

The adept nodded. "Yes, but prudently. I'd prefer not to disturb the High Initiate unless we must."

They began to move slowly and quietly across the floor. As they advanced, something loomed ahead of them in the mist, seven shapes, huge and as yet indistinct, and though he knew what they were and had seen them many times before, Carnon felt a familiar clenching of his stomach. Seven statues more than twice the height of a man, each depicting two figures standing back to back and blending in a bizarre and faintly disquieting way. The figures were to all appearances human, but closer scrutiny revealed a disturbing air of something far beyond mortality. There was an aura about the proud faces, an edge to the sculptured bones, a disdainful remoteness in the calm eyes and curved mouths that spoke of a deeply occult inspiration behind their creators' skill. The world's greatest artisans had carved these statues in homage to the dawning of Equilibrium, and now the seven lords of Order and the seven lords of Chaos gazed eternally and enigmatically down at the adepts who practiced here in their name.

Carnon had stopped and was still gazing at the statues with near-mesmerized eyes when Chiro's hand on his arm dragged his mind abruptly back to earth.

"Over there," Chiro whispered. "By the farthest of the statues."

Carnon looked, and saw a solitary figure crouched before the seventh carved form. A fur-trimmed cloak that looked too heavy for the frail body beneath covered him, and long strands of white hair fell over his hunched shoulders. He was motionless, silent, and as yet, Carnon surmised, unaware of their presence. Feeling suddenly uncomfortable, he looked at Chiro with uncertainty in his eyes.

"Chiro, we intrude. I think perhaps we should withdraw after all."

Before Chiro could reply, the cloaked figure raised his head and looked over his shoulder. Even at this distance the ravages of intense emotion were visible on his face, and Carnon felt shamed by the knowledge that they had interrupted such a private moment. But even as he started to step back, the crouching man rose awkwardly to his feet and turned to face them.

Keridil Toln, for sixty years High Initiate of the Circle and one of the world's triumvirate of rulers, stared across the Marble Hall at his two closest friends. Then tentatively, queryingly, he said: "Chiro?" His voice, as fragile as his frame, created whispering echoes through the hall.

Chiro inclined his head. "High Initiate . . . forgive us, we didn't intend to disturb you. But we were concerned."

"Of course." Keridil made a vague, placatory gesture. "I appreciate your thoughtfulness." His gaze slid to Carnon. "And yours, Grevard. You are very kind."

Carnon and Chiro exchanged an uneasy glance as they recognized the name. Grevard had been the castle's senior physician before either of the two men was born, and a good friend to the High Initiate through the turbulent time of Change. But Grevard had been dead for forty years; his was an old ghost and one that Carnon had thought laid to rest even in Keridil's shadowed mind.

He walked forward and gently took the High Initiate's arm, lending him the support that Keridil was too proud to admit he needed. Keridil's hazel eyes, faded with age but still intent and aware in the fallen, hollow face, met his and he said:

"She didn't come. I hoped that this time it might be different, but . . . she didn't come. I couldn't reach her."

"Keridil." Chiro had moved to stand on the High Initiate's other side. "There's a Warp on the way. If your business here is concluded, I think it would be as well to leave the hall."

"A Warp?" For a moment an ancient memory seemed to stir; then it flickered and faded and Keridil frowned. "It's been a long time, hasn't it, since we had such a visitation?" He looked back at the statues. "I wonder . . . but no." A shake of his head. "It won't make any difference, not now." He looked at Chiro, noting in a detached way that these days their eyes were on a level. Chiro wasn't an overly big man; not so many years ago Keridil had been half a head the taller. But age had withered his stature just as it had withered his mind.

He smiled sadly at the adept. "I think I've finally lost what talent I had, Chiro. I knew the day must come, but I tried to resist it. I think that was a mistake."

"Keridil—"

"No, no, hear me out and don't try to be kind. I'm eighty-four years old and my faculties are failing." The smile became dryly self-deprecating. "I'm well aware that just now I called Carnon by a dead man's name, and I'm equally well aware that there have been other such lapses in recent months. And tonight I've faced the final confirmation of my decline." He indicated the statues behind them. "Tonight I tried to perform a Higher Rite, something I've done more times in my life than I care to remember. But this time there was nothing. No trance, no psychic elevation: nothing. It's gone, my friend. My skill as a sorcerer, my power. It's gone."

"Keridil." Chiro took his hand, feeling the parchment-dry fragility of his skin. "It distresses me to hear you say such a thing. You're a seventh-rank adept, the highest—"

"In name only now. Chiro, your loyalty touches me but there are times when loyalty must give way to reason. I no longer have the ability to call on the powers I once possessed, therefore I no longer have a useful role to play in our occult activities. From now on someone else must represent me at all Circle rites."

Chiro looked in appeal to Carnon, but the physician refused to meet his gaze. Helplessly Chiro said, "Keridil, one failure doesn't necessarily mean that your skills have deserted you!"

"Oh, I think it does. And in this, at least, I can trust my own instincts." The High Initiate turned again to regard the seven statues. From the central plinth the two greatest gods of all gazed silently across the hall, the aquiline, cruel, yet darkly humorous features of Yandros of Chaos contrasting sharply with the sterner serenity of Aeoris of Order. But Keridil's attention wasn't on the highest of the gods. Instead he looked to the seventh and last carving. One of this statue's faces bore a close resemblance to Yandros's, but the eyes were more feline, the mouth narrower, and the expression more contemplative. Slowly the High Initiate walked toward the figure and stood looking up at the motionless, graven features.

"You took her life," he said, and his voice was suddenly harder, pain and anger replacing the quiet frailty. "You could reunite us, you have that power. But you maintain your silence. Sixty years, and still you maintain your silence in the face of everything I try to do. Even tonight when I thought that at last I might have an answer, you would tell me nothing, you only made me realize that I haven't the power or the strength left to even try to compel you. Is this your last joke on me? Is this the nature of your revenge?"

Chiro and Carnon didn't dare to meet each other's eyes. Though this was the first time either of them had been witness to the private rites that Keridil conducted in the Marble Hall, they'd known of them for a long time, and knew, too, the bitter story of Sashka, who had been betrothed to him before the Change. Her name was never

11

mentioned in the castle, but the story of how—and why—
she had died was no secret. Keridil had lived with the
memory ever since, but had never been able to eradicate
the hope, however futile, that one day the powers of Chaos
which had taken her from him would allow her to return.
And in all that time he had wanted no other woman.

Suddenly the High Initiate's shoulders slumped as
though in utter defeat. He turned sharply away from the
statue, and Carnon hastened forward, as it looked as if he
might lose his balance and fall. He gazed anxiously into
Keridil's face and for a moment saw no trace of recognition. Then abruptly the High Initiate's trancelike look vanished. He blinked, smiled, and Carnon realized soberingly
that he had no recollection of what had just occurred.

"Carnon?" Keridil said inquiringly. "Is something
wrong?"

"No . . . not at all. You were—" Carnon cleared his
throat. "You were speaking of Circle matters, the rites."
His glance warned Chiro not to make any protest.

"Ah, yes." Keridil's face finally cleared. "As I said, in
this I can trust my instincts. I choose you, Chiro, to be my
proxy." He looked up at the adept. "I think you know,
don't you, my good friend, what I'm saying to you?"

Chiro couldn't meet Carnon's eyes and couldn't make
any response. He stared down at the floor, and the High
Initiate continued gently, "I also want you to write two
letters for me, Chiro. One to the High Margrave's personal
envoy on Summer Isle and one to the Matriarch in Southern Chaun. Ask them to come to the Star Peninsula as soon
as convenience permits." He saw Chiro's stricken face and
added, "I know it's not a task you relish, but the protocol of
these matters forbids me from putting my own hand to the
letters."

"High Initiate, I—" Chiro fell silent as he realized
there was nothing he could say.

Keridil flexed his shoulders. "Well, now. It must be
late, and I've detained us all." He looked about him at the
hall's quietly pulsing mist. "I shall return to my rooms and
you should do likewise. I'm sorry to have kept you both
from your sleep for so long." Politely but firmly removing

Carnon's supporting hand from his arm, he started to walk with dignity toward the door, then paused.

"The Warp might well be overhead by now. It will be exhilarating to witness one again after so long. But from a safe vantage point, eh, Chiro?"

"Yes, sir," Chiro said pallidly. "From a safe vantage point."

Long after the second moon had slunk away into the west, a solitary light continued to burn at a window in the castle's north wing. The Warp had come howling overhead in a wild furor of brilliance and thunder and gone rampaging on into the south, but Keridil Toln still sat at the window of his private sanctum, elbows resting on the stone ledge as he hunched over his single candle and gazed out at the night. Dawn wasn't far away but he felt no wish to rest. His need and desire for sleep had waned with the years and this was the one time of the day when he could truly be alone without the constant ministrations of well-meaning servants or fellow adepts.

Though grateful for their concern, he was glad that Carnon and Chiro had gone. He hadn't been at his best tonight—mentioning Grevard had been an unforgivable mistake and he only hoped that that had been the worst of his errors. These lapses were occurring with increasing frequency; Carnon said that they were an inevitable part of his decline, but still Keridil found them intensely frustrating. Most of the time he was as lucid as he'd ever been, but it was becoming impossible to predict when his mind might slip into the murky no-man's-land between reality and imagination, twisting past and present together in an impossible meld.

He shouldn't have gone to the Marble Hall tonight. He should have accepted the truth long ago—that all the prayers and rituals in the world wouldn't achieve the one thing he longed for and which remained forever beyond his reach. Instead he'd been stubborn, he'd refused to listen to the inner warnings, and now he'd suffered the final humiliation of realizing that he could no longer command even the most simple occult skills. His power—such as it had been—was gone.

For one reckless moment he considered the idea of walking out of this room, saddling a horse, and riding away across the causeway that linked the castle to the mainland, without a word to anyone. His destination wouldn't matter, it would simply be a last taste of freedom. But no: realistically, he doubted if he had the strength to saddle a horse unaided, let alone ride one for any distance. And to be selfish now, with the end so close, would be to shirk his final duty.

Duty. He smiled at the thought. For more than sixty years, since the death of his father had catapulted him, young and inexperienced and idealistic as he was then, into the role of the world's occult and religious figurehead, he had put duty before all else. Duty to his father's example, duty to the Circle, duty to tradition . . .

He moved slightly, and at his shoulder something caught the candlelight with a small golden flicker. Keridil looked down and saw that the High Initiate's badge of rank was still pinned to his fur-trimmed cloak. He fingered it, feeling the contours of the symbol that even after all these years he still couldn't entirely accept. A seven-rayed star wrought in gold filigree, and bisecting the star, a golden lightning-flash. In the old days the lightning-flash had been set within a double circle, but since the Change it had been agreed that the star emblem of Chaos should be merged with that of Order to symbolize the Circle's official position as servants of both those titanic powers.

Keridil, who had looked on the face of Aeoris of Order and on the face of Yandros of Chaos, knew that in his heart his outward acceptance of Equilibrium was a sham. Long ago, when Chaos had emerged victorious from the last battle for ascendancy between the gods, he had answered Yandros's mocking challenge to his loyalty and avowed that he would not change allegiance to save either his neck or his soul. He had kept that vow for more than half a century and it was an ember of comfort in his last days. What would become of him after death, he didn't know. But his conscience, at least, was clear.

Or was it? Suddenly an old, old memory lurched into

focus in Keridil's wandering mind. A fellow initiate, his childhood friend, betrayed not through the duty that had been his lifelong yoke but for the sake of jealous love. A friend who, triumphant at the last and revealing his true power, had interceded with Yandros to spare Keridil's life and restore him to his place at the Star Peninsula.

And the being who had killed the only woman Keridil had ever loved.

The candle sputtered, hissing. Keridil blinked and realized to his chagrin that tears had started to roll down his face and fall onto the window ledge. Tears. Gods, they were an old man's last refuge. Yet why should he not cry? Why should he not mourn her? Whatever she had been—a schemer, a betrayer, even a murderess; oh, yes, there was no point denying the truth; everyone in the castle knew the story well enough—she had also been beautiful and enchanting, and he had loved her. But she'd died horribly, agonizingly, punished for the evil her twisted mind had wrought. All the ceremonies, all the rituals, all the pleas that disgusted his soul even as he uttered them hadn't brought her back, for only Chaos had that power, and Chaos was no friend to Keridil.

No friend?

It wasn't a sound, it was an intangible, supernatural breath that seemed to waft through the silent room, skimming the surface of Keridil's consciousness and making him start like an animal surprised by a hunter. The voice— it was imagination, he told himself, no more—had a terrible familiarity. Not Sashka's; her voice was beyond the reach of his memory now: but another, one he'd never been able to forget.

Keridil turned from the window and stared into the shadowed room.

"Tarod . . . ?" he said softly.

Silence answered him. The bed hangings shivered as though in a draft, then were still once more. There was no supernatural presence, no unseen hand at the latch, no flare of catlike green eyes and soft laughter with the black light of Chaos breaking through the human mask. Tarod, whose mortal form had disguised the soul of a god, who had sent Sashka to perdition, was no more present in this room than he had been tonight in the cold stone of the statue in the Marble Hall. Tarod dwelt in another realm now; he didn't hear, didn't answer. He had nothing to say.

The candle guttered suddenly—it was no more than a stump—and went out. Darkness descended on the room, obliterating Keridil's faint and insubstantial shadow, and just for a moment he felt grateful for the dark, for it was a place where he could hide.

However, there was nothing to be gained from sitting here to no purpose. There had been no visions, no visitations; the sun would rise soon enough, and another day would begin. Another day. There wouldn't be many more now. Tomorrow, good, dependable Chiro would write his two letters and the messenger birds would carry them away south. Their recipients would understand the meaning of the message, and would come to help him choose the man who, soon, would step into his shoes. Keridil would be glad, so glad, to relinquish that burden at last.

He rose and moved slowly toward the bed. Even if sleep wouldn't come, he'd at least be more comfortable among fresh sheets and pillows. And perhaps, for once, the gods would be kind to him, and just for a little while he might rest without dreaming of things that were best forgotten.

2

"She shouldn't have come." Sister-Senior Fiora leaned out a little from the inglenook to watch the girl, who, aided by a white-robed novice, was slowly and awkwardly climbing the stairs toward the inn's upper floor. "I'm sorry if I'm speaking out of turn, Matriarch, but I only voice what we've all been thinking. She's in no fit condition to travel. For her own and the child's sake, we should leave her here in the morning and go on without her."

The other two sisters who shared the table had cast their eyes down, unwilling to be drawn into the debate. Ria Morys didn't need her seer's skills to know what they were thinking, and she pushed her plate away with a sigh, motioning for someone to refill her wine cup.

"I know, Fiora. And if I could turn back time I'd revoke my decision and grit my teeth against the tantrums that would result. But it's too late now; if we leave her here, someone must stay with her, and you're the only healer in our party. It can't be done. No one else is senior enough to take your place at the conference." She sipped her wine, grimacing faintly both at the musty taste and at her own uncomfortable thoughts. "Wise or not, Avali must come with us to the castle."

Fiora bristled faintly and her plump hands clenched. "But, Matriarch, speaking *as* a healer, I must emphasize—"

"*No.*" Ria didn't often use the tone, but every sister in the Southern Chaun cot from the highest senior to the youngest novice knew better than to argue with it. Heads at nearer tables turned curiously, then looked quickly and respectfully away again; the innkeeper peered anxiously from behind his counter. Fiora flushed.

17

"Sister Fiora, I appreciate and share your concern." Ria lowered her voice and placed both palms firmly on the tabletop. "But Avali is here, and I already have enough to worry about without contending with a long list of ifs and buts and wherefores as to why she should not be. You will oblige me, *please,* by saying no more of the matter."

There was an embarrassed silence. Then Fiora said: "Yes, Matriarch."

A serving girl appeared at that moment to clear the plates and ask if there was anything more they wanted. Her arrival broke the awkward hiatus, and thankfully Ria leaned back in her chair, letting her head rest against the warm stonework of the ingle as she tried surreptitiously to ease the tension in her shoulders. She was overtired, she knew; contrary to predictions, the weather hadn't been kind to them, and eleven days' journeying through hailstorms and knifing winds had taken their toll of her energy. Tomorrow, with the mountain pass ahead of them, promised to be the worst of all, but by evening—barring mishaps, which didn't bear thinking about—they should reach their destination.

And then there would be another kind of tribulation to be faced.

The servant went quietly away and for a few minutes a relatively companionable silence reigned, only faintly tainted by the aftereffects of the altercation. Ria closed her eyes, aware that she could easily fall asleep and equally aware that for the sake of her dignity she must not. She suspected that in recent months she had begun to snore when she slept, though she had no husband to confirm or deny it, and none of her colleagues, if they heard, would ever dream of mentioning it to her. Another sign of impending age, she thought wryly. It would be unthinkable for the Matriarch of the Sisterhood to sit snorting and grunting like an overfed herdbeast in full view of an inn full of travelers. Better if she retired to her bed. The autumn days were short in this northern latitude, and they'd need to start out at dawn if they were to complete their journey without another halt.

She rose, with a grace that was only a little dimmed by advancing years, and smilingly said her good nights to her companions. The sisters rose and bowed to her; the four men provided by the Southern Chaun Margrave to act as their escort saluted gravely. They would relax and talk more easily without her, Ria thought, and she could take the opportunity to look in on Avali and see that all was well.

The tavern-keeper, gratified and awed at housing the person of the Matriarch, had given Ria his best room, which boasted a southerly and therefore sheltered aspect on the building's upper floor and which was also as far away as possible from the noisy taproom. Not wanting to offend him, Ria had surreptitiously reorganized the accommodation and given up her room to Avali, taking a smaller adjoining chamber for herself and placing Fiora on the other side in case her services were needed. Now, graciously declining the offer of a servant to light her way, turn her bed down, and make up the fire, she climbed the creaking wooden steps and walked—cautiously, for the floorboards were old and uneven—to Avali's door, tapped, and entered.

Avali was in bed, her riot of fair hair falling over her shoulders and the bulge of her belly clearly visible under the innkeeper's best blankets. The novice who had accompanied her and who was now laying out her traveling clothes for the morning bowed to Ria and, at a gesture, slipped out of the room, leaving them alone.

"Well, Avali." Ria sat down on the end of the bed, holding her hands out toward the fire that crackled in the hearth. "Are you comfortable? Do you have everything you need?"

Avali grimaced. "The bed's hard. Though it's better than I might have hoped for in this region, I suppose."

Ria smiled thinly. "West High Land isn't the most sophisticated of the provinces."

"No. I've often wondered why the Circle should have chosen to occupy such a barren place when they could have gone to Southern Chaun or Shu, or even Wishet."

"It was the choice of the gods, child, not of men," Ria reminded her. "Don't worry; it will be different when we reach the castle."

Avali was intelligent enough to recognize the gentle

rebuke. For a moment she hesitated; then her expression broke into a sweet and self-deprecating smile only faintly tinged with mischief. "I'm sorry, Aunt. I've been a great trial to you these last months, haven't I?"

The smile, the tilt of her head, were so reminiscent of her father, Ria's younger brother, that the Matriarch couldn't maintain her irritation. Avali had inherited that same natural charm which even when she was at her most exasperating could turn aside any anger, and Ria sighed, admitting defeat.

"I wouldn't go so far as to say that, my dear. But I will be thankful when this . . . interlude, shall we say, is over." She twitched a corner of the bed covering that wasn't quite straight. "I still wish that I'd stood firm and refused to bring you with me on this journey."

"Oh, Aunt." Avali looked at her with a disarming blend of contrition and sorrow. "Such an event will never happen again in my lifetime. If I'd missed it I couldn't have borne the disappointment!"

"Your parents will be a good deal more than disappointed if any harm befalls you," Ria said with feeling. Avali's protest was, she knew full well, a sham; the girl had no real interest in the conference at the Star Peninsula but had been motivated by a mixture of curiosity and whim, plus the fact that after four months in the quiet, orderly atmosphere of the Matriarch's Cot she was thoroughly bored.

Avali looked down at her stomach, and her face registered distaste. "No harm will come to me, Aunt. I'm disgustingly healthy and I've two more months yet before the baby's due to be born. Aile—she's my oldest friend, you met her last year at the spring Quarter-Day festival—Aile rode everywhere on horseback until just fifteen days before her child's birth."

"Your friend Aile had a husband to care for her. And she wasn't so headstrong as to attempt the pass through the northern mountains in her condition."

"I have you to care for me, haven't I? And Sister Fiora. Everyone knows she's the finest healer in three provinces." The firelight reflected in Avali's eyes as she shifted her position, and they glinted almost wickedly. "Dear

Aunt Ria, how *could* I not have come? To see, in person, the very same High Initiate who walked with the gods themselves all those years ago—"

"And who doesn't care to be reminded of it now," Ria interrupted sharply. "You're too free with your tongue, child. I've already told you that those events are not to be mentioned in the High Initiate's presence, and I'll thank you to obey me in that if in nothing else!"

"Yes, Aunt." She cast her gaze down. "I'm sorry."

The show of penitence didn't fool Ria for a moment, but she was too tired to press the point. Stiffly she rose to her feet.

"Well, then, if there's nothing more you need, best that we all try to sleep. You have your handbell?" She glanced at the bedside table, saw the small ornate bell within Avali's reach. "Good. But do try not to disturb Sister Fiora unless you really have to."

"Of course." Avali kissed the older woman's cheek as Ria bent over her; it was a formal salute but there was warmth in it. "Good night, Aunt."

If she'd been a wiser woman, Ria reflected wryly as she blew out the candle beside her bed, she wouldn't have made the mistake of opposing Avali's initial request to accompany her to the Star Peninsula. It was only that cussed determination to have her own way in all things that had made the girl so staunch in her resolve; if the request had been acceded to from the first, she would probably have lost interest and been content to remain safely at the Southern Chaun cot. However, at the first hint of opposition, Avali had used every wile in her repertoire —and, just like her father's, her repertoire was consider-able.

From the start of this whole affair, Ria thought, she should have told her brother Paon that Avali's foolishness in allowing herself to become pregnant out of wedlock was no concern of the Sisterhood's, and that no, she was not prepared to take the girl under her wing so that the baby could be quietly born and given away and Avali returned to the family fold with her marriage prospects unblemished. She should have stood up to him and refused to let him abuse the privileges of her rank. But she'd always been susceptible to Paon's blandishments, as she was now to Avali's, and his conspicuously generous endowment to the Matriarch's Cot had set a seal on the obligation. So four months ago Avali had arrived in Southern Chaun with a pack train of baggage, and since that day Ria's quiet, ordered life had been in upheaval.

It wasn't that Ria didn't love her niece. When she chose to, Avali could charm the birds from the trees, and though she had been shamelessly spoiled by her parents, her basically sweet nature hadn't been entirely ruined by their indulgence. But Ria didn't approve of allowing children such a free rein as Avali had always had, and certainly didn't approve of parents who allowed their unmarried daughters to broaden their experience of the world by taking lovers whenever and wherever the fancy struck them. Perhaps she was old-fashioned, but she had never been able to reconcile herself to the notion, however widely accepted it might be in the higher echelons, that there was no shame in a girl bearing a child or two before marriage, provided that such children weren't allowed to become a handicap to their mothers' later prospects. The unwanted babies could easily be adopted and forgotten, and Paon had suggested to Ria that the most convenient solution would be for the Sisterhood to take charge of Avali until the birth and thereafter find the child a good home. If it was a girl, he had suggested, they might even like to adopt it themselves and bring it up to train as a novice in their order.

Initially Ria had been shocked by the suggestion. The baby, she had pointed out, was Paon's own grandchild: did he have no personal feelings for it? And what of Avali's views on the matter? Patiently—he had always treated her as though she were a younger sister rather than six years his senior—Paon had explained that Avali had no wish to keep the baby and he wouldn't dream of trying to persuade her against her will. Besides, what better start in life could any child, let alone a child without a father, have than the wealth and security of the Matriarch's Cot?

It was this last and seemingly careless remark that had finally persuaded Ria to capitulate. If its own mother and grandfather weren't prepared to love the hapless infant, then she would. With grim amusement she reflected that she, a lifelong spinster with little experience of children, was hardly the ideal surrogate parent; but no matter. Her grandniece or -nephew would find a welcome under her roof and she would do the best she could.

Since making that decision, Ria had often wondered whether her motive was a little more selfish than she liked to pretend. Although there was no bar to marriage in the Sisterhood, the higher-ranking sisters rarely found it possible to combine their responsibilities with those of a husband and family, and certainly every Matriarch in the order's history, so far as Ria knew, had been single. In devoting herself to her work, she had sacrificed something that most women took for granted, and a part of her regretted it. The Matriarch's role, as one of the world's ruling triumvirate, was a lonely one; lonelier, she felt, than the lot of the High Initiate or the High Margrave, both of whom were expected to have families of their own. They, after all, were men, and as a fact of simple biology they were less intimately concerned with the rearing of their children. For a woman it was necessarily different, but though she had always accepted her destiny with a good grace, Ria's maternal instincts weren't entirely subdued. Perhaps, she thought with a small and unfamiliar surge of eager pride, she would at last have the chance to indulge those instincts through Avali's child.

The fire in the room's hearth was dying down to embers, casting only a dim, deep red glow across the lime-washed walls and ceiling. Ria settled deeper under the bedclothes, admonishing herself for allowing her wandering thoughts to keep her awake. If they were to complete the journey through the pass in one day, she shouldn't be wasting precious resting time in such self-indulgence or she'd be fit for nothing in the morning. Sleep, she told herself sternly. And stop being such a silly, sentimental old fool.

"Tell me about the High Initiate, Aunt Ria."

Ria looked over her shoulder to see Avali's staid gray mare drawing level with her own horse. In the late-afternoon sun that slanted down into the gorge, the girl's hair looked like spun gold, and her eyes were alight with excitement. The Matriarch smiled.

"My dear child, what can I possibly tell you?" She pursed her mouth in mock severity. "If you'd paid attention to your tutors when you were little, you wouldn't need me to remind you now of what you should have learned then!"

Avali laughed, drawing glances and smiles from the four armed men who rode with the small convoy. "Oh, I know all the *history*. My history tutor considered me his star pupil! But you've *known* the High Initiate for so many years—not as a figurehead, but as a person. That's what I want you to tell me about."

Ria looked at the track that wound on between the cliffs ahead of them. She estimated that they would reach the mountains' edge within half an hour or a little less: hardly enough time to recount her view of the most intelligent, complex, and yet ineffably sad human being that she had ever met. Besides, so many of her memories were rooted in the past, and Chiro's letter had warned her that Keridil had declined greatly in recent months. Perhaps it was to be expected in someone of his years, but nonetheless Ria grieved for the man he had been.

She said aloud: "Oh, my dear, how can I hope to encapsulate what Keridil Toln is—or was—in just a few words?" Her horse started to stray from the path, attracted by one of the few stunted bushes that somehow managed to grow among the shale, and she checked it back. "You see, he is one of the last people alive who remembers the days before the Change, when the gods of Chaos challenged the rule of the gods of Order and we mortals won the right to worship as we choose."

"The time when Equilibrium was restored?"

"Yes." So Avali hadn't entirely neglected her catechisms, Ria noted. "In our lifetimes, we have known no other way than that of balance. We say that Order rules the day, and Chaos the night, and that that is right and proper.

Try, though, to imagine how you might feel if you had been born in a time when there were no gods but Aeoris of Order and his six brethren." With a reflexive, unconscious gesture she held up a hand, fingers splayed, in the traditional sign of respect to the deities before continuing. "When Keridil Toln first became High Initiate, Yandros and the other lords of Chaos had no place in our world. They had been banished." She smiled, an odd little moue. "They were considered to be demons."

Avali's eyes widened and she, too, made the gesture, as though to ward off the gods' displeasure.

"Keridil was taught—as was every man, woman, and child—to worship Order alone, and to revile Chaos as evil," Ria went on. "For example, did you know that we used to be called the Sisterhood of Aeoris, rather than simply the Sisterhood?"

Avali shook her head.

"Oh, yes. We too served Order, and Order alone, however strange that may seem in these enlightened days. That's what I'm trying to explain to you, Avali. Our High Initiate was brought up to look upon Chaos as an enemy, yet for sixty years he has been the religious leader of a people who pay equal homage to both Chaos and Order. Can you even begin to imagine what that has meant to him?"

For a few moments there was silence but for the muffled, rhythmic beat of hooves. Avali's brow furrowed as she tried to grasp the import of what the Matriarch had said, and Ria realized a little regretfully that the lecture had no real meaning for her. To Avali's generation—and to the secular souls of Ria's, for that matter—the time of Change was too remote to have any relevance. Avali said her prayers to Aeoris in the morning and her prayers to Yandros at dusk, she attended the Quarter-Day rites which marked the changing of the seasons and the bounty of Equilibrium, but beyond that she had no concept of or interest in the religious structure of the world. In these peaceful days the gods demanded no more of anyone.

Ria added, "All I'm trying to explain to you, Avali, is that the experiences which Keridil Toln underwent so long ago must have left their mark on him. He has been a fine and noble High Initiate, but I think he has also been a very lonely man." Then she smiled wryly. "My position has brought me into close contact with Keridil over the years, but I couldn't truthfully say that I know him." She paused. "I rather doubt if anyone does."

An angry flicker at the periphery of vision drew her attention at that moment, and she looked up to see that the sun, swollen and crimson at this season and this latitude, was vanishing behind the huge granite crags that reared to either side of the pass. One sliver remained, burning hotly and etching the cliffs' edge with fire; then abruptly the gorge was plunged into intense shadow and a damp chill stole over them like a cloak.

Ria shivered. Far overhead the sky was still clear; the day was waning fast, but the weather, always unpredictable here in West High Land province, had held. She gave silent thanks for the gods' beneficence, then looked at Avali again. The girl was also staring at the point where the sun had disappeared, and her face was thoughtful. She said:

"The High Initiate has never been married, has he?"

"No, he hasn't."

"Then he has no son to succeed him."

"That's true."

"And that's why he's called this conference." She looked away from the clifftop, suddenly fixing Ria with an intense gaze. "To choose his successor. He's dying, isn't he?"

Ria shut her eyes. She'd deliberately said nothing to Avali about the reasons for her visit to the castle, but there seemed little point in trying to maintain the pretense now, and a sense of desolation took hold of her.

"Yes, child," she said quietly. "He's dying."

Ahead of them, a horse whinnied and a man's voice shouted, echoes bouncing back from the cliff walls and blurring his words. Ria's eyes flicked open and she looked along the track to see thir escort's leader gesturing to her and grinning.

"Matriarch!" This time she heard him more clearly. "The end of the pass is up ahead. We've arrived!"

Suddenly Ria realized that the scent of the sea was in

her nostrils. The dark spell broke and she urged her horse forward, aware of the others following suit behind her. The path turned sharply—and she heard Avali's gasp, echoed by the voices of the younger sisters, as they emerged from the mountains' shadow and the Star Peninsula lay spread before them.

The mountain range opened onto a sweep of giddying clifftops whose ramparts marked the northernmost edge of the world. From the riders' vantage, a sward of lush green turf rolled away in a gentle slope before narrowing to a buttress that jutted from the mainland into an ocean stretching before them into infinity. Beyond the cliffs' edge lay a vast and glittering horizon from which the setting sun seemed to explode as if from the dawning of the world. Gold, amber, and crimson stained the sky, merging into the sea's huge mirrorlike shimmer; headlands and small islands were silhouetted like scars on the titanic vista. And closer, blacker even than the cliffs against the sun's gory brilliance, stood their ultimate destination.

The Castle of the Star Peninsula reared from the bleak finger of a huge and ancient stack of granite that stood proud from the buttress's edge. The four great spires cut the sky's livid glare, and a massive shadow reached out toward them across the narrow and perilous span of a rock bridge that divided the stack from the mainland.

Mingled emotions moved in Ria as she gazed at the scene. The castle and its titanic backdrop were an awesome sight, and the awe didn't diminish with familiarity. How many hundred generations of men and women, whether pilgrims, prisoners, or seekers of arcane knowledge, had stood in this very space and felt the same sense of sheer insignificance that the castle had engendered throughout its long and turbulent history? No human hand had raised these massive, brooding stones; though for centuries before the Change it was the stronghold of those who worshiped Order, the castle had been created in an age long before the dawn of known history by the whim of Yandros, mercurial and unpredictable lord of Chaos, and for centuries—perhaps even millennia—its denizens had presided over a mad world in which Chaos was the only watchword. Those days were long gone, as were the days of Order's unopposed reign, but even now peace seemed to sit uneasily among the castle's towers and battlements. The black, sunless walls still held a powerful echo of ancient and ominous power that time had been unable to erase.

Ria's horse sidestepped suddenly, tossing its head with impatience, and the Matriarch realized that she had been sitting motionless, lost in her thoughts, for some minutes. Her companions were waiting dutifully for her order; she turned to them, smiling an apology, and gestured toward the dizzying span of the rock bridge.

"The crossing is a good deal wider than it looks from here, and quite safe," she said. "Our horses are locally bred and trained to have no fear of it, but if anyone would feel happier on foot or being led, she need only say."

One of the younger sisters immediately and gratefully dismounted, and Avali stared doubtfully at the bridge. Two stone cairns marked the beginning of the span; beyond them the ground fell away over a thousand-foot drop. Ria smiled sympathetically and held out a hand.

"Give me your mare's reins, child," she said. "Then you can close your eyes while I lead you. No one will think any the worse of you for it." Conspiratorially she added, "When I came here for the first time, my sister-seniors virtually had to carry me kicking and screaming to the bridge. You'll grow accustomed to it."

Avali bit her lip. Though she'd heard many dramatic tales of the castle crossing, she hadn't been prepared for the terrors of its reality. For a moment she wished she'd stayed in Southern Chaun; then the thought of what awaited her on the bridge's far side strengthened her resolve. She couldn't possibly turn back. If all the friends who envied her this chance of a lifetime ever got to hear of it, she'd never live down the shame.

She returned Ria's smile wanly, and nodded. "Yes, Aunt." The wind, a vicious and tricky little snap from the northwest, caught her hair and lifted it like a nimbus about her head; the gray mare stamped, and Avali shut her eyes tightly, praying silently to all fourteen of the gods to keep her safe as the horses moved off down the slope and out onto the great sweep of the Star Peninsula.

3

The first formalities of the conclave were to begin on the morning following the Matriarch's arrival. Ria was thankful to have no obligations on her first evening in the castle, for it gave her time to settle herself and her entourage in their quarters without undue haste. Her initial concern for Avali proved unfounded, much to her relief: her niece had suffered no ill effects from the journey and was enraptured by the castle's grim magnificence. She behaved perfectly, demurely charming to everyone she met, and after a substantial meal, served privately to the Sisterhood party, as they were too weary to face the more social atmosphere of the main dining hall, Ria gave private thanks that Avali was not after all proving to be a liability, and slept more soundly than she had done since leaving Southern Chaun.

The morning, though, brought a sobering of her mood. First, there was a brief but poignant meeting with Keridil, who had been too frail to greet her on her arrival the previous evening. She was shocked and deeply saddened by the changes in him, and when they kissed each other's cheeks she had to struggle not to let her expression betray her. Even the warning in Chiro's letter hadn't fully prepared her for the extent of the decline: it was as if the flame of Keridil's life had dwindled to nothing more than a barely glowing ember. He was not, she thought with a pang of grief, the man she had known and called her friend, but a stranger.

Upset by the encounter, Ria pleaded a headache and took a light lunch alone in her room, gently dismissing even Sister Fiora. She was still toying with the meal when someone tapped lightly on the door; expecting the return of Fiora—who could be very persistent—Ria called tiredly and a little testily, "Come in," and looked up to see a tall, spare man in his early fifties on the threshold.

"Matriarch." Her visitor smiled tentatively. "Carnon Imbro told me I might find you here. I'm sorry, do I disturb you?"

"Lias Barnack!" Ria rose, her irritation forgotten, and extended both hands. "Why, it must be near on five years!"

"Four and a half." His smile broadened as he took her fingers and bowed over them. "Sad to say, my duties don't allow me to visit Southern Chaun as often as I'd like."

"Well, it's a great pleasure to see you again. Sit down, sit down."

He hesitated. "I'm interrupting your meal."

"Not at all. I'm not hungry; I've only forced this much down to stop Sister Fiora from fussing." She relaxed back onto her chair, and he took another a few feet away. "I met the High Initiate this morning. The experience has somewhat diminished my appetite."

"Ah, yes." Lias inclined his head. His fair hair, Ria noticed with a twinge of envy, showed no signs of graying; he bore his increasing age well. "I had an interview with him yesterday." A pause, and he sucked breath in through his teeth. "Forgive me, Ria, but that's why I wanted to seek you out as early as I could. As we're both to be involved in this conclave, I felt it would be as well to discuss a few things in private, and candidly I think we'd be wiser to discuss them sooner rather than later."

Ria understood. Painful though they might be, the formalities must be completed, and it was obvious to anyone that Keridil had no more than a few days left to him. Her voice as Matriarch, and that of the High Margrave Solas Jair Alacar, would carry a good deal of weight in the election of the new High Initiate. Solas Jair Alacar couldn't attend the meeting in person, for by an old and established rule the High Margrave never left his court on Summer Isle in the far south except in the case of some dire emergency. The purpose and origins of that tradition were lost far back in the past—it was popularly supposed to stem from a more despotic age, when for a High Margrave to go openly among his people was to invite assassination—and Ria privately felt that in these enlightened times the rule was both nonsensical and an encumbrance. But somehow the precedent had never lapsed, and so Lias, as the High Margrave's envoy, was empowered to speak for his master.

She said: "I've made no secret of my own view as to who Keridil's successor should be. Chiro Piadar Lin is, I feel, the only wise choice."

Lias nodded. "Certainly Keridil favors him. I've also talked to a number of the senior adepts here at the castle—purely informally, of course—and I think the Circle Council will be almost unanimous in agreeing."

"And the High Margrave?"

She didn't miss the faint glint of cynicism that showed in Lias's eyes. "In truth, Ria, and strictly between the two of us, I don't think that the High Margrave has any real interest in who takes the reins at the Star Peninsula. Provided he can be assured that Chiro won't divert him from his parties and his pleasures, he'll ratify the choice and not think twice about it."

Ria looked at him shrewdly. "He has, I presume, been given that assurance?"

Lias shrugged. "Naturally, I felt it the merest duty to put his mind at rest. At a time like this, the last thing we need is any unnecessary complications. I've told Keridil that the High Margrave's view accords with the majority."

The Matriarch let out a small but emphatic sigh of relief. Privately, she didn't feel that either she or the High Margrave was qualified to have any say in the new High Initiate's election, and believed that it should be a matter for the Circle alone. They, after all, knew Chiro as no outsider could hope to do; his family had long-standing connections with the castle and he had lived from an early age among the men and women of the Circle. Keridil himself had initiated him at the age of fourteen, and only the Circle could truly judge his skills and his worth. But when the High Initiate had no son to follow in his footsteps, protocol dictated that the election of a successor must be a matter for wider debate.

The trouble was, she reflected, that of all the world's triumvirate of rulers, the High Initiate's role was the most

31

complex. First and foremost, he must be a master of the sorcerous arts, for he was the interlocutor between mortals and their gods, guardian of all aspects of religion and philosophy, and in arcane matters his word was law. These days he must also be a politician, a diplomat, able to counsel and support the High Margrave in more mundane matters, especially so when, as now, the High Margrave was either unable or unwilling to trouble himself unduly with the responsibilities of rulership. Keridil had been the perfect Lord Spiritual to the Lords Temporal personified in Solas Jair Alacar and his father, Fenar, before him, and Ria believed that Chiro would do justice to Keridil's example. But was she, or Solas, or anyone else outside the Circle for that matter, a fit judge? Certainly she had few illusions about her own place in the scheme of things; as little more than diviners, healers, and teachers of children, the Sisterhood carried far less influence than either the Circle or the High Margravate, and the Matriarch was the least of the world's three figureheads. How could she possibly presume to venture her opinion on who should lead the Circle, when she knew so little of its arcane workings?

Lias was watching her, and suddenly he said, "Ria, I suspect there's something wrong. You look as though you and your conscience aren't the best of friends."

She frowned, realizing that her expression had given her away, and silently wished a pox on Lias's shrewdness. Knowing that dismissal or dissembling wouldn't satisfy his curiosity, she sighed, and replied: "I was simply asking myself whether we outsiders have any right whatsoever to impose our views on what should be strictly a Circle matter."

"It's expected, Ria." Lias smiled sympathetically. "Above all else, the triumvirate must be seen to confer and agree. As a lifelong politician, I assure you that such a public show has a miraculous effect on the confidence and trust that the ordinary people place in their rulers. They see it as a safeguard against imbalance, and so they are content to pay their tithes and leave us all to perform our duties without interference."

"Lias, you're a cynic!"

"Nonsense. I'm a *realist*, not the same thing at all. But

32

seriously, Ria, I think you should banish your conscience back to where it belongs. I know Keridil has set a precedent that will be hard to follow, but it's obvious to everyone—the Circle included—that Chiro is admirably fitted for the role. You've made the right choice."

Her lower lip jutted. "I'm sure you're right. Yet I still have doubts about the principle of the whole thing. I feel that I'm meddling."

Lias chuckled. "If that were true, d'you think the Council of Adepts would sit back and let you dabble your fingers in their soup without argument? No: it's a showpiece, Ria, and everyone here knows it."

"Everyone except me, you mean," Ria retorted with some rancor.

"No, I do *not* mean. You simply have a more active conscience than the rest of us, and it's one of the many things we love you for."

The Matriarch treated him to an old-fashioned look. Then abruptly she laughed. "You're an unrepentant rogue, Lias. When all else fails, you fall back without scruple on your charm and your wiles. You remind me," she added with mock severity, "of my brother."

Lias pulled a face. "How is Paon these days? It's been a good many years since I last saw him."

"Oh, he doesn't change. His fortune grows bigger with every grape harvest, as does his good opinion of himself."

"Lord of all he surveys, eh? And the complete antithesis of his sister. Truly, Ria, I shall never understand how one family could have produced such a modest daughter and such an immodest son!" He grinned at her. "You almost outvie Chiro in your lack of self-esteem!"

"And the older you get, the more foolish you become," Ria rejoined tartly. "Chiro and I may lack the self-aggrandizement that's so beloved of you Summer Islers, but we're both sensible enough of our own qualities. And one of those qualities is to know our limitations."

Lias chuckled again. He and Ria had always enjoyed their half-serious sparring matches: over the years these had become an integral part of their friendship. "Mind you," he said, "Chiro must know that he's better qualified than anyone else to step into Keridil's shoes, even if nothing would induce him to admit it. Did you know, by the way, that he was recently confirmed into the seventh rank?"

"Was he? No, I hadn't heard." Seventh rank was the highest of the Circle's grades, and though the nature of the initiation trials was known only to the higher adepts, Ria was aware that very few ever achieved it. Even if he didn't have a spark of vanity in his soul, Chiro must be privately proud of the accolade.

"It's a splendid achievement," she said.

"A timely one too. Keridil, I understand, was especially pleased. The seniority it confers will make Chiro's future life that much easier when it comes to dealing with recalcitrant Province Margraves or argumentative scholars. No one would *dare* quarrel with a seventh-rank sorcerer for fear that he might send one of his tame demons to visit them when they least expect it!"

"*Really*, Lias!" However, Ria couldn't help smiling at his irreverence. "You are a very vexing man," she said. "I should be angry with you, but instead I find myself in your debt. You've cheered me considerably in the past few minutes and helped restore my sense of proportion." She looked at her plate, and prodded the cold food uncertainly with a fork. "I'm even beginning to feel hungry at last, though I can't say that this looks very appetizing now."

Lias smiled. "I've been too busy to beg a morsel since shortly after dawn. Do you think that if we go to the dining hall together and do our best to look lost and helpless, one of the stewards will take pity on us?"

Ria laughed. "I'm sure of it."

He rose, and indicated the door with a bow. "Then allow me to escort you, Matriarch. We'll feast and drink and enjoy an hour or two of satisfying gossip, then face the rest of the day's business with contented equanimity. Is that a bargain?"

The Matriarch beamed at him. "A bargain."

A banquet to welcome the castle's distinguished guests was held two days later. Although anticipation of the confer-

ence which would taken place on the following day subdued the atmosphere a little, it was still a splendid
occasion, and Ria found much to enjoy despite her underlying sadness. There were old acquaintances to renew,
new ones to explore, and above all the opportunity at last
to talk informally to Chiro Piadar Lin. The two of them
were old friends—they'd known each other since Ria's
earliest visit to the castle as a junior sister many years ago—
but thus far there had been time for no more than a few
brief encounters in the course of business, and Ria looked
forward to a more social meeting.

During the meal she was greatly complimented to
find herself placed on the High Initiate's right hand at the
banqueting table, with Chiro beside her. Keridil was the
perfect host, yet the strain of coping with the occasion was
obvious; he looked weary, spoke little, and against the
bright background of the castle's great hall, which was
aglow with torches and alive with music and the animated
conversation of the guests, he seemed a shadow figure, a
living ghost.

Chiro was keenly aware of the extent to which Keridil's decline had discomfited Ria, and though his gallant
determination to divert her was sometimes a little obvious,
she was grateful for the respite he provided. There was
also some comfort to be had from the knowledge that the
High Initiate was at least well enough to take part in the
festivities. Ria had presented Avali to him a little earlier in
the evening, and he seemed to have taken an avuncular
liking to the girl, so that when the feasting was over and
the celebration relaxed into more informal talk and
mingling, Avali was thrilled to find herself invited to sit at
the High Initiate's own table.

Once she had convinced herself that Avali wouldn't
drink too much wine and speak out of turn or indiscreetly,
Ria moved about the hall, greeting the few old friends
whom she hadn't yet had time to see since her arrival, and
ensuring that the other sisters were at their ease. Her
younger colleagues in particular were overawed by their
surroundings, but the warmth of their welcome and the
kindness of their hosts was breaking down the barriers,

and gradually even the most timid were overcoming their shyness.

Chiro intercepted her as she was returning to her own table after a brief consultation with Sister Fiora. Taking her arm, he guided her to one of the benches that flanked the walls, and indicated a flagon of wine and two cups that stood on a small table nearby.

"Especially for you, Ria." He smiled at her. "A flask of the Shu Celebration vintage."

"You remember that?" She was surprised and touched.

"Your fondness for that especial wine? Yes, I remember very well." He waited until she had sat down, then poured for them both and lowered himself onto the bench, handing her one of the cups as he did so.

"To your continuing good health. And perhaps I should add, to the health of your future . . . grandniece or -nephew, is it?"

Ria smiled. "Yes. Thank you."

He glanced to where Avali still sat with Keridil and his companions. "The High Initiate has taken a great liking to your niece. He told me earlier that he thinks her both pretty and intelligent, and a refreshing companion."

"How very kind of him." Ria was deeply gratified but felt in all conscience that she should add, "I do feel, though, that I really shouldn't have allowed her to come. It's a great imposition on the Circle's hospitality."

"Not at all. Keridil specifically wanted this conference to be a social occasion as well, and he's glad to have some new faces about him. If he finds your niece's company entertaining, then we're all more than grateful to you for bringing her." Ria smiled, and the adept continued: "Fiora tells me that the girl's staying at your Cot until the birth of her child, and that you're considering adopting the infant as your own."

The question, Ria knew, stemmed simply from friendly curiosity. Even so, to her own annoyance she felt her cheeks flushing.

"Well, yes, that's true. The child will be, as you say, my own grandniece or -nephew, and I do feel a sense of responsibility." She regarded him obliquely, then decided to be candid. "Especially as no one else seems to be concerned for its welfare."

"Ah. Then Avali doesn't intend to keep the child, or to marry its father?"

"No. In fact . . . no: I shouldn't say such a thing, Chiro, not even to you. It feels so disloyal. But . . ." It would be a relief to express herself honestly, Ria thought. She had grown tired of keeping her feelings to herself or pretending that they didn't exist. Chiro, of all people, would surely understand.

She continued, lowering her voice confidentially, "I mean that I don't know whether Avali even knows who fathered her child." There, it was out. "She won't tell anyone, not even her parents, and I suspect that she has been . . . somewhat liberal in the distribution of her favors."

"Ah," Chiro said again.

Ria made a helpless gesture. "I know it's not unusual these days, but there's something about such careless indulgence that discomforts me. I'm growing old and prim, I suppose, but I can't help it. It's as if Avali doesn't *care* about the new life she's responsible for creating."

"Part responsible," Chiro corrected with a thin smile.

"Well, yes. But you understand what I'm saying, Chiro, don't you? To Avali, the child is a nuisance to be tolerated for as short a time as possible, and then to be . . . foisted onto someone else and forgotten."

Chiro nodded. "I've encountered similar problems among some of the young women at the castle. Like you, I find it hard to understand their attitudes, especially so within these walls, where, if nothing else, we try to teach some kind of moral code."

"Perhaps that's a problem we both share. You in the Circle, I in the Sisterhood—perhaps we're living in an ivory tower."

Chiro smiled at her again, a little wistfully this time, she thought. "Is that such a bad thing?"

"Ohh . . . I don't know. So much has changed in the years of Equilibrium. I wonder if we older folk are in danger of becoming too anachronistic for the world. Maybe the Avalis of this age are in the right, and it's time for our tower to be demolished."

A short distance away, where a group of young men had gathered by the great hearth with its roaring fire, a burst of immoderate laughter broke out. Chiro looked pointedly at the group and the noise instantly subsided.

"I'm not sure that I can be that pessimistic," he said as he turned back to the Matriarch. "Our duty—the duty of the Circle and the Sisterhood, I mean—is to look to the future, and I don't think we've shirked it. In fact, I firmly believe that the likes of you and me still have a good deal to contribute."

Ria sipped her wine, and her eyes over the rim of the cup were suddenly warm. "Perhaps you're right," she said. "Perhaps I'm simply starting to grow nervous at the thought of trying to bring up a child at my time of life. I'm so *inexperienced*, Chiro. What does a confirmed old spinster know of child rearing?"

"In your case, everything she needs to," Chiro said firmly. "As a sister you've been concerned with children for most of your life. You've taught them their catechisms, sheltered them, guided them, trained them—and you have a natural way with them, as I've seen on many occasions. Don't fret so, dear Matriarch. The infant could have no better guardian."

"That's as may be, and I think you flatter me." Ria felt the time had come to change the subject, and added, "I've burdened you with my own tribulations for too long: this is the first chance we've had to talk in more than a year. Tell me of your own affairs, Chiro. How are Karuth and Tirand?"

He smiled, a rare smile of complete ease that transformed the sterner lines of his face. He was deeply and proprietorially fond of his two children, whom he'd cared for unstintingly since his wife's untimely death six years earlier. "They're both well," he told her. "Karuth is fourteen now, and quite the young woman. She's already reached second rank, and is studying with Carnon to become a physician."

"She's been accepted into the Circle? I didn't realize."

"She was initiated last year. Tirand will follow her after his next birthday."

"You must be very proud of them both."

Chiro looked embarrassed, then gave way and laughed. "Yes, I can't deny that I am."

"And with good reason. I imagine that Karuth will make an excellent physician-adept. She has just the right blend of dedication and curiosity. Does she still continue with her music?"

"Oh, indeed. In fact you'll hear her a little later. There's to be a musical entertainment before the evening ends, and the High Initiate asked especially that she should play."

"He was always very fond of your family," Ria said.

"Indeed, and he's been like a grandfather to Karuth and her brother. Tirand worships him." Chiro hesitated; then: "He'll take Keridil's death hard."

It was the first time either of them had made any direct reference to the real purpose of this gathering, and however reluctant she might be to speak of it, in the wake of her talk with Lias there was one question that Ria knew she must ask before tomorrow's meeting.

She said, "Chiro, I'm glad you said that. About Tirand's respect and admiration for the High Initiate. Because, as I'm sure you realize—"

He interrupted her. "Matriarch, I'd rather not—"

"No." She spoke emphatically, and saw his face flush at the gentle rebuke. "We can't evade the issue, Chiro. Keridil is dying and has no son to succeed him. Therefore a successor must be chosen from the ranks of the higher Circle adepts, and that is why this conference has been called." She met his gaze, her eyes quietly authoritative. "You must know that both the High Margrave and I want you to be the next High Initiate, and that we await only the Circle's agreement to ratify our choice. If you consent to the appointment, then Tirand will be your heir, with all the responsibilities that implies."

"Tirand is only nine years old."

"I know. But soon he'll be ten, and old enough to become an Initiate. Answer me truthfully, Chiro—is he aware of the strictures and demands that being the High Initiate's son will impose on him?"

Chiro considered the question for a long time. Then,

slowly, he said, "Yes. I believe he is. And—if it comes to it—he'll accept them."

"As you will?"

He looked at her unhappily, not wanting to admit what they both already knew. "Yes," he said at last. "As I will."

Ria let out a pent breath. She had the answer she needed, and when she spoke again her voice was gentle.

"We'll need a man of your caliber in the days to come, Chiro," she said. "Don't feel that you're betraying Keridil by acknowledging that while he still lives."

She knew from Chiro's pallid smile that she'd read his thoughts accurately. He took her hand and held it tightly for a few seconds.

"Thank you, Ria. I'm very grateful for your kindness. And for your honesty."

"Nonsense." Ria was suddenly embarrassed, and looked away. "Drink your wine and let's refill our cups. Tonight, as you pointed out earlier, is a festive occasion, and I want to propose a toast."

The vintage bubbled from the flagon, sparkling in the light of the hall's myriad torches. The Matriarch touched her cup to Chiro's and the small sound rang pleasingly.

"To the future," she said. "Whatever it may hold."

Chiro smiled, and the smile broadened into a grin as he allowed himself to relax. "Yes. To the future."

The senior councillors rose as one from their seats on the high dais, and the sound of a heavy staff rapping three times on the surface of the great table brought silence to the hall.

"The vote is completed." Carnon Imbro, who combined his duties as physician with those of council spokesman, turned and bowed to Keridil, holding out the High Initiate's staff of office in a formal gesture. "The Council of Adepts now respectfully requests that Keridil Toln, High Initiate of the Circle, shall ratify the decision taken by this conclave."

The entire assembly rose to their feet, and Ria allowed

herself to exhale a small sigh of relief. Not one vote had been cast against Chiro Piadar Lin, and though the High Initiate had the power of veto should he choose to use it, she was certain—*almost* certain, she amended, not wanting to tempt fate—that nothing would go amiss now.

Keridil stood up. One hand gripped the table edge to steady his uncertain balance, and with the other he held up the staff so that all present could see it clearly.

"My friends." His voice caught; he coughed, cleared his throat. "The unanimous vote of this conference is that seventh-rank adept Chiro Piadar Lin shall be named as heir and successor to the position of High Initiate of the Circle. It only remains for me to . . ." He frowned, hesitating; Ria felt her pulse skip and tried not to catch Lias Barnack's eye, but then Keridil's face cleared again as the confusion passed. "It only remains for me to express my wholehearted agreement with the vote, and to set my seal upon the ratification of the council's decision."

The silence held as the High Initiate bent forward. A signet ring glinted in the torchlight, Carnon dripped wax onto the document that lay on the table, and with great solemnity Keridil pressed the ring's seal firmly into the molten pool.

It was done. Ria shut her eyes, feeling relief flood her as a susurration of approval rippled through the hall. Chiro, to his embarrassment, was being urged forward from his place, and as he stepped up to the table the High Initiate embraced him as though he were blood kin. Keridil's gnarled fingers squeezed the younger man's upper arms, and, unheard by anyone save Chiro, he said softly:

"The gods go with you, my son. I pray there'll be greater peace in your time than there was in mine." He looked up, and Chiro saw the true extent of the weariness in his eyes. "Thank you, Chiro. Thank you for releasing me."

Though she wasn't privy to the exchange, Ria felt moved in a sense she couldn't define even to herself as the the two men stepped apart. At the far end of the hall the double doors were opening, and with the inrush of fresher air from the passage outside came a palpable release of tension. People were flexing stiff shoulders, moving from their seats, mingling, talking: she heard someone give vent to the sheer relief of laughter, and the careful formality of the meeting collapsed into thankful relaxation.

It had been, Ria thought, a taxing day. This morning, Carnon, diplomatically apologetic, had informed her that the banquet's exertions had taken a toll of the High Initiate's strength. Keridil would, he hoped, be well enough for the conference, but a postponement might prove necessary. Ria had spent the morning in prayer, asking the gods' indulgence in granting the High Initiate a respite, and thankfully the gods had been kind. As the assembly milled around her, some already making toward the doors, she glanced back to where Keridil sat at the table with Carnon and Chiro at his side. They were talking together; she saw Keridil smile, heard his laugh, as quiet as the rustle of falling leaves, and gave silent thanks. The worst was over. Her party would rest here another day, perhaps, and then—

"Matriarch!"

Ria turned. Sister Fiora was weaving through the throng toward her, and as soon as she saw the healer's expression she knew that something was amiss.

"Fiora?" She started toward the other woman, colliding with someone in her sudden haste and bowing a quick but purely reflexive apology. "What is it?"

Fiora was flushed and breathless, her eyes alarmed. "Matriarch, it's Avali. Is Physician Imbro here?"

Ria threw a swift glance back to the dais. "He's with the High Initiate. Fiora, what—"

"I must speak to him, Matriarch. I think Avali's time has come."

"Her *time?*" Ria was stunned. "It's only seven months!"

"I know. But an hour ago she began to complain of pains in her back, and then . . ." Fiora shook her head. "I believe the baby's about to be born and there may be serious complications. I would have come to you earlier, but I couldn't gain admittance to the hall while the conference was in progress." She gestured helplessly.

Ria cursed under her breath. Fiora was a skilled healer and knew the precise extent of her abilities. If she needed

Carnon's help, then something must indeed be very wrong.

She said: "Is Avali in her room?"

"Yes, Matriarch."

"Go back to her, quickly, and do what you can." Keridil would understand, she told herself. "I'll bring Carnon to you. Go, now!"

Whey-faced, Fiora hurried away, and Ria hastened toward the dais. To her relief, there was no question or confusion: Carnon Imbro heard her request and instantly excused himself, calling as he followed Ria down the hall's central aisle for someone to fetch his medical bag and bring it to Avali's room.

The castle corridors seemed endless. Ria tried to tell herself that both she and Carnon were too old to run, but by the time Avali's door came in sight they were both moving at undignified speed.

And even from the far end of the passage they could hear the girl screaming.

Fiora met them at the door, and her face was by now drawn with stark fear. "Matriarch . . . Physician Imbro, she's in such pain, I don't know what—"

Carnon didn't wait for further information but shouldered past Fiora and into the room. Avali lay spread-eagled on her bed, her face contorted into a mask of blind panic. Her mouth hung open and the sounds coming from her throat were the pleadings of blind, mindless agony. Two of the younger sisters were trying to hold her down, but her back was arching spasmodically, her limbs thrashing and flailing as she tried to escape her pain.

Appalled, Ria turned on Fiora as the physician hurried across to the stricken girl.

"How long has she been like this?"

"I don't know, Matriarch! When I left her to find you, she was in pain but calm. Then, when I returned—"

Her words were drowned as Avali's voice rose to a shriek that cut the air like a blade. Through it Ria heard Carnon's voice soothing, saw him bending over the bed, then abruptly Avali's screams ceased and she slumped back, her breast heaving violently as the spasm passed and gave way to exhaustion.

43

Ria approached the bed. "Carnon? What is it? What's wrong with her?"

The physician gave her an uneasy look. "I don't know yet, Matriarch. But her child will be born tonight, and I fear the birth won't be normal."

Ria drew breath between clenched teeth. "What can we do?"

Before Carnon could answer, running footsteps sounded in the passage and a tall, gawky girl in her early teens entered the room with his medical bag. Karuth Piadar, Chiro's daughter. He'd mentioned that Carnon had recently taken the girl on as an apprentice, Ria recalled, and with an exclamation of relief she hastened to take the bag from Karuth and pass it to the physician.

"Can I help, sir?" Karuth asked. Her gray eyes were wide with a mixture of sympathy and professional interest as she looked at Avali and her anxious attendants.

Carnon shook his head. "Not now. Wait outside—I'll call you if I need you." He looked up, scanned the worried faces of the sisters as though he'd forgotten they were there, then focused on Ria. "In fact, Matriarch, I'd prefer it if you and your ladies left—except for Sister Fiora, that is. There's nothing you can do, and you'll be more comfortable in your own chambers."

"If you're sure we can't—" Ria began worriedly.

"Quite certain. If you please, Matriarch . . ."

Ria didn't argue; he knew best. Followed by Karuth, she shepherded the sisters out and closed the door behind them. As the other women entered the adjoining room, Karuth touched her arm respectfully.

"Physician Imbro will do whatever's right, Matriarch. He's probably the finest physician in the whole world."

"Bless you, child, I know." Ria forced a wan smile, touched by Karuth's fierce loyalty. She started to follow the sisters, but slowly, reluctant to leave in case—a foolish feeling, probably, but she couldn't help it—Avali should call out for her. Karuth kept pace with her, glancing back every few seconds at the closed door, and in an attempt to distract them both from thoughts of what was taking place in Avali's room, Ria said:

"Your father tells me that you intend to become a fully qualified physician, Karuth."

The girl blushed. She had always been a shy child, Ria recalled, and dawning adulthood hadn't yet given her the confidence to overcome it. "I . . . hope so, madam. If Physician Imbro considers I have the ability."

"I'm sure he does. Still, I hope your studies won't force you to neglect your other talents." Ria's smile grew warmer. "I did so enjoy your playing at the banquet, my dear. They say the manzon is a hard instrument to master, but your skill is quite remarkable."

Karuth's flush deepened and an extraordinary mixture of pleasure and acute embarrassment showed on her face. "Th-*thank* you, Matriarch," she managed at last. "I don't deserve your praise."

"Nonsense: there's no need to be so modest. You're a highly gifted girl in many ways, Karuth. You should thank the gods for it. Your talents will be of great value to the Circle now that your father—" She stopped as she saw Karuth's eyes widen. Of course: the girl hadn't been present at the conference, so couldn't yet know the outcome.

"Oh, dear," the Matriarch said wryly. "I'm sorry, Karuth. This is hardly the most apt time or place for you to hear of it, but . . . yes, your father will be the next High Initiate."

The dark, heavy curtain of Karuth's hair swung across her face as she turned her head away, and her angular shoulders relaxed visibly. After a moment she looked back at Ria and returned her smile.

"I'm glad you told me, Matriarch. I'd been thinking about it, wondering, but with this emergency I didn't like to ask anyone."

"Are you glad?"

A pause. Then: "Yes . . . yes, I *am* glad. And so proud for Father."

"He was Keridil Toln's own choice. The vote was unanimous."

"Was it?" Warm pleasure suffused Karuth's face. "That's very gratifying."

She was genuinely delighted, but at the same time Ria saw that her solemn, serious mind was already projecting into a future that had suddenly taken on new and far-reaching obligations. Karuth had a deeply ingrained sense of responsibility, a result perhaps of her mother's early death, which had cast her effectively into the role of nurturer to her father and younger brother. That responsibility would be redoubled now. She would be Chiro's helpmeet, and when the time came for Chiro to be called to the gods, she would transfer her loyalty from father to brother and be a pillar of strength to Tirand too. She would have been a great asset to the Sisterhood, the Matriarch thought. Yet she couldn't help a sense of regret for the woman that Karuth might have become, had her future not been quite so bound to the demands of duty. There were uncomfortable parallels with the pattern of Ria's own life, though the child was too young and too inexperienced to see them as yet. Ria only hoped that in the years to come, Karuth wouldn't have cause to regret her father's elevation.

She put the thought from her mind and was about to make some innocuous remark to continue the conversation when a cry, unhumanly inarticulate, cut through the corridor from the room where Avali lay. Ria jumped like a shot bird, involuntarily clutching at Karuth's arm. "Sweet gods, what—"

There was a flurry of sound, and the door opened to reveal Carnon Imbro's taut face.

"Karuth!" He hesitated as he saw Ria staring at him in shock, but in an instant his composure returned and he beckoned cursorily to the girl. "In here. Quickly!"

Karuth started forward, and Ria felt as though the ground were falling away from under her feet. "Carnon, what's happening?"

"Please, Matriarch." He held up a hand, palm out, excluding her. "Go to your bedchamber. You can't help Avali at the moment."

"Surely there must be something—"

"Pray," Carnon said tersely. "For the moment, I can think of nothing else that might help her."

4

Avali died at midnight, as the second moon reached its zenith. Her child—a girl, tiny and almost hairless and barely able to summon the strength to cry—was delivered from her lifeless body by Carnon, Karuth, and Fiora, and carried to the next room to be laid beside the fire in a blanket-lined basket while the sisters sat weeping beside her.

Ria was in shock. At first she stubbornly refused to grieve openly, and refused, too, the sedative that Carnon tried to give her; all she could do was sit in a high-backed chair clutching her upper arms and rocking her body back and forth as the guilt to which she couldn't give voice shone miserably from her eyes. It was Karuth who finally persuaded her to drink the draft and who helped her, fully clothed, into her bed, summoning a castle servant to watch over her as she slept.

Leaving the Matriarch's room at last, Karuth paused in the corridor to compose herself a little before returning to join Carnon in the room where the dead girl lay. She had attended dying patients before now—Carnon didn't believe in shielding his apprentices' finer feelings—but the sight of that poor broken creature, scarcely older than herself, finally succumbing after hours of agony had upset her in a way she'd never experienced before. Such a tragic *waste*. As for the tiny, helpless child: she'd heard a rumor that its father was unknown, and now its mother, too, was gone. What would the future hold for it?

Karuth shivered, and rubbed fiercely at her eyes. She was tired, and would have liked nothing better than to

47

retire to the warmth and security of her room, where she could hide from the cruelties of life for a while, but that was out of the question. Sister Fiora was with the baby, and so Physician Imbro would need her to help with the laying-out. Her own needs must wait.

She drew a deep breath and opened the door to Avali's room.

There was a faint, musky perfume in the air. Carnon had lit incense in a small brazier near the fire, and smoke curled lazily up, already beginning to form a thin canopy across the ceiling. Karuth's task, which she didn't relish but had learned not to shrink from, would be to dress Avali in a purple funeral gown, brush her hair for the last time, and paint her face with the sigils that would speed her journey to the gods. Then she must fetch Sister Fiora, and the three of them—by custom, all those who had been present at the moment of death—would sit in silent vigil by Avali's corpse until break of dawn.

She set quietly about her work, murmuring prayers to Aeoris and Yandros, and was peripherally aware of Carnon's soft-footed movements in the background. Her sense of time was out of kilter, distorted by her tiredness and the room's dimly lit silence; one hour or four might have passed before at last the task was done and Sister Fiora came in and they took up their stations around the bed, heads bowed in respect and contemplation.

Time moved on and Karuth's weary mind lured her into a world of drifting phantasms midway between dream and waking. Only once did she start momentarily from the first grasp of a nightmare and look up, blinking sleepily, to see the room undisturbed and hear the faint sputtering of the brazier. The window in this room faced westward, so she couldn't see the first sliver of the sun's fire that appeared, at the moment she stirred, far away to the east over the sea. But in the slowly awakening castle one man saw the dawn's glimmer, and saw too the faint shimmer of an unearthly light, colorless and yet hinting at every shade of the spectrum, that darted between two of the castle's great spires. It was gone in an instant, like a distant reflection of lightning, but the glimpse stayed in his mind. It told

him something that he had been waiting to learn. And it
stirred another, stranger intuition. . . .

The light touch of a hand on the doorlatch stirred Karuth
to full wakefulness, and she raised her head as the vestiges
of sleep slid away. Daylight was trickling into the room,
the brazier was dark, and the fire had almost burned out.
Opposite her, beyond the smoothed covering of the bed,
Sister Fiora rubbed at her eyes. Carnon, also stirring, sat
back and stretched stiffened arms—then froze as he saw
Keridil Toln standing on the threshold.

"High Initiate . . ." Carnon rose, Karuth only an instant behind him, and Fiora, looking quickly over her
shoulder, scrambled to her feet and made a hasty bow.

"Carnon." Keridil's faded eyes held a peculiar intensity. "Ladies." He looked at the bed, studied it carefully for
a few moments. "I am so sorry to hear of this tragedy. Poor
child: she was barely eighteen, I understand." Now his
gaze left Avali's still form, flicked swiftly to the vigilants
one by one. "I know you did everything possible to save
her. This must have been a grievous night for you all."

Karuth and Fiora cast their eyes down. Carnon nodded somberly. "Thank you, Keridil. I'm touched by your
kindness."

"Kindness?" Keridil's look became faintly quizzical.
"Ah. I wonder . . ." He stepped forward so that he could
see Avali more clearly. "The child lives, though?"

"Yes. A girl. Premature, but I think she will survive."

"Ah," Keridil said again. He was now at the foot of the
bed. Fiora had moved aside to let him pass, and his gnarled
hands gripped the bedrail, the knuckles whitening.

"Omens." Slowly the puzzled look faded, to be re-
placed by a frown. Karuth dared to glance up at Carnon;
his eyes met hers and she saw, as she had anticipated,
unease on his face. He made as though to take the High
Initiate's arm and guide him back, but Keridil spoke again,
forestalling him.

"No, no. That time is long past." Suddenly, chillingly,
Karuth felt that he was addressing someone who was not in

the room. Then he shook his head and smiled thinly. "If there *are* omens, let others find them. I thank the gods that I will no longer have to take that responsibility."

"Keridil," Carnon interjected gently, "you should rest. We should all rest. It's been a long night."

He slipped a hand under Keridil's arm. Keridil acquiesced, allowing himself to be drawn away from the bed and turned toward the door—then as they started across the room together he suddenly stopped and looked hard into the physician's eyes, and Karuth saw Carnon recoil.

"But which gods, Carnon?" Keridil said harshly. "Can you answer me that? *Which* gods?"

The High Initiate's face was turned away from Karuth, and she didn't know, nor would she ever dare to ask, what Physician Imbro had seen in that moment. But as Keridil began once more to move slowly, wearily toward the door, Carnon looked back at her and she read the message in his eyes.

"Go to your room, Karuth," he told her quietly. "Sleep, while you can. I think I will have need of you again before long."

"I'm so sorry, Matriarch, that I must be the bringer of yet more sad news." Chiro Piadar Lin took Ria's hands in his own and squeezed them gently. "But he is asking for you. He wants only his closest friends now, and it would be a great kindness."

Only his closest friends . . . Did he, then, count her among that number? Ria was deeply moved and shut her eyes tightly to stave off fresh tears. This morning the dam within her had broken and she had at last been able to cry for Avali. Crying had helped to blunt the knives of grief and guilt within her, at least enough for her to recover her composure and present a calm face to the world around her. She had even begun to consider the grim necessities that must follow her niece's death. The breaking of the news to her parents, arrangements for the funeral, the future of the baby: all these were her responsibility and her burden, and she must face them and be strong.

Now, though, in the aftermath of one tragedy came another.

It was a further cruel blow but she wouldn't shirk it. Keridil had asked for her, and she couldn't refuse his last wish.

She rose, smoothing her robe and with it the embroidered purple sash that was a symbol of mourning. "Of course, Chiro," she said, and was relieved to hear no tremor in her voice. "Should I come with you now?"

"Carnon thinks it would be best."

A tiny snuffling noise on the far side of the room made Ria turn her head. From here she couldn't see the baby in its basket; two sisters were bending over it, crooning soft, reassuring noises, and on a chair between them the wet nurse smiled down. The Matriarch didn't speak to them— at this moment she wouldn't have known quite what to say —but let Chiro escort her from the room and out into the corridor.

Sunlight slanted in at the tall windows; servants went about their business; in the courtyard several children were playing. On the surface it seemed an ordinary, unremarkable day, but Ria was all too well aware of what lay beneath the veneer. Last night the gods had laid the whisper of death on one soul; today the whisper would come again, and to Ria the bright day seemed incongruous. Yet Keridil wanted it this way. They could extinguish the lights, he had said, and silence the castle, and mourn him as they pleased once his spirit had left on its last journey, but while mortality still held him, he wanted no sorrowing. Perhaps, she thought, his was the wiser counsel, for what use was grief to the dying or the dead? Avali had no need of her weeping, or her conscience. And there was a new life to consider, a precious new life. *Out of sadness,* she thought, recalling the catechism she'd taught to so many novices in her time, *may yet come joy. Out of the darkening of winter comes still the greening of spring. . . .*

Chiro said: "Avali is at peace, Ria. We can be sure of that. And her child will flourish."

He had guessed her thoughts yet again, with that strange skill he had, and Ria smiled.

"I know, Chiro. And Keridil—"

"Looks forward with gladness. An ending, but also a beginning. For all of us."

They walked a few paces in silence, then Chiro said: "Have you decided what to name her?"

"The baby?" Ria was taken aback by his abrupt change of tack, then glad of it. "I haven't really given it any consideration. The sisters favor Ygorla, but . . ." She bit her lip. "I wish I could know what Avali would have liked. She never talked about names; she . . . Oh, dear." She wiped her eyes with the sleeve of her robe.

He put an arm about her and squeezed her shoulders gently. "Ria, you mustn't torment yourself. You heard what Carnon said—you can't be held to blame in any way. Avali's condition couldn't have been diagnosed or predicted, and the rigors of the journey here made no difference."

"I know. Carnon explained it all to me this morning. I know, too, that she could have had no better care in all the world. Far better than if she'd stayed in Southern Chaun. Yet I can't help thinking . . ." She shook her head helplessly.

"You must stop thinking it. Truly, Ria, you must," Chiro told her sternly; then his expression softened. "Do you remember what we said to each other at the banquet? Do you remember your toast?"

She did, and thought that perhaps he was right. They had the future to consider. *Out of the darkening of winter* . . . Sorrow must fade eventually and she *did* still have much to give, not least to the tiny orphan now sleeping in the east wing. This unhappy time would soon be over, and life would return to normal.

But all the same, as she looked up at the bright sun, Ria felt something chill and fearful touch her with a cold hand.

Keridil hadn't wanted to die in his bed. He would have preferred to spend his final hour sitting in his favorite chair by the fire with his closest friends and colleagues beside him, but at the last his body proved too frail, and reluc-

52

tantly he bowed to Carnon's will and instead lay propped up by pillows in the great canopied four-poster that had couched him for most of his life, and countless predecessors before him.

As soon as she entered the room with Chiro, Ria knew that death was very close to Keridil. The old High Initiate's skin had taken on the peculiar translucence that so often heralded the departure of the soul from its mortal frame. When he turned his head and smiled at her, she saw certainty in his eyes.

"Dear Matriarch." He held out a hand; the grip was surprisingly strong, yet somehow ephemeral. "Thank you for coming to see me."

Ria couldn't speak, but she raised his fingers to her lips and kissed them. Chiro moved forward to crouch down by the bed, saying something for Keridil's ears alone, and as she stepped back Ria saw that there were only three other people in the room. Carnon, as she would have expected, and by the window, holding each other's hands, Chiro's two children, Karuth and her brother, Tirand.

Tirand, only nine years old but already the image of his father in his youth, met the Matriarch's gaze briefly and nervously before looking down once more at his own feet. He was unsure of protocol, knowing he should have bowed to her, yet aware of the solemnity of this occasion, and taking pity on him, Ria edged quietly across the room until she could reach out and squeeze his free hand.

"How are you, Tirand?" she whispered.

"Well, thank you, madam," the boy whispered back. "At least . . ." His face froze unhappily and he looked involuntarily toward the bed.

"It's all right, child. I understand what you mean. And the High Initiate doesn't want us to be sad. Though we are to be left behind, this is for him a time of joy, for he will be at peace."

She wondered for a moment if the words rang hollow, but the change in Tirand's expression from unhappy confusion to tentative relief banished the doubt. Over the boy's head she looked at Karuth, and caught the girl assessing her with a concerned, professional eye. She smiled.

"I am much recovered, Karuth. Thank you for your kindness."

"I'm glad, madam. Is the baby well?"

"She thrives, thanks to the gods' benevolence."

Karuth nodded toward Keridil's frail figure. "The High Initiate was asking after her, Matriarch. Before you arrived. He seems concerned for her."

Ria had been told of Keridil's unwonted dawn visit to Avali's vigil. Perhaps, she thought, Keridil saw the child as a symbol of new hope, a new beginning.

The thought broke off abruptly as Karuth suddenly reached past Tirand to clutch her arm. "Matriarch—"

"What?" Then Ria felt it too, a chill breath that flicked past them and across the sunlit chamber. Instinctively she looked toward the bed, and was in time to see Keridil's eyes widen perceptibly and their focus change so that he seemed to be looking with intense clarity and sudden re-awakened intelligence at a point precisely between the bed foot's twin posts. And—later she thought she might have imagined it, but she could never be certain—at that point there seemed to be the faintest of shimmerings, and the sense of a presence, an *intelligence*, that filled the room and reached beyond its physical dimensions into another, unimaginable plane of existence.

Instinct swelled into certainty and, unable to check the impulse, Ria started forward. "Keridil—" The words stopped in her throat.

Keridil sat upright. The vivid intelligence in his eyes intensified, and suddenly there were happiness and pain and an extraordinary understanding vying for precedence on his face. Ria felt Karuth at her side, clinging to her, saw Chiro draw back, heard Carnon's sharply indrawn breath.

"Wait." It wasn't the familiar voice of the High Initiate, but stronger, younger, changed almost beyond recognition. "There's one thing I must—"

"Keridil, don't exert yourself!" Carnon took him by the shoulders, trying to make him lie back. To the physician's astonished chagrin, Keridil threw him off. He was still staring fixedly at that same point between the bedposts. Carnon and Chiro both followed his gaze and saw nothing, while Ria and Karuth could only sense an edge of light blending with darkness, the presence of immense power.

Keridil, however, saw with far more than his physical senses. As the frail thread that linked him with the mortal world shivered and began finally to fray, he looked beyond the room, beyond the castle's ancient stones, into a realm where strange colors shifted and changed in a vast, coruscating rainbow, and he looked at the tall figure, haloed in an eerie spectrum, that stood before him and slowly, slowly, raised a hand to beckon and welcome him.

"Ah, yes." He uttered the words aloud, heard them drop away like stones cast from a cliff and falling, falling, toward a distant and ever-hungry sea. If his friends and companions in this world, those he was leaving behind, heard or understood, he didn't know, and the question was no longer relevant. Sixty years had fallen away and Keridil Toln spoke once again to a being of another order, who at last had come to call him home.

Hair like molten silver rippled over high shoulders, eyes like twin golden furnaces gazed through skin and flesh and bone, an exquisitely symmetrical mouth smiled. Keridil raised one arm, reaching out to the apparition—

Suddenly a new flicker on the periphery of vision drew his gaze. He turned his head sharply, and saw another figure, even more familiar, standing where moments ago the anxious faces of Chiro and Carnon had hovered.

Keridil felt something deep within him relax. This was the moment his intuition had told him would come. This was the one last thing he had to do, the message he had to give. For the sake of an old and ravaged friendship, for a loyalty that he had waited sixty years to repay.

Green eyes, invisible to all senses but his, gazed down at the dying High Initiate, and he felt once more, after so long, the presence of the friend he had betrayed, the friend who had regained his true identity and returned, at the dawn of this world's new age, to the realm to which he owed his existence.

Mortal man and lord of Chaos regarded each other across the gulf of time and memory, and Keridil Toln spoke his last words.

"She isn't like Sashka. Have a care, Tarod. Have a care."

Thin lips curved, the eyes like emeralds closed, and the vision was gone. Keridil turned his head once more and looked to where the shining silver-haired apparition still stood, still waited. He heard the final breath that exhaled gently—not a rattle, not the way the physicians might have expected—from his lungs, and with the exhalation the room took on new dimensions, as his consciousness slipped free of its shell.

He rose. The body, the husk, that he was leaving behind shuddered once and then sagged slowly back against the pillows of the bed. Keridil's outstretched hand reached forward and clasped the other, unhuman fingers, and he didn't hear the soft sound of a woman's weeping as he passed beyond the constraints of the world.

———————————————

Seven prisms of blinding light turned slowly above a shifting landscape, their iridescent colors flashing and merging into a vast rainbow that shivered across the restless sky. A sound rose on a long, eldritch note, shattered, fell away to silence broken only by the intermittent moan of the wind.

From where he stood, on a towering black cliff that in its tortured way echoed the granite stacks of the Star Peninsula, the mortal world was a tiny candle flame hovering on the edge of perception, all but lost against the titanic and ever-changing backdrop of Chaos. In the heart of that flame a human soul was drawing its final breaths, and its flickering transition from life to what awaited it beyond life had sounded a chord that awakened memories.

His form was as mercurial as his Chaotic mind but with the stirring of the memories he took on the appearance of a man. He alone among the Seven had once known what it was to be human; this manifestation was a tribute to those old days and, though a little ironically, a tribute to the dying man at the Star Peninsula, for he was the last survivor of the Change, the last of the mortals who had looked upon the face of a Chaos lord. Wild black hair streamed back from a proud and ascetic face, green eyes turned calmly to watch the High Initiate's final moments, and thin lips smiled with something that hovered between pity, contempt, and affection.

He could have called Keridil Toln to Chaos. It was within his power, for the balance between the gods, which men and women in their naiveté called Equilibrium, had been weighted from the fondly remembered day when Yandros had triumphed over Aeoris of Order and had refashioned the laws of the mortal world to Chaos's own purpose. But, however great the temptation to indulge that whim, he was content to allow Keridil's own choice to be the final arbiter. Sixty years ago, as mankind reckoned time, it had amused Chaos to overturn the strictures long laid down by the lords of Order and grant the world a level of freedom unknown in its history. Opposition, as Yandros had once observed, was a valuable factor in preventing any power from becoming complacent. Now each individual was free to choose his or her own allegiance, and Chaos, perversely, as befitted its nature, had been steadfast in maintaining its pledge to stay its hand and not manipulate their lives. Though outwardly he had played his dutiful part in giving both factions their due, Keridil Toln had in his heart remained faithful to Order. Let him go to Aeoris, as he had prayed to do for so long. Once he had been a friend, and though friendship had ended in betrayal, Tarod bore him no grudge.

But as the spark that was Keridil's life dimmed, it seemed suddenly that something was trying to cry across dimensions, to reach out and touch for one final moment the echoes and the memories that had once bound the dying High Initiate to another allegiance. Time collapsed, and from the bed in the quiet room in the castle a face from which the ravages of years had been abruptly stripped away gazed out, and a mind racked with old guilts and longings and confusions projected a last urgent message.

She isn't like Sashka. Have a care, Tarod. Have a care.

The words struck like a cold barb, and the wind that soughed through the Chaos realm rose momentarily to a hurricane shriek. Tarod raised an arm, quieting it, then his hand clenched, enclosing the candle flame of the world as though he held a firefly in his palm. His consciousness shifted, refocused, and he gazed down at the old man, his onetime companion, and saw the faded hazel eyes widen with recognition and with the knowledge that his words had been heard.

The contact lasted only a moment. Another presence was waiting for Keridil's soul, and gracefully Tarod withdrew, leaving only a faint disturbance in the air of the quiet bedchamber and a lingering touch in the High Initiate's mind that was his own form of farewell. It was over. The last upholder of the Circle's old ways was gone, and the future lay open to new influence. It would be, he thought, an interesting time.

As he turned away, leaving the bleak cliff behind and allowing it to flow back into the constantly changing spectrum of light and dark from which he had created it, he considered Keridil's strange message to him. *She isn't like Sashka.* The reference intrigued him, for it had been a long time since he'd had occasion to recall that name, and for curiosity's sake he formed an image from the shimmering mists around him, of a tall and lovely young woman with brown eyes and a cascade of rich auburn hair. As an example of human self-interest, greed, and corruption, Sashka had had no rival. She had also possessed rare beauty, rare intelligence, and the ability to blind men to the truth lurking behind her mask. She had been—an amusing thought when he considered the accusations made in her time against his own kin—evil.

But Sashka was long gone from the mortal or any other world. Even the maggot at the heart of her soul must by now have decayed to nothing in the dimensionless hell to which he'd sent her. A pity that Keridil had been unable to sever the last links and abandon his vain hope of finding her again. He'd deserved better: but even with his last breath he'd still uttered her name.

She isn't like Sashka. Idly Tarod wondered what delusion, what distorted fantasy, had been in Keridil's mind at that moment. It was as though he'd tried to express a warning but his thoughts had been too feeble and too confused to form it with any clarity. Some ghost of the past? Some demon lover of his mind's own creation? Tarod smiled a little pityingly. Chaos had nothing to fear from ghosts.

He dismissed the beautiful, slowly pirouetting image of Sashka, and looked up to the brooding sky. Blood-red lightning exploded across the firmament, and on a whim he hurled his consciousness up to meet and join with it, the shards of his human form spinning away like a million diamonds. One of the seven prisms that still pulsed their slow, relentless rhythm on the vast horizon flickered suddenly and briefly, then the lightning shouted again, cracking the sky's bowl, and a dark shadow took wing over the shifting, shimmering landscape to vanish into the coruscating rainbow far above.

5

"I don't see *why* I should have to know!" Blue eyes, in a heart-shaped face whose childish beauty was at this moment spoiled by a show of petulance, glared accusingly at Sister-Senior Corelm Simik. "I don't *care* whether I can name all the provinces and their Margraves and get every one right! And I don't care about the High Margrave either, or his father and grandfather! I don't care if they *all* go and—"

"Ygorla!" Sister Corelm's lips pursed tightly and she rapped out the reprimand with far more than her customary sharpness, slapping her hand down on the table for emphasis. Yet behind the anger in her eyes lurked weary despair, and she suspected that her ten-year-old pupil was well aware of it.

"Ygorla," she repeated, regaining her rigid self-control, "I shan't tell you again. I will *not* tolerate such rudeness, nor such disrespect to the High Margrave! You are here to learn, and the fact that the Matriarch has granted you the privilege of studying at the Cot rather than attending the Sisterhood school with other children doesn't mean she does not expect high standards of you. Quite the contrary." She stood up, the long white skirt of her robe whisking as she paced across the small schoolroom; then she stopped and turned to fix her charge with a stern look. "Do you *want* to be uneducated, Ygorla? Do you want your peers to point at you in the years to come, and laugh behind their hands at your ignorance?"

The barb struck home and the child hunched defensively, though her eyes were still resentful. "But it's so *dull*," she protested.

"Dull or not, it's necessary if you're to hold your own in the kind of society that befits your station in life." Sister Corelm detected the first sign of weakening and pounced on it; it was, she had learned, the only way to cope with Ygorla. She allowed her voice to soften a little. "My child, when I was your age I didn't enjoy my lessons any more than you enjoy yours now, but I assure you, you'll thank me for my diligence in years to come. When you reach marriageable age—"

The child's head came up quickly. "*I* shan't ever marry."

"Well, you're but ten years old; it's hardly a subject that need concern you yet."

"It concerns Aunt Ria. I heard her say so to Sister Fiora."

Sister Corelm's patience began to wane again. "Now, Ygorla, that is quite enough! The Matriarch's private discussions with Sister Fiora are not for the ears of small girls, and you shouldn't have been eavesdropping on matters that you're not old enough to understand."

"I couldn't help it." Ygorla looked up at her, blinking. "It was late one night, I couldn't sleep, and I went to the refectory to get a cup of water. I had to go past Aunt Ria's study, and she and Sister Fiora were talking about me. I couldn't *help* hearing what they said. I'm sorry, Sister Corelm."

Her expression was utterly guileless and Sister Corelm sighed. She hadn't been close to the child's poor mother during her stay here, and it didn't do to think ill of the dead, but she remembered that sweet, innocent look all too well. Avali Troi had been quite unscrupulous in using charm to turn aside censure, and her daughter had clearly inherited that trait from her, if little else. When Ygorla put on what Corelm called her "penitent face"—even if it was a sham—it was impossible to remain angry with her.

Corelm returned to her chair and sat down. "Well, as long as you promise me that you won't do such a thing again, we'll say no more about it."

Ygorla's face brightened. "I promise."

"Very well. Then go back to your lesson, and in a few minutes you may close your book and I'll test you on the provinces and their Margraves."

Obediently the child bent her dark head over her lesson-book, and for a while there was silence. Sister Corelm turned her attention to her own work, the marking of a test she had set for her more senior students a few days earlier. Looking at the sprawling hands, making sharp notes beside some of the more asinine answers, she reflected wryly that despite her mulish resistance to formal schooling, Ygorla was blessed with far greater intelligence than most. If only she would apply herself, and really *work*.

She had the sudden discomfiting feeling that she was being watched, and looked up quickly to see Ygorla gazing solemnly and thoughtfully at her. Sister Corelm sighed and set down her quill. "What is it, child? Is there something you don't understand?"

"No, sister." Ygorla smiled sweetly. "I was just thinking about who I might marry if I ever decided I would."

Corelm raised her eyebrows at the dubious grammar, but let it pass. There was, she realized, little point in trying to steer the child back to her studies; once her mind was distracted, it was impossible to recapture her attention, and she gave in.

"And who," she said with dry amusement, "engages your fancy at this moment?"

Ygorla's small shoulders lifted in a coquettish gesture. "Ohh . . . I think I would consider Blis Alacar. I might like to be High Margravine one day. Or perhaps the High Initiate's son, Tirand Lin, though they say he isn't very handsome."

Corelm touched a hand to her mouth to disguise a smile. "Well, my dear, you're nothing if not ambitious. But Blis Alacar is twenty-six now; I think that by the time you're old enough to wed he will have found a wife. Perhaps you'd do better to consider his younger brother?"

Her irony was lost on Ygorla: either that, or she chose to ignore it. Tilting her head on one side, she regarded her teacher with eyes that were suddenly very intense. "Perhaps. Mind you, Blis Alacar will become High Margrave *very* soon."

Cold, claylike fingers stroked Corelm's spine and she said sharply, "What do you mean?"

Ygorla shrugged. "Solas Jair Alacar's going to die," she stated flatly.

"Nonsense! What are you—"

"He is. I dreamed about it: that's how I know."

This was too much, Sister Corelm's sensibilities protested. First disrespect, and now claims to prescience that were disturbingly close to downright ill-wishing—it could not be tolerated.

"Ygorla!" Her voice cracked across the room like a spear of ice. "I have heard *enough!*" She rose like an avenging angel and strode to the table, snatching up Ygorla's books and slamming them down out of her way before leaning menacingly over the tabletop, knuckles whitening as they gripped the edge. The child recoiled as though frightened, but this time Corelm was too angry to be swayed by her.

"You will listen to me, and if you have any wits at all, you'll take heed!" she said savagely. "I will not, and I repeat *not*, have you making such wild and unfounded statements! *Dreams*—dear gods, such a thing's little short of treasonous!" With an effort she collected herself as she realized that her tone was becoming shrill, and pushed herself away from the table, folding her arms.

"Our High Margrave Solas Jair Alacar is but fifty-seven years old," she continued, calmer but still waspish. "He is in the best of health and by the grace of the gods will live for many years to come, as you know full well from your catechisms. It is *not* the place of a spoilt and wayward child to indulge her spiteful imaginings in this disgraceful way! Do you understand me, Ygorla? *Do* you?"

Ygorla's small dark head nodded once. "Yes, Sister Corelm."

"Good. Now, as penance for your behavior, you will remain here alone until you have written, seven times seven times, the names of each of our provinces and their Margraves. The door of this room will be unlocked in one hour's time: I will then expect you to bring your work straight to me and I will expect it to be flawless." She paused. "I trust I have made myself clear?"

"Yes, Sister Corelm."

Meekness, capitulation. Corelm paused tensely for a few moments, the suspicious side of her nature anticipating some new ploy on Ygorla's part, but it seemed that for once she wasn't going to argue. Satisfied, if not entirely convinced by the show of shame, the sister collected the lesson-books, leaving Ygorla only with writing materials and her own memory to aid her task, and left the room, locking the door behind her.

In the comparative cool of the whitewashed corridor Corelm stopped and shut her eyes tightly for a moment, pinching the bridge of her nose in an effort to banish the headache that stabbed sharply through her skull. Tension vibrated the length of her spine, and her pulse was over-rapid and refused to settle back to its normal rhythm. She knew she was a fool to allow a mere child to upset her so, but Ygorla seemed to become more intractable with every day that passed, and was fast developing the knack of finding and exploiting every chink in Corelm's armor. This morning had been the final straw: something would have to be done, or she would be forced to resign her role as Ygorla's tutor and insist that the child be given into sterner hands.

Her wooden-soled shoes clacked briskly on the stone floor as she moved off down the passage, and the hard sound made Corelm's head throb anew. She should take one of Sister Fiora's herbal powders before the pain incapacitated her; she knew these headaches of old. First, though, while this latest incident was still fresh and clear in her mind, she *must* speak to the Matriarch. It was long overdue.

Despite the fact that it was almost midwinter, the southern sun still had a trace of warmth and was a pleasant balm to Corelm as she emerged from the low building and began to cross the courtyard to the Matriarch's house. In the shelter of the gabled wall that fronted the Hall of Prayer, bells jingled with a faint, sweet sound and Corelm saw a falconer with one of the trained messenger birds that were used to convey urgent letters between the provinces. A bird had come in earlier this morning, she recalled, with dispatches for the Matriarch, and for a moment her steps faltered as she wondered whether Ria would be too busy to see her. But surely a few minutes could be granted. She needed no more than that.

The Matriarch's house was a white-painted single-story building set on the west side of the courtyard, where its tall windows would catch the evening light. The main door stood open as always, and Corelm walked as quietly as she could through the entrance hall and then along the flagged corridor that led to the Matriarch's study.

The study door, leather-clad to muffle sound, displayed a small bunch of twigs above the latch—a sign that Ria was at her desk and willing to receive callers. Relieved, Corelm knocked politely, waited for the response—which was a few moments in coming—and entered.

"Corelm." Ria looked up from the single sheet of parchment unrolled before her, her brows knitting together in surprise. "Is this something urgent? I really don't want to be disturbed."

Puzzled, Corelm gestured toward the door. "Forgive me, Matriarch, but the sign—"

"Is it still there? Oh, dear, I thought I'd removed it. No," as, embarrassed, Corelm turned to go, "no, Sister, don't worry. The error is mine entirely." She forced a smile. "What can I do for you?"

The years had been kind to Ria. Though she was now well into her sixties, a handsome bone structure had stood her in good stead, and her face was lined only by the marks of graceful aging and the southern sun. The rheumatism that plagued her generation further to the north was all but absent in Southern Chaun's kindly climate, and though her hair was gray, she wasn't above using the occasional herbal concoction to give the illusion of the color she'd once possessed. Age had its benefits, too; not least of them the wisdom and experience to see at a glance that Sister Corelm was very distressed.

She said kindly, "Sit down, my dear. Something's troubling you?"

"Well . . ." Corelm sank onto a chair, twisting her hands together. "I don't want to burden you, Matriarch, especially so if you're already occupied with other matters . . ."

"Other matters." Ria repeated the words as though they had some unwitting irony, and looked at the spread parchment again. "Sadly, there's nothing that I can do to change this grievous news, so—"

It was unthinkable for a sister to interrupt the Matriarch, but at that moment a terrible premonition put Corelm's tongue beyond her control, and she said in a tight, peculiar voice, "Grievous news, madam?"

"Yes. Ah, you may as well know, Corelm. I will be making an announcement to the entire Cot within the hour." Ria laid a hand on the parchment and suddenly Corelm felt like a swimmer carried without warning into a current that threatened to sweep her away and drown her. She heard the Matriarch's next words as though in a gathering nightmare.

"I have just received a message from the Summer Isle, Corelm. Two days ago, our High Margrave was killed when he fell from his horse while riding in the grounds of his court."

Corelm stared at her as the world seemed to fall away into an abyss.

"Corelm?" Ria's expression froze and she started to get to her feet. "Corelm, are you all right? What is it?"

Corelm made a sound that couldn't even begin to express the blind, black mayhem that was surging up from the pit which her mind had become. For a single instant she saw again Ygorla's face and wide, innocent blue eyes, and heard again the prediction delivered in the childish but utterly confident voice, before—for the first time in her adult life—she fell to the floor in a dead faint.

"A sound night's sleep, and tomorrow morning in bed." Fiora closed the door of Corelm's room and smiled reassuringly at Ria as they walked toward the main door of the sister-seniors' quarters. "She simply needs the rest, Matriarch. And a chance to recover from this rather unpleasant shock."

Ria nodded acknowledgment, but her face remained somber as she thought back on the story that Corelm had told them when she came round from her fainting fit. Fiora, who perhaps knew her better than anyone else in the Cot, waited, knowing that she'd say what she had to say in her own good time. At length Ria spoke.

"This still leaves us with the problem of Ygorla."

"Yes, Matriarch." Fiora had anticipated this, and anticipated, too, the arguments that would counter what she had to say. Nevertheless she felt she must speak frankly. "I think you know my own feelings, and I'm afraid that this incident only serves to strengthen them. I truly believe that Ygorla has a very powerful innate talent. I also believe that once she grows beyond adolescence, the Sisterhood won't be enough to satisfy her."

Ria nodded. "I'd rather hoped that she would choose a more secular path and make a good marriage in a few years' time, but it seems that isn't to be. A pity."

Fiora smiled dryly. "If you mean that there'll be a great many disappointed young men in her wake, Matriarch, then certainly I agree with you. She's already broken several hearts, and she's only ten. Even so . . ." Her gaze slid obliquely to the Matriarch's face and she hesitated. "Please pardon my presumption in speaking so bluntly, but I really wouldn't have thought that you of all people would wish Ygorla to become simply a wife, rather than make full use of her talents."

"I take your point, Fiora. However, at the same time, I wouldn't want her to deny herself what is, after all, the natural expectation and delight of any woman." She was tempted to add: *as I did*—but restrained herself. Fiora knew exactly what she meant; it was an old sore and the healer was well aware of it.

Fiora said gently, "You're thinking of Karuth Piadar, at the castle?"

Fiora, Ria thought, had always been a skilled diplomat. "Yes," she replied, allowing herself the faintest of smiles, just enough to tell the other woman that their understanding was mutual. "I'm thinking of Karuth, of course. So much time and energy dedicated to the demands of her work and her responsibilities that even at twenty-four it seems she's destined to be a lifelong spinster. I wouldn't

want to see Ygorla propelled in the same direction unless
it's what she truly wants."

"But if it is?"

"Then I shan't stand in her way. I only want her to be
sure."

They lapsed into thoughtful but companionable silence until they had reentered the Matriarch's house and
stood in the high-ceilinged hall. Then, clasping her hands
before her, Ria turned to face her old friend.

"Whatever the future may hold for my niece, Fiora,
it's a matter that must wait for further consideration. For
now, we have more sobering work to attend to. I want you
to assemble all the sisters in the refectory in twenty minutes' time, and I will address them and break the news of
the High Margrave's death. We'll have the knell rung at
noon and the mourning rituals will begin immediately afterward. Oh, and in Sister Corelm's absence you'd best ask
Sister Mirrio to ensure that word goes out to close all the
Sisterhood schools as a mark of respect." She looked about
the hall, seeming to focus not on the clean, modest lines of
the walls but on something beyond them, something hidden to Fiora. "I hardly knew Solas, and it seems barely any
time at all since we marked the passing of his father, Fenar.
I suppose that's one of the penalties of our High Margrave's seclusion on Summer Isle; we see him so rarely that
he's merely a name to us rather than a man. Ah, well . . .
the gods grant him rest."

Fiora made the splay-fingered sign of reverence. "Indeed, Matriarch. And Ygorla?"

Ria sighed. "Let her out of the schoolroom, and set her
to some task that will keep her out of mischief for a while."

"Should she come to the refectory with the others?"

Ria frowned, considered for a moment. Then: "I think
not." She raised her head, and her eyes were suddenly
sharply candid. "In fact, I'd prefer to keep this news from
her for as long as possible. I don't know what instinct or
seeing power prompted her to predict Solas Jair Alacar's
demise so startlingly, but I don't want her to find out yet
just how accurate that prediction was." She hesitated for a
moment, then added: "I think it would be as well to keep
the truth from her for a while. For her own sake."

Word of the High Margrave's death reached the Star Peninsula a day later. Once he had taken in the news and announced it with appropriate solemnity to his fellow adepts, the High Initiate Chiro Piadar Lin reluctantly applied himself to the practicalities of the southward journey that now loomed ahead of him.

The fact that a part of him resented this ritualistic necessity caused Chiro more than one pang of conscience. But in truth he'd hardly known the High Margrave— they'd met on three occasions, all told—and he hadn't liked the little he had seen. Solas had inherited his father's weakness of character, and to Chiro he had seemed something of a dilettante, more concerned with the trivial diversions of court life than with statesmanship, of which he had no real grasp. His son Blis, though young, would be a wiser and more dedicated ruler. Privately, Chiro suspected that he wouldn't be the only mourner at the funeral rites whose grief was more dutiful than genuine.

Nonetheless, the forms had to be observed. He didn't relish the prospect of traveling through the northern mountains at the height of winter; though the passes were —just—negotiable, snow and ice would make the journey both hazardous and extremely uncomfortable. And there was so much to attend to at the castle. There was always so much to attend to, but at the moment fate seemed to be in a particularly perverse mood, for as well as the seasonal infections which seemed to be afflicting half the Circle, a new intake of students was also about to arrive to begin their three years of tutelage in the arts and sciences taught by the Circle's scholars. Yet he had no choice but to go. For the High Initiate not to be present to speed Solas Jair Alacar's soul to the gods was unthinkable.

It was Karuth, as usual, who soothed Chiro's worries and finally convinced him that the entire social fabric of the castle wouldn't collapse during his absence, so that at last he and his entourage rode across the causeway on a bright, brittle morning with the sun glaring down on them like a furious red eye. From the wall above the castle gates

Chiro's son, Tirand, watched their departure, then, rubbing his hands together—even through thick gloves the winter cold bit like serpents—climbed down and crossed the courtyard to enter the High Initiate's study.

Karuth was there before him. She was straightening papers on their father's great desk, not fussily, but with quiet, reassuring efficiency. She'd built up the fire, Tirand noticed with gratitude, and he paused to pull the gloves off and warm his hands before the blaze, smiling at her.

"They're away safely. The gods speed them well—it won't be a pleasant journey."

Karuth nodded soberly. From a leggy and gauche adolescent she had grown into a tall, graceful young woman with a handsome if slightly heavy bone structure, fine gray eyes, and a luxuriance of warm brown hair. Never flamboyant in her dress, she was today wearing a plain wool gown decorated only with a gold adept's badge, while the mass of her hair was confined into a single, practical plait. And the changes of the last decade went deeper than mere appearance, for the shyness that Ria Morys had once observed had given way to an outwardly quiet but inwardly strong and decisive personality to which eleven years of Circle training had added its own confidence. She was a fourth-rank adept now—only two degrees short of the highest she might hope to achieve, for though the Circle had seven theoretical grades, in practice no one in living memory had attained the formidable skills of a seventh-ranker, and the accolade was largely an honorary one reserved for the High Initiate or his prospective successor. She was also a member of the Council of Adepts, though her involvement with the council was sporadic, as two years ago she had qualified as a fully fledged physician, and now that Carnon Imbro had virtually retired she was effectively the castle's senior healer.

"I've put out the notes that Father made for your welcoming address to the new students," she said. "I think it might be best to make the speech during the feast in the great hall; that way you can combine both occasions into one and it'll be less of a drain on your time."

Tirand walked to the desk and looked down at the

parchments a little uneasily. "I'm sure to make a poor job of it. I'll never be a natural orator as Father is."

"Nonsense, you'll do very well." Karuth patted his arm in the faintly proprietorial way that she'd developed in childhood. To her, Tirand knew, he was and always would be the little brother, to be cherished and supported and gently, subtly guided. Now that he was twenty and childhood far behind him, he sometimes found her patronage amusing, but it enhanced rather than lessened his affection for her.

He ran his hands through the crisp dark curls of his hair and said, "Well, I suppose I'd best settle down to work. We've a Lower Rite at dusk, an elemental conjuration to see if we can find out what's behind these unexplained floods in Wishet province." He looked up at her. "You'll be attending that?"

"Oh, yes." Karuth's particular talent for treating with the lower elemental spirits was unusual, and invaluable to the Circle. "I have some letters to write and see dispatched this afternoon, but I'll be there."

"Letters?" Tirand had begun to flick through the papers awaiting attention. The pile seemed dauntingly thick.

"To the sponsors of would-be candidates for the Circle. We've a number of requests awaiting replies; Father didn't have the time to see to them before he left."

"Ah. Any interesting prospects, do you think?"

"I don't know yet, I've barely read through them. Besides, we can't judge a potential initiate from a single letter. We'll have to postpone any interviews at least until the spring Quarter-Day festival, or possibly later if Father is delayed in the south. Oh, but . . ." She turned, searching on the desk, and pulled out a rolled parchment that still bore traces of a broken seal. "While we're speaking of candidates, a letter came late yesterday, from the Matriarch."

"The Matriarch?" Tirand looked up. "Has Father seen it?"

"No—but as it's only her general seal, I took the liberty of opening it in case it should need an urgent reply." Karuth smoothed the paper. "It concerns her grandniece, a girl of ten. Do you remember, Tirand, years ago the

Matriarch visited the castle and brought a young girl with her? The girl was pregnant and the baby was born here."

Tirand frowned. "I recall something of it. Didn't the mother die?"

"Yes." Karuth's expression grew reflective. "It was at the time of the old High Initiate's death. It's strange, isn't it, how when death's in the air it always seems to call us back to other dyings at other times. The Matriarch adopted the baby and I think there was some mystery surrounding the father's identity, though I was a little young then to know much about such things." She regarded the parchment again thoughtfully. "The child's ten years old now. And the Matriarch has asked Father to consider her for possible initiation into the Circle."

"At ten? That's very unusual for a candidate from outside the castle."

"Yes." There was an odd edge in Karuth's voice: most listeners would have missed it, but Tirand, who knew her better than anyone else, did not. For a few moments she seemed to be silently debating whether or not to speak her mind; then honesty won over caution.

"Tirand, I can't pinpoint it, but I detect great concern underlying the Matriarch's letter. She says the girl is unusually gifted—that may well be true, yet I feel there's more to her request than that."

Tirand looked keenly at her. "Your instinct's usually trustworthy."

"Perhaps, but . . ." She shook her head. "I don't know; I truly don't know." A pause. "Something very strange happened on the night that the child's mother died. I was keeping vigil with Carnon and Sister Fiora, the Southern Chaun healer. The High Initiate visited us unexpectedly and—"

"Father did?"

"No, no, the old High Initiate, Keridil Toln. He said something about omens. I can't remember now exactly what his words were, but they sent a chill through me, Tirand. A sense of premonition. I've never understood what they meant and I haven't even thought about them for years. Now, though, now that the memory's been stirred . . ." She turned, as though looking about the room for something that wasn't there, and to Tirand her eyes seemed suddenly haunted. "I feel it again. I don't know what it is, but I *feel* it."

Tirand might have treated the statement with healthy skepticism, had it been uttered by anyone but Karuth. And though innate psychism wasn't among his occult talents, he felt, as she spoke, as though something dark and cold and unimaginably ancient had exhaled a gentle but icy breath into the warm room.

Karuth had let the Matriarch's letter drop back onto the desk. Reaching out, Tirand picked it up and looked at the neat, familiar writing.

"My greatniece Ygorla . . . natural gifts . . . I would not wish to stand in the way of her development . . . the adepts' assessment of her potential . . . if she is willing . . ." He looked up.

" 'If she is willing.' " He repeated the last phrase aloud. "It seems to imply that the Matriarch is more anxious to see her ward settled safely within the Circle than the child is herself."

Karuth nodded gravely. "I have the same impression. And I keep asking myself why that should be."

"The Matriarch wants only the best for the girl. Surely that's understandable?"

"Of course. But there's more to this. Even if Ria Morys herself doesn't know it, there's more. I think . . ." Karuth hesitated, then continued with new and abrupt conviction. "I think that Father should be persuaded to defer the matter, at least for the time being. Something tells me . . ." Her voice trailed off, and after a moment Tirand prompted:

"Something tells you . . . ?"

Karuth nipped at her lower lip. "Call it instinct; I wouldn't care to put it more strongly than that." She looked directly at him, and her gray eyes were candid and troubled. "But something tells me, Tirand, that the Circle shouldn't risk bringing this child into its midst. Not yet. Not until we can be sure that it's the right thing to do."

6

In a world which had been at peace with itself and with its gods for more than seventy years, the everyday concerns of human existence had the opportunity to grow and flourish in a way that would have been impossible in an earlier age. Since the time of Change, history had been largely unremarkable, so that such mainstays of small gossip—births, marriages, deaths, scandals, minor achievements—played a reassuringly prominent role in the dealings of everyone from the highest to the lowest.

As predicted, the reign of Solas Jair Alacar's son Blis was proving to be thoroughly if quietly successful. In the years since his father's death he had inaugurated a number of modest and popular reforms and had a ready, sympathetic ear for the problems of the lesser Margraves and the ten provinces they ruled. Though thirty now, he hadn't yet chosen a wife, and speculative hope was rife in the higher echelons among families with eligible daughters.

Blis Alacar's continuing bachelorhood wasn't something of particular concern to Ria Morys; but in the autumn of the fourth year of his reign she was preoccupied with the topic of marriage, albeit with a different goal in mind. Ygorla was approaching her fourteenth birthday, a multiple of seven and therefore a theoretical milestone in her life. Traditionally the future of a wellborn child should be lengthily and seriously considered and, with the gods' grace, finalized at such an age, but in Ygorla's case Ria was forced to admit that the future looked anything but certain.

The High Initiate's punctiliously diplomatic refusal of

her request for her grandniece's early admission to the Circle had disappointed Ria, though it hadn't entirely surprised her. Chiro Piadar Lin wasn't a man to go against protocol, and protocol dictated that no child of ten, unless born and bred to castle life, could be either mature or stable enough to embark on the rigorous training of an initiate.

In a way, the collapse of her hopes had been a blessing in disguise, for as time passed, Ygorla showed no sign of settling into a more adult attitude, nor of tempering her fickle inclinations to a steadier ambition. As a novice in the Circle, the Matriarch was forced to admit, she would have been a dismal failure—but the vexed question of what her future *did* hold still remained unanswered. As she put the finishing touches to the guest list for the party that would mark her grandniece's birthday, Ria offered a silent prayer to both Aeoris and Yandros—though her fundamental loyalty was to Order, she acknowledged that, in this matter at least, Chaos might lend a more sympathetic ear—that at long last there might be a glimmer of dawn at the end of a long and dark night. From the ranks of the higher families of four provinces she had counted fifteen unwedded and potentially desirable sons. Surely one of them, at least, would take Ygorla's fancy? For it seemed that, indifferent as she was to the idea of joining either the Circle or the Sisterhood, marriage was the only remaining option if she was to make anything of her life.

The birthday celebration was to be an opulent event. Ria felt obliged to provide the best, and had dug deeply into her purse to ensure that the occasion would be the talk of three provinces for a good while to come. For protocol's sake she sent invitations to her brother and his wife—as Ygorla's grandparents, it would have been unthinkable to leave them out—but secretly she was relieved when they politely declined. Since Ygorla's birth the family had staunchly refused to do more than barely acknowledge her existence; obliquely they blamed the child for her mother's untimely death, and any meeting between them would have been, to say the least of it, fraught. Besides, in recent years Ria and Paon had become increasingly estranged and the Matriarch admitted privately that she was becoming heartily sick of her brother's posturing and pretension. Old age didn't suit Paon, she told herself. The eccentricity it brought sat awkwardly on his shoulders, and he was becoming, to put it bluntly, an intolerable bore. The party, she decided with satisfaction as she tore up his declination and consigned it to her wastebasket, would go perfectly well without him.

"So your . . . great-aunt's sister must be your . . . grandmother?" The young man smiled helplessly, his blue eyes pleading for assistance. The hall was hot, the company daunting for an unfledged nestling of a minor but ambitious Wishet-Province family, and he was acutely aware of his own mother's hawklike eye fastened on him from a distance and watching his every movement.

Ygorla's rouged mouth curved into a sweet bow and she said, "No."

A fresh wave of perspiration broke out on the young man's face. "Ah." Further words failed him, and shame followed the confusion. She was so lovely and so supremely self-confident; it was all too easy to forget that she was four years his junior and that he should be leading her in conversation rather than she leading him and tripping him at every turn. He swallowed, and tried again. "Then your grandmother must be . . ."

"My grandfather's wife." Ygorla's eyes, which were a far more intense blue than his, regarded him with steady and faintly amused contempt. "It's perfectly simple, if you've the wit to comprehend it. I was given my great-aunt Ria's clan name because my grandfather—her brother—doesn't wish to acknowledge me. You see, I am a bastard."

Her companion's face turned crimson. To admit in private that there was no stigma in being born out of wedlock was one thing; to hear the status proclaimed with such blatant relish was quite another. He made one last desperate effort to redeem the topic but it collapsed into a stammering mumble. Mercilessly Ygorla watched him in silence until at last he faltered to a hopeless halt; then she lifted her bare white shoulders in a careless shrug.

"I'm sure that you're not in the least interested by my origins," she said in honeyed tones. "After all, you care only for what your mother says you must care for, and in her world status carries far more weight than background, doesn't it?" She yawned ostentatiously. "I think I shall find a more entertaining companion. Good night."

She didn't look back as she walked away. She didn't need to, she knew without the evidence of her eyes what his expression would be. Chagrin, shame, frustration, and disappointment. He must be the third, perhaps even the fourth hopeful suitor whom she'd crushed with her tongue tonight, and Ygorla felt a glow of perverse satisfaction warm her. It was the only entertainment she'd so far found at this tedious celebration.

She was making her way toward the end of the refectory hall where four long tables had been lavishly laden with food and drink, when a girl some three years her senior intercepted her. Shar Veryan was a novice in the Sisterhood and, insofar as Ygorla was willing to be friendly with anyone, the two had struck up a companionable relationship since Shar's arrival at the Cot.

"Ygorla!" Shar kissed her cheek. "I'm sorry to be so late. My parents are here and I've been trapped in *interminable* small talk with them." She drew back, holding Ygorla at arm's length. "Oh, but you look wonderful! You put us all to shame—felicitations on your auspicious day!"

Ygorla felt a little of her pent anger ebb away, and she said, "Thank you, Shar. You look uncommonly fine yourself." The compliment was genuine enough, especially so as she knew that she could afford to be generous; by comparison to her own slender, dark beauty, Shar was an ox. And red certainly didn't suit her.

Shar clasped her hands together and gazed rapturously around the room. "Such a splendid occasion! The Matriarch has spared nothing, and rightly so." Her voice became conspiratorial. "I saw you dancing a while ago with the Margrave of Prospect's eldest son. What is he like?"

"He's tedious," Ygorla said with rancor. "All he can

talk about is his father's estates and how he intends to improve them when the old man dies and he inherits his role. He's so *parochial*. I don't believe he's ever strayed beyond Prospect's borders in his life before tonight."

Shar raised her eyebrows. "He's handsome, though. You have to allow that."

"Handsome." Ygorla repeated the word with studied contempt. "Oh, yes. He's handsome. But so is a good horse, and I wouldn't converse with a horse from choice."

A faintly uncomfortable silence fell. Then Shar said gently, "Oh, dear."

Her tone raised Ygorla's hackles, and with more venom than she'd intended she fired back, "Oh, dear, *what?*"

Shar sighed. "You're not enjoying the night, are you? No, don't try to deny it—I know you too well by now and it's just what I feared. Ygorla, can't you try? For the Matriarch's sake if nothing else? She only wants the best for you, as we all do!"

The small, tight knot of utter darkness that had been pent deep within Ygorla's mind since the celebration began suddenly burst and flowered into rage. She turned on Shar, and had the satisfaction of seeing the other girl recoil before her furious, ice-cold gaze.

"Very well," she said savagely. "Very *well*. I'll tell you the truth, Shar, if that's what you want. I *hate* this celebration! I hate every crude, pitiful attempt to please me and to manipulate me. I hate everyone here—I hate the Margraves and the merchants and all their simpering sons, I hate Aunt Ria, I hate Sister Fiora and Sister Corelm and all the twittering crew—and if you're not careful I'm going to hate you as well, because you don't possess enough sense to see through this whole charade!"

"Ygorla!" Shar was shocked and dismayed. "You don't mean that."

"I *do!*" Suddenly Ygorla didn't care who might be watching or what punishment she might receive in the cold light of dawn, and she stamped her foot, turning heads all around them. The fury was loose, she couldn't control it and didn't want to, and she turned with a dramatic gesture, letting her voice carry shrilly through the crowd. "I hate you all! I hate *everything!*"

And under the stunned stares of a hundred guests she hitched up the skirt of her expensive silk gown and ran from the room.

———————————⟩ ⟨——————————

The autumn chill was like a slap in the face as Ygorla rushed pell-mell out of the hall that led from the refectory and into the quiet night. She stumbled a few paces across the courtyard, then regained her balance and her dignity and halted, drinking in the sharp air and letting its soothing balm wash over her.

Damn them. She'd meant what she said, every word of it, and the hate was a precious jewel inside her. She hadn't wanted this celebration, which had been designed solely to force her into a mold to which she didn't want to conform. *Marriage.* What did she want with marriage? To be the chattel of some stammering fool who wielded power without the sense to understand what power could really mean. Or to take the white veil of the Sisterhood, or the gold badge of a Circle initiate. They, too, were only marriage in another guise. To be forever second, to be subject to another's will. She didn't want that. She wouldn't *tolerate* it.

She started to stamp across the courtyard, heading toward the small annex attached to the Matriarch's house, where she had her own private quarters. A long shadow cast by the two moons, which were almost in conjunction, fell across her and she slowed, looking up at the simple column of white marble some thirty feet high, that stood at the court's exact center. The column had been erected over seventy years ago as a commemorative monument to the Change. It was supposed to symbolize the purity of balance between Order and Chaos, though for the life of her Ygorla had never been able to comprehend how such a dull, featureless object could be said to symbolize anything at all. For years now she had loftily ignored the monument, but for once she stopped and stared at it, and her anger focused tightly on its smooth, passive lines.

"What do *you* know?" she hissed under her breath, challenging the fourteen gods and feeling a delicious sense of pure heresy as she spat the words. "What use are you? Aeoris and Yandros and all the gods of light and dark— what have you ever done for *me?*"

There was no bolt of lightning, no instantaneous retribution for her impertinence. If there had been, if she'd been struck down where she stood, Ygorla doubted if she would have cared anyway. Damn Aunt Ria, she thought again. Damn the gods too. Damn *everything.*

Behind her in the refectory, torches and candles blazed and music played on. She could see through the fogged windows the blurred forms of the party guests dancing, the swirl of mingling colors. Food and wine and laughter and revelry, and she, for whose benefit in theory this entire farce had been arranged, was out here alone and lonely in the night, miserable and uncomforted and angry. It wasn't *fair.*

But the gods, like the stars that twinkled remotely in the clear autumn sky, weren't concerned with her desires, and that knowledge only served to increase Ygorla's anger and strengthen her determination that, tonight of all nights, when she was fourteen and almost an adult in her own right, she would bow the knee to no one. Let them continue with their celebration if that was what satisfied them. She would have no further part in it.

There was no light in her quarters, but she wanted none. Years of familiarity had accustomed her to the exact placing of every item of furniture, and she picked her way across the room, unfastening the party gown—how she *hated* it at this moment, despite the fact that she knew how well it enhanced her burgeoning beauty—as she headed for her bed. The dress fell from her, crumpling to the floor with a silky rustle that only increased her irritation, and, dressed in her smallclothes, Ygorla flung herself facedown among the pillows and burst into furious tears.

"Damn *everything!*" Her frustration was at such a pitch that she could think of nothing more satisfying than to repeat her earlier expletive, though it didn't help. Given the chance, she told herself savagely, she'd burn it all down. The Cot, the simpering sisters, her great-aunt, the party guests, and most of all that complacent, thrice-cursed monument, which she could feel *staring* at her through the window as though passing silent judgment. *Rot* it. *Cess* to it. *Putrefaction* take them all—why wouldn't they just *die?*

At her back, Ygorla heard the soft sound of a door opening.

She tensed instantly. Her immediate reaction had been to assume that the sound came from her own door, that someone had seen her run from the refectory and had followed her. But another, deeper instinct following on the heels of the first told her it was not so.

Slowly, and very cautiously, Ygorla raised her head from the pillow and turned to look.

There was light in the room where before there had been only darkness. It hung, a perfect, dimly phosphorescent oval, a handspan above the floor, and peculiar shadows spread out from it to lurk and flicker on the walls. The door whose latch she had heard was suspended in the center of the glowing oval, and as she stared with growing astonishment at it, the door began to swing open.

A bizarre spectrum of colors flickered about the door's outline for a brief moment, then faded, leaving only the steady, opalescent glow. Ygorla saw a hand, its knuckles distorted as though with some wasting disease, slip around the doorframe. A new shadow fell across the floor, seeming to quiver in the nacreous light. A voice laughed softly.

"Wh . . ." Ygorla took a grip on herself. Shocked she might be, but she wasn't afraid; intuition told her that whatever this phenomenon might be, she had nothing to fear from it. She tried again, and this time her voice was clear and sharp. "Who's there?"

Silence. The echoes of the laugh had faded; only the hand remained, gently, gently pushing the door further open.

She saw his eyes first. They were like banked fires burnt almost to embers, hot and crimson and searing. The eyes smiled at her, laughed at her, and the full, sensual mouth below the hook of a nose smiled too. Hair that gleamed like a newly minted copper coin hung in wild tangles around the blade-sharp face and over shoulders distorted by a terrible hunch; the white torso beneath was naked, wizened and carried on spindle shanks with splayed, clawed feet like the legs of some bizarre bird.

The gnarled hands gripped the spectral doorframe and the figure stepped through, out of the shimmering oval, to land lightly in the room.

Ygorla didn't shrink back. She remained motionless, knowing with a blend of instinct and learning what manner of creature this was. Human—or near-human—though it might appear, it was not born of the mortal world but came from a dimension beyond this world's reach. Not a god, not this warped thing. Even Yandros, the most unpredictable and mercurial of all the fourteen deities, had his vanity. Nor an emissary of Aeoris, for Order abhorred such misshapen ugliness. No: this was a being of another kind entirely.

The room was claustrophobically still. The nacreous oval still glowed in midair, but the door within it had vanished. There was just the night and the silence. And her supernatural visitor.

With clear and utterly calm emphasis Ygorla said: "Who are you?"

A sharp, quick smile; the hot eyes flickered briefly with something that might have been amusement. The being had peculiarly white teeth, the canines abnormally long, like the fangs of a predatory animal. Then he spoke, and the voice that issued from the smiling mouth was the most intelligent, most persuasive voice that Ygorla had ever heard.

He said: "My name is Narid-na-Gost."

A sensation that was fire and ice together touched her spine with preternatural fingers. The name meant nothing, and yet in a part of her mind that she could neither fathom nor control, it had the thrilling ring of familiarity. And its nature—the hard syllables, the faint slyness implicit in its pronunciation—turned suspicion into certainty.

Ygorla's vivid eyes narrowed. "Narid-na-Gost." She tried the name out on her own tongue, and the sound of it pleased her. "Why should Chaos have decided to send one of its demons to visit me?"

For a moment her visitor's expression registered surprise. Then he laughed, a quiet laugh and one that many mortals would have found chilling. Ygorla, however, didn't flinch. She simply smiled with the satisfaction of her small triumph, and as his laughter subsided, Narid-na-Gost bowed sardonically.

"I salute your perception, Ygorla, though I must correct you in one particular. I am, as you say, of Chaos; but Chaos didn't send me. Indeed"—he began to pace slowly across the room, looking at her assessingly as he moved—"my masters"—a faint twist to his lips now—"are unaware of my presence here. My business with you is strictly personal."

Ygorla didn't reply. Her pulse had quickened to the point where it was almost painful, but she was determined to maintain her outward calm. Inwardly, though, her thoughts were seething. A demon who claimed to have a personal concern with her—and this was her fourteenth birthday, an occasion of great significance. There must be a connection. There *must!*

"The day is significant." Narid-na-Gost stopped, then chuckled again as he saw her dismay. "No, Ygorla, I can't read every nuance of your thoughts. But your eyes are windows through which your mind shines like a beacon." He began to move again, now walking with his odd, ungainly gait toward the window. Reaching it, he stared out into the courtyard, past the white stone monument to the lit windows of the refectory.

"I have waited fourteen years for this night," he said, not looking at her. "More than fourteen years, for I have been waiting and watching since the night in Prospect province when a young blade in his cups set himself to seducing a wealthy and wayward girl of seventeen." He paused, and the embers of his eyes met hers again. "Or is this not a fit subject for one of your tender years?"

Ygorla smiled superciliously. "I'm not a child. I know perfectly well what men and women do in the pursuit of pleasure."

"Yes. I thought you might." Narid-na-Gost turned away from the window at last and surveyed the room. Its Spartan furnishings, which Ygorla had always loathed, seemed to amuse him. "Then you may also have gathered from the whispered conversations of your elders that your mother conferred her favors very generously before her untimely demise. A pretty face, some pretty manners, a few pretty compliments"—again he made no effort to hide his contempt—"were quite enough to ensure that she'd be obliging to a would-be lover." He paused, and an intuition far beyond her years told Ygorla that this was a challenge, a gauntlet. He expected her to rise to the bait as any dutiful child would do. She smiled.

"My mother was a slut, and I'm the bastard daughter of her whoring. Don't hesitate to say it; it's no less than the truth."

As she spoke, she experienced a quick, sharp flood of adrenaline. Never before in her life had she dared to utter such words to another soul, though she'd lost count of the times when she had longed to shout them, spit them in the faces of her great-aunt or Sister Corelm or any of her clucking tutors and peers. However delicately others might try to couch it, she knew the truth and wasn't ashamed of it. Indeed, the knowledge had always evoked a sense of perverse pride in her, for if nothing else, her mother had at least been unconventional.

Narid-na-Gost inclined his head, acknowledging the point. "Do you hate her for that?"

"Not for that." Ygorla's shoulders lifted carelessly. "Only for dying and leaving me to the mercies of the Sisterhood."

"Ah. You have no ambitions, then, to become a novice?"

Ygorla's eyes grew steely. "None."

"Or to find a handsome and wealthy husband?"

The girl's lip curled. "Show me a handsome and wealthy man in this or any other province, and I'll show you a fool."

"Such cynicism in one so young." The demon made a show of regret, but it didn't deceive Ygorla for a moment. Then his expression hardened. "Though it's nothing less than I would have expected from you. In fact, I am glad— *very* glad—to hear it." He took a pace toward her and seemed pleased when she didn't shrink back. "Yet you must have some ambition. What is it, Ygorla? What do you want, above all else in the mortal world?"

For the first time since this bizarre encounter had begun, Ygorla was suddenly unsure of herself. The demon's face was only inches from her own, and his eyes held her, mesmerizing her as a snake might mesmerize its intended prey. She gazed into their depths, beyond the glowing crimson irises, beyond the black pinpoints of the pupils, and for a moment that robbed her of breath she seemed to see into another, impossible dimension where something akin to madness reigned. In those depths a worm of desire stirred and raised its ugly head.

She knew the answer to the question he had asked, and she dared not lie to him. Nor, she realized with sudden cold clarity, did she wish to.

She said: "I want *power.*"

For a long, racking moment there was silence. Then Narid-na-Gost exhaled a breath that seemed to take life of its own, whispering through the room and filling it with rustling echoes.

"Ah, Ygorla. How that pleases me. How that *pleases* me." He raised a hand and held it out to her. The gesture was gentle yet commanding; though she didn't consciously will it, Ygorla found her fingers joining with his. His skin was warm and smooth, like old, cherished parchment. The rough-edged fingernails grazed her palm.

"Your mother took her pleasures where she found them," Narid-na-Gost said softly. "But the young man who courted her on that night more than fourteen years ago was too far gone in his cups to take advantage of the favor she conferred on him. So while he snored his drunken stupor away, another opened the door that he had left ajar. And Avali Troi, also inflamed with wine but without sharing its unfortunate consequences, welcomed that other one in the fond belief that he was her chosen lover."

Ygorla continued to stare at him as the truth slid like a knife into her brain. She couldn't speak, she was beyond words. Only her eyes, widening with the suddenly kindled flame of understanding, mirrored the inchoate shock of the revelation.

Narid-na-Gost raised her hand to his full lips and

kissed it. When he spoke again, his voice was a sibilant whisper that thrust a spike of ice and fire through her heart.

"I have waited fourteen years to make myself known to you, Ygorla. For you are my daughter."

7

"Then I am . . ." Ygorla didn't recognize her own voice. It came from too far away, it was too alien, and suddenly she felt as though huge invisible hands had taken hold of her and ripped her in two. One part, the earthbound, frustrated adolescent whose world revolved however unwillingly around the Sisterhood Cot, could only flounder in the throes of numbing shock. But the other part—and that, she *knew,* was the real Ygorla—felt a headlong rush of wild excitement that pitched her mind into a world of awesome possibilities.

The glorious exultation lasted only a moment before reason jerked her mind back to coherence. This was *madness.* A jester's story, incredible, impossible. She couldn't believe it. She *dared* not believe it, not without proof, and suddenly her excitement was eclipsed by searing disappointment.

She said harshly, *"No!"*

"No?" Narid-na-Gost repeated the word very gently. He had watched her struggling, watched the rapid play of emotions on her face, but his own expression gave nothing away.

Ygorla's lips tightened to a thin line. "I don't trust you! How do I know that this isn't some game you're playing with me? You may not be what you claim at all. You may be some incubus come to dupe me as you say my mother was duped!"

"Is that what you believe?"

"I . . ." Then Ygorla stopped as she realized that she couldn't answer his question. She simply didn't know. And her confusion was made all the worse by the fact that, with a yearning that was almost a physical pain within her, she wanted what he had told her to be true.

Narid-na-Gost said softly, "I can prove it."

Her head came up quickly and she looked at him with suspicious eyes. "How?" Her heart was pounding.

The demon gestured toward the window. "By showing you something of the power that lies dormant within you and waiting to be awakened." A thin, vulpine smile. "You say that power is what you desire above all else. You have power, Ygorla. More power than the miserable meddlers who call themselves adepts of the gods. More power than the High Initiate and all his acolytes. More power than any mortal in this world. All you lack is the knowledge that will enable you to use it."

Ygorla drew breath slowly between clenched teeth. "Then," she said with an icy calm that she was very far from feeling, "show me. Prove it to me—if you can."

The demon chuckled. "You doubt my promise. Good. I would have thought the less of you without it. Come to the window."

She began to move, then hesitated. Narid-na-Gost regarded her quizzically, head tilted like a bird's. "What are you afraid of? Failure—or success?"

Ygorla's chin jutted. "I'm not afraid!" She snatched at her underskirt, pushing its folds clear of her ankles, and strode to stand beside him. Their faces were on a level. Narid-na-Gost smiled.

"Look out of the window, Ygorla. Tell me what you see."

She turned her head. "The courtyard, The refectory windows. The monument."

"Ah, yes, the monument. I sense your contempt for that memorial to human piety. Burn it. Call on your power, and burn it to ashes."

Quickly, startled, Ygorla looked at him again. *"Burn* it? That's impossible! Stone doesn't burn."

"Not with mortal fire, perhaps. But the flames of Chaos are another matter." The demon smiled again. "Burn it, Ygorla. Face your true heritage and learn what it means!"

As he spoke, the crimson embers of his eyes flared like a fire newly stirred, and Ygorla felt a surge of energy cleave through her as the demon's mind locked with hers. For a fraction of a moment the sensation was shockingly alien—and then an incredible feeling of familiarity hit her, as though a key had turned in the lock of her awareness to fling open the door to her deepest self. She cried out, shock turning to monstrous exultation, and her own eyes blazed as something vast, uncheckable, unhuman, blasted through her consciousness, focused—

The monument erupted in a sheet of blue-green fire. Dazzling light slammed against the window and into the room, and a roar like a cataract shook the walls. Ygorla reeled back, staggering and shouting as the power that had ripped from her mind loosed its hold on her. She spun around, cannoned into a chair, and fell to all fours, then looked up to where Narid-na-Gost stood gazing impassively down at her. A hellish dance of glare and shadow from the Chaos flames lit the demon's twisted form, turning his skin a bizarre and nightmarish piebald. She knew now that he had told her the truth.

"*I* . . ." But there were no more words to say; that statement of herself, her identity, her knowledge, was all. She wasn't fully human. She was the seed of Chaos. She bridged the awesome gulf between mortals and their gods. At last, at long last, after fourteen years of waiting without knowing it, she was *alive*.

Her head jerked around in a reflexive spasm as new sounds broke in on the wave of stunned understanding. Voices yelling, screaming; the party guests had seen the conflagration in the courtyard and a tangle of shadowy figures was pouring from the refectory. One voice in particular strove to make itself heard over the mayhem, and Ygorla recognized the frantic tones of her great-aunt calling for water and fire brooms. Ygorla's mouth stretched into a terrible smile. Water and brooms would avail them nothing—the monument was burning with a fire that couldn't be quenched, and that knowledge brought a wild surge of laughter bubbling up within her. She flung her head back, her black hair reflecting a hundred colors as the hellglow played on it, and the laughter burst savagely, joyfully from her throat. Through it, and through the flames' crackle and the cries of the panicking sisters and their guests, she heard Narid-na-Gost's voice, harsh and triumphant.

"Now you understand! Don't you, my daughter—*don't you?*"

"Yes!" She cried the affirmation. "Oh, Father, *yes!*"

She didn't hear the crash of the outer door. She had regained her feet and run back to the window, her face exultant as she drank in the frantic scene outside, and the sound was only one more discord lost amid the general clamor. Only when running footsteps sounded in the corridor, growing rapidly louder and closer, did she turn her head alertly. As she swung away from the window, the door of her room burst open, and Ria Morys, hair awry and the hem of her robe torn, appeared on the threshold.

"Ygorla!" Relief broke through the fear in the Matriarch's voice. "Thank Aeoris and Yandros you're safe! I thought—" Then abruptly she stopped as she saw Narid-na-Gost for the first time. The hectic color drained from her face and she flung up one hand in a sign against evil. *"Sweet gods—"*

The emotion and the reaction which followed it hit Ygorla like a Warp. *Hatred.* It focused on Ria, on all that Ria stood for, and she felt the power roaring up again from the depths of her soul. It coalesced into a bolt of howling energy, and the Matriarch shrieked as a white fireball exploded in her face. Flames leapt to the ceiling, fastening on her body; her clothing and hair disintegrated with a flash and a murderous thud of devoured air, and the shriek rose to a hideous pitch as Ria's flesh burned from her bones. Somewhere, the child that Ygorla had once been was screaming in horrified harmony with the writhing Matriarch, but that child was drowning in the power, in the triumph, of the demon's daughter who opened her mouth and yelled with unholy glee as the woman who for fourteen years had been her nurturer screeched her agony to the gods, and died.

Suddenly, with an enormous concussion, the flames punched their last fury to the ceiling and went out. Lights danced before Ygorla's eyes as gloom shot only with the capering glow from the courtyard crashed down on the room—but this time she didn't stagger, didn't reel: she simply stood motionless, utterly controlled, and stared down at what she had wrought.

It might have been a human corpse, or an animal, or a pile of discarded, charred rags. She drew a deep breath and smelled the sick-sweet stench of roasted flesh, which to her was like the scent of a rich and heady wine. She felt no remorse, only satisfaction, and with it an awesome awareness of her own potential. Narid-na-Gost had taken no hand in this. The power had been hers alone. And now that she had tasted it, she craved more. Chaos was awake within her, and its flames, like the flames that devoured the monument, couldn't be extinguished.

She raised her head from the smoking thing on the floor at last, and met Narid-na-Gost's smoldering crimson gaze.

"Others will come," the demon said gently.

Ygorla smiled, showing her teeth. "Let them. I will deal with them as I have dealt with *that.*" One hand made a careless gesture toward the corpse.

The demon shook his head. "No, daughter. That time is not yet."

Triumph had made her reckless; she tossed her head defiantly. "What? Do you think I can't—"

"Hear me." Abruptly the tone of his voice changed as he interrupted her, and a spike of pure ice cut through the burning heat of her delight. For one moment an appalling image that she couldn't even assimilate, let alone name, flickered across the periphery of her consciousness, and for the first time she felt fear. She battled against the sensation that seemed to crush her vitals, but the demon's eyes were steady and her will crumbled before the threat of panic. Perspiration beaded her forehead; she clenched her fists, forced herself to look away.

"That's better." Honey laced Narid-na-Gost's tone now, but the threat still remained and Ygorla dared not move a muscle. "You will listen to me, daughter, and you will pay heed. Yes, you are powerful, but as yet your skills are nothing to mine. You have a great deal to learn, and I have not waited through all these years to see you cast your heritage away as a mortal drunk on new wine might cast away his fortune. Do you understand me?"

Something was trying to lock her jaw, but she fought it. "Y-yes. Yes . . . Father."

"Good. Then listen to me, and obey. The time has come for you to leave this pitiful place and make your home elsewhere. No"—as her eyes widened—"not the realm of Chaos. Not for many years yet." He held out one arm commandingly. "I have other and greater plans for you. Take my hand, Ygorla."

Her whole body was beginning to tremble. She told herself that it wasn't fear, merely a reflexive reaction, and forced her fingers to intertwine with his. His hand seemed to burn into her flesh, and he smiled.

"Make your farewells, my daughter. If you see your friends again, it will be under very different circumstances."

Ygorla looked quickly about her at the room that had been her sanctuary for so long. Her possessions—clothes, letters, ornaments, souvenirs, all the tiny mosaic pieces of her life—for a moment she felt adrift. These were the sum of all her memories and experiences, the physical reflections of her identity and place within the world. Without them she would have nothing to anchor her, no point of reference. Then abruptly, doubt fled. The Matriarch was a blackened husk on the floor at her feet, and outside these enclosing walls, fire was burning and voices were screaming. She, *she* was the architect of this mayhem, and with such power at her command, what else could she possibly need to tell her what she truly was?

The last of her uncertainty collapsed before new understanding, and joy flooded her like a rising tide. She met the demon's gaze with a terrible, avid smile.

"Yes, Father—I am ready!"

Narid-na-Gost looked up toward the ceiling, and suddenly the roof of the Cot seemed to dissolve so that her room stood open to the vast night sky. Cold air with a distant hint of frost and sulfur swept through the chamber as though an invisible giant had exhaled, and an ominous shadow fell across Ygorla. The atmosphere was darkening, thickening, beginning to agitate; the demon gripped her other hand, pulling her toward him, and she heard a faint, hollow howling like a far-off whirlwind. The floor beneath her lurched—and then they were rising, her feet flailing as they left the ground, spearing up, up as the great black wing of power took hold of them and thrust them like two leaves in a gale away into the night.

Amid the furor that gripped the courtyard, it was some minutes before the Matriarch's absence was noticed. Only when Sister Corelm, tending the burns of one of the hapless firefighters, realized that Ria hadn't returned from her search for Ygorla was a young novice dispatched to the girl's room to see if all was well.

The novice's screams brought Corelm and four companions running to Ygorla's quarters. Later, with the novice heavily sedated and the blackened stump of the monument smoking like a small malevolent volcano, Corelm at last found time to let the tears come as she crouched in her own infirmary and vomited the bile of delayed shock and horror in the first chilly glimmer of dawn.

Now she knew how a falcon must feel when it broke free from the confinement of dull earth to soar across the world. The Cot had fallen far behind them, its buildings reduced to tiny white dolls' houses that whirled away into the distance, the burning monument a last angry, winking eye until it too was lost in the dark. They flew high above the fertile meadows of Southern Chaun, over vineyards and farms and the cold, shining ribbons of rivers, and Ygorla laughed in harmony with the voice of the wind that bore them, her hair streaming behind her, her arms upraised to the heavens, and the demon's taloned hands tight upon her waist. Past Wester Town, the gracious old province capital with its Margrave's grand residence aloof on the central hill. Only a bare few lights glimmered at this dead hour, and she longed for Narid-na-Gost to hurl down a lightning bolt of their contempt to shatter the town's slumbering serenity, but the demon's face was impassive, and already Wester had become a diminishing blur behind them as they speared onward faster than any mortal creature could fly. Ahead now was the province border and the huge, chill mouth of Prospect Estuary, where the river met the sea in a glittering mirror. On then into Prospect itself, its forests spread like a black cloak to the south, and then skimming the edge of a gleaming coastline where breakers showed silver on the ocean's shifting surface. Then there were moors, bleak and empty but for the pale, isolated line of a lonely drove road. And at last, shining in the distance like a beacon, the lights of the town that never slept, the greatest and busiest harbor in all the world: Shu-Nhadek.

New excitement gripped Ygorla and she twisted her upper body to look at Narid-na-Gost's face. The demon was smiling, his crimson stare fixed on something still far ahead of them, too far for her to be able to discern. But she thought she knew at last what their destination was to be. Not Shu-Nhadek itself, but what lay beyond Shu-Nhadek, out over the glittering southern sea.

Her lips parted and she cried two breathless words. *"Summer Isle!"*

Narid-na-Gost smiled and said, "No."

Hope and imagination crumbled into confusion. They were above the town now, the harbor lights blurring into vivid streaks with the speed of their passage. On the horizon, where the sea met the sky at an incalculable distance, a thin, phantasmic aurora danced across the heavens, and distant thunder rolled as a storm—a natural storm, not a Warp—gathered. Ygorla didn't understand. She had been so sure that their destination could only be the Summer Isle, seat of the High Margrave himself, but beyond Shu's coast there was nothing else but the end of the world.

Shu-Nhadek was falling behind, night swallowing the lights and the wharves and the ships bobbing at anchor in the shelter of the bay. Summer Isle, she knew, lay away to the west, invisible in the darkness, but there, a jewel, a goal. But ahead, another island was looming—and suddenly an old catechism slipped back into Ygorla's memory, a story from the time of Change.

And so it was decreed that these three, on whose shoulders the fate of the world might ultimately rest, should meet together in solemn conclave, in the place appointed by Aeoris of Order to be his stronghold and his pledge. And there upon that isle, which is known to us now, as it was in those days, as the White Isle, did the High Margrave and the High Initiate and the Matriarch make their fateful appointment with the gods themselves. . . .

She could see it now. It rose from the sea like a blunt, accusing finger pointing heavenward, harsh and barren against the tide's black swell. Waves crashed savagely against the jagged cliffs that formed ramparts at the island's feet, and towering above those ramparts was a single titanic, jagged crag. Aeons ago the sea had given birth to the White Isle in a roaring cataclysm of fire, but now, its fury long extinct, its fearsome life extinguished, all that remained of the ancient volcano was this single dead cone.

But this, Ygorla knew, was—or had been—far more than merely a lifeless basalt island. For it was here that Aeoris had placed a sacred artifact in the care of his human worshipers, a golden casket, which in a time of great peril when the rule of Order was threatened might be opened by the High Initiate in conclave with the High Margrave and Matriarch to call the lords of Order back to the world. On this site, in the barren bowl of the ancient crater, Keridil Toln had set his hand to the sacred casket, and thereby played his part in the last supernatural battle that had brought about Equilibrium.

Ygorla's already thundering heart gave a great lurch as the White Isle loomed closer and she saw the crater clearly at last. Its north face had split, gaping to the night like a vast, slack, idiot mouth, and she remembered the stories of the final conflict between Chaos and Order. Legend had it that the hand of Yandros himself had smashed through the cone as he confronted his archenemy Aeoris, and images of mayhem rioted in her imagination. Such a time that must have been, such a power that must have rampaged through the world—

She realized abruptly that their wild flight was slowing. Narid-na-Gost's hands pulled at her, turning her in the air, and the physical sensation brought her mind back to the moment. They hovered high over the angry sea, and now she could hear the rumbling hiss of the waves as they beat against the cliffs. The shattered cone yawned before them, shockingly close; eastward, a spear of lightning flashed silently on the horizon, and beyond the lightning the sky was beginning to pale to thin silver-gray with the first hint of dawn.

Narid-na-Gost smiled at her and nodded toward the crater. He didn't speak; she was sure of his intention now, and there was no need for words. They began to descend, gliding downward in a gentle, effortless spiral. The sharp, unfamiliar tang of salt and seaweed filled Ygorla's nostrils, and with it came a pang of terror: born and bred far from any coast, the sea was to her both hostile and implacably alien, and she felt a dizzy rush of near-panic as its huge swell seemed to surge toward her. Then the scene tilted as Narid-na-Gost turned again in midair. A paler blur loomed before her, and suddenly the waves were out of sight and they were above the volcano itself, drifting across the cone's broken lip to hover over the crater. Again they began to spiral downward, the rock walls rising to enclose them and cutting off the threatening noise of the sea. She could see streaks of darkly livid color in the walls, and below her the great crater bowl was barren and deserted, with massive chunks of rubble littering the petrified stone floor.

Her feet touched ground. Briefly, perspective swelled and warped as the last vestige of the Chaos power that had carried them here relaxed its grip; then the giddiness fled and her senses righted themselves as she stood, swaying, on solid ground.

Narid-na-Gost's hands fell away from her body and she stepped back. There was something akin to humor in his hot eyes as he said, "Welcome, daughter, to your new home."

Ygorla sucked in a long, deep breath. She could still smell the sea even though she could no longer hear it, and mingling with its scent were the odors of ancient rock and damp, musty decay. She gazed around her, then at last looked at the demon again. Her voice was thin and bewildered.

"This?"

Narid-na-Gost smiled. "Yes, Ygorla, this. Not prepossessing, I grant—but it has one advantage which no other place in the mortal world can offer."

She frowned uneasily. "I don't understand."

He paced across the floor and stopped beside a large and peculiarly symmetrical boulder which seemed to have been sheared in two. One foot prodded the stone, and the demon uttered an unpleasant, throaty laugh.

"So much for the vanities of the gods," he said with sweet venom. "Do you know what this is?"

Ygorla shook her head.

"This worthless lump of rock," said Narid-na-Gost contemptuously, "is all that remains of my lord Aeoris's claim to rulership of this world. In years gone by, when Order was complacent and Chaos had no power to challenge its reign, this island was sacred"—he emphasized the word with withering scorn—"to Aeoris and his insipid brood. And on this stone Aeoris placed an artifact for his human slaves to revere."

"The Casket," Ygorla said softly.

The demon looked sidelong at her. "So the pious sisters taught you that much?"

"They taught me what they wanted me to know." Her tone was resentful as she remembered the many questions she had asked and which her tutors had refused to answer.

"Of course." Narid-na-Gost walked slowly around to the far side of the broken slab, then suddenly, like a snake striking at a victim, bent swiftly and plucked something from the litter of smaller debris that surrounded it. He straightened, clenching his fist; then his fingers opened again and he displayed his prize on an open palm.

Hesitantly Ygorla went toward him, and saw what he had found. Glimmering dully, its brilliance dimmed by the thin predawn shadows, a small gold brooch lay in his hand. It was fashioned in the form of a single circle bisected by a lightning-flash.

"It looks like—" Then she stopped as she realized she was wrong.

Thunder rumbled distantly, though no flicker of lightning had been discernible in the crater. The demon smiled. "What does it look like?"

Ygorla shook her head. "I thought it was a Circle initiate's badge of rank. But the design is wrong. It doesn't show the star of Chaos."

"No, Ygorla, *you* are wrong. It is indeed an initiate's badge, but no initiate has worn such a one as this for nearly a century. In fact, the last mortals to set foot here who might have carried such a badge at their shoulders were those who witnessed the opening of the sacred casket and the vanquishing of Order's rule."

Ygorla's eyes widened. "At the time of Change?"

"Exactly." Narid-na-Gost uttered his throaty laugh again. "What a relic this would have made to grace the altar of some devout religious, if anyone had been observant enough to find it! Instead it has lain here undiscovered, a pitiful and unsung memorial with no one to marvel over it. Now, perhaps, you see why I've chosen this place as your refuge." Carelessly he tossed the gold brooch away, then made a sweeping gesture that took in the sere and empty entirety of the bowl. "The casket of Aeoris is gone. The altar is broken, the eternal votive lamp extinguished, and the ascetic men who once dedicated their lives to guarding the shrine are all long dead. The White Isle has become nothing more than a place where historians can come to indulge their curiosity, and even curiosity has faded to indifference with the years." He turned, and his eyes appeared to focus on a ledge some two hundred feet above the crater floor. Behind the ledge was what looked like a tunnel entrance, but the tunnel was empty and Ygorla couldn't imagine what might be there to capture his attention.

"It has been nearly a decade since any human foot sullied this island," Narid-na-Gost continued. "No one now remembers what happened here, and so no one cares." A faint, sly smile began to creep across his face. "Even my own masters, I suspect, have all but forgotten the Isle's existence. Doubtless they have higher matters to contemplate—which is just as I would wish it." The smile became a vulpine grin. "Solitude, Ygorla. Freedom from prying eyes and curious minds. *That* is what the White Isle offers, and that is why you are to make your home here."

Again Ygorla looked around her at the crater's bowl. Any normal child of fourteen summers—and a good many adults—would have been appalled by the prospect of life in such a grim place. To exist alone among these towering, echoing rocks, without human company or human comforts, would be a sure gateway to breakdown and insanity. But, though embryonic as yet, Ygorla's deepest psyche was stirring her to excited anticipation. She trusted Narid-na-Gost. He had already shown her something of the potential that lay within her soul, and if this was the price she must pay to learn more, then she would welcome the White Isle and solitude with open arms.

She turned to the demon and said eagerly, "What will I do here, Father? What plans do you have for me?"

Some moments passed before Narid-na-Gost answered. The dawn light was slowly growing stronger, and by its all-but-colorless illumination she saw that his crimson eyes had a distant look, as though he contemplated something beyond the reach of human senses. At last, though, his mind seemed to return to the present and he looked at her once more.

"How great is your ambition, Ygorla? Is it, I wonder, as great as mine?"

"What do you mean? I don't understand."

"Of course you don't. And I am not yet ready to tell you everything." Abruptly his eyes became twin furnaces. "First you must learn what you are, and learn how to control the power you have and mold it to your will."

Frustrated, Ygorla started to protest. "I can control it! Last night I—"

"Last night you used your talents randomly and without coherence. That will not do, daughter. For example, how would your unfledged skills cope with *this*?" As he spoke he made a rapid, complex gesture—and Ygorla yelled in fright as, with a screech that echoed around the bowl, a chimera exploded into being above her head. A ghastly meld of eagle, hound, and serpent, it beat its great wings, sending up a storm of dust and debris that blinded Ygorla and caught suffocatingly in her throat. She cried out again, and the chimera answered in a horrible, mocking parody of a human scream as it plummeted, talons outstretched, down toward her.

"No-o-o! No, please!" She stumbled and fell, flinging up her arms in a frantic effort to protect her head—

The chimera vanished. Dust settled, and Ygorla, on her knees, stared up at Narid-na-Gost and prayed silently that she wasn't going to be sick.

"You see?" The demon's voice was deceptively mild. "No thought, no control; you simply reacted like the frightened animal you are."

Fury and fear battled for precedence in Ygorla's mind. She tried to speak but couldn't. And though she railed against it, she had to admit to herself that he was right.

Capitulation showed in her eyes. Narid-na-Gost smiled thinly, then extended a hand toward her. The air seemed momentarily to blur, and when Ygorla looked again, she saw that he was holding a brimming wine cup.

"Drink," he said. "It will restore your composure."

She needed no second telling. Still queasy with shock, she gulped at the wine, shutting her eyes as it went down her throat and began to soothe her frayed nerves. It tasted like nothing she had ever encountered before: sharp yet with a peculiar background sweetness that bore no relation to the sweetness of grapes. She suspected that this was no earthly brew, but something from Chaos.

"You have a great deal to learn," Narid-na-Gost told her, "and your training will take time and resolution and courage. The art of sorcery is not a game for children, and the sorcery in which I shall instruct you is very far removed from the posturings of the human fools at the Star Peninsula. You will look into the face of Chaos, Ygorla, and you must be prepared to meet it without fear."

Her pulse quickened to a rapid, erratic beat. "You mean to take me to the Chaos realm?"

"Ah, no, you misunderstand. *I* shall be your sole mentor, and our work will be done only in the mortal world. My masters"—again there was contempt in his tone, and with it a hint of venomous bitterness—"know nothing of your heritage, let alone my plans for you, and I shall ensure that you are shielded from their attentions until the time is right."

"*What* time, Father?" Ygorla pleaded. "Please, tell me!"

"No." The demon shook his head emphatically. "I will tell you only when I am certain that you are ready to know. Meanwhile, though, I promise you this. If you are diligent and obey me in all things, and if you fulfill the promise that I have seen in you, then before many more years have passed you will have power beyond your deepest dreams. Will that content you for a while?"

Ygorla was silent. As Narid-na-Gost spoke, she had felt a shuddering inner furor, as though a fire had blazed up in her vitals. What he had promised, she knew with unerring certainty, was no idle boast: and in his oblique, savage reference to the gods of Chaos he had hinted at some far darker machination than a mere wish to train his own half-human child in the sorcerous arts that were her birthright. There was more to this, *far* more, and everything within her screamed with the silent frustration of not knowing the whole truth. But she dared not press him. Last night, she reminded herself, she had been a prisoner of the Sisterhood's well-intentioned but suffocating control, hedged about with rules and regulations, treated as a child, *caged*. Now Narid-na-Gost had unlocked the cage and granted her undreamed-of freedom. A tiny voice of dissent tried to argue that she had done nothing more than exchange one jailer for another, but she scornfully dismissed the idea. Narid-na-Gost would not clip her wings: on the contrary, he would teach her to fly. If that meant that she must quell her avidness and learn patience, so be it. It was a small price to pay.

She said at last, "Yes, Father. It will content me."

"Very good." The demon stepped toward her. "Then for a while now I will leave you to contemplate your future."

"Leave?" She was dismayed.

"Indeed." His smile this time was sly and conspiratorial. "I must be prudent, and return to Chaos before my absence is noted. But I will soon be back." He touched her arm, then paused. "Your skin is cold."

Louise Cooper

With only her smallclothes to cover her, Ygorla was in fact chilled to the marrow, but she had been too preoccupied to notice. She shook her head. "I am well enough."

"Nevertheless . . ." His hand stroked across her shoulder to her small breasts, and a long cloak materialized around her, enfolding her body warmly. Startled, Ygorla stared down at herself. The cloak looked and felt almost—but not quite—like rich fur, and its intense blackness was stippled with a soft, opalescent sheen. She moved her shoulders, delighted by the shimmering ripples that flowed down the length of the garment in response, and Narid-na-Gost laughed gently.

"You will want for nothing here, Ygorla. Fine food, fine wine, fine clothing; whatever you desire, it shall be yours. I will have nothing but the best for my beloved daughter."

Light played suddenly across the crater walls, and moments later thunder spoke grimly, echoing in the empty rock chamber. The first drops of rain began to fall. Narid-na-Gost took Ygorla's hand and pointed to the ledge she had seen earlier.

"There is a path to the ledge, and the tunnel beyond has many caves leading off it. Choose one as your sanctuary, and when you have chosen, speak my name aloud. All the mortal comforts you could wish for will appear. Enjoy them until we meet again."

The rain was rapidly growing heavier, hissing on the floor of the bowl. At Narid-na-Gost's back the air shimmered and distorted, and the door through which he had entered the mortal world appeared once more, suspended in midair. A spectrum of dark colors agitated around the portal, and it swung silently open.

The demon drew her toward him. "Farewell," he said, "for now."

Their faces were on a level. She could see the pocks that ravaged his pale skin, and the scent of musk hung about him, mingled with something redolent of hot iron. For a moment the coals of his eyes burned into her own; then his lips parted and he kissed her, fully and deliberately and with relish. For an instant she was shocked—and

102

then something within her responded and she returned the kiss with a greed that matched his.

At last Narid-na-Gost drew away. He said nothing, only smiled with utter satisfaction, then stepped back into the shivering oval of light. The oval turned blood-red, casting a grisly radiance over the demon's hunched form as he stood poised in the doorway. Then a soft, implosive sound impinged on the hiss of the rain, and Narid-na-Gost and the portal vanished.

Ygorla stared through rain-blurred eyes at the place where the door had been. In the wake of her father's parting kiss her mind was numb, unable to assimilate the thoughts and reactions that rioted in her head. Only when water began to stream from her soaked hair and down her face did she at last lurch back to reality, and a shudder ran through her as her senses returned to conscious control.

The rain was a downpour now. Ygorla looked up in time to see lightning flash brilliantly in the sulfurous sky overhead, with the thunder only an instant behind. The storm was almost above the island, and she drew her fur-like cloak closer about her body, turning toward the path that would lead her to the ledge and shelter. As she turned, something on the ground winked gold in the momentary glare of a second lightning-flash, and she paused.

The initiate's brooch. Her father had cast it contemptuously away, but Ygorla bent to snatch it up. A souvenir of a lost age, the symbol of Order triumphant. Who, she wondered, had worn this badge on the day that the gods walked in the world? Could it even have belonged to Keridil Toln himself? It hardly mattered: High Initiate or mere minion, his bones were moldering now, his dreams turned to dust, and a slow, cruel smile began to form on Ygorla's face. She would keep this little trinket as a souvenir. She would pin it on her shoulder in mockery of the proud men and women who had thought themselves so wise and invincible, and who had been so wrong. She, alone in this bleak place, solitary Margravine of the White Isle, sorceress, *demoness*—she would wear the symbol of Order, and laugh in Order's face as she claimed her heritage of Chaos.

Her fist closed tightly around the brooch as thunder shook the crater walls again. Then she hitched up her cloak and, laughing at the storm and at her own wild thoughts, began to run through the pelting rain toward the path.

8

"Ladies, gentlemen." The High Initiate sat back in his chair. "I think our business is finally concluded. We've been over the known facts in fine detail, and I believe that there's nothing more any of us can add that might shed further light on the matter." He smiled a weary apology at the small group around the table. "I'm only sorry to have detained you all for so long."

There were murmurs of thanks and agreement, and the atmosphere in the room eased a little as the company allowed itself to relax. Tirand, at a gesture from his father, crossed the floor to pull back the heavy curtains and open the window a crack. Moonlight and cold night air slid into the room, sending smoke from the dying fire ceilingward in a quick eddy. Rubbing at the misted glass and peering out, Tirand saw that the first moon had set and the second was beginning to slip below the high castle wall. They had talked long into the night, but he wasn't tired. He felt too disturbed for tiredness.

Chiro rose from his chair. "Let me at least offer you all some refreshment before we retire to our beds." He moved to an ornate cabinet at the far side of the room. "I'd suggest mulled wine to warm us . . . here, Tirand, riddle up the fire and I'll mix some mead with a flask of the Han province vintage and set it on the trivet to heat. Now, where did Karuth put the mulling spices? . . ."

Cups were filled, and the High Initiate resumed his seat with a sigh. Everyone sipped appreciatively and for a time there was silence. The lamps were burning low and the atmosphere was soporific; with only eight people to be accommodated—and that reduced to seven when Karuth had been called away on a medical matter—Chiro had chosen to hold the meeting in his own study rather than in the vast and drafty council hall, but now he realized that it would be all too easy to doze off if he wasn't careful. He was trying to think of something to say to keep himself awake, when Lias Barnack cleared his throat.

Lias was well on in years now, close to retirement, Chiro surmised, but as the High Margrave's senior envoy he had considered it his duty to attend this conference in person rather than send a less experienced subordinate. He'd stayed largely in the background during the discussion, intervening only now and then to offer some information as to the militia's actions or to ask a pertinent question, but Chiro knew from his shrewd eyes that he'd been attending more closely than appearances suggested.

Lias said: "High Initiate, this may not be the most opportune moment to voice what's in my mind, but . . . well, I think I need to be frank."

Everyone looked at him. Sister Fiora, who sat between Sister Corelm and one of the two senior Circle councillors present, shivered a little and adjusted the purple mourning sash at her shoulder. Lias fingered the stem of his cup.

"I have to confess," he continued, "that in the light of all I've heard tonight, I hold out very little hope that the child will be found. The militia have stinted no efforts in their search, and both the Circle and the Sisterhood"—he nodded gravely to Fiora and Corelm—"have employed their skills on other planes, and all with no result. I have to say that I believe the girl must be dead."

The silence this time was stark. No one seemed to want to meet anyone else's gaze, and at length Lias made a helpless gesture. "I'm sorry, my friends, but I see no point in dissembling about it."

"You're right, Lias." Chiro looked at the rigid, unhappy faces around the table. "I think that even if we're reluctant to admit it, in our hearts we all agree with you." He waited. Tirand and the other adepts nodded curtly, Corelm stared at her wine cup, and Fiora put a clenched fist to her mouth and made a small sound that might have been a sob. The High Initiate's gaze returned to Lias and he saw what he had suspected reflected in the other man's eyes. Lias never said or did anything without good reason, and Chiro believed he knew what had prompted this.

"I think, Lias," he added gently, "that your thoughts and mine have been running along parallel paths."

"That isn't for me to say, Chiro. I wouldn't presume to speak for you—or for the Circle."

The hint was clear. Chiro nodded. "Very well. I hadn't intended to air this now, as the hour's late and I don't want to provoke further discussions until we've all had some sleep. But perhaps it's only fair that I should tell you of the proposal which I plan to put to a full meeting of the Council of Adepts tomorrow."

Tirand glanced sharply at his father, and the other adepts watched the High Initiate alertly. Chiro hesitated for a few moments, then said:

"My friends, I'd be a fool to pretend that I'm not deeply worried by the possible implications of this tragedy. In fact I consider them serious enough to justify the performance of a Circle ritual to call directly on the gods for their inspiration."

Tirand felt a sharp, chilly thrill of trepidation run through him. Lias nodded; the sisters' faces became still masks. Only the two councillors seemed impassive, and Tirand suspected that they'd anticipated this all along. He himself had felt from the start that it would be a wise if drastic move, but, knowing his father's innate caution, he hadn't expected that he would make a decision so quickly.

"You think, then," Lias said, "that there *is* something in the idea that some supernatural agency has been at work?"

"Yes, I do."

"And do you yet have any thoughts on what its nature might be?"

He was blatantly probing, but Chiro refused to be drawn. "No," he said, and Tirand knew that he was deliberately guarding his tongue, and also knew why. "But with the gods' grace, I hope we'll find out."

Realizing that he'd learn nothing else as yet, Lias gave way and said no more, but Chiro's revelation had soured the atmosphere a little. The adepts were prudently keeping their own counsel, reserving their reactions for later and less public airing, and the two sisters, feeling out of their depth, had nothing to contribute. The mulled wine was finished in subdued quiet, and at last, with evident relief, the small group rose from their seats, wished each other good night, and took their leave. Lias was the last to step out into the dimly lit corridor; he clasped Chiro's arm in a farewell gesture and gave him a faintly ironic smile.

"I'm sorry if I let a cat loose in the dovecote, Chiro. It wasn't intentional."

The High Initiate shook his head. "No, Lias; you were quite right to prompt me. And I'll be able to tell you more of my plans in a day or two. You'll be staying for a while?"

"Oh, yes; if I don't wear out my welcome. I mean to spend some time with young Calvi. He's greatly missed on Summer Isle, and the High Margrave wants me to take home a full report on his progress."

"I'm sure Calvi will be delighted to see you." Chiro smiled tiredly. "Good night, Lias."

"Good night, my friend."

Chiro closed the door and turned back to the room. Tirand was clearing the cups and setting them on a tray ready for a servant to take out in the morning, and the High Initiate removed the trivet from the hearth and set about banking down the fire. For a while neither of them spoke, but Chiro was aware that his son had something on his mind. At length he said:

"You may as well speak it as think it, Tirand. What's troubling you?"

Tirand had finished with the cups and was now straightening papers on the desk. He paused and looked up, his brown eyes serious.

"The ritual, Father. I was just wondering which gods you intend to call on."

"Ah." Chiro steepled his fingers and touched them to his lips. "Yes. So you too caught the drift of Lias's probing?"

Tirand nodded. "He shouldn't have tried such a tactic. He ought to know better."

"It's a privilege of his rank, Tirand; and besides, I don't doubt that he has strict instructions from the High Margrave to turn over every stone that might yield another scrap of information."

"But to try so blatantly to inveigle you—"

"There's no harm done. Anyway, I suspect that in truth Lias only wanted confirmation of his own feelings." Chiro closed the doors of his wine cupboard and locked them. "Equilibrium notwithstanding, it's all but impossible for any mortal man or woman not to feel a bias in one direction or the other, and I've known Lias Barnack long enough to be aware of where his loyalties lie. He doesn't need to hide them; but, as you know only too well, my position is very different. As High Initiate I give equal fealty to Order and to Chaos, as my duty demands. But as a man I can't shake off more fundamental loyalties, and one of those loyalties is rooted in my memories of Keridil Toln."

"You know I feel the same way."

"Of course you do; you, too, remember Keridil, even though you were only a child when he died. However, we haven't the freedom to express our feelings as Lias and others like him may express theirs. We must maintain the balance and show the world that our dealings with the gods aren't colored by prejudice."

"But in private . . ." Tirand said.

Chiro regarded him gravely. "In private, Tirand, I don't think I need to spell it out to you, or to remind you that what I'm saying is for your ears alone. The facts are quite simple: I suspect the hand of Chaos in this unhappy affair."

Tirand sucked air in between his teeth and tongue, then let it slowly out again. "Then you'll call on Aeoris for aid?"

"No. I'll appeal to Aeoris and Yandros equally."

"Surely, though—"

"Put out that lamp, will you? It's empty and the wick's beginning to burn." Chiro waited until the light had been extinguished, bringing shadows closing in. "I'll appeal both to Order and to Chaos because that is how it must be. I have no proof of my suspicions, after all."

Tirand shook his head. "Is proof needed? The burning

of the monument—and the way the Matriarch died—" He shuddered.

"Demons come in many guises, Tirand. Whatever my personal views, I *dare* not make assumptions without evidence." He moved across the room and began to turn down the second and final lamp. Dim gloom sank onto the room, relieved only by the fire's last, sullen glow, and the High Initiate moved wearily toward the door.

"Go to bed, my son, and try not to lie awake asking questions that can't yet be answered." He yawned, and pressed the palms of both hands to his eyes.

Tirand moved to open the door for him. "I'll try, Father. Good night."

The High Initiate nodded and smiled. "Good night, Tirand. What's left of it."

On the way to his own bedchamber Tirand decided on the spur of the moment to make a detour past his sister's room. He had little hope that she'd be awake at this hour, for the small emergency that had called her away from the meeting couldn't have taken long to attend to and he surmised that she must have gone to bed rather than return in the midst of the discussions and disrupt the proceedings. Still, there was a chance, albeit a small one, that she might still be awake, and he wanted to talk to her. Simply, he wanted company, because sleep was beyond him.

To his surprise, he met Karuth in the corridor outside her room. She was in her night shift with a robe loosely belted over it, her hair was tousled, and there were heavy shadows under her eyes. In the dim glow given off by the one guttering torch that hadn't been extinguished, she peered into his face, then laughed softly and with relief.

"Tirand! I wondered for a moment who in the world it could be at this hour. Please don't tell me I'm needed again, or I'll be sorely tempted to throw myself off one of the spires!"

"The meeting's only just ended." He took her arm companionably and they walked toward her room. "Have you been called out a second time?"

She grimaced. "As if the first wasn't enough. One of the servants overturned a pot of boiling water in the kitchens and badly scalded himself. I'd just fallen asleep after salving Calvi's wounds, and—"

"Calvi?" Tirand interrupted her. "I thought it was a brawl between two of the servants."

"No, no. The duty steward—Reyni, and you know how slight he is—tried to intervene, and received two cracked ribs for his trouble." They reached her door; she opened it and he stood back to let her enter the room before him. She stumbled against something in the dark, swore under her breath, and found flint and tinder. "Three of the younger students had an argument in the dining hall, and words led to blows."

"Calvi was one of them?"

"Yes." A spark flickered and Karuth lit three candles in a sconce. "Gant Harlon was also involved, and that red-haired boy from East Han—I can't remember his name. But before you ask me, Tirand, I don't know who started it or who was at fault. By the time I arrived on the scene, you'd think someone had stitched their lips together; no one was willing to take or apportion blame."

Tirand sighed exasperatedly. "What was the quarrel about?"

"A girl. What else could be important enough to reduce three studious young men to a kicking and punching tangle on the dining-hall floor?"

Tirand quelled a snort of laughter; the matter wasn't funny. "Their tutor must be told," he said. "This sort of behavior can't be tolerated."

"I don't think we'll have any more trouble." Karuth carried the candle sconce over to her bedside table, set it down, and sank gratefully onto the bed. "I took care to use a salve that stings, and I think that'll be lesson enough for them." She smiled. "Calvi, at least, has already apologized for putting me to trouble."

Tirand grunted, not entirely mollified. "I suppose they'd been drinking?"

"Yes, of course they had." She saw his expression. "Don't think too harshly of them, Tirand. They're young

111

and unfledged. We weren't so very different ourselves at their age."

"All of eight or ten years ago?" Tirand raised an ironic eyebrow. "We *were* different, Karuth. We'd never have dreamed of behaving so disgracefully."

Karuth's face sobered. "No," she said thoughtfully, "but then, perhaps we never had the opportunity."

"Well, I think we should see to it that this sort of thing doesn't occur again. I'll speak to Father if need be—and I'll certainly have stern words with Calvi. What would the High Margrave think if he heard about it? His brother, entrusted to our care to learn philosophy, only to end up brawling over some wretched girl." He shook his head. "It won't do."

Karuth lay back among her pillows and shut her eyes. "For now I want to hear no more about it. I've had quite enough of quarreling students for one night." She shifted her position to one of greater comfort. "Tell me about the meeting. Did I miss anything of importance?"

Tirand subsided onto a chair, straddling it and resting his chin and arms on the high back. "No, you didn't. It was very much as we'd expected; no one had any new evidence to offer that might help us solve the mystery. And Lias Barnack voiced a feeling which I think we all share—that the Matriarch's grandniece must be dead."

Karuth's eyes opened again. "Then there's still no trace of her?"

"No, and no clue as to what her fate might have been. Father is certain that some demonic agency has been at work. He means to perform a Higher Rite, to ask the gods for their inspiration." He paused, watching his sister's face. "You don't seem surprised by the news."

"I'm not. But I am relieved—I'd hoped that it might happen. I just didn't think the council would agree so quickly to such a proposal."

"They haven't agreed yet; Father hasn't put it to them formally. But I had the impression that Keln and Arcoro at least share his view."

Karuth hesitated for a moment, then swung her legs over the bed's edge and sat up. "We must do what we can to persuade the others. I feel . . ." She stopped.

"Karuth? What is it, what's wrong?"

She shook her head. "Perhaps it's nothing. I don't know."

"Tell me."

"Well . . ." Abruptly she looked at him, and her eyes were very intense. "Tirand, you know, don't you, that I've always had a peculiar feeling about that child?"

He was taken aback. "Always? I recall you mentioning it once a few years ago, but that's all."

"Then maybe I've thought about it more than I've cared to admit until now. It all harks back to the day the girl was born, and the incident with the old High Initiate—"

"Ah, yes." He remembered what she had told him once before, and his tone grew wary.

"Keridil Toln was a wise man," Karuth went on. "And I think he had that abnormal insight which the gods often grant to wise men in their last days. *He* knew that something was amiss. Then, when the Matriarch proposed that the girl should be admitted to the Circle, I too felt a similar disquiet. Now"—her shoulders lifted, as though she was hunching against cold—"I have that feeling again."

Tirand didn't speak for some moments. He was thinking about what their father had said during their last, brief discussion before parting, and wondering if it might have any bearing on Karuth's unease. For himself he could see no possible connection, and though the thought was unworthy, he believed that Keridil Toln's strange reaction after Ygorla Morys's birth had been nothing more than a delusion of an old and failing mind. Still, he trusted Karuth's psychic talents. If nothing else, her suspicion should at least be investigated.

He said at last: "If you're concerned about this, Karuth, then there's one other thing I should tell you. Father thinks that, whatever happened to the girl, Chaos might have had a hand in it."

Karuth had been fiddling with the belt of her robe; abruptly she stopped. "Chaos?"

They looked at each other. Tirand knew that his sister didn't share his own and Chiro's private leanings toward the gods of Order. Since she was old enough to make a sound judgment in such matters, she had always seemed to have no personal bias in her loyalties to one side or the other: but now, as he tried and failed to interpret her expression, Tirand began to wonder if that assumption had been entirely accurate.

He put the thought aside. Karuth had as much right to her preference as anyone else, and if she was more inclined to call on Yandros than on Aeoris in a time of trouble, he, with his own prejudices, was hardly in a position to criticize.

Karuth said: "When is the rite to be performed? Assuming it goes ahead, that is."

"Nothing's been decided yet. I suspect Father will prefer to wait until Lias Barnack is safely on his way back to the south."

"Mmm." She acknowledged the point thoughtfully. "A few days yet, then."

"Probably. Why?"

"Ohh . . . just a thought that's crossed my mind. I wonder if it might be prudent to make a few preliminary investigations."

Tirand regarded her shrewdly. "Of your own devising?"

"Yes." Karuth's face took on a peculiar expression that he couldn't quite interpret, then cleared. "I'm sorry, Tirand, I don't mean to be cryptic. It's this mystery of the girl's disappearance; it's preying on my mind and I can't help thinking that there's some dimension to it which none of us has yet grasped."

Tirand sighed. He trusted his sister's intuition even if he couldn't share it, and anything that might help in their current predicament would be doubly welcome. He said, "Explore it, Karuth. If there's anything at all you can learn—"

"I can't make any promises."

"I know. But—"

"But I'll try." She stood up. "Tirand, forgive me, but I think I'd rather you left now." She met his gaze, her gray eyes steady and suddenly very alert. "I won't sleep tonight; it's so near dawn that there's little point in trying. So I might as well try to make some use of my time, don't you agree?"

He nodded. "Thank you. You know, if only——"

"Don't." She laid one finger on his arm. "Please. You've said it before and it isn't true."

"Oh, but I think it is." Tirand also rose, and walked toward her, stopping when they were only inches apart. "I think you're far better qualified to succeed Father when the time comes than I am. I'm only sorry that it can't be."

"Well, I'm not," Karuth said firmly. "Seriously, Tirand: I don't want to resurrect that old ghost again, and particularly not now. I've quite enough to fill my plate without it." She looked at him again, then leaned forward and kissed his cheek. "Go away, little brother. Go and fulfill your duties, while I fulfill mine. If I'd wanted fame and glory, I'd have joined the Sisterhood and set my sights on the Matriarchy."

"Perhaps you should have done."

"No. I'm a physician and a sorceress, not a teacher and politician. I wouldn't want to be Matriarch. And I wouldn't want to be heir to the High Initiate's role either, even if you offered me an entire Southern Chaun vintage for the privilege."

"All the same——"

"A cat's curse for all the same. That's your responsibility, not mine, and I'm thankful. Go away, Tirand. Sleep soundly."

Showing his feelings didn't come easily to Tirand, but on impulse he hugged her. "Don't take any risks."

"I won't. And if I learn anything, you'll be the first to know. Good night."

The door closed quietly behind him. Karuth stood motionless until the sound of his footsteps had faded along the corridor; then she turned to where the sconce stood and extinguished two of the candles, leaving one solitary flame guttering uneasily. The fire in her hearth had gone out; she'd dismissed her servants early and there had been no one to replenish it, so now the room was lit only by the single candle's dim glow. Well and good; she needed little illumination for what she meant to do.

She wished that Tirand hadn't chosen to remind her of

the old sore. Even if precedent hadn't made it impossible, she wouldn't have wanted to be High Initiate when the time came. Nor Matriarch, nor High Margravine, nor Grand Lady of any title that the world could devise. She was Karuth, and at times that in itself was a greater responsibility than she felt she could bear. So many disparate influences pulling her this way and that, so much she wanted to do, to explore, and never sufficient time. Now, yet again, Tirand was relying on her, and through Tirand her father. Physician, sorceress, adept . . . The gods didn't grant enough hours for it all, and certainly not enough hours for her, once in a while, to be herself. Sometimes, she thought with an uncharacteristic bitter edge, she wondered if she even *had* a true self anymore.

Reflexively, almost without realizing it, she had moved across the room to where a small, ornately embellished wooden box stood on a table under her window, and her fingers lifted the lid before she became conscious of what she was doing. A smell of spice and resined mustiness made her nose wrinkle; it was so familiar that she almost— but not quite—laughed.

Responsibility. She'd fulfilled her responsibilities tonight, first to the squabbling students, later to the scalded servant. Now another duty. Self-imposed perhaps, but why else had Tirand sought her out? He was too scrupulous— and too inhibited—to ask directly for her help, but the plea had been clearly visible in his eyes. Besides, she too wanted answers to the same questions, or she wouldn't sleep easy in her bed.

She had begun to sort through the box, instinctively dismissing most of its contents and searching for the few ingredients she needed. Incense: it had no real arcane value, but it would help to set the right mood. Substances to represent the elements: she considered for a few moments, then chose air and fire. Water and earth were too solid; this matter sprang from a more ephemeral dimension. Then last a small bottle made of opaque amber glass. Her crucible was ready, as always; the candle would be sufficient to heat it, and she set the little tripod over the flame before shutting the lid of the box.

The ritual she intended to perform was a simple piece

of low magic, nothing taxing and nothing that needed more than the most arbitrary preparation. She was too tired to embark on anything more complex—though weariness could be an asset under some conditions, it could become dangerous if it went too far—and besides, she didn't feel that anything more would be needed. She had always worked well with elemental forces, and elementals were an invaluable source of information, for they had no especial loyalties either to Order or to Chaos. It made a change, too, to be working alone rather than as one among a group of her peers. Chiro didn't encourage solitary sorceries among the adepts, but, although nothing would have induced her to confess it to her father, Karuth sometimes found the rites of the Circle a little tedious and long-drawn. She understood and accepted the need for precaution and established routine in high magic, where the forces being conjured were so much more powerful, but for more modest purposes she preferred to practice without others to help her.

Silence descended on the room as the crucible's metal bowl began to darken, and Karuth turned to where a carafe of seawater and a cup stood on her bedside table. She had long ago made it a rule to drink a dose of this brine every night before retiring, as a buffer against winter rheums; now, though, she poured just a small quantity of the water into the cup and added three drops from the amber vial. She didn't normally use this shortcut to induce the necessary mental state for occult working, as it was all too easy—as she knew from past experience—to take too much of the narcotic and lose direction, or, worse, control. Tonight, though, she had neither the time nor the patience for the slower and more orthodox methods, and without ceremony she drank the cup's contents in one draft, grimacing at the unpleasant combination of salt and the drug. Then she set the cup down and turned to the crucible.

For a while the silence held, its intensity deepening as the draft began to take effect. Karuth's breathing settled to an even, controlled rhythm; then, when she judged the moment to be right, she brought both hands forward to meet over the flame and dropped a few grains of incense from either palm into the small vessel. The crucible hissed like an angry cat, and smoke roiled toward the ceiling as the two incenses coagulated and formed furiously spitting droplets that rolled and bounced in the bottom of the bowl. Karuth closed her eyes and inhaled deeply, letting the aromatic smoke fill her throat and lungs and seep through to her mind. The room's walls seemed to recede, becoming remote and unreal; she caught mentally at the sensation, encouraging it to grow stronger as awareness of her surroundings began to waver and fade. Her lips moved, mouthing the old chant that had been used for centuries by adepts to engender the trance state. Another deep breath, the incense acrid in her nostrils now, and she felt a sharp, vicious gust of wind snatch at her hair and heard the distant crackle of fire. Slowly, very slowly as the trance deepened, her hands came together before her, one fist clenched above the other as though she held an invisible wand between her fingers. She pictured the wand in her mind's eye, flickering with the pale, elusive colors of air, the hot hues of fire, and refined the image until she could almost feel its physical presence. Slowly she opened her eyes again, resisting the drag of the trance that made her eyelids feel intolerably heavy. Between her fingers the image of the wand shimmered like uncertain lightning; beyond, the room's dimensions had distorted into abnormal and grotesque angles. A sound so low that it bordered on the audible threshold hummed in her ears; then she felt a sharp, painful jolt as the ephemeral and ethereal corridor between the physical world and the elemental dimensions sprang open.

In the air before her a face appeared. It was composed of flames, gold etched with flickering crimson, small and sharp and smiling. The empty sockets of its eyes regarded her and a voice spoke in her mind.

You call me. I answer.

Karuth hissed between clenched teeth. The language of elementals bore little resemblance to human speech, and to communicate with this tricky and capricious creature of fire and air taxed her tongue and her vocal cords. Nevertheless she formed the words, the command, the question.

"I summon you with the flame and I summon you with

the gale. I will have truth, and nothing less will content me."

The savage little face wavered, and a tongue of fire spat silently from the elemental's mouth. *By what right and what geas do you bind me?*

Karuth smiled, her expression making her look un-human in the smoking gloom. "By right of mastery and by geas of obligation I bind you. I am fire and I am air. I am earth and I am water. My bones and my flesh are one with all that the gods have created, and I summon you and bind you in the name of Yandros and in the name of Aeoris. Hear me, friend and servant of the flame and of the gale. Speak of what you know, and speak as I command you." She drew breath, tasting sulfur and the ice-cold searing of a northerly wind in her throat as the bridge between dimensions shuddered and shifted. A word, two otherworldly syllables, the utmost syllables of command to such a being, formed on her tongue: she uttered them aloud.

A high, shrill whine vibrated in her head, and her ears ached with the unearthly frequency. Terrible transformations shot through the elemental's image; she forced herself to pay no heed to them, knowing the test, knowing she wouldn't fail it. At last the sound died and the shimmering, feline face was still again.

I acknowledge your mastery. Ask what you will.

Another Karuth, far away in another world, gave fervent thanks for the strength which had allowed her to prevail. Such beings as this had no loyalty to mortals, and they could maim, or in some circumstances kill, the adept whose will slipped even for a moment. After a time one became used to the risk, but never quite inured to it.

"There have been disturbances in Southern Chaun," she told the being. "The forces which govern the equilibrium of your kind and mine have suffered an unwonted disruption."

The elemental's tongue flickered like a snake's. *This I know.*

"Then you must also know that the Matriarch of the Sisterhood is dead, and that a child has disappeared from the eyes of mortals."

A pause, and a cold breath of air caressed Karuth's

face. *Yes, I know this too. But your Matriarch's fate is of no concern to me. Another will follow in her stead. It is of no moment.*

Karuth frowned, partly at the elemental's lack of respect but partly because she thought she'd detected something untoward in the tone of its reply. An issue, perhaps, which the creature was anxious to avoid?

There was more than a hint of threat in her voice as she spoke again. "It is the child and not the Matriarch who is the subject of my questioning. What do you know of her fate?"

Silence. The elemental's form wavered briefly; for an instant the face became something nightmarish. Karuth frowned. "Speak, servant. Or you will rouse my anger."

Hot colors chased one another across the sharp little face, as though flames had abruptly sprung up about the being. At length the catlike mouth opened.

I cannot tell you what became of the child. I do not know.

Was it a lie? Karuth thought not, for when such creatures lied, a skilled adept could detect changes in their auras, and there was no such change now.

"Very well," she said. "I will not test your veracity—at least, for now. Tell me instead, what was the nature of the force which disrupted the elements from their appointed places on the night that the child disappeared?"

Again, silence. The room felt suddenly deeply claustrophobic.

"Servant." Karuth's voice was malevolent. "You are bound by that which you cannot gainsay to obey me! I will have your answer!"

Instantly she felt as though a thin, red-hot knife had been plunged into the deepest levels of her brain, and she gasped with shock and pain. For a dreadful moment she thought that she'd lost control and that the elemental, seizing its chance, was attacking her—but then the sensation vanished and she realized what had caused it. The being was *afraid.* And she, attuned to its mind, had felt at second hand the sharp and agonizing thrust of its fear.

The shimmering face still hung suspended before her, though the colors of its aura had become sickly and pale.

The elemental's mouth opened and closed rapidly, but no voice echoed in Karuth's mind.

"Servant." She was implacable. "Speak. Or must I chastise you?"

The face distorted again. The elemental was in great distress. *I . . . cannot speak. I cannot do what you ask.*

"I do not ask, I *demand*. Answer me—or earth shall be your prison and water your bed. By the power of mastery that the gods have granted me, I shall extinguish your flame!"

A thin, mewling cry echoed in the room, a signal of pain and fear and misery. *Ah, no! Do not condemn me! I have no choice in this!*

Karuth hesitated. "Explain."

Awful colors flickered in the elemental's eye sockets. *Be merciful, lady*, it said piteously. *I cannot obey you, for I dare not! Another and greater power than yours has set geas upon me, and if I speak of what I know, I will suffer a more dreadful fate than any you can devise!*

Karuth's frown deepened and she tried to ignore the unease that crawled through her. "What is this power that binds you?"

I cannot say. I dare not say. I will serve you willingly in all else, but I cannot serve you in this. Have pity— release me from my obligation!

On the verge of uttering an angry anathema on the creature, Karuth paused suddenly as a new thought struck her. She composed herself, reasserted calm over her anger, and spoke again.

"You have brothers of air and fire, and you have cousins of earth and water. How would those others of your kind answer me, were I to demand the same of them?"

There was a pause. Then the elemental said:

They would answer you as I have answered. We were defied. We were overcome. The geas is upon us all, and we have no power to gainsay it. The child is gone, lady, and there is nothing to be done. I beg you again, release me, please!

Karuth stood very still. She had no doubt now that the elemental was telling her the truth, for she could feel its terror leaching like poison from its mind into her own.

Elementals ranked low among the legions of the unhuman beings which spanned the gulf between gods and mortals. Their domain was confined to the world they shared with humankind, and as such the great lords of Chaos and Order disdained any interest in their activities. However, in the strata between highest and lowest there were many orders of creation with the power to bind the elements under geas, and any one might be behind this extraordinary development. How could she find out what manner of force was responsible? And, more vitally, *why* had this geas been evoked?

Gone, it had said. *The child is gone.* An ambiguous statement. . . . She opened her mouth to speak, then looked at the elemental again and realized that under these circumstances any further questioning was pointless. She could carry out her threat to bind it with the forces of earth and water that were inimical to its existence, but she'd gain nothing from such torture. The creature would face destruction at her hands rather than break the injunction which had compelled its silence. There was nothing she could do.

She sucked in air that tasted hot and dry, and spoke to the elemental again. "Very well. It seems there is nothing to be gained from prolonging this encounter. I shall be merciful and release you without penalty. But I will have one last thing from you."

Ask it, lady. If it is within my power, I shall give it willingly.

If nothing else, Karuth thought ironically, she had secured its gratitude, which might stand her in good stead at some time in the future. She said: "Then in the name of Yandros and in the name of Aeoris, I claim from you one riddle. Speak to me as fire and speak to me as air, and let your riddle be true and without deceit. This can be done without breaking your obligation, and I demand it as my price for your dismissal."

A pause, while the elemental considered this. Then: *Yes. It can be done.* It looked up and its eyes took on the colors of newly fueled flames.

This, then, is my riddle. Fire was the schemer's weapon, and air was the schemer's steed. But the one who sits at the schemer's feet shall have greater weapons and fleeter steeds than any of our making.

Karuth repeated the words in her mind, committing them to memory. As yet, they meant nothing to her, but she could ask for no more. Bound by the old spell and by its own kind's love of the cryptic and the occluded, the elemental had given her no more and no less than she asked for, a true riddle which contained a clue, however obscure, to the answers she sought. It was up to her to make of it what she could.

She stepped back and took up the flagon of seawater, then held it over the crucible on its trivet. "Your work is done," she said formally. "I therefore dismiss you from my presence until I should require your service again. Servant, begone!" With this last command she tipped the flagon over the crucible, at the same time uttering a sibilant alien word.

The crucible hissed, metal pinging against metal as it reacted to the violent assault of the cold water. Steam boiled up in a dense plume, and the elemental flickered, flared, and vanished. Karuth felt the fire-and-ice rush of its departure, a sharp, momentary sense of the room contracting and expanding. She blinked, and her vision cleared as proportion and perspective returned to normal.

Water was threatening to bubble over the crucible's edge; hastily she rescued the candle before it was extinguished, and waved away the cloud of steam. Her back ached and she felt exhausted—it must be close to dawn, she thought, and soon the castle's earliest risers would be stirring. She needed sleep. And until she had slept and was refreshed, she didn't want to consider the implications of what she had learned tonight.

With a fastidious care born of long training, Karuth tidied away her paraphernalia, returning the incenses and the amber vial to their box and setting the crucible and trivet aside to cool thoroughly. When that was done she moved to her writing desk, took a hide folder from one of the drawers, and shook out the papers inside. These were her personal magical record, a chronicle of every sorcerous operation she had performed since her first initiation into the Circle. No matter how tired she might be, every detail of tonight's ritual must be carefully noted before she could even think of sleep.

She prepared her pen and ink, and began to write. It was a familiar chore, but reassuring, for it disciplined her mind to the strict regimen of her training and allowed her to shift her preoccupation away from the thoughts that were trying to break through the barrier she'd imposed against them. When she was done, she turned at last toward her bed—then paused.

A sound outside her door. It was faint but just audible, a querying mew. Then seconds later she felt a new presence in her mind, a tentative probing. Karuth's shoulders relaxed fractionally and she crossed to the door to open it.

Outside in the darkened corridor two cats, one white, the other marked with gray and brown stripes like a small wildcat, sat watching her, their lambent eyes filled with interest. Karuth smiled and pulled the door wider, allowing them to slip past her into the room. She should have anticipated this; it was all but impossible to perform any occult rite without attracting attention from at least one of the castle's many feline inhabitants. Half-wild and half-domesticated, telepathic, insatiably curious, the cats were drawn to the scent of ritual like moths to a flame, and she watched as they began to explore, sniffing about them, occasionally uttering a soft chirrup. The white animal—a female, if she recalled rightly, with a new litter of kittens hidden somewhere in the castle kitchens—approached her and rubbed against her leg. She bent to stroke it, eliciting a loud, thrumming purr, then climbed into her bed. The cats' silent meanderings wouldn't disturb her, and their presence would be comforting. Better by far, she thought, than being entirely alone.

Karuth could still hear the white cat purring as she snuffed out the candle and settled down to sleep.

9

". . . and so if I hear word of one more such disgraceful incident—just one, mark you—I shan't hesitate to report you all immediately to the High Initiate." Tirand paused, staring hard at the three young miscreants of the previous night, who stood in line before him in one of the anterooms behind the castle's main hall. None of them had the temerity to return his gaze. "I don't think I need spell out to any of you the steps he might deem it necessary to take as a result. Do I make myself clear?"

There was a mumble of affirmation, and from one a gruff "Yes, sir."

"Very well. Then you may consider the matter closed. Count yourselves lucky that this time you've been let off with no more than a reprimand."

They turned and began to shuffle toward the door, but Tirand said suddenly, "Calvi."

"Sir?" The smallest and youngest of the trio stopped and looked back. His blue eyes, under a thatch of fair hair, were wary.

"A further word, if you please." Tirand realized suddenly that his own expression was still sour, and forced his face muscles to relax into more benign lines. Calvi Alacar, the High Margrave's fifteen-year-old brother, had been studying philosophy at the castle for nearly a year now, and though he hadn't the sorcerous aptitude to gain initiation to the Circle itself, Tirand believed he had great promise as a secular teaching master. Calvi had been afforded no special privileges here—the castle judged its students strictly on merit and not rank—but Tirand felt that a degree of special interest in the boy was warranted, if for no other reason than to maintain good relations between the Star Peninsula and the Summer Isle court. He didn't like the association that seemed to be growing between Calvi and some of the rowdier elements among his fellow students, and though he knew that the subject must be approached with caution, he was anxious to nip any potential trouble in the bud.

Calvi hesitantly approached him, and he drew the boy toward the hearth, where a fire was blazing to ward off the morning's autumnal cold. The door had by now closed behind the other youths, and Tirand laid an avuncular hand on Calvi's shoulder.

"I shouldn't strictly tell you this, Calvi," he said, "but I think you've learned your lesson and I see no point in prolonging your discomfiture any further. I just want to say that I think it's very unlikely that word of this incident will reach Lias Barnack's ears. So you can rest assured that the only report of your progress he'll carry back to the High Margrave will be a favorable one."

Calvi's pale cheeks, already flushed with shame from the dressing-down he'd just endured, colored an even deeper crimson. "Thank you, sir." He stared at the floor.

"But," Tirand continued, "I do know that your brother would be very distressed if he thought that you weren't making the most of your opportunities here." He smiled. "He's proud of you, and anxious that you should have every chance to develop your talents to the full. I know that you don't want to let him down."

At last Calvi managed to meet his gaze. His answering smile was hesitant, but Tirand thought that the homily was getting through. "We, too, have a lot of faith in you, Calvi," he added. "Don't squander what the gods have granted you, but make sure that you settle your priorities and keep to them."

"I will, sir. Thank you."

Tirand nodded. "Well, then, best get yourself off to the dining hall while there's still some breakfast to be had." He waved toward the door. "Go on."

When Calvi had left, Tirand turned back to the fire with a sigh. He hadn't conducted the last part of the inter-

126

view well: he'd intended to offer friendly advice but had put it across in a way that to a boy of Calvi's age must have seemed stiff and pompous. Wryly he reflected that he'd never had and never would have Karuth's natural facility for putting others at their ease, and he only hoped that in speaking to Calvi he hadn't done more harm than good.

All in all, he reflected, it hadn't thus far been an auspicious day. He'd barely slept last night, for questions raised by the meeting and by his later talk with Karuth had been crowding his mind like a swarm of bees. He'd risen at dawn, filled with pent energy for which he could find no outlet; he'd wanted to see Karuth and learn the results of her conjuration, but couldn't dream of disturbing her at such an hour. His father, too, was still abed, and only a few heavy-eyed servants were about in the castle, and finally Tirand had forced himself to accept the fact that he must allow events to move at their own pace, and had tried to salve his restlessness by taking an early walk outside the castle walls.

He'd left by the main gates and crossed the sward toward the narrow rock span that separated the Star Peninsula from the mainland. The rising sun was glorious in a clear sky, turning the eastern sea to silver and making the frost that sheened the grass sparkle like hard gems. Tirand breathed deeply, enjoying the raw sharpness of the air in his throat and the tingling sensation that the cold brought to his face and hands; then stopped as he reached a patch of sward which stood out from its surroundings in a peculiar, isolated rectangle. The grass was a lusher, darker green here, as though some eccentric gardener had carefully and deliberately tended this one patch while neglecting the rest, and tentatively Tirand stretched out one foot to rub at the thin coating of frost.

The Maze. It hasn't been used in his lifetime, nor, as far as he was aware, in his father's, and he wondered if there was an adept left alive who knew the spell that would bring it from dormancy. Many centuries before the earliest records began, when the gods of Chaos—who then had held unchallenged sway over the world—called the castle into being, it had pleased Yandros to set the great building a fraction out of kilter with normal time and

127

space, so that to enter its portals was to step into a dimension that had shifted slightly from the norm. The Maze bridged the two realities as the rock span bridged the mainland and the peninsula stack. When open, it meshed the castle with the rest of the world, but when closed it reestablished the dimensional shift so that the castle could be entered only by those who knew how to negotiate the barrier. According to Circle records, when the Maze was closed, the castle was invisible to anyone on the far side of the rock bridge, and Tirand turned, looking back at the great looming black bulk and trying—though imagination failed him—to picture how the stack might look without its brooding presence. Before Equilibrium, the Maze had been kept closed as a matter of course, except when some great event had drawn large numbers of outsiders to the Star Peninsula. But in latter years, with the castle open to incomers as it had never been in the past, the tradition had lapsed and the Maze had lain idle now for more than half a century.

Tirand withdrew his foot and stared at the narrow trail he had flattened in the grass. The castle held so many secrets that its inhabitants didn't begin to understand, even though they had learned to harness them for their own benefit. What other, unknown properties, Tirand asked himself, might lie untapped and unrealized within the walls or beneath the foundations? It was a familiar speculation, but now as he looked down at this only overt sign of the Maze's existence, it troubled him in a new way that he couldn't explain to himself. As if, somewhere behind the jumble of thought and speculation, lay the answers to a good deal more than one idle question.

A vicious breath of wind blew in from the sea, whipping Tirand's hair across his face and carrying a hint of deeper and more bitter cold. He raised his head and turned to scan beyond the castle; clouds were massing on the northern horizon and taking on tinges of the telltale pinks and purples that presaged bad weather. Their livid, disturbing colors reminded him of the first heralds of a Warp, and though he knew that this was a more natural phenomenon, still he found it disturbing, and he set his face back toward the castle, retracing his steps and walking under the vast black arch of the main gates.

In the mere few minutes since he'd left its precincts, the castle had begun to awaken, and Tirand's restlessness at last found an outlet. He had washed, shaved, then summoned the three miscreants, and for a while had been able to sublimate his unease in mundane matters. Now, though, with the lecture over and nothing else to demand his attention, the disquiet was forming again, insidious and refusing to leave him alone.

Noises from the dining hall were beginning to filter into his consciousness, gradually rising in volume as more and more of the castle's residents found places at the long tables for the communal morning meal. Tirand left the anteroom and walked along the short connecting passage, pushing open the hall's double doors and entering. The hall was no more than a quarter full, most people choosing seats close to the fire that crackled vividly in the vast hearth, and he looked about, scanning faces in the hope that Karuth might by now have woken and come down.

She wasn't there, but she arrived half an hour later as Tirand was finishing the last of his food. He saw her and signaled; he was sitting alone, having politely fended off any would-be companions, and she approached his table and sat down, shaking her unbound hair back and running her fingers through it wearily.

"I feel as though I haven't eaten for three days," she said. "What's the fare? Anything appetizing?"

Tirand beckoned a servant to bring a tray, and Karuth selected a bowl of sweetened oatmeal, some game pie, and a slice of dried-fruit cake. Tirand poured ale for them both and tried to check his impatience while she ate. Watching her face, he thought that she looked drained and a little haggard this morning, and felt a twinge of guilt. At last she finished and pushed her dishes away with a sigh.

"I don't know why, but I always wake ravening after any sorcerous operation," she said. "Last time I spent the entire following day stealing back and forth to the kitchens and nibbling. It's a wonder I'm not as fat as an old mare in a cornfield."

Tirand looked at his clasped hands. "Solitary workings

129

always take a far greater toll of one's energy than an orthodox Circle ritual. I shouldn't have asked it of you. I'm
sorry."

"No, no." She shook her head, dabbing at her mouth
with a napkin, then looked up at him intently. "After what
I learned last night, I'm thankful that you did. There's
something afoot, Tirand, something strange. I don't like
the feel of it."

He frowned. "What happened?"

Karuth told him, recounting the elemental's fear and
its unwillingness or inability to answer her questions despite the threats she'd made, and finally repeating the
peculiar riddle that the being had given her.

"The schemer . . . and the one who sits at the
schemer's feet." Tirand was nonplussed. "I can't imagine
what it might mean."

"Nor I. Unless it has some direct reference to the girl
herself."

"That *she's* the schemer, you mean? It seems unlikely.
She's a mere child of fourteen. Or was."

"I know; it isn't a likely avenue, is it?"

Tirand started to reply, but his words turned into a
startled exclamation as something pushed against his leg
under the table. He looked down, and met the intense
green stare of a white cat.

"What is it?" Karuth asked.

"Nothing." He laughed as the momentary shock evaporated. "Just one of our resident scavengers looking for a
soft heart and a full plate."

Karuth's expression changed rapidly. "The white female?"

"Yes. Why?"

"She came to my room last night, with another cat."

Her voice was suddenly tense, and Tirand said, "Well,
you know the way they are. They can sense when any of us
are working, and they're drawn to it."

"I know that. But she was still there when I woke, and
she's been following me about ever since. She stares at me;
I can feel her mind probing, as if she's trying to tell me
something. And I keep thinking about a remark you made
last night." She looked up. "We know that cats are crea-

tures of Chaos rather than Order; it's in their fundamental nature. Last night you told me that Father thinks Chaos might have had a hand in what happened at the Matriarch's Cot."

Tirand hissed softly between his teeth. "You're saying that perhaps it was Chaos that put a geas on the elemental? That we might do well to look in that direction for the 'schemer' of the riddle?"

"I don't know, Tirand. But it's the only other possibility I can think of as yet."

They were clutching at straws, Tirand thought. And yet . . . He said, "Have you told Father about this?"

"I haven't had the chance. Apparently he's been breakfasting in his study with Lias Barnack, and it certainly wouldn't have been prudent to approach him there."

"Not with Lias's sharp ears to overhear, no," Tirand agreed. "Nevertheless, I think we should speak to him, Karuth. This could have a strong bearing on the council's attitude toward the Higher Rite."

She sighed. "I wish I could agree with you, but I doubt if there's anything of value in it."

"It's still worth exploring." Tirand turned around, narrowing his eyes to look through the sunlit window and judge the hour. "Father should have finished with Lias by now. Let's find him."

They rose and made to leave. As Karuth turned away from the bench, the white cat suddenly jumped up onto the table. Its tail was held upright, its whiskers quivered as it gazed at her, and it uttered a plaintive cry. For a moment Karuth returned its stare, trying but failing to understand what the animal was attempting to communicate. Then, with a nervous, ungraceful movement she pulled her shawl more tightly around her shoulders and followed Tirand from the hall.

"Aeoris, lord of the daylight hours; Yandros, lord of all the hours of darkness; O thou greatest of the gods, whose supernal hands set and hold the scales of Equilibrium: in true and rightful reverence we make our obeisance and our salute, and we give due thanks for your justice and enlightenment." Chiro Piadar Lin raised his hands high, and his arms, as the wide sleeves of his ceremonial robe fell back, were patterned by the faint nacre of the Marble Hall's shifting mists. "By the power and duty invested in me in the name of Order and in the name of Chaos, I close this circle and bid all servants of the higher and lower ethers to depart hence to their dwelling places. Air and Fire, Earth and Water, Time and Space, Life and Death: I constrain all watchers to obey me, for I am Order and I am Chaos, and I am the chosen avatar of the gods' work and word within the mortal realm. Servants, aroint!"

The High Initiate clapped his hands with a sound like a whip cracking, and Tirand felt a rush of energy that seemed to implode through the hall with his father's rigid figure at its core. The mists twisted into a hundred whirlwind columns, images distorted, and something like a huge unhuman sigh echoed from all about him. Then abruptly his vision cleared, the mists settled while the mosaic floor regained its normal proportions, and he came back to earth to feel his palms clammy with sweat as he released the hands of the adepts on either side of him and let his arms fall to his sides.

There was silence for perhaps a minute. Looks were exchanged, but, as was demanded by a Higher Rite, no one would speak until the entire company had left the hall and reached the exoteric realms of the library beyond the shining corridor. Tirand could see Karuth between two of the older adepts on the far side of the circle. She was rubbing her upper arms as though they ached; he hoped she might look in his direction so that he could judge something of her thoughts, but she only gazed down at the floor beneath her feet. As Chiro turned, the adepts moved into two lines on either side of him. The High Initiate didn't so much as glance at anyone, but walked briskly down the aisle they formed and away toward the silver door. Just before he turned to follow, Tirand cast one last look at the seven massive statues looming in the haze. It was pure imagination, he knew, but it seemed to him that the face of Aeoris was a little more stern than usual, and the smile of Yandros a little more sardonic.

Karuth, passing, brushed his arm with her fingers and he realized that others behind him were waiting for him to precede them. Hastily Tirand tore his gaze from the carved figures and walked quickly after his peers.

The library was empty and lit only by a single candle, enough to lift the room from darkness to dusty shadows, but no more. The adepts gathered in a group before Chiro. Though the rule of silence no longer applied, it seemed that no one was eager to be first to speak, and at last the High Initiate broke the hiatus.

"My friends." His voice was somber, and the candle-light reflected from beads of perspiration on his forehead. "I can only confirm what you've already seen for yourselves. The gods have granted us no sign tonight. It may be that a later and perhaps cryptic sign will come, but I'm not optimistic, for I sensed no divine presence in the Marble Hall. Reluctantly I must suggest that Aeoris and Yandros have not chosen to answer our plea, and conclude either that the matter is beneath their notice or that, for reasons which aren't for us to question, they have deemed that we must solve the conundrum for ourselves. Either way, there is nothing more that the Circle can do. I thank you all, and wish you sound sleep."

There were nods and murmurs, but no one had anything to say. As he turned to lead the way from the library, Chiro caught Tirand's gaze briefly, and an almost imperceptible movement of his eyes signaled his wish for a word in private. The small procession climbed the stairs and emerged into the chill evening; with muted goodnights exchanged, the group broke up and the adepts went their separate ways.

Tirand hung back, waiting for Karuth. The courtyard was as deserted as the library had been, though the darkness was relieved by the splash of lights from many of the castle's windows. The air smelled frosty beneath the ever-present tang of salt, and the sea's deep, restless voice seemed preternaturally clear and close. Their footsteps echoed sharply as Tirand linked arms with his sister and they walked toward the main doors.

"Father wants to speak to us alone," Tirand said in an undertone.

"I know, I saw his signal." Karuth's gaze lingered for a moment on the figure of Chiro ahead of them. "Best wait until the others have dispersed, then we'll go to his study." She paused; then, "So: the gods were silent."

"Yes. And I think it's shaken him. It was a powerful rite; it *must* have been noted in the higher realms, or all our tenets and beliefs are a mockery. Yet there was nothing, not even a whisper of any power beyond the level of the elemental guardians. I don't understand it, Karuth."

Karuth began to reply, then stopped, stiffening. "Look." She had halted abruptly, and pointed to the first of the colonnaded pillars that flanked the wall. Tirand was in time to see a flicker of movement in the gloom, something small and pale slipping quickly out of sight.

"It was that cat again," Karuth said softly. "It must have been waiting by the outer door while the Rite was conducted. Tirand, it *knows* something, I'm certain it does!"

Even Tirand's initial skepticism about the cat's peculiar behavior was beginning to falter. For three days now it had followed Karuth wherever she went, watching, listening, probing. Karuth had tried to make some sense of the unsettling signals that she felt emanating from its mind, but her efforts had been fruitless. She had no especial talent for telepathy, and besides, even the most gifted human psychics could glean very little from the alien territory of a cat's consciousness.

Tirand squeezed her arm firmly. "Leave it be," he advised. "There's no point in fretting over something that can't be resolved."

A little reluctantly Karuth tore her gaze from the spot where the cat had been sitting, and they walked together up the steps toward the double doors. At the top of the flight she looked back over her shoulder. But the courtyard was empty.

Chiro was waiting for them in his study, and what he had to say was brief and without preamble.

"It's a matter of simple logic," he told them. "The gods have not seen fit to grant us enlightenment or aid, and it isn't for us to question their wisdom. I'm calling an end to any further investigation." He looked at them both in turn and his face was bleak. "We've tried to solve the mystery and we've failed. There's nothing more we can do, and this tragedy has already given rise to more than enough disquiet. People are looking to the Circle for reassurance, and in the absence of any guidance from the higher realms, our first duty must be to calm unease and allay groundless fears."

Karuth said, "Groundless?" and Chiro looked at her wearily.

"I know what you're thinking, my child, and of course you're right. We can guarantee nothing. But then again, we'll achieve nothing by allowing rumor to feed on rumor to no good purpose." He turned to his son. "You understand me, don't you, Tirand?"

Tirand nodded. "Yes, Father, and I agree." He ignored the sharp glance Karuth gave him. "People want to look forward, not back. There's much practical work to be done in the wake of this tragedy, and I feel strongly that we should turn our thoughts to that rather than dwell on what can't be changed."

"Exactly."

"But, Father," Karuth protested, "what about Ygorla Morys?"

The High Initiate shook his head sadly. "She's dead, Karuth. She must be." He looked up at her, and his brown eyes were both sorrowful and candid. "Forget about her, my dear. There's nothing any of us can do for her now, and unhealthy speculation will only bring harm. Grieve for her and for the Matriarch, but don't dwell on their fate or try to solve an insoluble conundrum. There's no point."

Later, alone in her bed, Karuth brooded over Chiro's words. It wasn't easy to quash her private feelings about the mystery or resign herself to abandoning her own investigations. There were avenues that she hadn't yet explored, and even if some carried too many attendant risks to be worth serious consideration, she didn't like the thought that they must now be closed to her. Yet how could she go against the stricture? Chiro was not only her father but also High Initiate of the Circle to which she was bound as an adept; she was therefore doubly constrained to obey him. But every instinct within her protested against letting the matter drop.

The root of her dilemma, Karuth knew, was an illogical but stubborn conviction that Ygorla Morys wasn't dead. What that implied, she didn't know, but the ambiguity of the elemental's statement, *she is gone*, worried at her mind with small, sharp claws. Could the creature have been trying to convey something that it dared not say directly? *Gone*. Not dead: *gone*. They were not of necessity the same thing. Then there was the cryptic riddle it had given her, which, she was certain, had far more bearing on the missing girl's fate than she or anyone else could imagine. But the clues were too slight—she needed more information if she hoped to unravel the mystery. Before the Higher Rite and her father's subsequent pronouncement, she had thought of speaking to Sister Fiora and Sister Corelm, to glean what she could about Ygorla's background and character. That was out of the question now; they would be leaving tomorrow and she couldn't and wouldn't openly defy Chiro's order. If she was to do anything at all, it must be done in secret and without the aid of any other soul.

Yet what *could* she do? Karuth turned over and hugged her pillow, feeling restless and unhappy. There were rituals and summonings that went far beyond the minor working she'd performed three nights ago, and higher beings than elementals who might bring her closer to the answers she sought, but she didn't know if she had the courage to delve into those perilous realms alone. If she should overestimate her skill and her strength, she might find herself confronted with something far too

deadly to cope with. Better—for the time being, at least—
to concentrate her efforts as far as she could in the more
mundane planes.

She exhaled breath in a long sigh and shut her eyes,
trying to will her body to relax. Unbidden, an image of the
central statue in the Marble Hall formed in her inner vision and she saw again the faces of the two greatest gods,
Aeoris and Yandros. Yandros's graven eyes seemed to be
watching her, emphasizing the malevolent humor of his
smile, and she sighed again.

Ah, great one, do you find me amusing? she thought.
*Perhaps I should share the joke, and laugh at myself and
my foolish preoccupation. You mocked us all with your
silence tonight, Yandros. Are we so far beneath your notice
that we're not worthy of reassurance? Or do I flatter myself
in believing that you trouble even to watch us and know
what we do?*

The image persisted; she received, as she had expected, no answer. But the carved faced of the great Chaos
lord seemed for a moment to take on a more human aspect, contrasting suddenly and sharply with the stone indifference of Aeoris—and his smile had vanished. Karuth
started, her heartbeat missing painfully for a moment.
Then a shadow passed before her closed eyelids as though
a hand had moved across her face. She thought she felt the
faintest movement of displaced air, but before she could
wonder at it or look for its source, darkness muffled her
mind and her consciousness sank away into profound
sleep.

Outside, on a narrow ledge that was part of its mysterious and inaccessible night world, a small ghost-white form
blinked its brilliant eyes and turned its head away from
Karuth's window to stare across the courtyard and beyond
the black walls to where both moons hung low in a sky
alive with stars. The chilly light reflected in its irises, and
the cat seemed for a moment to be looking beyond the
firmament to another dimension before it twitched its tail,
rose, and padded away with the supreme confidence of its
kind along the byroads of its rooftop sanctuary.

Innate instinct told Yandros of his brother's approach, and his form and surroundings changed violently before narrow eyes that flickered with every color in the spectrum turned to regard the fire arch behind him.

For a moment Tarod was a silhouette, casting five shadows that loomed on the translucent walls as though they had independent life. Then his tall figure emerged from the flames and he smiled a greeting before turning to usher in his companion, who took the form of a small thin young woman with luminescent white hair and disconcertingly vast amber eyes. Seeing her, Yandros rose and bowed with punctilious courtesy; she bowed in return, inclining her head gravely.

Tarod crossed the shifting floor and gazed through a window that looked out on a mind-numbing vista. "The Circle seem very agitated by this affair in Southern Chaun," he said.

"Yes." Yandros conjured a sweetmeat and chewed it reflectively. Food was an irrelevance in the Chaos realm, but now and again it amused Yandros to mimic human ways.

"Why did you choose not to answer them, Yandros?"

Yandros studied the vista beyond the window for a moment, then made a slight movement of one hand. The scene altered, and rolling downland stretched away under the light of three iridescent blue stars. "I was in two minds about it," he said at length. "I'll confess that there's something in the mystery that interests me. But the Circle are so unsubtle and unimaginative in their approach—they look immediately to us for aid and guidance without even pausing to consider how they might solve the conundrum for themselves. It's a tiresome trait, and it makes a mockery of the pride they profess to take in their freedom."

Tarod smiled thinly. "And the fact that the High Initiate also called on Aeoris and his anemic kin no doubt adds its own sour spice?"

"I wouldn't phrase it quite so strongly." Yandros raised an ironic eyebrow. "But if the High Initiate chooses to be so rigidly impartial, then I'm inclined for once to sit back and let Aeoris have the pleasure of helping him."

"If he can," Tarod observed. "Personally, I doubt that

the lords of Order know anything more about the mystery than we do. It *is* an intriguing puzzle, Yandros. If the child had any innate power, where did that power come from?"

Yandros shrugged. "Not from Aeoris, you can be certain of that. And not from us. I imagine it was the influence of some mischief-making elemental or other lower being." He smiled wolfishly. "If she was as forward as some of the brats spawned in the provinces, it wouldn't surprise me in the least if she fell foul of an incubus or something similar. That's happened before, when curious children have tried to experiment with matters they don't understand, and it only takes one false move for their playthings to turn on them and on anyone else who happens to be in the way. But frankly, my brother, I neither know nor care. Whatever the truth of it, it's none of our concern. If mortals want the freedom we've granted them to manage their own affairs, then as long as those affairs don't affect us, they can cope with their own troubles as they please. Let the Circle draw whatever conclusions satisfy them, and have done with it. Doubtless the girl's dead, and once Chiro Piadar Lin and his friends embroil themselves in wrangling over who should succeed the Matriarch, they'll forget her soon enough."

Tarod smiled faintly at the rancor in his voice. "The High Initiate is proving to be something of a disappointment, isn't he?"

"He's not of the same mettle as Keridil Toln, certainly. Even in his last years, I confess I had certain respect for Keridil, for at least he had firm principles and refused to compromise them. He might have been a fool, but he certainly wasn't a hypocrite. Chiro's a different matter altogether. We know perfectly well where his real loyalties lie, but he insists on maintaining a facade of giving equal reverence to us as well as to Order, and personal principle comes a poor second. I find that degree of pragmatism contemptibly weak; I'd much prefer an outright adversary like Keridil to a man who pays us lip service for safety's sake."

"If nothing else, his tenure should be relatively quiet," Tarod said. "Barring any further incidents like this one, I doubt if the Circle will trouble us unduly for the next decade or two."

The amber-eyed woman, who thus far had listened to the conversation without comment, said suddenly, "I'm not so certain that that's true."

Yandros turned and regarded her quizzically. "Cyllan, you surprise me." Then his eyes narrowed. "What makes you unsure?"

Rainbows of light reflected in her hair as she shook her head. "I don't know, my lord. But I sense—I *feel*— that all is not entirely well in the mortal realm, even if the signs of it haven't yet manifested." She glanced up at Tarod, then met Yandros's gaze and ventured a thin smile. "Perhaps it's a resurgence of old human intuitions."

Yandros, too, smiled. "Of course: these days I tend to forget that you were mortal once." He looked at Tarod. "What do you think, Tarod? Is Cyllan right to be concerned?"

Tarod slipped an arm across Cyllan's shoulders. "What she says is worth keeping in mind. In human affairs, her intuition might be a surer guide than our own knowledge —and I learned long ago never to underestimate the deviousness of some mortals. But in all honesty, I don't think we need trouble ourselves overmuch. If there is anything more to this affair in Southern Chaun, we'll learn of it in good time. I'd simply suggest that we keep a casual watch for any further developments in that particular province."

Yandros nodded. "I think you're right. Well, then: we'll leave the Circle to their own devices, but we won't entirely neglect our interest in Southern Chaun." He glanced at the window again. Storm clouds were gathering, moving with unnatural speed, and blotting out the three blue suns. "If nothing else, it will make an amusing diversion."

10

Yandros's casual prediction about Chiro Piadar Lin's tenure as High Initiate proved true enough. The Circle's investigation into the grisly events at the Matriarch's Cot was officially halted, and though some members of the Sisterhood were unhappy at the abrupt closing of the book, they had neither the confidence nor the conviction to argue with Chiro's decree, especially when Blis Alacar let it be known that he agreed with the High Initiate's view.

Ria's successor as Matriarch was Shaill Falada, a popular and respected senior from Wishet province. Behind a ruddy face and a very down-to-earth manner she was an eminently sound choice, and once the pomp and ceremony of her inauguration was over, she settled down to rule her order of women with quiet efficiency. A small memorial to Ria was created in the garden of the Matriarch's Cot, but Ygorla, though dutifully mourned as protocol demanded, was soon forgotten, and the more immediate concerns of everyday life seeped back to their old, ascendant place.

In the winter of the third year after Ria's death the fishermen of Shu and Prospect provinces came home to harbor with tales of unusually fierce and localized storms in the Bay of Illusions. One boat had been driven onto rocks in the Summerisle Strait and sunk with the loss of three crewmen; five days later a larger smack met an unexpected squall in the same area and was forced to run to Summer Isle itself, arriving with her sails in tatters and her hold awash. Barely seven days at a time went by without the storm cones being hoisted on the quays at Shu-Nhadek, and when prayers and rituals to bring calmer weather failed, many crews of the smaller fleets and individual boats philosophically resigned themselves to being landbound until the peculiar season passed.

But, as always, there were braver—or, cynics said, more foolhardy—souls who refused to bow to the elements. With half the province's craft idle in port, fresh fish was in short supply and commanding high prices, and that was temptation enough for a poor man or an opportunist. So when the *Smiling Girl* put out from Shu-Nhadek one bright, hard-lit dawn, her crew unfurled the sails with eager anticipation, proud of their enterprise and the courage that prevailed where others had faltered.

There was a heavy swell, choppy in places, but the sky was clear and the wind fresh, and soon *Smiling Girl* was bearing eastward on a course that took her slowly away from Shu's coastline and toward the rich fishing grounds southwest of Summer Isle. By midmorning they could see the stark cliffs of the bay's other landmark, the White Isle, rising on their starboard quarter and crowned by the truncated peak of the dead volcano, and the skipper paused idly at the wheel to wonder, as he'd often done before, what might be seen on that ancient deserted rock. As a boy he had heard tales of the place from those who had gone out on one of the chartered pilgrim boats and returned with awed descriptions of the vast staircases and labyrinthine caves carved from the rock, but though the skipper had promised himself that someday he too would assuage his curiosity and see the Isle for himself, he had never done so. Now the pilgrim boats no longer sailed, for there wasn't sufficient interest in the island to make them profitable, and no right-minded seaman would attempt to negotiate a smaller craft around those rocks with their treacherous tide races. The skipper shrugged, forgetting the Isle and his youthful fancies, and turned his attention back to more practical matters.

The warning came minutes later from the lookout posted in the prow to watch for the telltale signs of a shoal, and when the skipper heard the shout of *"Storm!"* his blood seemed to slow to a crawl in his veins. Anger quickly followed, a fearful, instinctive reaction. The sky was as clear as midsummer, not a cloud on the horizon—there could be no storm!

Then he peered through the wheelhouse window to starboard again, and saw the massive piles of anvil-headed cloud rising beyond the White Isle.

The oath he tried to utter died in his throat as he stared at the banking, roiling mass. It wasn't *possible*! Not out of a clear sky, not out of nowhere—

The first huge breath of wind struck *Smiling Girl* broadside-on, and the skipper staggered as the deck heeled beneath his feet. A cross wave rose, smacking heavily into the boat's side and setting her rocking wildly; hastily recovering his wits, he yelled for the crew to jump to the sails and began to swing the wheel, trying to bring his craft around head-on to the wind. But suddenly *Smiling Girl* wouldn't respond. More cross waves were following in the wake of the first, battering the hull, and in what seemed like only seconds, the wind had become a gale. The sun vanished as the rising cloud mass swallowed it, and a vast dark wing of shadow swept across the sea from the direction of the island, turning the water's surface to an oily, murderous black. Rain and hail began to bombard the boat, and the waves swelled and humped to toss her like a cork. There were yells of terror from somewhere astern, the thumping splash of a freshwater barrel breaking loose and falling overboard, then over the shriek of the wind came a deep, ominous creak as the mainsail began to beat like a monstrous wing, and the boom, out of control, came swinging around in a scything arc to smash against the wheelhouse and hurl the skipper sprawling out onto the deck.

Mayhem broke out as fear erupted into blind panic. The skipper, clinging helplessly to the rail as a massive wave tried to drag him with it down into the sea, saw blurred, flailing shapes staggering by him, heard screams of terror and a lethal tearing sound as the sail, defeating all efforts to furl it, ripped free and went whirling away on the hailstorm. The boat's prow plunged down, reared up; she was turning full circle and the boom swung savagely back, mowing down two men in its path and sweeping them over the side like broken dolls. Somewhere in the depths of his tortured mind the skipper still struggled to protest the impossibility of this hideous assault, but there was no time for reason, no chance to assimilate the horror of what was happening to them. Leaping now like a mad horse, *Smiling Girl* plowed into another trough, and when she rose again with water cascading from her deck, the skipper saw a vast wall looming out of the chaos toward him. *The island*—he tried to yell a warning, but a flurry of hailstones scourged his face and turned the cry to a howl of pain and shock. *Rocks!* his brain screamed, *the rocks!*—but no one could hear and no one had the power to stop the boat's wild, careering rush toward destruction.

Smiling Girl struck the first of the underwater reefs with a tearing, groaning judder that rattled the skipper's teeth in his skull. She slewed violently through ninety degrees as the rocks gashed half the length of her hull, and the deep, terrifying rumble of water bursting into her hold echoed up through the deck planking. Someone started to screech *"Abandon ship!"* but the skipper never knew whether the cry was heard or obeyed. He saw the boom coming toward him again and flung up his arms as both it and a cataract of water crashed down together; then he was flying, slowly, it seemed, so slowly, through the howling air, and the sea was rising to meet him, and there was a roaring in his ears and—

He came to facedown on a ledge just above the sea's reach. One hand, cramped rigid, was locked around a broken splinter of wood, and rain was beating down on his unprotected back. The storm's racket had ceased; now there was only the relentless boom of a sea flattened and tamed by the downpour, and the crags of the White Isle rearing vertiginously against a blank gray sky.

He couldn't remember getting to shore. He had no memories at all from the moment that the great wave had broken the boom from its mooring and washed it over the boat's side, carrying him with it. As some semblance of rationality returned, he reasoned that he must have clung instinctively to the spar and by a miracle been carried through the reefs to the shelving foot of the island, where he'd somehow found the wherewithal to drag himself clear of the water before he lost consciousness. As for the others . . .

He didn't want to look, yet the compulsion was too great to resist. Through the rain's blur he saw among the teeth of the rocks the broken mast and sections of timber which were all that remained of *Smiling Girl*. A few pieces of flotsam bobbed near the edge of the reefs; further out, he thought he could see something larger floating, but he turned his head quickly, not wanting to acknowledge what it was. Along his ledge, which stretched around the island's curve, nothing else moved or broke the rocks' symmetry. He was alone.

The skipper began to shiver uncontrollably, and it was some while before he could bring the reaction under control. Without knowing the sun's position, he couldn't tell the time of day, and neither could he judge whether the tide was rising or falling. He had no survival equipment, no flares, no rope, not even a drop of fresh water, let alone food, and the odds on any other vessel coming within hailing distance were ones that no sane gambler would take. If he stayed where he was, he would die. He *had* to try to reach the island's interior.

When he struggled to his hands and knees, he found that although his body was bruised, cut, and battered, no bones seemed to be broken. Shutting his eyes, the skipper offered fervent thanks to the gods, then added a prayer that, having brought him this far, they might continue to look mercifully on him for a while yet. If he could get to a high vantage point and find some means of making a fire, then surely, *surely*, before too long the smoke would be seen and a vessel would come to investigate? He didn't want to die. Not here; not like this, alone and unmourned and frightened.

Painfully slowly he began to crawl along the ledge, hardly knowing what he hoped to find but desperately scanning the sheer wall beside him. At last he came upon what appeared to be a break in the cliff face where the rocks had cracked and split, forming a steep path leading upward. For a long time he could do no more than sit and stare at the crevasse, asking himself what he would do if after a grueling climb he found himself at a dead end. But the question was irrelevant. He had no other choice but to try, so at last he inched his body into the fissure and, hand over hand, started to pull himself with grim, almost mesmerized determination up the path toward what he fervently prayed would be sanctuary.

On another part of the island, a pair of startlingly blue eyes gazed into a small mirror and watched the stricken sailor's progress with intent fascination. At last, judging that the crawling man would reach the path's end within a few more minutes, small, pale hands put the mirror aside and the White Isle's sole inhabitant rose from her couch.

At fourteen Ygorla had been pretty; at seventeen the last traces of childishness were fading to reveal a girl of extraordinary beauty. Her skin was flawless, her hair like a rich black waterfall framing a delicate heart-shaped face. And where three years of solitude in this bleak place might have taken an ordinary mortal over the brink of insanity, Ygorla had thrived and blossomed. Her father had been true to his promise; she had every luxury she could desire —and besides material trappings she also had a secret and burgeoning talent which, even after just three years of study and practice, had already outstripped the wildest dreams of her childhood. Her training wasn't complete yet, not by a long way; but she could with confidence call herself a sorceress. And though her skills were small by the standards her demon father had set, they would have stunned the Circle's highest adepts had the Circle known of her continuing existence.

Yet in all this time the one thing she had *not* had was the sight of a human soul. In truth, she hadn't missed mortal society; Narid-na-Gost's visits were frequent, and besides, in Southern Chaun she'd found the company of others more of an irritant than a pleasure. But this new development intrigued her. She hadn't expected anyone to survive the wreck of the boat, and the fact that the fisherman was still clinging doggedly to the tatters of his life had aroused her curiosity.

She looked around her, then snatched up a black fur cloak from where she'd carelessly cast it some days before.

Her sanctuary was only one among the many caves that honeycombed the White Isle's interior, but its humble origins were invisible beneath the opulent trappings that her father—and latterly she herself—had created. Throwing the cloak about her shoulders, Ygorla paused to stare at the chamber for a few moments. She would need more space. Another cave, perhaps one like the smaller antechamber that connected to this by a short tunnel, where her most private studies and experiments were conducted. On her return she'd think more closely about it. First, though, she must attend to her more immediate concern.

With a rustle of silk she whirled away along the tunnel that led to the outer wall of the crater and an unadorned foursquare portal worn smooth by centuries of erosion. Above the lintel it was just possible to make out a carved design—an unblinking eye with a lightning-flash spearing from the pupil, the old symbol of Aeoris of Order. Decades ago, when this island was a sacred and taboo place, the design had been picked out in gold leaf, but any traces of the gold which less scrupulous pilgrims hadn't stolen as a souvenir had flaked away and vanished. Ygorla smiled up at the carving, resisting a childish impulse to poke her tongue at it, then stepped out from under the portal and into the open air.

The rain was still falling heavily, but no water touched her as she gazed down on what she had come to think of as her domain. From the portal, which once had been the guarded ceremonial entrance to the crater itself, a gigantic stairway fell away down the volcano's flank. According to legend this great flight had been created by Aeoris in the days before recorded history, and the stairs were cut on an unhuman scale as though to accommodate the feet of a giant. The view was breathtaking: far, far below it was just possible to make out the narrow inlet of the island's one harbor, little more than a cleft in the high cliffs and unused now for decades, and beyond that the vast gray sweep of the southern ocean reached away to merge with the horizon. On a clear day she could sometimes make out the shape of Summer Isle shining in the distance, but today there were only the sea and the clouds and the rain.

Ygorla paused for a moment, studying the staircase

and the network of cave entrances that showed as darker pocks in the rock walls. Then she began to descend, jumping from step to step like a gazelle and pausing every now and then to tilt her head to one side as though listening for something. At last she found the right vantage point, near the mouth of one of the wider adits, and there she stopped. The rain continued to pour down around her, but, still untouched, she ignored it. Smiling as though at some private joke, she sat down on the stair to wait.

***

Throughout his agonizing, crawling climb, the fisherman had prayed ceaselessly that his efforts wouldn't prove to be in vain, and when he saw the tunnel mouth before him the shock of relief was so great that it almost stopped his heart. For a few moments he lost control of his limbs, his body collapsing nervelessly as he tried to slow his stertorous breathing and regain a little strength. Then, mumbling incoherent thanks to the powers which had saved him, he pushed himself forward into the tunnel.

The rain stopped beating on him and he felt dry dust under his clawing hands. Almost immediately the tunnel floor leveled out, and when he peered into the gloom he thought he saw a glimmer of light far ahead. He rubbed at his eyes to clear away a mixture of rain and tears, and, fighting a desire simply to curl up and sleep, pressed on.

For a while there was nothing but the shuffling sound of his own slow progress. His mind was too numbed even to guess at how much distance he had covered, and whenever he looked up and ahead, the gleam of distant light seemed no brighter. He persevered, knowing he couldn't go back, trying not to lose heart . . . and then, suddenly, stopped.

Had he imagined that faint, untoward sound that momentarily cut across the muffled noise of his hands and feet? His pulse quickened erratically and he peered about him. Nothing to see; just the tunnel, wider and higher now, but still featureless. It must have been a reverberation, perhaps from some small hollow beyond the wall. He made to move on—

148

And yelped aloud as a vicious gust of wind came whirling up the tunnel from behind him and sent him sprawling.

The echoes of his shout bowled away along the tunnel in the wind's wake, and as they faded he heard—or thought he heard—a soft giggle of laughter at his back.

For what seemed an age he was held in a dreadful limbo, trapped between terror of looking behind him and the equal horror of not knowing what might be there. At last, hearing no more sounds, he forced himself to turn his head.

At first he though the tunnel was empty, but as he let out his pent breath and prepared to crawl on again, a shadow lurched across the wall. Then the skipper's eyes bulged in their sockets as the shadow resolved into something more solid and he saw what was prowling along the tunnel toward him.

His scream was deafening, dinning in his own ears and escalating fear into panic. Scrabbling to his feet—the roof was just high enough now to allow him to stand, albeit bent nearly double—he began to run, zigzagging along the tunnel, stumbling, tripping, rebounding from the walls, staggering on. Behind him he heard the soft pad of paws, trotting at first, then running, and he could hear *it*, the *creature*, panting and slavering. Through his mind roiled images of the one glimpse he'd had of it: black, sleek, cat and yet somehow not cat, not real, not *mortal*. It was something from another, hideous realm, fire-eyed, fire-mouthed, laughing and snarling and gaining on him—

Suddenly light flared ahead and the tunnel curved sharply so that he almost lost his footing as he careered around at a sharp angle. As he righted himself, his eyes and brain had time to register the shock of the tunnel's abrupt end before, with a yell, he missed his footing, flailed wildly, and stumbled out of the tunnel mouth to measure his length on solid ground that knocked the breath from his lungs. He felt a rushing at his back, the sense of something dark, and vaster than its physical bulk implied, leaping over him with a wave of searing heat and streaking away. Then cold rain was pelting down on him, and he raised his head, blinking, to focus on a pair of black-slippered feet not a single pace from where he sprawled.

Black slippers, the hem of a rich blue silk gown, black fur that shimmered as though it possessed an inner light . . . The fisherman's straining eyes rolled upward and he saw clearly the figure who stood over him.

"Oh, you poor unfortunate!" Wide blue eyes in a face that might have been made of the finest porcelain; the man groaned, certain that this was some appalling delusion sent to taunt him in the last moments before he was torn apart and devoured. He couldn't assimilate her youthful loveliness, couldn't believe in it; she was a phantom— she *must* be.

Yet the slim hand that reached out to touch his hair was real enough, and a sharp tingle ran from his scalp down the length of his spine. He'd *dreamed* of women like this. Was she another dream? . . .

"What have you suffered, poor helpless man?" Ygorla's voice was honey and her fingers traced a complex pattern over his right cheek, making him shudder instinctively with delight that he couldn't control. She swooped like a dark bird and her fur cloak enclosed him in headily scented folds. "You've nothing to fear now. You're *mine* now."

A cold stab of intuition struck terror into the man's brain as he heard the words, but shallower and more powerful reactions drowned the doubt. She was so very beautiful. He couldn't resist her, didn't *want* to resist her.

"I will keep you here with me. You will be my pet." Now Ygorla's voice was changing, honey tempered by something else that in his confusion and shock the man couldn't quite comprehend. Hunger—but laced with another emotion, another desire. *Greed*, a part of him that was still sane said. *Power*.

"*Unuhhh . . .*" It was an inarticulate protest but the best he could contrive. Cold and exhaustion and fright were combining in an irresistible meld, and when she leaned further over him and her pale fingers began to play in his hair and pull at his clothing and the skin beneath, he could only twitch helplessly as animal desire and blind panic warred for precedence.

"I shall keep you and hold you and play with you when I please. I can show you so *much.*" She thrust three fingers under his chin, forcing his head up, hurting him, and he moaned as he saw her lovely face drawing closer to his, her lips parting to reveal perfect teeth and a tongue ready for a shattering, agonizing kiss—

"Daughter!"

Ygorla whirled. Two stairs above her, shrouded in an aura that pulsed darkly crimson, stood Narid-na-Gost.

"Father . . ." Instinct and old habit made her draw back and rise to her feet, pulling the fur cloak tightly about herself. A high flush of color burned in her cheeks.

The supernatural door through which he'd stepped slammed and vanished, and the demon stared at her, his crimson eyes alight. "What is this, Ygorla?" He gestured toward the groveling fisherman, who had frozen rigid and was staring at him in horror.

Ygorla lifted her small shoulders, but there was suddenly a nervous glint in her eyes. "Nothing of any importance, Father. A mere diversion." Her voice took on a note that was both defensive and faintly pleading. "I was bored."

The demon turned slowly on one heel, and the fisherman recoiled as the terrible, unhuman eyes seemed to glare through his skull and into the roiling brain beyond. He tried to shout a protest, knowing that this must be some appalling nightmare from which he would soon wake, but all his throat and tongue could conjure was a feeble croak.

"Bored," Narid-na-Gost said contemptuously, and the dark aura flickered about his twisted form. "So you squander your powers to wreak some petty havoc with a boat and with this squirming creature, just to satisfy a childish whim!" He swung to face her again, and fury erupted in his voice. *"Have you learned nothing?"*

"Father—no, please—" Ygorla backed away as the demon raised his left hand. Something that looked to the petrified man like chained lightning spat across the gap between father and daughter, and Ygorla screamed, spinning around and falling to her knees as the bolt struck her. Her hair flew out in a nimbus about her head, spitting sparks, and lights danced in the crackling fur of her cloak.

"*Ahh . . .*" Her body heaved convulsively as she tried to struggle up. The demon moved to stand over her.

"I punish you for the fool that you are!" he said savagely. "I have been patient and indulgent, but I will not tolerate this! Do you think I've nurtured you and taught you, just to see you jeopardize your destiny and mine by these pitiful, self-aggrandizing entertainments? Storms and wreckings—how long do you think it will be before the world realizes that something is afoot? And when the world knows, the gods will know! But no; you have to flout my authority and play games to satisfy your vanity!" He dropped to a crouch and took her chin viciously between his clawed thumb and finger. "Do you know what it has cost me to enclose this island in a shroud of secrecy? *Secrecy*—that is our watchword, Ygorla! Whose power has maintained that secrecy? Whose power has kept all knowledge of our activities even from Yandros himself? *Answer me!*"

Tears of pain were streaming down Ygorla's cheeks; she grated through clenched teeth: "Y-yours."

"*Mine.* And if you forget yourself again, if you *dare* forget yourself, I will not be so lenient a second time!"

"I'm s-sorry . . . I'm sorry, I'm *sorry!*"

There was genuine contrition behind her fear, Narid-na-Gost saw, and his voice became calmer. "Very well. Vanity has its place, child, but not in this way. Do you understand?"

A nod.

"Good." In a cold, unhuman way the demon's fury had evaporated as swiftly as it had come, and he rose to his feet, glancing again at the fisherman, who throughout the exchange had been unable to move, speak, or even think coherently. Narid-na-Gost made a careless gesture toward him and said, "Kill that."

The man's eyes widened. "N-nh—" It *was* a dream, *had* to be—he was struck down by fever, he wasn't in this mad place, but lying sick and injured on the ledge above the sea, and this was a nightmare, it wasn't real, *it couldn't be happening!*

Ygorla sniffed and said in a small voice, "Could I not

keep him, Father? My pet . . . I thought he could be my pet . . ."

"And if you were to relax your vigilance and allow him to escape, what then?" Narid-na-Gost's eyes began to catch fire once more. "What then, daughter?"

"He couldn't escape. There's no way by which he could leave the island."

"Maybe so—but we can afford to take no risks. None whatever."

She hung her head. "Yes. I understand. Forgive me."

"Then do as I bid you. Or have you not the stomach?"

She masked her resentment quickly. "I've the stomach, Father. But I don't know if I have the power. Not like this, not yet."

"Ah." Narid-na-Gost spoke softly. "So you *are* wise enough to know your limitations. That is better; that pleases me. Very well, then." He turned toward the fisherman, and the man's brain locked into a rictus of sheer terror. In his mind he was screaming and babbling, words tumbling over one another, *no, please, I'll do anything, I'll worship you whatever you are, don't, please, have mercy, let me—*

The incoherent plea would never be uttered. He saw the crimson light and he felt the searing fire, and he had time for one insane shriek of agony before the thread of his life was severed.

———————— ⚬ ⊃ ⊂

Ygorla stared down at the charred corpse with a kind of emotionless fascination. She felt vaguely regretful at the loss of her plaything, but her father was right; they could take no chances. She'd been foolish to think otherwise.

"Come, daughter." The demon took her arm. "Come with me. There is something I wish to show you."

She turned away from the dead man, and as she did so, two shadowy forms materialized and padded silently toward the remains. The demon-cats she had conjured to drive her prey here were little better than phantom creatures, but even phantoms craved sustenance, and her creations would feed well on the corpse. The fisherman was nothing to Ygorla now, and, forgetting him, she followed her father as he began to climb the titanic stairway. When they reached the top of the flight and the great square portal, Narid-na-Gost stopped and turned to stare out across the island and the sea beyond.

"Look into the distance," he said softly. "Tell me what you see."

She peered through the rain. "The ocean."

The demon chuckled and, moving to stand behind her, touched his fingers to her temples. "Look again."

A shuddering thrill ran through her, the sense of power awakening deep within her soul, and suddenly the scene before her focused into incredible clarity. The rocks of the White Isle dazzled her vision; she saw through the rain, through the gray clouds to where the sun hung livid in the sky. And far, far off she saw a white shimmer that broke the horizon, reflecting the dreary daylight like a beacon.

"Summer Isle . . ." Her voice was awed and enraptured.

"Yes. Look well at it, my daughter; drink in the vision. Do you remember how I told you that one day you would have power beyond any mortal dream? There is the hub of that power, Ygorla; there is the seat of your future domain."

She drew in a sharp, excited breath, feeling the orgasmic shudder run through her again. *Summer Isle.* It was the crown of human might and majesty, the ultimate goal of mortal achievement.

"Yes, it is all that and more." Narid-na-Gost knew her thoughts and his lips parted in a feral, deadly smile. "But for you it will be only the beginning. The time is drawing nearer, Ygorla. Each day that dawns brings you one step closer to your destiny."

He drew back, leaving her to stand alone for a few moments as his quiet words reverberated in her mind and took root. He could see her hands quivering as the feelings within her all but overpowered her, and he smiled again, a more private smile, a smile of satisfaction. She was deeply excited by what he had told her, but what he had told her was only a small fraction of the truth. The rest—and in particular the final revelation—would come in time. But not yet. Not yet.

He stepped forward once more and laid his hands upon her shoulders. "You are due for your next lesson, Ygorla."

She turned, and he laughed softly, inwardly, as he saw the hunger and the ambition and the delight that shone in her brilliant eyes. "Yes," she said eagerly. "Yes, Father. Show me—teach me all I can learn!"

Narid-na-Gost's crimson gaze grew hot with pleasure. He was proud of his child. She wouldn't fail him. And in the times to come, the mortal world—and more, far more than the mortal world—would learn to fear both her name and his own.

11

Even Karuth Piadar had long forgotten about Ygorla. As years went by and the Southern Chaun mystery faded into the distance, other demands on her time and attention had gradually eroded her early concern, until even the elemental's cryptic riddle was no more than a vaguely and infrequently recalled memory.

There were many other preoccupations to fill her days. Shortly after her thirty-second birthday she passed—as everyone in the Circle had expected—the trials that elevated her to fifth rank among the adepts. And a month later she received a more secular distinction but one which, her father and brother teased, probably meant more to her than any Circle accolade, when the Guild Academy of Musicians bestowed on her the title of Mistress of the Musical Arts.

Despite the teasing, Chiro was deeply proud of his daughter's achievement, for he knew how much music meant to Karuth and knew, too, that she sometimes felt keenly the frustration of having so little leisure time to devote to her playing. He was worldly enough to be aware of a certain amount of political maneuvering behind the award, as the Guild knew full well that to honor his daughter would win the High Initiate's favor; but nevertheless the accolade was richly deserved. Chiro also hoped that Karuth's new status in the Guild might help persuade her to devote a little more time to private pursuits and a little less to her duties at the castle, which in his view she took just a shade too seriously. Neither of his children was yet married. In Tirand's case that was all well and good, for it was expected that the High Initiate's son and heir should dedicate himself solely to preparing for the position he would one day inherit. He'd make a suitable match when the time was right; until then there was no cause for concern. Karuth, however, was another matter. To begin with, she was five years older than her brother, and while a man might wait even until middle age before finding a wife, for women it was, Chiro believed, altogether different. What disturbed him most was the feeling that Karuth had no intention of marrying either now or at any time in the future. The thought troubled Chiro, for above all he wanted her to be happy. And though she wouldn't admit it and couldn't even be persuaded to discuss it, he had the distinct feeling that at times her single status was something that Karuth desperately regretted.

But the subject remained unaired, and Karuth continued to pursue her duties as single-mindedly as ever. Calvi Alacar, who had been home to the Summer Isle for a year, returned in the following spring, skin browned and hair bleached by the southern sun, and a good inch taller. He was twenty now and turning from an awkward youth into a slim, spare, and attractive young man; he was also gaining self-confidence, modest charm, and a level of achievement in his chosen studies that fully justified Tirand's early faith in him. Life at the castle was peaceable and good.

Then in the summer of that same year came the blow that no one could have foreseen or expected, when at the summer Quarter-Day celebrations Chiro rose in the banqueting hall to address the Circle and their guests, stopped in mid-sentence, frowned as though puzzled, and collapsed face-forward over the table. Karuth, scattering plates and cups in all directions, laid him out on the board and pummeled his chest in a frantic effort to start his heart beating again, but even her skills weren't enough, and amid stunned silence the High Initiate was pronounced dead.

When she finally realized the truth, Karuth fainted for the first time in her life. Her assistant, a quiet, capable young man named Sanquar, directed servants to carry her to bed and see that she stayed there, then, with the help of several high adepts and a senior Sisterhood healer who was fortuitously present, set about making the necessary preparations for the death vigil.

More than two hundred people sat silent in the great hall throughout that short, warm summer night. Tirand, shocked and barely knowing what he was doing, had been led with somber ceremony to sit at the center of the high table, and felt strangely remote and detached and tearless as he looked at the sea of stricken faces illuminated by the glow of torches. The real grief, he knew, would come later, when the first shock passed, but for now his mind clung stubbornly to only two disconnected yet obsessive thoughts. A part of him said silently: *so many of them are crying; they all must have loved him.* And another part asked helplessly: *sweet gods . . . what am I to do now?*

Chiro Piadar Lin was sent to his final rest with all the solemn ceremony that the castle could muster. His two children attended the funeral, Karuth with her face veiled, Tirand wearing the purple sash embroidered with the gods' sigils that was the emblem of a High Initiate in mourning for his predecessor. Messages came from all parts of the world; every provincial Margrave sent personal condolences, and a sealed letter from Blis Alacar, in his own hand, paid a tribute to Chiro that privately reduced even Tirand to tears. At last, though, the grieving was done, and as the first colder autumn winds began to blow, Tirand Lin was officially inaugurated as the new High Initiate of the Circle.

That same night Karuth turned down a proposal of marriage from the man who for the past seven months had been her lover, and gently ended their liaison.

Tirand and her father had been aware of the friendship but Karuth had taken good care to hide the fact that, for a while at least, it had been something more than that. She knew that every man she had looked on fondly in the past ten years or more had been, in Chiro's eyes, a prospective son-elect, and hadn't wanted to disappoint him yet again. But now that he was gone, the possibility of her marrying was more remote than ever. Tirand, thrown so suddenly into his new responsibility, would need her help and support as never before. She couldn't think of herself; duty must come first, and if for a while she must suffer the pangs of regret, well, she had suffered them before and they would be no worse now.

So throughout the autumn and winter that followed her brother's inauguration, Karuth dedicated her every waking moment to her work. There were no new lovers. Even her assistant, Sanquar, who adored her and whom under happier circumstances she might have been tempted to look on as more than a colleague, met with a kind but firm rebuff when he shyly tried to express his hopes. She could afford no new complications in her life; while Tirand and the Circle needed her, they must come first.

However, the strain of the changes wrought in their lives was telling on both Karuth and Tirand. The Matriarch, on an official visit to the Star Peninsula toward the end of winter, said firmly that they looked peaky and pallid and in need of a rest—little wonder when one considered the burden that had been laid on both their shoulders. But though her advice made sound sense, the idea of a break of any kind was unthinkable. In addition to his greater duties, which in themselves were onerous enough, Tirand found that a High Initiate had countless other and lesser calls upon his time; minor niggling but necessary matters which he'd been ignorant of while Chiro was alive. And Karuth, dividing her days between her own work and helping her brother in any way she could, had no more chance than he to consider any prospect of leisure. She was, however, aware that the Matriarch had told them both a few home truths. Tirand in particular was working too hard, even with the Council of Adepts to help him and secretaries and servants to share the everyday burden, and she herself hardly dared look in her mirror these days, hating the shallow, heavy-eyed stranger she knew she would see there. But the days wore on and there was no respite— until, as the hard northern winter drew to its long-awaited end, a letter from Summer Isle arrived at the castle.

The invitation came by messenger bird during the first few days of the spring thaw. The castle falconer who retrieved the hawk as it spiraled down to the courtyard saw the High Margrave's personal seal on the small scroll and carried it immediately to Tirand. As soon as he read the news it contained, Tirand sent a servant running to fetch Karuth from her infirmary.

In Tirand's study Karuth read the message with surprise and delight. "It's splendid news!" Her tired face broke into a smile. "Blis Alacar to marry at last—we were all beginning to wonder if he'd end his days as a bachelor!"

Tirand took the letter back and scanned it again. "His bride-to-be is Jianna Hanmen. Hanmen . . . I know the family; they're from East Han, aren't they? One of the oldest clans in the province. But I can't place a Jianna."

"The Chaun Margrave's eldest daughter married the Hanmen Charises' son last year," Karuth said. "I think Jianna might be his sister, though I couldn't tell you what she looks like."

"Well, we'll find out for ourselves soon enough." Then Tirand frowned worriedly. "Though I must admit that from a practical viewpoint this couldn't have come at a worse time. There's so much to be done here that I'm not sure if I can in all conscience leave the castle."

"You can't possibly decline," Karuth told him firmly. "It would be an insult to Blis—it's unthinkable."

"You could stand for me."

"I'll do no such thing. No, Tirand, we must both go. It will do us good—we both need a rest, and this will provide it without damage to our consciences." She peered over his shoulder at the invitation again. "Seven days of festivity, and it's also to coincide with Calvi's twenty-first birthday. It will be a magnificent celebration."

Her voice betrayed her eagerness, and, looking at her, Tirand saw that her eyes were alight with the old enthusiasm that had been sorely lacking lately. He reminded himself that they'd had no recreation in the months since their father died, and however stoically he might accept his lot, it was unfair to expect Karuth to sacrifice her own pleasures indefinitely. She was right, it *would* do them good to get away from the stern life of castle and Circle for a while, to emerge from this enclosed eyrie and see something of the world. For her sake, if nothing else, he should put aside duty for once and enjoy this opportunity for a change.

———————————➤ ◁———————————

They left the Star Peninsula twelve days later, a large and impressive company consisting of Tirand, Karuth, Calvi Alacar, and some twenty of the Circle's higher adepts whom the invitation had encompassed, together with servants and a long baggage train. Word of the High Margrave's wedding had by now spread throughout the world, and each province was planning its own celebrations so that in every town and village they found bonfires being built, flags being raised, garlands decorating the streets. They traveled through West High Land, joining up with a party from the main Sisterhood Cot, then on down through Chaun and into Prospect, where by prearrangement they met the Matriarch and a group of her seniors, and finally to Shu-Nhadek, from where they would take ship to Summer Isle.

In Shu-Nhadek the festivities were already in full swing. The townspeople had always felt that their proximity to Summer Isle gave them a privileged link with the High Margravate, and therefore considered themselves somewhat superior to the rest of the world: likewise they were determined that their celebrations would outdo all rival events, and the town was alive with color and noise. Tirand had never felt at ease in the midst of revelries, and was privately relieved to learn that the province Margrave, who was also attending the wedding, had offered to accommodate the High Initiate's party at his own house in its secluded grounds on a hill above the harbor. Their ship was due to leave on the morning tide, and Tirand hadn't looked forward to a sleepless night in an inn with the celebrations continuing noisily in the streets outside.

The Margrave and Margravine were renowned for keeping a good table, and after a magnificent meal and a little too much wine the guests retired to their rooms. Karuth was sharing a bedchamber with Sister Fiora, who was now elevated to the rank of the Matriarch's immediate deputy. Karuth hadn't seen Fiora for a long time, and both enjoyed this rare chance to exchange news and gossip, so that it was late into the night before they finally extinguished the room's candles and settled down to sleep.

Just as dawn was breaking, Karuth woke with a shriek.

"Karuth!" Fiora, shocked awake, sat bolt upright with her heart pounding beneath her ribs. "What is it—what's to do?"

Karuth had flung herself out of bed and was on her feet before consciousness jolted her into awareness of the physical world. She stood swaying, her mouth working soundlessly; then abruptly she gasped and sat down hard on the edge of the mattress.

"My dear, whatever was it?" Fiora's long years as a healer had instilled in her an ability to snap quickly into full wakefulness, and she grasped Karuth's shoulders, squeezing gently. "A nightmare?"

Karuth clenched her teeth as they threatened to start chattering uncontrollably. "I don't know. I thought—" She collected her wits with an effort, then gently freed herself from Fiora's grasp and stood up, crossing to where a jug of water was set on a table.

"You should tell me about it," Fiora said. "It's always advisable to earth these dreams by recounting them aloud."

Karuth took a drink of water, privately wishing it was something stronger. "I'm not sure if I can, Fiora. I'm not even sure that it was a dream."

Fiora leaned forward, alerted. "A seeing?"

"No, I don't think so. That's a province of the Sisterhood rather than the Circle, and I've never had a talent for seeing or scrying anyway. It was more like . . ." She pressed a finger to the bridge of her nose, trying—though a little reluctantly—to bring the memory back into focus. Then she frowned sharply.

"I can't recall it. It's gone." She sounded bemused, and the sister hastened to her side, leading her back to bed as though she were a feverish child.

"Sit down, my dear, and give yourself a chance to recover." She smoothed the coverlet, and Karuth sat. "It must have been a dream, Karuth. It's happened to me on more occasions than I care to remember; a violent night-mare, which vanishes from memory the moment I wake."

"It wasn't that." She might be sure of nothing else, Karuth thought, but she was certain that this had been no normal dream.

Fiora pursed her mouth. "Perhaps I should wake Sister Mysha? She's a skilled psychic; she might be able to help you unravel the threads and remember."

Karuth shook her head. "Not at this hour." She smiled pallidly. "I can guess the time; I haven't forgotten how much earlier the sun rises here than at home at this season. No, Fiora, I'll be well enough. Let's try to get a little more sleep, and forget about it."

Fiora was dubious, but Karuth could be firmly persuasive, and at last the sister reluctantly gave way. Yet though she made a pretense of settling again, Karuth's thoughts were still in turmoil. She couldn't recall the detail of her vision or whatever it had been, but she felt the essence of it like something lurking and predatory at the back of her mind, and she was certain that it had been a presentiment —or, more accurately, a warning.

But a warning of what? She turned her head and looked at Sister Fiora in the other bed. She appeared to have fallen asleep, and Karuth let her breath out in a long, quiet sigh. Perhaps she should consult Sister-Seer Mysha as Fiora had suggested. Dream-interpreting was a skill that the Circle, whose disciplines encompassed sorcery and high occult ritual rather than the lower and more personal psychic arts, had always left to their colleagues in the Sisterhood. As diviners the sisters had no equals, and Mysha was one of the most highly respected scryers in the land. Yet what could even Mysha possibly tell her that would be of any use? Though Karuth's training—which had taught her early on the folly of ignoring possible omens of any kind—counseled against it, something else within her argued that it would be better to dismiss the incident as meaningless, a momentary aberration of her subconscious mind brought on by unfamiliar surroundings and too much rich food. She didn't want to probe any deeper; she wanted simply to believe that there was nothing more to the matter than that. Forget it, she told herself, firmly quashing the small inner voice that cast doubts on the wisdom of such an attitude. *It means nothing. Put it aside and sail for Summer Isle with a quiet mind.*

With the aid of a few small tricks that calmed ruffled mental waters, Karuth was able to doze again until a servant came to rouse her. It was only when she was going down to breakfast with Fiora that she remembered what had hovered on the periphery of consciousness just before she rose, and wondered why, after all these years, she should have chosen this unlikely time to dream of Ygorla Morys.

They sailed as the tide turned, just before noon, leaving the festive harbor and the noise and mill of the crowds for the calm brilliance of open sea. It was a perfect morning, and as she stood at the ship's rail watching the glittering slide of the water under the keel, Karuth felt sorry for Tirand, who had never been a good sailor and was already confined belowdecks with seasickness. He'd tetchily refused her help, wanting only to be alone with his misery, and so she had joined a group of sisters who like her had never before visited Summer Isle and were attending to Calvi Alacar's enthusiastic commentary on the seascape.

Calvi was in his element. Vividly excited by the prospect of seeing his home and family, he had emerged from his normally diffident shell and was eagerly describing the features of the distant Shu coastline, which lay basking in the haze to larboard. Karuth listened for a few minutes, shading her eyes against the glare of sun on water; then suddenly Calvi swung about and pointed eagerly toward the ship's bows.

"There!" he said. "There it is—d'you see, just visible on the horizon ahead? That's the White Isle."

The sisters obediently turned to look, but as Calvi spoke, Karuth felt a sharp chill run through her. It took her completely by surprise; startled, she collected herself swiftly and followed the direction of the others' gazes. There was nothing remarkable to see, only a shadowed smudge that broke the line between ocean and sky, but as she looked at it she felt the inexplicable frisson again.

"How close will we sail to it?" She didn't know why she had asked the question; it had crept unbidden from some uneasy corner of her mind.

Calvi calculated. "Oh . . . I'd say we'll pass about ten miles off its northern tip." He wasn't aware of her disquiet. "If we were sailing in a direct line to Summer Isle, we probably wouldn't even glimpse it, but there's a strong prevailing current here that makes it worth our while to curve around and approach the strait from the southwest." He glanced at her, smiling. "I suppose you haven't seen the White Isle before?"

"No, I haven't." And she thought: *and I don't want to see it now.*

"It's a familiar sight to all the seamen in these parts," Calvi said proudly. "Not that anyone ever sets foot there now, of course. When I was little I wanted to go, but I was never allowed to." He grinned. "Perhaps one day I'll revive the old custom and make a pilgrimage to the site of the gods' great battle. And perhaps I'll persuade you and Tirand to come with me?"

Something deep in Karuth's psyche recoiled, and she forced a hasty answering smile before her eyes could give her away. "That would be . . . very interesting."

"Not this time, though. Imagine what Blis would say if we all arrived late for his nuptials! By the way," he went on, blithely ignorant of anything amiss, "where *is* Tirand? I haven't seen him since we left harbor."

Karuth nodded toward the companion hatch. "He's below in one of the cabins, and not at all well. In fact"—it would give her an excuse, she thought, to get away, not to have to look at the approaching White Isle—"I should go and see how he's progressing and if I can do anything for him." She smiled again, making a better pretense of it this time. "If you'll all forgive me . . ."

She walked away along the deck, balancing with the roll of the ship, and hastened down the companion steps. At the foot of the flight she paused to get her breath and hastily wipe away the film of perspiration that slicked her brow and the palms of her hands. What was the matter with her? Why did she fear the White Isle? It was ludicrous —there was no possible link between that deserted rock and the terror that had woken her at dawn, and yet she felt illogically that they were somehow connected.

A crewman came hurrying along the passage toward the steps and touched his forelock respectfully as she stood back to let him pass. His appearance broke the hiatus, and Karuth forced herself to relax. This was ridiculous. She was letting imagination run away with her to the point where it threatened to swamp common sense under a tide of unfounded speculation. It *must* stop, or she'd be seeing demons in every corner before long.

She took another long, slow breath, felt her pulse slowing at last, and with relief turned toward Tirand's cabin. But before she moved off she slipped her hand into the reticule at her waist and drew out a small gold ring which, on pure impulse, she'd decided to take with her at the last moment before leaving the Star Peninsula. The ring had been given to her long ago by her predecessor and mentor, Carnon Imbro, who, perhaps knowing her better even than her father and brother did, had been more aware than most of her nature and her instinctive loyalties. The ring was set with tiny gems which formed the seven-rayed star symbol of Chaos, and Karuth had always treasured it as something more than a simple adornment. A talisman, perhaps. . . .

She slid it onto the middle finger of her left hand and went in search of Tirand.

Ygorla stood under the great stone portal, gazing past the giddying sweep of the giant staircase and over the harbor to the sea. Her hands worked feverishly, turning something over and over between her pale fingers. Gold glinted in the sunlight.

"The High Initiate himself . . ." She spoke softly, huskily, and an unholy light shone in her eyes. "Oh, Father. It would be so *simple*."

"No, daughter." There was no censure in Narid-na-Gost's voice, but his tone was implacable. "Not this time."

166

He showed his teeth in a slow smile. "Let them have their pleasure for now. You must be patient just a little while longer."

She sighed and stopped turning the golden badge in her fingers, looking down as she pinned it back onto her bodice and wondering yet again if it had ever belonged to that other High Initiate, Keridil Toln. The emblem of a dead man and a dead reign. Order's emblem. An anachronism now, like its once proud wearer. Like the Circle, like the Matriarchy, like the High Margravate.

Her perfect lips curled in a sneer, and she let the sorcerously enhanced vision slip from her so that the distant ship with its scarlet sails reverted to nothing more than a faraway pinpoint on the sea. She had learned so much, gained so much power and so many skills, that the frustration of having to stay her hand was as keen as a sword-thrust inside her. Still, the knowledge of what she could have done to that ship and its passengers, had she chosen, was a balm to the sword. She had been patient thus far; she could, as her father said, be patient for a little longer.

The sneer became a smile and she said, "They are so weak."

"Yes. And we are strong, and growing stronger. But"—the demon reached out and stroked her cheek with proud affection—"we will be stronger yet, and our final strength will be beyond their imagining."

He moved into the shadows of the portal. For perhaps a minute longer Ygorla continued to gaze at the sea and the distant ship now veering away toward Summer Isle. Then she turned her back on the brilliant day and on her racing thoughts, and followed Narid-na-Gost away down the tunnel toward the crater.

12

The flames of the bonfire leapt high into the night, challenging the rising first moon and bringing a rapturous cheer from the crowd that thronged around the High Margrave's palace. A second later the great building gave its own answer to the flames as countless facets of quartz buried in its walls caught and reflected the firelight in a glittering flash, a beacon signaling across the high slopes of Summer Isle. On a promontory two miles away a second fire sprang to life, then another, and another, a chain lighting across the island as from a high tower at the shimmering palace's heart bells began to ring out to proclaim and celebrate the marriage of Blis Alacar and Jianna Hanmen.

In the palace's great hall, brilliant with the flare of torches and the magnificence of ceremonial robes, the procession was forming up to lead the wedding guests out to the grounds where the nuptial feast was ready to begin. In the confined space the cheer that greeted Blis and Jianna was deafening, and Karuth, caught up in the glory and excitement of the occasion, added her voice to the rest as the gold-robed couple passed down the aisle formed by the watching throng. Behind them walked Calvi, his face lit by an uncontainable grin, with his mother the dowager High Margravine on his arm; and then came an older pair—Jianna's parents—and behind them Tirand, escorting the Matriarch in her silver ceremonial veil. Karuth saw the glad smile on Tirand's face and found time to give thanks to the gods that her brother was in such good spirits. The Star Peninsula belonged to another world and could be forgotten for a while; all she wanted now was to enter into the festive spirit and enjoy herself.

Someone nudged her elbow, and she looked around to see Lias Barnack smiling at her.

"Physician-Adept Karuth, may I have the honor of escorting you?" The old politician's eyes glinted with mischief and open admiration, and Karuth laughed, thinking that despite his years he was still handsome—and still a rogue.

"The honor is mine, sir." She made a mock bow and he settled her arm over his as they took their places in the procession. A fanfare rang out from the gallery at the far end of the hall, the great doors were opened, and as they began to move, Lias raised his voice a little to be heard over the triumphant notes.

"You look lovely tonight, Karuth. Casting away the cares of the world for a while, eh?"

Her shoulders shook with muted laughter. "For a while, Lias. And I won't deny that it's doing me more good than any of my own nostrums!"

"So it should. Life's too short for its pleasures to be neglected. Which reminds me—I hope we're to hear something of your talent during tonight's celebrations?" He pointed to the engraved brooch that she wore pinned beside her adept's badge at her breast. "It's a rare thing to have a Mistress of the Musical Arts among us."

Karuth's cheeks reddened and she almost—but not quite—regretted having worn the token, of which she was privately so proud. "Well . . . the High Margrave *has* asked me to play a piece. I'm deeply flattered by the accolade."

"Nonsense; *we're* deeply flattered to have the chance to hear you. It's a rare treat for us benighted southerners!"

Karuth laughed at his teasing, and they moved on. As others fell into step behind them and the great company surged through the doors, a pair of hazel eyes watched Karuth's back with sudden quizzical interest, and a hand reached up to touch an identical brooch at the observer's shoulder. So that was the High Initiate's sister. Older than he'd imagined her, and though she wasn't a beauty in the classical sense, she was quite handsome in her own way.

Light brown eyebrows lifted faintly under the brim of an overornate hat, and the observer wondered if she merited her rank in the Guild Academy or if it had simply been a political honor. Perhaps later he'd find out. Or perhaps, he thought with sudden dry amusement, he might conduct his own form of investigation.

———————————⟶ ⊂——————————

Tirand was surprised when in a momentary lull he realized that he was thoroughly enjoying the celebrations. The wedding feast had been eaten, and for the past hour the guests had been dancing on the smooth sward of the palace lawns. Tirand had never been much of a dancer, but, persuaded by Karuth and the Matriarch, he'd joined in the livelier reels, which didn't demand too much grace or coordination, and soon found his inhibitions crumbling before the sheer exuberance of the occasion. It helped, too, to be free for once of any official obligations, for much to his relief, Blis Alacar hadn't asked him to solemnize the marriage. It was believed that to be joined in wedlock by a blood kinsman brought good luck; the High Margrave had therefore chosen his own elderly and distinguished second cousin, a fifth-rank adept, to witness the sacred vows and commend him and his bride to the gods, and so for once Tirand had been able to forget rank and duty and become simply one among the throng of celebrants.

The dancing ended at last. Later, when the guests had been fortified with more food and had drunk enough to dispel any last traces of formality, the truly uproarious revels would begin, the serpent dances and jump dances and cross dances, culminating, as dawn broke, in the great and riotous Double Circle, in which everyone in the palace must join. Until then the company would be entertained more restfully by a number of invited singers and musicians.

As the night was fine and warm, the recitals were to take place on one of the palace's formal lawns, which had been strewn with rugs and cushions to make a comfortable setting. Karuth, breathless and flushed still from the last dance, paused for a moment on her way to the anteroom set aside for the players and gazed appreciatively at the torchlit scene. People were taking their places on the grass; on the far side she saw Tirand and the Matriarch together, trailed by a gaggle of young women who doubt-less hoped to catch the eye of the eligible High Initiate. Karuth smiled mischievously, then turned away, beckon-ing to the servant who followed with her manzon, and walked through the open doors into the anteroom. She found a suitable place to sit, dismissed the servant, and began to tune the seven-stringed instrument. One string stubbornly resisted her efforts to bring it to perfect pitch, and after fingering several melodies and arpeggios and trying between each one to correct the problem, she shook her head in irritation. It could be her own fault—she'd had a few cups of wine tonight, and too much could blunt the ear's accuracy—but it was more likely that the instrument was making its own protest against the neglect it had suf-fered in the past few months. She should have oiled the fingerboard more often, and polished the soundbox; above all she should have *played* the damned thing, even if only for a few minutes, at least once a day instead of in erratic and increasingly rare snatched moments. She made an-other fine adjustment, listened intently to the harmonic. Dammit again, it was *wrong*—

"Perhaps if I were to sound my third string, we might hear where the disharmony lies?"

Karuth's head jerked up in surprise and her fingers caught two strings with an unpleasant discord. She quickly silenced them, and stared at the stranger who had moved up on her so quietly and who now stood holding his own manzon carelessly in one hand. She couldn't see his face clearly, as much of it was shadowed by the wide brim of a hat trimmed ostentatiously with lace and feathers, but the smile beneath the shadows was broad and openly friendly. A Guild Academy Master's badge was pinned at his left shoulder.

Her own shoulders relaxed, and she returned his smile. "Thank you. I think the night air must have affected it." Then, more candidly she added, "That, or my own neglect. I should have prepared more thoroughly."

The stranger dropped to a crouch and balanced his

own instrument over his knees. "You must have had very
little time for such pleasures under recent circumstances."
Eyes of a color she couldn't quite judge glinted under the
hat brim. "I'm not sure of the protocols, so I don't know
which I should offer first: commiserations on the death of
your father or congratulations on your Guild accolade."

"Ah." Some of Karuth's tension returned. "Then you
know my name. You have the advantage of me."

He laughed quietly. "Hardly an advantage, lady
Karuth. My name is considerably less elevated than yours."
He pulled off the hat and made a small bow. "My friends
call me Strann."

Hazel eyes, a small bony face dominated by a nose that
rightly belonged on a far bigger countenance, a generous
mouth, unfashionably long hair the color of a mouse's fur,
which he'd made only a small attempt to comb and trim.
He was, she surmised, about her own age, and his clothes
were a peculiar blend of the theatrical and the strictly
practical, gaudily colored, yet—apart from the hat—by no
means new. An itinerant, Karuth guessed. But clearly no
ordinary travelling player. The badge, and his presence at
this auspicious gathering, gave the lie to his appearance
and she found herself both baffled and intrigued.

Strann brushed a suntanned hand across the strings of
his manzon. "So. May I be of service?" The smile, which
had never quite faded, suddenly became a broad grin.
"I've done nothing but stand and stare since my arrival
here. If I can make myself useful, I might feel a little less
out of place among such high company."

Karuth wasn't quite sure whether the gentle gibe was
directed against himself or against her, but pragmatism
prevailed and she said, "Thank you. I'd certainly appreciate a second opinion."

He nodded, pulled up a chair for himself, then sat
down and plucked his manzon's third string. Karuth did
the same, and Strann's eyes narrowed. "Sharp. Just an
iota." He watched as she adjusted the tuning fractionally,
then listened again. "Better—no, that's too far. Yes . . . a
little more. More—that's it. Play it again." The grin returned. "There."

"Perfect!" Relief colored Karuth's voice. "I'm very much obliged to you!"

He shrugged modestly, or with a pretense of modesty. "A pleasure, lady." Then he looked up at her and she detected a hint of mischief in the look. "Though I think we should test the two instruments together, to be certain." And before she could respond, he fingered a series of quick, dazzling notes on the manzon in his hands.

Karuth stiffened as astonishment and chagrin struck her in equal and unexpected measure. In the space of a moment Strann had revealed himself as a breathtakingly skilled musician—and at the same time he had broken every rule of protocol with a blatant and shameless challenge. In the Guild they called it the Hand Speech, a sophisticated code—almost a language in itself—by which the academy's more accomplished students could converse through musical notes. Karuth had studied Hand Speech as part of her training, and she instantly recognized the message that Strann had played. It meant: *if your skill can match mine, then I shall consider you worthy of me.*

Her cheeks burned with high, angry color. How *dared* he throw down such a boastful gauntlet? And to use the strictly circumscribed Guild code—he was flouting every rule, every stricture . . .

Then suddenly she began to see the funny side of it, and had to repress a desire to laugh aloud as she realized what lay behind the challenge. Strann was testing her. He knew who she was, knew that she had been accorded a rank equal to his own in the Guild, and he wondered whether she truly deserved her position or if she was simply privileged by the lucky accident of birth.

She flexed her fingers, and met his eyes with a challenge of her own as she played a rapid response in Hand Speech. *The judgment of worth is the privilege of those who are themselves worthy.*

Strann inclined his head, acknowledging the point. *My lady speaks truth,* he played. *Will she, therefore, consent to sit in judgment upon me?* He finished the sequence of notes with an embellishment that made Karuth draw her breath in admiration.

She couldn't match him. She was an accomplished player, but it had taken no more than a few moments for her to realize that Strann was a natural master, and she shook her head, allowing the smile she had been repressing to show on her face at last.

"No," she said aloud. "I will not sit in judgment upon you. I wouldn't *dare.*"

He looked surprised, then bowed his head. "Madam, you flatter me."

"I do no such thing," Karuth said. "I'm not such a fool that I don't know when I'm outclassed, nor so vain that I'm not prepared to admit it." She set her instrument down and sat back in her chair. "I'm only surprised that I haven't encountered you before. Two years ago, at the Guild conclave—"

"I wasn't there." Strann smiled. "I'm afraid I've always made a habit of failing to attend the Guild's official functions."

"But I've never even heard your name mentioned."

He laughed. "I'm sure it's mentioned often enough, lady, but probably not in polite company. In fact, I suppose I should be honest and confess that as of last winter Quarter-Day, my Guild membership has been a thing of the past."

She was taken aback. "You've resigned?"

"Well . . . it might be more accurate to say that my name was erased from the rolls by mutual agreement. 'Bringing the Guild into disrepute' was the phrase the elders used." Strann chuckled. "I was flattered to know that my disgraceful reputation had spread wide enough to warrant their concern."

"What did you do to upset them?"

"Oh, no one thing in particular. But I never could bring myself to obey all the rules." He gave her a broad grin and began to count on his fingers. "I didn't pay my Guild tithes, I didn't practice the Guild's code of conduct, and I most certainly didn't uphold its high moral standards." The grin widened still further. "My brief but thoroughly delightful affair with Elder Kyen Skand's daughter removed the final foundation stone and brought the tower of official outrage down on my head, and it was suggested that I might prefer to pursue my future career without benefit of the Guild's protective embrace. Very politely suggested, of course."

Karuth put a hand to her mouth to suppress laughter. "Of course," she said dryly. "However, you still retain your title?"

"Master of the Musical Arts? Oh, yes, they can't revoke that, no matter how much they might like to. I must give them credit; they do at least honor genuine talent rather than selling their accolades to the most influential bidder."

Karuth couldn't decide whether that last statement was blatant arrogance or simple honesty. She let it pass; it was, after all, a backhanded compliment to herself.

"So," she said, "what do you do now?"

"What I've always done. I travel, I play my music and sing my songs, and I carry stories and gossip from one province to another. Sometimes this little badge at my shoulder opens doors that would otherwise be closed to me"—he indicated the room around them with a quick, expressive flicker of his eyes—"and I'm most certainly not above taking advantage of that. We all need bread and meat to thrive, after all, and I have a very healthy appetite." The grin flashed again. "I suppose you might call me a professional opportunist."

Karuth couldn't imagine how it must feel to be so footloose and so careless, and for a brief moment she wished that she could experience that freedom for herself. "Duty" was a word that didn't seem to exist in Strann's vocabulary; an acute contrast with the encumbrances of her own life at the castle. In the past few days she'd probably seen more of the world than in the previous thirty years of her existence, and it had made her realize just how limited—and limiting—her own background was. Strann, she reflected wryly, was her complete opposite in almost every way, and she could very easily envy him.

A palace steward appeared at the door to announce quietly that all was ready, and a middle-aged man whom Karuth didn't know picked up his lyre and followed the steward out to the waiting guests. Strann watched him go, then said in an undertone, "Ah—that's Cadro Alacar, he's a cousin of the High Margrave. It seems that rank's taking precedence over ability tonight."

"Well, I'm thankful for that, if you're not," Karuth said with feeling. "I wouldn't care to have to follow your performance with my meager efforts."

"You do yourself an injustice." Strann paused; then: "Though it occurs to me that the entertainment might be livened up a little if someone were to break with the accepted order. Tell me, lady Karuth, do you know 'Silverhair, Goldeneyes' from the *Equilibrium* epic?"

"Yes, though it's a long time since I've played it."

"Play it with me, here, tonight."

Her eyes widened. "Oh, no—I couldn't *possibly*!"

"Why not?"

"Because . . ." Karuth groped for the right words, for an argument that he wouldn't be able to counter. *Equilibrium* was one of the most famous major musical works of the past century, the story of the great battle between the gods. The whole epic was scored for upward of thirty musicians and singers, but it contained numerous individual vignettes, some of them extremely demanding. The duet to which Strann referred was one of the most difficult of all; the theme of the drover girl Cyllan Anassan, who had played such a major part in the historic conflict and who, according to legend, had been accorded a place among the gods as her reward. It was one of Karuth's favorite pieces, but she couldn't play it now. Not in front of such an audience—and certainly not with a partner as skilled as Strann.

She said at last, "No. Thank you, but I can't accept."

Strann's expression changed and he nodded. "Of course, lady," he said stiffly. "I appreciate the difficulty. It was presumptuous of me to ask you." He made to rise and walk away.

Karuth felt mortified; he'd misinterpreted her meaning entirely, and hastily she too got to her feet. "Strann, please—you misunderstand—I wasn't implying that your rank . . ." And she stopped in mid-sentence as she saw impish humor in his eyes and realized that she'd walked neatly into his trap.

Strann grinned and bowed. "Then, lady Karuth, you'll

acknowledge that you have no possible excuse for refusing to play the duet with me."

She flushed. "Oh, but I have."

"I can see no other barrier." One eyebrow went up, a trick which Karuth had wished from childhood that she could do. She sighed.

"Very well, then, if you insist on forcing this admission from me: I don't relish the idea of having my shortcomings revealed to the entire company by playing with you, and that's the truth of it."

Abruptly Strann's face became serious. "Madam," he said, "if you honor me with such a compliment, then you must surely also have some faith in my judgment of your talent. I heard you playing, remember, before I had the temerity to introduce myself, and that told me all I needed to know." He reached out and, with no regard for propriety, took her hand. "Besides, what possible reason could I have for wanting to humiliate you?"

Karuth opened her mouth to argue, then realized that he was right. A small, reckless voice within her was goading her, saying, *yes, accept, play the duet. How many opportunities do you have to perform with such a brilliant partner? And if you do fail, who on this happy night will notice or care?*

Strann was looking at her, still holding her hand, and she dropped her gaze as the balance between inclination and caution began to tilt. "Well . . ."

"A bargain," Strann said firmly. "And a rare treat for this exalted company! I suggest that we dedicate the piece to the High Margravine Jianna in person, to please our hosts."

Karuth laughed. "You *are* an opportunist!"

"Of course I am. I can't afford to be anything else. And now, as well as delighting the High Margrave, I've also ingratiated myself with the High Initiate's sister." His infectious grin returned. "A thoroughly satisfactory night's work, don't you think?"

Karuth wondered what Tirand would have said in the face of such a barefaced admission, and suppressed more laughter. She liked Strann. He was uncomplicated and refreshing, such a change from the sober company in which she normally spent her time. If he led her down a reckless path, if she made a complete fool of herself tonight, for once she didn't care.

She sat down again and picked up her manzon, setting it across her knee.

"Very well," she said with mock severity. "You've persuaded me. But I think we'd better rehearse the piece—or you might end the night by bitterly regretting your rashness!"

A ripple of surprised murmurs rose among the assembled company on the lawn as Karuth and Strann walked out together. Karuth was tense and excited; the impromptu rehearsal had surprised her out of her pessimism and she felt at this moment as though she could have conquered any obstacle. As they took their places and settled their instruments, she glanced surreptitiously around and saw Blis Alacar—Blis Hanmen Alacar, she corrected herself, using his new married name—leaning eagerly across to speak to his bride and gesturing toward them. Clearly he, at least, knew Strann's abilities, and Karuth's stomach fluttered queasily with momentary stage fright. But then she saw Tirand and the Matriarch, Tirand puzzled, the Matriarch agog, and her nerve steadied. She wouldn't let her brother down. She'd show that she was worthy.

Strann smiled at the assembly, then addressed them in a richly cultivated voice trained for public appearance and startlingly different from his normal tones.

"My exalted lord and lady, revered High Initiate, beloved Lady Matriarch, honored friends all. Words cannot express my joy on this auspicious night, and so I hope that where words fail, my humble offering of music might suffice in some small way to convey my deep and respectful felicitations." He bowed in the direction of the bridal pair, and Karuth saw the new High Margravine smile happily and squeeze her husband's hand. Strann paused long enough for the reaction to be noted and approved, then continued: "To that end, I am greatly honored to announce that the lady Karuth Piadar, Mistress of the Musical Arts and sister of our High Initiate Tirand Lin, has graciously consented to join me in a duet which we wish to dedicate, with love and respect, to our High Margravine Jianna Hanmen Alacar, who in her turn is beloved of the gods as was that other great and courageous lady of our noble history. Friends all, we shall play for you a piece from the *Equilibrium* epic. 'Silverhair, Goldeneyes'—Cyllan's theme."

The High Margravine gave a delighted little cry, audible over the ripple of surprised approval that susurrated around the torchlit lawn. Karuth shut her eyes, forcing down the bubble of laughter that threatened to overtake her in the wake of Strann's showman's flamboyance, and listened as he began to play the slow, melodic solo introduction, the shimmering, glass-bright tones of his manzon flowing out into the warm night air. She felt the familiar stirring within her, the captivation of music, the eagerness, the urge to be a part of that creative power—her fingers moved and the drone strings of her own instrument added a plaintive counterpoint to the melody, a gentle yet insistent rhythm, setting the mood for what was to come. Her eyes opened once more; Strann caught her gaze, smiled so openly and warmly that confidence flooded through her, and their fingers moved faster, quickening the tune, modulating into a more urgent melody as they created the images of the girl with the silver hair and the golden eyes, of pain and of love, of betrayal and loyalty, of the storm that gathered over the world. Cyllan, who had loved a lord of Chaos, who had been ready to sacrifice not only her life but also her very soul for his sake—pictures were forming in Karuth's mind as so often happened when she played with all her heart, and she could almost see those scenes of long ago and feel the agonies of the simple, uneducated innocent whose courage had helped to change the world. *If she could have been like Cyllan—if she could have known that love, that passion—*

Karuth's fingers were flying now as Strann led her into the dazzling dance figures that portrayed Cyllan's desperate flight across the world to find her lover and restore to him the glittering but deadly stone that contained his soul. Her hair flew about her face, blurring the torchlit scene around her, and her consciousness took wing and soared with the music as it moved toward its climax. Then she let out her pent breath as the last loud, triumphant chord rang out, and Strann plucked the single note that shivered across and through it in startling disharmony, growing dominant as the chord faded, modulating the theme, holding the harmonic that would introduce the final eerie melody that told of Cyllan's transformation from mortality to something beyond human experience. Karuth was all but lost in the images her mind had created; she was only barely aware of Strann's foot tapping, counting the beats before the melody began—

A gargantuan flash lit up the lawn, and Karuth started so violently that she nearly dropped her manzon. She heard cries of shock among the crowd, and seconds later the distant rumble of thunder echoed from far out over the sea. Heart pounding, fumbling to regain her poise, Karuth looked up quickly when Strann kicked her ankle.

"Don't stop!" he said in a harsh stage whisper. "Play on—finish! One . . . and two . . . and—"

How she gathered her wits in time, Karuth didn't know, but somehow her hands, if not her brain, reacted instinctively and she was with him once more as they played the final slow, shimmering movement, which at last died away into silence.

For some moments there was no reaction from their audience. Then, so suddenly that Karuth jumped again, a storm of applause broke out all around them. The clapping of hundreds of hands sounded like a resurgence of the thunder, and some, their inhibitions loosened by wine, were cheering and shouting for more. Strann got to his feet, pulling Karuth with him when she seemed too surprised to move, and they bowed first to the High Margrave and Margravine, then to the company at large, and finally Strann made a flourishing sign of obeisance to the fourteen gods, which was greeted with renewed fervor.

"Well, well." His tone was droll and low-pitched enough to be for Karuth's ears alone. "I do believe they liked us!"

Excitement, embarrassment, and gratification were battling for precedence in Karuth's emotions. But underlying them was a gnawing edge of disquiet, and as the applause finally began to subside, she looked obliquely at her partner.

"Thank you for saving me," she said quietly. "I lost my head for a moment." She paused. "What was it?"

He bowed to the crowd again, and replied out of the corner of his mouth, "Lightning, over the sea."

"That was what I thought. But lightning doesn't strike from a clear sky."

Strann straightened and met her eyes. "No, it doesn't."

"Then what—"

He interrupted before she could finish. "Lady, you're a fifth-rank adept of the Circle; you're far better qualified than I'll ever be to answer such a conundrum." He made another bow to their audience, and hastily she followed suit. Then he took her left hand. She was still wearing the ring that Carnon Imbro had given her, and Strann saw it. The tiny gems forming the seven-rayed star of Chaos winked in the torchlight, and with a very deliberate gesture, in full view of the assembly, Strann raised her hand to his lips and kissed her fingers and the ring lightly.

"Perhaps," he said very quietly, "it was a sign of approval from Yandros?"

"Is that what you believe?"

He hesitated, seemingly reluctant to let her hand go. Then at last he released her, and his own arm fell to his side.

"No," he said soberly. "It's not what I believe at all. But it's the only explanation that doesn't make me feel more uncomfortable than I care to admit."

13

"My dears, it was a simply splendid performance!" Shaill Falada kissed Karuth's cheek, then turned to clasp Strann's hands warmly. "*Splendid*. The High Margravine is still talking about it; she was *so* touched by your kindness in dedicating that special piece to her."

Strann had the grace to redden slightly, and Karuth smiled. "Thank you, Matriarch." She glanced at her fellow musician. "I won't deny, though, that I was very nervous about dueting with such a master."

This time Strann said something under his breath and turned away, and Karuth allowed her smile to broaden to a grin. The Matriarch chuckled. "Don't affect modesty with me, Master Strann; I'm well aware of your reputation in more ways than one. Now, you'll oblige me by agreeing to visit us in Southern Chaun for the summer Quarter-Day festivities. We could do with someone of your caliber to enliven our celebration."

Strann recovered his composure instantly, and bowed. "Madam, you're too kind."

"Indeed I am, and I pay well for good measure. So the summer Quarter-Day it is, and don't you dare forget." She turned to look across the lawn, where the energetic country dances were now in full swing. "The storm came to nothing, thanks be. I thought when we had that isolated thunderclap that the night would be ruined by rain, but there's not a cloud in the sky now. Mind you, the spring weather here is always unpredictable."

Karuth glanced at the second moon, which was dropping toward the western horizon against a background scattering of stars. There hadn't been a cloud in the sky, either, when the lightning bolt had flashed out over the sea, but it seemed that neither the Matriarch nor anyone else except for Strann had noticed that. She quelled an impulse to say something to Shaill, deciding that it was better to keep her uneasy thoughts on the subject to herself.

Apart from that one unnerving moment, the impromptu performance which she and Strann had given to the wedding guests had been a triumph. By demand they had improvised two encores, and afterward, in the midst of the congratulations, Karuth had seen the High Margrave take Strann aside, grip his hand warmly, and present him with a fistful of coins, including, she noted, a good measure of gold. She was aware that she had been of more than a little value in helping him to ingratiate himself with such an influential patron, but she didn't begrudge Strann a single gravine of his earnings. And when, flushed with his success, he returned to her as the dance musicians struck up once more and demanded that she partner him in the first of the new sets, she had agreed with a broad smile. He was a fine dancer as well as a fine musician, she discovered, and the first set had merged into the second and then the third before Karuth declared herself too breathless to continue. Now they had found places near the tables, where more food and wine were being served, and Strann showed no inclination to leave her side, though she'd noticed with amusement how his hazel eyes roamed about the company, lighting on a pretty face here, a trim figure there. He was obviously popular with the young women of the assembly, and Karuth knew that but for her daunting presence the girls would have flocked about him like pigeons around a shock of corn. For the moment, though, Strann clearly felt that to be seen in the company of the High Initiate's sister was more worthwhile than to pursue any other kind of assignation.

"Your plate's empty, lady Karuth." His voice broke her reverie and he reached out to take the platter from her. "May I fetch you something more to eat?"

She smiled. "No, thank you. I've had more than my fill."

"Another cup of wine, then." He snapped his fingers at a nearby servant—something, she suspected, that he wouldn't have had the temerity to do earlier in the evening—and their glasses were refilled. The Matriarch had left them, drawn away by an acquaintance, and for the moment there was no one else in earshot.

"A toast," Strann said, raising his glass. "To music, and to its most talented mistress. I salute you—and I thank you for your kindness to me."

"Kindness?" She was surprised.

"Yes. You've been kind enough to indulge my self-seeking ambitions tonight, and thanks to you, it seems as though I won't go short of a crust for a good while to come." He gave his broad, contagious grin. "I suppose you wouldn't consider becoming my official patron?"

Karuth laughed, turning heads. "I don't think you need a patron, Strann. It would only cramp your natural flamboyance."

"Ah, well." He made a pretense of dismay, but before he could say any more, a cheer from the company on the lawn made them both turn their heads. A new dance was beginning, and to shouts of approval, Blis Hanmen Alacar was leading the Matriarch into the middle of the formed-up dancers.

"It must be almost dawn," Strann said, and clapped his hands above his head to add his own approbation. "These are the last ritual pairings—it'll be time for the Double Circle dance soon, and then those of us who haven't collapsed with exhaustion can at last seek our beds." He smiled. "I won't deny that I'll be thankful. It's been a long night."

"But a memorable one."

"Oh, yes." His expression sobered suddenly and a faint frown appeared on his face. "Certainly that."

Before Karuth could query the unexpected shift of mood, a movement among the people thronging the lawn's edges caught her eye and she saw a small group coming toward them. In the lead was the High Margravine Jianna, flanked by Tirand and Lias Barnack and followed at a diffident distance by a small, dark-haired, and pretty girl whose name Karuth didn't know but whom Tirand had partenered several times during the earlier dances. Jianna quickened her steps as they approached, and both Karuth and Strann bowed to her.

"Karuth—may I call you Karuth?" Jianna's face was flushed with happiness; her hair gleamed gold in the light of the torches. *"Thank* you for your playing tonight. It was *entrancing.* And, Master Strann—you were magnificent, and your reputation does you less than justice! Tirand tells me that the two of you hadn't so much as met before tonight. I can barely believe it; you played together as though you had dueted all your lives."

"Madam, you honor us." Strann bowed again, and Karuth concurred, casting her gaze down.

"I mustn't linger. I'm to dance this set with my father, while Blis partners the Matriarch. Thank you again. Thank you from us all. Thank you!" Jianna had probably drunk a little more than she was accustomed to, Karuth thought; it enhanced her radiance but she was youthfully overexcited and garrulous. She hastened away in a whirl of gold cloak and shimmering hair, and Lias Barnack smiled at her departing back.

"Our new High Margravine will bring a breath of fresh air to this fusty court, if I'm not mistaken," he said. "Aeoris and Yandros bless her!" Then he turned. "As for you two—I can only add my own humble gravine's-worth to the accolades you've already received. You were both inspired."

Karuth was surprised and warmed by such uncompromising praise from Lias, who made a profession of his cynicism. Tirand, too, added his compliments, though she detected a note of reserve in his voice and saw his gaze flick to Strann's face with more than a hint of suspicion. The dark-haired girl had hung back, and Tirand made no attempt to introduce her; instead he turned at length to face Strann and address him directly.

"You're a Master of the Musical Arts, I see." His tone wasn't overly friendly. "I'm surprised that, as the High Margravine said, we haven't met you before."

Strann made a self-deprecating gesture. "My links with the Guild have never been strong ones, High Initiate. I'm nothing more than a peripatetic entertainer."

"If an unusually skilled one," Lias observed.

Tirand ignored the comment. "And your clan name?"

"Like my Guild involvement, a thing of the past."
Strann met Tirand's eyes and smiled. "I suspect that my
people in Wishet are as thankful as I am to have severed
the old links."

"A shame." Tirand returned the smile coldly. "There's
a great deal to be said for the security and protection of a
close-knit family, don't you agree?"

"Indeed, sir, and I envy those who have that comfort."
Strann's gaze didn't falter; then abruptly he bowed. "I've
intruded on you all for too long. Lady Karuth—" He
turned his back on Tirand and took Karuth's hand. "Thank
you again for the privilege you've granted me tonight.
May the gods continue to smile on you." He kissed her
fingers very deliberately, then bowed again to the others.
"High Initiate, Master Lias, good night to you."

Karuth watched him walk away, feeling anger mount-
ing inside her. Lias had prudently drawn back and was
inviting the dark girl to dance; after a few moments the
two of them moved off into the throng and Karuth and
Tirand were alone.

There was silence for a few seconds. Then Tirand said
explosively: "Gods blind me—the *impudence* of that posturing jongleur!"

Karuth felt the muscles in her jaw tightening. "Don't
be ridiculous, Tirand," she retorted.

"*Me*, ridiculous?" Tirand snorted. "He was trying to
make a fool of us both! Damn him, he *used* you, Karuth! He
had the blatant arrogance to try to put himself on your
level, to ingratiate himself—"

"Does that matter?"

"Of course it matters! If you saw through his charade,
then I'm astonished that you allowed it to continue. Kiss-
ing your hand as though he were an intimate friend, and
monopolizing you through three dance sets—"

Karuth was growing angry. "Just as you monopolized
that pretty little girl whom Lias has just tactfully steered
away. But I suppose that's different?"

"Yes, it *is* different. Ilase is—"

"Oh; Ilase, is it?" Karuth said acidly. "You didn't favor me with an introduction."

Two patches of hectic color flamed on Tirand's cheeks. "No, I didn't, because while I might have wished to introduce her to my sister, I had no intention of presenting her to a man who isn't worthy to carry her baggage!"

Karuth stared at him. "I see. So Strann's talent counts for nothing; it's only his rank that matters. I suppose that I brought disgrace on our name and on the Circle by consenting to duet with him?"

"That isn't what I meant!" Suddenly Tirand's indignant fury faltered, and he continued more subduedly: "It isn't that, Karuth. The music was magnificent, I'm not trying to deny it for a moment. But Master of Music or no, the man's nothing more than a cynical opportunist and I don't like to see him trading on your position and using you as a foil to advance himself. It's *wrong*, and it demeans you."

"Oh, Tirand." Karuth sighed heavily. "Do you really think I'm that gullible? Do you think I didn't know exactly what Strann was trying to do?"

"Not only trying. He was succeeding very well, from what I saw."

"Again, does that matter? Entertaining is his profession; he relies on it to make a living. Do you expect him not to take advantage of an opportunity wherever he can?"

"Not at your expense!"

Her anger flared again. "For Yandros's sake, Tirand, it *wasn't* at my expense! I enjoyed playing with him, and I enjoyed dancing with him, and I found his company pleasant and amusing. Any benefit he might have derived from attaching himself to me was quite mutual, I assure you!"

Tirand glowered at her. "That's all well and good—just so long as he doesn't let it go to his head. If he thinks you've given him the smallest encouragement, then the gods alone know what liberties he might consider himself entitled to next."

"Tirand." Suddenly Karuth's tone was dangerous, and her brother stopped short. "Strann took no liberties, but *you* are taking them! How *dare* you say that to me? What manner of fool do you take me for?"

"Karuth, I'm only—"

"Only nothing!" Aware that people were looking at them, she dropped her voice to a sharp, furious whisper. "I'll listen to no more of this, Tirand! If I didn't know you better, I'd believe you were drunk: as it is I'll assume that you were simply trying misguidedly to protect me against a threat that exists purely in your imagination." She paused for a moment, her mouth tightening into a hard line. "And I'll remind you that even if your suspicions had any foundation, how I choose to conduct my private affairs is entirely my own business!"

She thought for a moment that Tirand would continue to argue, but abruptly his shoulders sagged and he turned away.

"I don't want to quarrel with you, Karuth. I don't want to quarrel with anyone, not tonight of all nights." He glanced back, his eyes appealing to her. "It's just that I was *worried* for you."

"I know that," she said, more gently.

He nodded, biting his lip. "You're right, I overreacted. I'm sorry. I didn't mean to upset or insult you."

Karuth sighed. "I understand, Tirand. Don't think I don't appreciate your concern, even if it's misplaced. Let's say no more about it, shall we? Let's forget that this conversation ever took place."

Tirand was relieved. "I think that would be wisest." He hesitated; then: "Will you dance with me? The night's almost over; let's patch up the rent and enjoy what's left."

There was still a sour, rankling note in Karuth's mind, but she thrust it away. She'd enjoyed the celebrations so much until this had happened; she wanted to recapture that pleasure and not let anything mar the memories she would take home. "Yes," she said, trying to banish the last lingering edge of hostility from her voice. "I'll dance with you, little brother."

The sunrise on the eastern horizon promised another fine day, but Karuth was too tired to feel more than a faint twinge of envy at the south's kindly climate as she made her way along the palace's broad corridors toward her room and a welcome bed.

She was among the last of the wedding guests to retire. The newly married couple had been escorted to their private apartments an hour ago and some of the older celebrants had admitted defeat long before that. Only a few diehards, reluctant to allow the memorable night to end, had stayed on to toast Blis and Jianna, and each other, and the dawn's first glimmer, and any other pretext they could think of before finally making their weary way from the opulent halls to seek sleep. Karuth had sat for some time in the garden where the musical entertainments had taken place, enjoying the early cool and listening to the first stirrings of birdsong. Tirand had left the gathering, and she was glad to be free of his presence, which since their sharp exchange she had found a little stultifying. Tirand wasn't to blame. He had only tried to do as he thought best, and Karuth knew that she should have been gratified by his protectiveness toward her. But somehow, in the warmer and more liberal atmosphere of Summer Isle, which contrasted so sharply with the stiffer mien of the Star Peninsula, her brother's punctilious concern galled. So she had escaped to the peaceful privacy of the garden to give herself a little time to relax and soothe her irritation before retiring.

She hadn't spoken to Strann again. She'd glimpsed him once in apparently intimate conversation with a pretty girl, and the two of them had disappeared from the gathering shortly afterward. Karuth wasn't disappointed— she was too old and too worldly-wise for such foolish notions—but she regretted, just a little, that she hadn't had the chance to say a kinder good-night to him.

But her regrets together with all other thoughts were submerged in a pleasant haze of tiredness as she neared her room. The passage was still dark; the highest-ranking guests had been housed in the palace's west wing, where their slumbers wouldn't be disturbed by the morning sun, and now that the torches had been extinguished, there was only a faint, pearly glow to relieve the gloom. She climbed a short flight of steps, then turned immediately into a narrower corridor that led off to the left at the top of the flight.

Her room lay near the far end of this passage, and she was counting doors when she felt a prickling sensation at the back of her neck, the small hairs at her nape rising as though lightning had flickered silently behind her.

Karuth's steps faltered, and in the sudden stillness as her footfalls ceased, she stood listening. There was no sound, no furtive movement. Yet she knew with emphatic certainty that she was being watched.

Remembering the most fundamental lessons of her adept's training, she let her breathing settle to a slow, shallow rhythm that calmed her overrapid heartbeat. Logic said that there could be no danger here, but nevertheless she was reluctant to look over her shoulder. She chided herself for allowing her imagination to intimidate her, set her shoulders, and turned in one quick, economic movement.

There was nothing there. Karuth watched the dimly outlined angles of the walls while she counted calmly to seven, then turned away.

And as she moved, a violent emerald glimmer flicked on the periphery of her vision.

"Who—" The word broke from her throat before she could swallow back the rest of the question, and reverberated away into the background silence. She reached out, pressing her palm against the wall to steady her body as well as her mind, and began to move slowly, cautiously back toward the junction with the main passage. The gloom seemed doubly intense after the momentary vividness of that emerald flicker, and though the darkness ahead looked as empty as it was silent, Karuth's skin still crawled with psychic disquiet. Two more paces, three. She reached the junction where the stairs led down at a right angle, and forced herself to step out into the broader corridor.

The stairs dropped away to her right. At the foot of the short flight, a young woman stood looking up at her.

Karuth felt thoroughly foolish. All this drama, this fraying of nerves, only to find that her mysterious follower was simply another late—or early—reveler seeking her own bed. Tension loosed its hold and she raised a hand in salute, opening her mouth to offer a whispered and con-spiratorial good-night.

Then stopped as her brain interpreted what her eyes took in.

The shadows at the foot of the stairs were so intense that it should have been impossible to see more than a vague image of the other woman. Yet every detail of her face and figure was utterly clear. She was haloed in a faint, oddly hued aura that seemed to emanate from *within* her, highlighting her pale, ragged hair and giving a chilling cast to her unnaturally large eyes. Moreover, her red silk gown was cut in an old-fashioned style that hadn't been worn for fifty years or more.

Karuth clutched at the wall, her gaze riveted by the apparition and a terrible sense of recognition surging to-ward the surface of her mind. She fought it back, refusing to acknowledge it—and the woman smiled a wide-mouthed smile, mischievous and knowing and not quite human.

And vanished.

"Aah!" Karuth jerked backward and almost lost her footing as one shoe caught in the hem of her gown. Recov-ering her balance, she stared into the darkness of the stair-well, unable in the first few stunned moments to believe that she hadn't hallucinated. Eventually, though, reason struggled through to force the truth on her. She hadn't imagined that pale, elfin figure, nor was this a waking dream. She had just seen a clear and emphatic vision—of someone who in human terms had been dead for near on a hundred years.

No life portraits existed, for that white-haired, amber-eyed girl had left the mortal world before any such tribute could be paid to her. But the old stories passed down from those who lived through the Change had preserved mem-ories of her image. And that smile, so wise yet so mocking —that smile had had the stamp of Chaos.

Karuth felt sudden nausea as a shaft of primal fear seemed to open like a gaping mouth within her. She swung around and plunged into the side passage, running toward her room, careless of the noise she made. She flung herself through the door and stumbled to the bed with its opulent canopy, and only when she fell full-length onto the rich coverlet and felt the bed's solid contours beneath her did the terror recede and rationality creep back.

The window was open and a gentle breeze wafted into the room, freshening it and carrying scents of blossom and scythed grass. Patterns of daylight were banishing the shadows, and Karuth rolled over and sat upright, drawing up her knees and hugging them as she stared toward the peaceful world outside.

Her mind was suddenly reasoning coldly and clearly in the wake of her panic, and she knew that the fear she'd felt hadn't been triggered by the fact of what she had seen, but by its implications. She didn't fear Chaos; as a fifth-rank adept she had had enough dealings with its lower and less predictable denizens to have lost the terrors that might beset ordinary mortals, and she had no reason to believe that Yandros looked unfavorably on her. But in the years since the Change, the gods had kept their promise to take no direct hand in human affairs; for nearly a century now they had stood apart and aloof from the world. So why, she asked herself, *why* on this night, in this place, had one who could only be an avatar of Chaos returned to the mortal realm?

The ring with its seven-rayed star, Carnon Imbro's old gift, felt tight on her finger, and Karuth twisted the shank to ease the discomfort, though she stopped short of taking it off. She was exhausted, but she was also reluctant to lie down and close her eyes. Her psychic senses were awake and working at a feverish level; she knew she'd dream and that her dreams would have meaning, and she didn't want to face what sleep would bring.

She and Strann had played Cyllan Anassan's theme tonight, a tribute to that long-dead woman and to the new High Margravine. Was the vision she had seen simply an acknowledgment from a higher realm for that tribute? Or was there some subtler connection that she couldn't divine? She recalled her disquiet when the bizarre and isolated lightning bolt had flashed out over the sea as though something were delivering a warning. Strann, too, had been disturbed by that incident, and Karuth suspected that even if he was unwilling to admit it, he, too, had been alerted on a subconscious level to the suspicion that something was wrong.

But what? She couldn't answer the question; she hadn't even the smallest clue to guide her. Only instinct and speculation, and they weren't enough.

At last Karuth pulled back the coverlet and drew it over herself. She should have undressed, washed, combed out her hair, but she couldn't bring herself to turn to such mundane tasks. She felt so weary; her body demanded sleep, however unwilling her mind might be to comply.

Images formed in her inner vision when she closed her eyes. She saw again the woman's pale face, her smile, the strange, dim aura that had surrounded her. Karuth clenched her fists, the ring digging painfully into her palm as she tried—it was a contradiction, but she had few resources left now—to force herself to relax. Sleep was waiting like a predator; she felt it stealing up on her, dimming her senses, pulling her away and out of the physical world. Her last conscious thought was: *why? Why have you come back, after all this time? And what are you trying to tell me?*

A thin white hand curved up and two pairs of eyes, emerald and amber, watched the streamers of unnameable color that flowed away from Cyllan's fingertips and merged with the shifting, shimmering mists of Chaos. The place they had chosen was quiet, undisturbed but for gentle eddies caused by breezes which sprang from nowhere and faded into nothing. There were no eyes to see them, no ears to hear their conversation. Now and then sparks of elemental energy would flicker toward them, drawn by their presence and hovering like tiny jewels in hope of some recognition or reward, but a mild command from Tarod's consciousness sent them dancing away again on their mindless course. Normally he paid no attention to such barely sentient things, but at this moment they were an intrusion and he wanted no intrusions.

He said: "So there is something out of kilter?"

Cyllan shrugged her bare shoulders, and her silvery

hair rippled. "Yes, I think there is. Though as to its origins . . . I don't know, Tarod. I couldn't even begin to guess. I could find nothing concrete, and yet there are undercurrents in some of the more psychic mortal minds: strange dreams, unsubstantiated fears, suspicions. But I don't have your powers. I can't be sure that it's not simply a harmless ripple."

Tarod sighed. "We can't take a direct hand without breaking our old pledge. They haven't called on us to intervene—and if they did, I'm not sure that Yandros would be willing to respond."

"Even if the appeal were to come from someone like Karuth Piadar?"

He considered this, then shook his head. "I doubt if it would make any difference. I know she's well-disposed toward Chaos, and she has the potential to become a worthy avatar. But she's never used that potential; she's overcautious and much of her natural talent goes to waste. A pity. I'd hoped for better from her."

"I had wondered," Cyllan said, "if any one of the three who saw something untoward in the night might possibly be prompted to call upon Chaos for enlightenment." She smiled thinly, with that same impish quirk that had chilled Karuth's blood in the dark corridor of the High Margrave's palace. "Karuth was my strongest hope; but you're right, she chose to take the prudent course and do nothing. I suspect that she's too strongly influenced by her brother's attitude."

"Ah, yes, the worthy Tirand. He grows more stiff-necked with every season, doesn't he? The responsibilities of leadership seem to have snuffed out any spark of independence he might once have possessed. At this rate, he'll become nothing more than a simulacrum of his father."

Cyllan gazed into the middle distance. "It can't be easy for him. To have such a burden forced on him at his age—it's enough to crush the spirit of any man. And his sister's very loyal to him; she must be keenly aware of how important it is not to undermine his authority."

Tarod's fingers twined with hers and he squeezed her hand gently. "You're always ready to see virtue and make allowances for fault."

"In mortals like Tirand and Karuth, yes." She smiled at him, a very private smile that conveyed old, shared memories. "As were you when you lived among them."

He returned her smile. "That's as may be . . . still, whatever the case, I don't see that we can pursue this any further for the time being. You've visited the mortal world and discovered no fire behind the smoke; certainly nothing that we can act on. We can do no more." A pause; then he added, "I only wish I could rid myself of the suspicion that there's some connection between this matter and that old incident in Southern Chaun."

Cyllan looked at him keenly. "I though you'd dismissed that matter long ago."

"I had, but now I'm beginning to wonder. There have been one or two odd coincidences: certain individuals in the mortal world were plagued by nightmares at that time, and those same individuals are being plagued by nightmares again now. We also know that there *is* a disturbance in the psychic currents of that world. It's small, but strong enough for us to have sensed it and be prompted to look a little closer." He paused, considering his thoughts, then continued. "We chose not to answer the High Initiate when he asked for our help five years ago. I'm not saying that we were wrong, but I *am* saying that the human mind doesn't dredge up these subconscious patterns without a reason."

"The lords of Order have shown no sign of interest, either then or now," Cyllan pointed out. "Surely if Aeoris felt there was something afoot, he wouldn't have maintained his silence?"

"In the past, Aeoris was a complacent fool; he may not yet have learned his lesson. I'm concerned to ensure that we don't make the same mistake as he once did, by ignoring something that might have some foundation." Tarod rose, drawing her up with him, and they began to walk slowly across the shifting ground. "The furor over the old Matriarch's death settled down a long time ago, but the mystery has never been solved. We considered it too trivial a matter to be worthy of further attention; now, though, I think we should perhaps ponder it again." He stopped and turned to look at her, cupping her face lightly in his hands.

"I've nothing to guide me other than my instinct and yours. But there *is* a link, Cyllan. I feel it. And I don't like the feeling."

She considered this for a few moments. Three more elemental sparks came flickering toward her and settled on her hair; Tarod moved as though to brush them away, then changed his mind and let his hand fall to his side.

"What should we do?" Cyllan asked at last.

"Watch," Tarod said. "Be alert for any untoward signs in the mortal realm, and alert, too, for any hints that Aeoris and his brood are stirring from their lethargy." He looked about him, his green eyes narrowed. "I'll say nothing to Yandros at present: there's little point until and unless we have something more concrete to tell him. It may be that there's nothing amiss after all and we're pursuing a meaningless speculation. Nevertheless, I think it would be prudent not to assume that just yet."

The three golden sparks fell from Cyllan's hair as she and Tarod moved on. A capricious eddy caught them and they spiraled away into the mist, spinning and flickering at random. These tiny beings were the lowest manifestation of life on this plane, like plankton in the great shifting sea of Chaos. Barely sentient, their lives were a mindless cycle of drifting and dancing on whatever currents might come to carry them along, reflecting but not comprehending all that passed by them. They were baubles, trifles, beautiful and utterly harmless.

Utterly harmless . . .

From the mist a shape took form where moments before there had been nothing. The three sparks quivered, attracted by this new presence; a small zephyr of a breeze sprang up, buffeting them, and they danced toward the figure, which stood waiting. The newcomer held up a twisted hand, letting them gyrate on his palm, and as they danced and glittered, his crimson eyes watched them intently and he saw a little of what they had seen, and heard a little of what they had heard. It was a fragmented jigsaw with no coherence and no reasoning, but it was enough to alert him.

He tossed the elementals away. They flew, separating, vanishing, and Narid-na-Gost turned his head to stare at the place where the Chaos lord and his lady had sat. His eyes burned with bitterness, with hatred, and with new urgency as a worm of unease moved within him. Then he turned away. For a moment the mist grew ragged and dark like blown smoke or a scudding rain cloud. When it cleared, the demon was gone.

"My brother?"

A pure shaft of light slanted in at the tall window, pooling on the mosaic floor and highlighting the pattern's perfect symmetry. The visitor received permission to approach, and glided to where the greatest of his brethren stood gazing out across the pastel landscape.

Aeoris raised his head. His eyes, pupilless, were twin golden spheres in his skull; his white hair flowed over his shoulders, framing the harsh but lovely features. He didn't smile; he rarely smiled. But his jawline tightened a fraction as though with repressed eagerness.

"What news?" he demanded.

His brother, whose appearance was identical to his in every way, shook his head. "Something is stirring in Chaos, there's no doubt of it. Last night they sent an envoy to the mortal realm—"

"They broke their pledge?" Aeoris interrupted sharply.

"No, no; it was a creature of a lower order, not one of Yandros's filthy kin, and no attempt was made to intervene in human affairs as far as we can ascertain. Even so, they wouldn't have taken even such a small step without good reason, and it bears out our own suspicions. There's something afoot, and it may bode ill for Chaos."

Aeoris turned back to the window, considering this news. To outward appearances he seemed calm, but his brother saw the telltale whitening of his knuckles as he gripped the window ledge, and sensed the new excitement within him.

"I would give a great deal to know what they have discovered," Aeoris said at last, and there was an undercurrent of deep frustration in his tone. "But we can no more penetrate their realm than they can penetrate ours." Abruptly he looked at the other lord of Order again. "What of the mortal world, Ailind? Are there any new developments there?"

"None that we weren't already aware of," Ailind told him. "There's a sense of foreboding among some more sensitive souls, though neither they nor we—nor, it seems, Chaos—can give it a name or a cause. However, the Circle show no signs of concern."

Aeoris pondered this for a while. "Very well," he said at last. "Then we will continue to do as we have done thus far: we will wait." His eyes took on a disturbing new light. "We may be wrong, Ailind. This may come to nothing. But if there is a chance—one chance, however small—to strike against Chaos, I want to ensure that we're ready to grasp it." His fists clenched and he stared down at them, controlling his voice with an effort. "I owe Yandros a debt of vengeance that I *burn* to repay. If there is trouble in the Chaos realm, then I'll be waiting to take advantage of it. One error, one moment of complacency, and I'll deal Yandros a blow that will smash his arrogant supremacy and bring him crashing down to crawl at my feet!" He drew in a long, slow breath and forced himself to relax before regarding Ailind again, this time more calmly. "Watch, Ailind. That's all I ask for now. Watch." At last he did smile, a chilly, ferocious curving of his lips. "And be sure that you miss nothing."

14

The Circle party's return journey to the Star Peninsula was not the festive progress that their outward journey had been. The lengthy wedding celebrations had been followed by a grand party to mark Calvi's twenty-first birthday, so that by the time all the feasting was done they had spent a total of eleven days on Summer Isle, and for Tirand that was more than enough. He was beset by a growing anxiety for what might be happening at the castle in his absence, and as the days passed he began to fret and grow impatient to be away. Karuth would gladly have stayed on for a while longer to enjoy this rare chance for peace and relaxation in the delightful southern climate: the Matriarch and her party had no plans for an immediate departure and Karuth saw no reason why they shouldn't follow her example. But Tirand refused to consider the idea, and even the High Margrave couldn't persuade him to change his mind. Duty called him home, Tirand said, and duty must take precedence. So reluctantly Karuth packed her bags and made ready to leave.

The sea crossing was a bad one. The good weather had finally broken, deteriorating to squalling rain and blustery northwesterlies that turned the Bay of Illusions into a churning gray nightmare, and by the time their ship reached Shu-Nhadek after battling for many hours against the prevailing winds, even the hardiest sailors in the party were seasick and unwilling to face the next stage of the journey without a rest. Then, once recovered and embarked on the overland trek, it seemed that everything was conspiring against them. Horses went lame, hired

199

bodyguards proved unreliable, spring floods on the plains of Han forced a long and irksome detour. And the mood of the company was further soured by the High Initiate's increasing moroseness and Karuth's apparent preoccupation with some private matter which she seemed unwilling to discuss with anyone.

Karuth *was* preoccupied, and for the first time in her life had found that she couldn't bring herself to discuss her troubles with Tirand. Her reluctance had nothing to do with their quarrel at the wedding feast, which as far as she was concerned was past and forgotten; it stemmed simply from a dismaying realization that Tirand would not understand the nature of the problem that faced her. If she tried to explain, she feared that he might feel obliged, out of misplaced concern, to forbid her to pursue any investigations on her own.

Sheer chance had led Karuth to discover that her disturbing vision on the night of the wedding hadn't been an isolated incident. She'd seen Strann only once more before his departure for the mainland—as a hired player rather than a guest, he hadn't been invited to stay on—and during their brief exchange of farewells he had suddenly said something that shocked Karuth to the marrow. She could recall his words now, and see again his foxy face suddenly stripped of its usual carefree smile.

"I think," he had said, "that I'll be a little less ready to show off my skills by playing 'Silverhair, Goldeneyes' again in the future." Abruptly the smile had returned, but it was just a little strained. "Music and wine are a heady mixture, lady Karuth, but I can honestly say that I've never been quite so drunk as to suffer such a visitation in my sleep before."

Karuth's face had become very still, and she had asked, "What do you mean?"

"Oh, it's nothing of any moment, I'm sure. The lady seemed to mean me no harm; she even smiled at me, though I'm not sure if I want to dream such a smile again. Still, I shall take it as a compliment, and say a few prayers to Chaos to be on the safe side." He bowed over her hand. "Farewell, madam. The gods go with you."

With that he had left, giving her no opportunity to ask

any more questions. His words had been cryptic, but Karuth was in no doubt of what must have happened. And when later that same day Calvi Alacar had sought her out and asked her for a draft that might help to stop frightening dreams, the mental alarm bells had sounded yet again.

She'd been more successful in drawing the truth out of Calvi, and discovered that his vision—which, like Strann's, had come to him in a dream—had been almost identical to her own. A white-haired woman with strange bronze-colored eyes, Calvi said, waiting for him in the palace gardens at dead of night, and smiling. He didn't seem to have any idea of who she was, but the dream had terrified him, and for Karuth it was final confirmation.

Herself, Strann, now Calvi. Might there be others? She didn't know and could think of no way to find out that wouldn't arouse suspicion. But again and again the question reverberated in her mind: *why?* Why had Chaos chosen to send the same vision to three such disparate people? And what was the message that the vision had wanted to convey?

She had had no further visitations since then, and neither, as far as she was aware, had Calvi. Nevertheless the experience haunted her as surely as if it had continued to recur each night, and it had given rise to other, unexpected recollections. There was no obvious link between them, but Karuth couldn't rid herself of the suspicion that a connection existed and that it was in some arcane and disturbing way relevant. Her dreams at the High Margrave's house in Shu-Nhadek on the night before they'd set sail for the island. Her irrational fear of the distant and deserted White Isle. Further back, and the affair of the old Matriarch's grisly death and her ward's disappearance. Further still, and she arrived at the childhood memory of Keridil Toln in his last hours, standing at the bed of Ygorla Morys's dead mother and uttering his oblique observation.

It was strange, she thought, how those particular memories stood out so clearly among all the countless incidents and milestones in her life. Though five years or more must have passed, she could still recall the words of the riddle that the elemental she'd conjured had set her, and which, like the mystery at the Matriarch's Cot, had never been solved. Could it be that the incidents of the past few days were a new link in that old chain? There was no logical connection, yet Karuth felt in her bones that the events of past and present weren't quite as disparate as they appeared.

There lay the nub of her problem. The rational, sensible thing would be to discuss her suspicions with Tirand. Not only was he the close confidant of a lifetime, he was also her High Initiate, and this ought to be a matter for the Circle. However, she knew Tirand well enough to realize that his reaction to her story would be, at very best, equivocal. He would want something more than her flimsy and unsubstantiated suspicions before he agreed to sanction any investigation, and he would in any case probably argue that the Circle had already been through such an investigation five years ago, with no result. She might persuade him to direct a dream interpreter to make some small sortie on the lower astral planes: on the other hand, he might be so set against any resurrection of those old, forgotten questions that he would forbid any further probing of any kind. If he did that, her hands would be tied, unless she chose to break the adept's oath of loyalty and defy him.

She was therefore alone with her dilemma, and as each day brought the party nearer and nearer to the castle, she felt increasingly oppressed by her own thoughts. Tirand, too, spent his waking hours in a dark fugue, but while Karuth seemed unaware of her brother's mood, he by sharp contrast was acutely aware of hers and had put an entirely wrong interpretation on the reasons behind it.

The High Initiate was deeply and resentfully angry with his sister. Their quarrel at the wedding had been trivial and short-lived, yet now it seemed to him that despite her assurances that she bore no grudge, Karuth was sulking. She had been distant and evasive ever since that night, and as they drew closer to home, she was growing more and more sullen. It wasn't like her, and he found it impossible to believe that she could truly have taken something so petty to heart. A few sharp words over the presumptuous behavior of that self-aggrandizing balladeer— what in the name of all the fourteen gods, Tirand asked himself indignantly, was the matter with the woman?

What did she think he was? A small boy still, ready to defer to his sister simply because she was a few years his senior? She had no right to behave in such a way. No right, and no cause.

Yet though he ached to express his grievances and try to clear the air, he couldn't bring himself to tackle Karuth. Something in her manner precluded even the most tentative approach, and adding to Tirand's turmoil was an inescapable feeling that anything he might say would only provoke another argument. He didn't want to quarrel with her again, he only wanted to close the rift and return to normal. But in Karuth's present mood it seemed that was impossible. And lurking like a shapeless, venomous predator in the very darkest corner of Tirand's consciousness was a fear that something had happened to his sister on Summer Isle. Something that might widen the rift instead of closing it, and which, one dark day, might threaten to take her from him once and for all.

So, silenced by complete misunderstanding of each other's plights, Tirand and Karuth rode on with their entourage across the northern tip of Chaun province and finally into West High Land and the last leg of their dismal journey. The weather was foul, as though the northern elements were stubbornly refusing to acknowledge the approach of summer, and several of the party had fallen prey to a feverish illness which had recently arisen in Empty province and begun to spread westward. Knowing these virulent agues of old, Tirand decided to press on to the Star Peninsula rather than divert the party to the nearer West High Land Sisterhood Cot. If the entire company came down with the fever, as seemed likely in their current run of misfortune, the castle was better equipped and its healers better qualified to deal with any epidemic, and though the sisters would be more than willing to tend the sick ones, it would be unfair to bring the fever into their midst unnecessarily. He only prayed gloomily that no one would die before they could reach their destination.

No one died, but when the party finally arrived at the Star Peninsula in driving rain on a sodden and miserable evening, no one felt remotely like celebrating their return home. Six people had the fever by this time, including

Calvi, who sat swathed in blankets on his horse, shivering and looking jaundicedly at the perilous rock span which separated the castle stack from the mainland. They made the crossing in silent single file, Karuth with a sharply anxious eye on one or two sufferers whose minds had begun to wander in their illness. As they neared the end of the rock bridge, everyone heard the first faint wailing sound that came echoing out of the north, far beyond the rainswept horizon.

Tirand, in the lead, swore under his breath, narrowing his eyes against the rain as he stared out to sea. At first he saw nothing but featureless grayness, and for a few moments as the sea's roar drowned the distant grim echoes, he hoped that he'd imagined that telltale warning. But then, dim against the cloud-racked sky, the first terrible, unnatural colors began to form, and the slow-turning bands of light and shadow began to wheel across the heavens as the thin howling swelled toward something more dreadful.

"Warp!" Tirand cupped a hand to his mouth and yelled back at the party, though by now everyone had seen the approaching horror for themselves. "Get to the castle —*quickly!"*

The horses, goaded by a fear far greater than caution, broke into a rapid trot. Tirand was the first to gain the safety of the stack, and he halted, turning to watch and count heads as the cavalcade streamed past him and on toward the open castle gates. Only one rider lagged behind, and he saw Karuth, her mount sweating and stamping as she held it on a tight rein and stared fixedly at the darkening, murderous sky.

"Karuth!" The wind snatched Tirand's voice and flung it toward her, but she paid no heed. *"Karuth!"*

Still she ignored him, and, cursing, he spurred his own reluctant horse back toward her. As he approached, she snapped out of her trance, and the wide eyes which stared, shocked, into his were momentarily the eyes of a stranger.

"Gods—" Suddenly she was aware of the danger, and loosened her reins. The two horses galloped in the wake of their companions, and as the first bolt of emerald lightning spat across the sky, they plunged under the great black

arch and into the familiar castle courtyard, while men ran to close the gates at their backs. Servants and grooms hastened to greet the party; a babble of talk broke out as people dismounted, baggage was unloaded, and the fever sufferers were helped toward warmth and shelter. Karuth sat in her saddle, staring about her as though she didn't recognize her surroundings. She didn't react when a groom came to help her down, and Tirand slipped from his own mount and hurried toward her.

"Karuth? Karuth, what's wrong?"

She looked down at him and frowned. Then, abruptly, refusing any assistance, she swung her leg over the saddle and slid to the ground.

"Nothing's wrong," she said in a peculiarly remote voice. "I'm just tired."

"Go up to your room and rest. I'll have some food sent to you."

"No." She looked at him wearily and, he thought, a little bitterly. "There are sick people to see to and it's my duty to supervise their care. Duty must come first, after all."

Before Tirand could reply, she turned and walked away toward the main door.

Karuth didn't want to attend to her work. All she wanted was to lie down and be oblivious of the world until the aching in her muscles and the dragging exhaustion in her bones went away. But she couldn't do that. She had obligations. Six down with the fever, and she must attend to their initial needs and see to it that her subordinates knew what to do thereafter.

She regretted speaking so sharply to Tirand, and hoped he hadn't taken her comment about duty as a personal gibe. She hadn't meant it in that way—its intention had been sympathetic rather than critical—but she wasn't sure that her brother would realize and understand.

The window of her room was shuttered and the curtain closed, blotting out all sight of the Warp that now rampaged overhead. But even through the castle's thick walls she could hear the terrible, eerie singing, and, far worse, she could *feel* its presence pervading her body and mind. Try as she might, she had never been able to shake off her innate fear of these Chaos-driven storms and the sense of helpless insignificance that they evoked in her. She felt exposed to powers beyond her comprehension, let alone her ability to control, and she disliked the feeling intensely.

There was a faint knocking at her door. She looked up, sighed, and called, "Enter."

Sanquar, her senior assistant, came into the room. He hesitated when he saw that she hadn't yet finished changing out of her traveling clothes, and the wistful glint that showed in his eyes before he could hide it didn't escape her. She turned her back on him and picked up the gown she'd laid ready on the bed, pulling it on over her small-clothes.

"Are our invalids comfortably settled?" she asked levelly.

"Yes, Karuth. I . . ." Since her rejection of him some months ago, Sanquar had been a little ill-at-ease with her, and now he was all but stammering. "I came to say that all's well and that there's no need for you to trouble yourself by attending them. They'll sleep until morning for the most part, and you must be very tired."

Karuth belted her gown, cinching the buckle more tightly than she needed to. Her hands were clenched, the knuckles white. She forced her fingers to relax.

"I'll look in on them all the same." She sounded waspish, she realized; she hadn't meant to, and she took a deep breath before speaking again. "And I want to check the pharmacy. I gather that we're low on supplies of some of the febrifuges."

"I can gladly do that for you."

Karuth's self-control lapsed again as his tone, his anxiety to please, grated irrationally on the raw edges of her patience, and she turned on him with acid in her voice. "Thank you, Sanquar, but as I apparently couldn't trust anyone to ensure that our stocks were replenished while I was away, it seems that I'd better see to it myself."

She immediately regretted her harsh and unfair retort, but at this moment she didn't have the heart to retract what she'd said or to apologize for using Sanquar as a scapegoat. She pushed her feet into her slippers, tossed her hair, uncombed and clammily wet from the rain, back over her shoulders and headed toward the door. Sanquar, his face flushed, stood aside—and on the threshold Karuth stopped.

The white cat sat in the corridor outside her room. It was long past its kitten-bearing days now and living out a comfortable old age among the humans who shamelessly indulged it. Karuth's gray eyes met its brilliant green ones, and the cat opened its mouth, showing small teeth and a pink tongue in a welcoming mew.

Karuth shivered. She was fond of cats, but her relationship with this particular creature had been ambiguous since that elemental conjuration of five years ago. She'd never been able to shake off the conviction that the cat knew something which it was either unable or disinclined to communicate. Its appearance now, confronting her, reminding her of that uneasy undercurrent, was the last straw.

She turned on her heel and stared at Sanquar. "Take that animal to the kitchens and see that it stays there. I don't want to find it up here again."

Sanquar and the cat both stared after her as she stalked away along the corridor. She felt Sanquar's dismay, felt the cat's open curiosity, and crushed the shuddering that threatened to rack her. Her head ached, her limbs ached; she wanted *rest,* she wanted *sleep.* But she couldn't rest, not while the Warp was still howling over the castle and not while her every nerve felt frayed and tattered and stretched to the limits of endurance. Perspiration beaded her face, although the passage was chill, and she realized abruptly that she was suffering the first symptoms of the fever. She'd feared this; now she knew it, and it explained, if not excused, her mood. *Curse* it. She'd do what she could before it incapacitated her, and then when it grew too much for her, she'd face the ague and the weakness and the delirium and try to fight her way through it as soon as possible.

The main stairs were ahead of her. They looked faintly

unreal in the torchlight, perspective distorted, a faint halo hazing around everything on which her eyes focused. She sensed the Warp vibrating through the floor, through her bones, and she was beginning to feel sick. She wouldn't give in to it, she told herself. She *wouldn't*.

The stairwell loomed at her. Karuth caught hold of the banister to steady herself, and the momentary dizziness receded, leaving her with a small feeling of triumph. She was well enough. It hadn't overcome her yet.

She took three sharp, savagely controlled breaths and began to descend to the ground floor.

Kiszi was sulking. She knelt on the bed in her skimpy chemise, one well-rounded leg thrust out at a provocative angle, and peered resentfully through the thick, tumbling curls of her hair at her lover, who sat cross-legged on the floor with his back to her.

At last she couldn't keep silent any longer. She'd argued with him; that hadn't worked. She'd tried to cajole and seduce him out of his preoccupation; that, too, had met with failure. And the prolonged frosty silence that had been her last weapon had had no more effect than the presence of a fly on the face of a granite cliff. She rolled over onto her stomach with a groan and laid her chin on her folded arms.

"How *much* longer?" She sounded both wheedling and resentful.

Strann didn't turn his head. "I don't know. A few minutes, maybe. Be patient."

"I've *been* patient! I've been patient since it got dark, and that's *hours* now!" Her lower lip quivered with self-pity. "Oh, Strann, this is so stupid! You don't know what I had to go through to get out of the house without Father knowing. I must go back long before dawn if I'm not to be found out, and this is our very last night because tomorrow you're leaving, and you won't even tell me why, and there's no *need* for you to leave, and . . ."

Her voice tailed off. Strann had turned around to look at her, and in the light of the one candle sconce which she'd artfully placed by the bed foot, his face wore an expression of weary patience.

"I told you, Kiszi. I just don't want to stay in Shu-Nhadek any longer. I don't even want to stay in the province; I need to get away."

"Why? You haven't done anything." She gave him a lascivious smile. "Or at least, you haven't been caught doing it."

"Nonetheless, I want to go." A pause, a faint challenge in his hazel eyes. "I've invited you to come with me."

Her mouth turned down. "And you know full well I can't do any such thing. Father would have the militia out searching for me before we were a mile along the road."

"Well, that's the price you must pay for being a wealthy girl."

"I didn't ask to be wellborn!" She was nearly in tears now, tears of furious frustration. "I hate being wealthy! I wish—"

"Kiszi, Kiszi." Strann stood up with a sigh and crossed to the bed. Kiszi's eyes brightened instantly and she turned over onto her back, but he merely sat down on the edge of the mattress and took hold of one her hands.

"I'm sorry, little kitten."

"Don't call me that!"

"But you are." His fingers caught a strand of her hair and teased it. "A little kitten. A little yellow-furred cat."

Kiszi began to scent victory, but she wasn't willing to give way entirely yet. *"Golden*-furred," she corrected him with mock asperity.

"Ah, yes, of course. Whores have yellow hair, rich girls have gold. I'd forgotten that fine distinction."

"Ohh . . ." Kiszi's coquettish pretense crumbled; now she really was angry with him, and bitterly disappointed. "You *pig!* You've no right to sharpen your knives on me, it isn't *fair.* Just because something dislikable happened on Summer Isle and you came scurrying back to Shu-Nhadek before the celebrations were over—"

"I wasn't invited to stay, if you recall," Strann interrupted. Then his look became peculiarly introverted and he added under his breath, "and nor would I have wanted to."

"What do you mean?"

Strann opened his mouth to make an acid retort, but closed it again as his innate sense of justice struggled to the surface. He *was* being unfair. Kiszi wasn't to blame for the uneasiness that had dogged him since the night of the High Margrave's wedding, and to make her the butt of his ill humor was shameful. Yet he couldn't explain the convolutions of his present mood to her, for in all but the most obvious ways, Kiszi was an innocent, and she simply wouldn't understand.

He looked back to where the little pyramid of coins he'd built sat incongruously on the floor. Earlier, downstairs in the inn's taproom, before Kiszi's secretive arrival and their hasty flight to his bedchamber, he'd been running the old fairground trick over in his mind. He hadn't wanted to experiment with it then, not in the full gaze of the other drinkers, who would only have pestered him for a public performance, but he'd remembered it, largely, he suspected, because it was the one trick in the repertoire he used to know which he'd never been able to perform successfully. According to the old woman who had first demonstrated it to him, more years ago now than he cared to count, it was a debased version of a genuine psychic skill practiced by the stone readers of the Great Eastern Flatlands. A lot of hucksters' "miracles" had started life that way, but that one trick, despite Strann's sleight-of-hand, had always seemed to resist its debasement—as though, he'd often thought, something stranger, something less explicable, lay just a little too close to the surface and would not consent to be misused.

Tonight, for no logical reason, he'd remembered the trick and had an intuition about it. He wasn't entirely sure that he liked the feeling, and he had tried to dissuade himself from making the experiment. But curiosity—which, he reminded himself, had been the downfall of greater men than himself—had got the better of him as it almost always did, and he hadn't been able to resist the temptation to try. Something, the nagging instinct told him, would be different this time. Something would happen.

Yet nothing had happened. He'd tried to show the

trick to Kiszi, who had assumed it was some silly game as a forerunner to their love play and initially had joined in willingly enough. However, just as in his old fairground days, Strann hadn't been able to make the sleight work. At first he'd treated his failure with a casual shrug, resolving to try again just once more before dismissing his feeling as a piece of foolishness and turning to more pleasurable matters. But when the second attempt also failed, resolve had given way to pique. He wouldn't be bested. It was nothing more than a conjurer's frippery, and he was as skilled a conjurer as any—he'd always prided himself on his ability; dammit, before his talent won him admission to the Guild, he'd *lived* on it.

Even as he tried again and again to complete the trick successfully, a small, thin inner voice had been telling him that this was ridiculous. Two paces away a pretty, loving, and increasingly impatient girl waited in his bed, and this was his last chance for a few secret and delicious hours with her. What kind of madness was it to squat on the grubby carpet wrestling with a piece of worthless nonsense, a trinket, a toy? He'd probably drunk too much again last night, the drink had brought back the dreams, and the dreams had brought back the memory of a pile of coins and a sleight that wouldn't work. And here was Kiszi, who, by the time he returned to Shu-Nhadek—and who could say when that might be?—would probably have found herself a wealthy young husband and would have forgotten their brief but happy liaison. His last chance, and he was squandering it. *You,* Strann said to himself, *are a fool.*

He looked down at Kiszi again. "I'm sorry, little kitten. You're right: I am a pig, and worse." He glanced toward the window. "What do you think the hour is?"

"Early enough." She reached up for him, her arms twining about his neck. "Put your tricks away, Strann. *I've* a trick to show you now."

Strann started to move toward her, then paused. Those wretched coins: they winked in the candlelight like disembodied cats' eyes watching him. . . . Swiftly he bent to give Kiszi a kiss that promised much more, then propelled himself from the bed and across the floor, scooping

211

up the little heap of silver in one deft movement. Unable to resist it, he tossed the seven coins with a juggler's confident dexterity, watching them glint and spin and return to his hand. Then his fist closed on them and he grinned.

"A pox on conjurer's tricks," he said, and with another flick of the wrist flipped the coins from the back of his hand in a careless arc. They flew upward—and stopped in midair. Then, so fast that Strann couldn't react and Kiszi could do no more than utter a stifled yelp of shock, they began to spin and twist and dart in a pattern of their own.

"Great gods!" Strann couldn't recover his wits in time to stop the reflex that made him grab for the flying coins. Something ricocheted off his thumb with a violent, stinging pain and he jumped back, cursing. The coins whirled faster, faster, blurring as they meshed with their own afterimages—and suddenly he saw a face form in the midst of their tiny mayhem, colorless silver-and-shadow, lips smiling sardonically, eyes—huge eyes—gazing into his and seeing beyond them into his soul.

Strann yelled aloud. And the face vanished as the seven coins dropped to the floor with a dead metallic rattle.

His shout reverberated away into an appalling silence and he stared at the coins as though they were venomous snakes. They didn't move. They were lifeless now, their momentary animation halted as suddenly and as violently as it had begun. But they formed a pattern, and Strann recognized it instantly. A musical notation: the short sequence that, in the Guild's hand-speech code, meant: *I am watching.*

An inarticulate sound from behind him broke Strann's thrall. He spun around and saw Kiszi sprawled across the bed, limbs threshing as she propelled herself without any coordination toward the far side of the mattress, where her gown and shoes lay discarded.

"Kiszi—" He started toward her even as she snatched up her dress and started to flail it over her head. "Kiszi!"

"I'm not staying here!" Her muffled voice was shrill with terror. "I'm not, I'm *not!*" Her head emerged from the dress's folds and her wide, wild stare fastened on his face. *"What did you do?"*

"I did nothing! Kiszi, you saw it, you saw what happened!"

Kiszi gagged as though she were about to be sick, and fought her arms into the sleeves of her gown. Groping frantically, she found one shoe, thrust it onto the wrong foot, said a word that would have appalled her parents, and fumbled for the other shoe.

"No!" as Strann tried to intercept her. "I'm *going!*" She scrambled off the bed, caught her foot in the gown's hem, and fell to one knee; Strann heard expensive fabric rip. Then she was up again, stumbling to the door and scrabbling at the latch until it opened.

"I'm sorry." Her eyes met his again as she stood for a moment shivering on the threshold. She looked like a young and badly frightened child. "Something's happened to you, Strann. I don't know what it is and I don't think you do either. I've felt it since you came back from Summer Isle. Something's *touched* you. And I don't want to find out any more!"

She left the door swinging on its strained hinges and he heard her feet clattering along the landing and down the back stairs. *Something's happened to you, Strann.* She'd found the core of it, unknowingly and in her innocence. A snatch of wisdom, a snatch of insight, so unlike her that it had sounded alien on her lips. *Something's happened.* He knew it, and it struck a deadly cold into the pit of his stomach.

Behind him the candles in the sconce were guttering as an unwonted draft from the landing distorted their flames. The coins lay on the floor, still forming their pattern. *I am watching.* Strann crossed the room in two strides and raised one foot to kick at the silver pieces and scatter them, but at the last instant he held back. He didn't want to touch them. Let them lie. Let them *rot.*

His belongings were few enough; a rolled blanket, a pack containing a few essentials, and his precious manzon. In his customary way he'd stacked them neatly by the window, always ready to be hefted and shouldered and carried to his next destination. Where that would be, he didn't know, and at this moment he didn't care; all that mattered was to get away from Shu-Nhadek without any further delay. He'd stayed for the sake of Kiszi's bright eyes and welcoming arms, though instinct had told him to go. Now he wished heartily that he'd listened to that instinct, for if he had, by now there would be a good many miles between himself and this town. Or, more to the point, between himself and Summer Isle. Indeed, he wished that he'd never accepted the invitation to set foot on Summer Isle in the first place.

But if a wish were a good horse, Strann reflected wryly, then by now he'd be halfway to Empty province on the best steed ever bred. It was too late for regrets. Done was done, and the only thing that made sense now was to set his back to the south and be on his way. He could probably reach the junction of the main drove roads by dawn if he walked briskly, and from there it shouldn't be difficult to barter a ride on some carter's wagon to Han province or even further. Beyond that, he could only hope —not pray, for above all else, he didn't want to attract the attention of any of the fourteen gods—that in leaving Shu-Nhadek he would also leave behind the unnameable, unquantifiable taint of supernatural machination that had dogged him since the night that he and Karuth Piadar had played their duet on Summer Isle.

Strann was not a religious man. Forced to a choice, his nature would have inclined him more toward Chaos than toward Order, but since reaching an age when he could comprehend such things, he had maintained a pragmatic determination to adopt no loyalties and take no sides. Beyond the occasional small offering to both Yandros and Aeoris at the Quarter-Day festivals, he paid no particular attention to the gods, and he had always trusted that in return they would pay no particular attention to him. Now, though, he was beginning to wonder if he could still rely on that trust.

But why me? logic asked. He might play at vanity now and again, but beneath the surface he was wise enough to know that there was nothing about him to interest the greater powers. He was no sorcerer, no psychic. He didn't lust for power or for arcane knowledge. He didn't preach. He was simply a maker of songs and stories, albeit—for Strann wasn't given to false modesty any more than to vainglory—an especially talented one. He was no threat to anyone, and no one's pawn. Whatever was afoot in realms beyond his understanding, he wanted to play no part in it.

But, want or no, something had touched him. And it had begun on Summer Isle, when the High Initiate's sister had agreed to play that rare and difficult piece of music with him and when lightning had struck, once, out of a star-filled sky.

Strann took a last look around the room that had been his home for the past twenty-two days. For the first time he saw how shabby it was, how the carpet was worn to holes in places, how the furnishings were battered and chipped and crying out for paint, how the curtain rail had been fixed at a slight angle to the frame of the window so that it took on a drunken, disorienting list. Even the bed where he and Kiszi had taken their pleasure was lumpy, uneven, thoroughly uncomfortable if truth be told. He wouldn't be sorry to leave.

The candles were still burning, though lopsidedly now, wax dripping down the sconce and pooling. The seven silver coins glinted where he'd left them. The landlord would doubtless find them in the morning, and they'd be payment enough for Strann's account.

He stepped out onto the landing. The taproom was silent; even the diehards had staggered home to their own beds. A part-open window at the landing's far end rattled in a sudden breeze and Strann's nostrils flared as he caught the smells of brine, tar, old fish, and older seaweed from the harbor. He didn't want to see the sea again, not for a while. And though he dismissed the thought as quickly as he was able, he couldn't help but wonder briefly what strangeness might be haunting Karuth Piadar's dreams tonight.

He closed the door and moved softly toward the stairs.

15

The marriage of Blis and Jianna Hanmen Alacar heralded
—fortuitously, according to the seers and readers of augu-
ries—a quiet and uneventful year. The spring fever took a
minimal toll, and that mainly among the old and weak,
which was no more than anyone had expected. As summer
waxed, the provinces settled to their customary seasonal
routines, with no major upheavals to mar the long warm
days.

The only small disappointment in society's higher echelons during that pleasant summer and the autumn and
winter which followed was that as yet there was to be no
new heir at the palace on Summer Isle. An announcement
was eagerly awaited, but even after a year had passed, no
announcement came. However, it was widely agreed that
the High Margrave and his wife were young enough yet
and that matters would take their own course in their own
time, and—except in a few gossip-ridden quarters—preoccupation with the affairs of the Margravate died down.

Life was quiet, too, at the Star Peninsula; in some ways
perhaps a little too quiet, for the rift between Tirand and
Karuth, though healed on the surface, seemed to have left
an underlying scar. Nothing was ever said, but both were
aware that their relationship had altered in some subtle
way, creating slight tensions that had never existed before.
However hard they tried, it seemed impossible to shake off
entirely the old quarrel's effects and return to normal.
Close friends and their more psychically sensitive colleagues in the Circle had also noticed the change, and it

216

cast a small but tangible cloud over the atmosphere within the castle walls.

But if the unresolved trouble caused them discomfort, Tirand and Karuth were determined that it shouldn't have an adverse effect on their responsibilities and duties. If anything, they both applied themselves with more dedication than ever, submerging personal feelings in the distraction of work. In the following spring, a year after his brother's wedding and his own coming of age, Calvi Alacar passed—with honors—his qualifying examinations in philosophy and natural sciences. At the party held to celebrate his own and his fellow students' successes, Calvi got up on a table in the dining hall and made an enthusiastic if none-too-sober speech in which he thanked the High Initiate in particular for his unstinting help and guidance throughout the years of his studies. Tirand, though horribly embarrassed, was also privately touched by Calvi's paean of praise. In the last year or two he *had* taken an especial interest in the young man's progress, for he believed that Calvi had the makings of a highly gifted philosopher and teacher, and in addition the two of them had developed a strong mutual liking and respect. Tirand was glad to find his view of Calvi vindicated, and he was doubly delighted when Calvi announced his intention to stay on at the castle and study for higher accolades.

So another spring passed, another summer flowered and began to fade. Far to the south, on the small island which the rest of the world believed uninhabited, Ygorla Morys, too, had proved herself a more-than-diligent student, though in a very different field. Her father, she knew, was pleased with her progress. And though his visits to her hideaway on the White Isle had become less frequent of late, she looked forward to each occasion with increasing eagerness, for she knew that before too much more time had passed there would be great changes in her life.

Narid-na-Gost came to her one bright morning as autumn began to impose its first influence on the world. She had been waiting for him, knowing he would come but not knowing precisely when. Her intuition, honed now over more than six years to catlike accuracy, still wasn't equal to her father's unpredictable and mercurial nature, and even her best efforts could do no more than sense his presence in the minutes before the shimmering door between the mortal world and that of Chaos appeared in the crater bowl.

This time, though, she was aware even before Narid-na-Gost's arrival that something was different. She sensed it as a tingling sensation insinuating like ice spiders along her spine, and when she emerged from her cavern as the sun's rays began to crawl over the crater's highest reaches, she felt it, physical, almost visible, in the air. Peculiar colors crackled on the periphery of her vision, perspectives were distorted, half-formed faces flickered and gibbered among the rock walls, vanishing like the illusions they were whenever she tried to face and challenge them. There was power in the atmosphere, and for once it was none of her own doing.

Standing before the old shattered altar that had once supported Aeoris's votive light, Ygorla smiled. Something was afoot. Something was shifting in her father's realm. Though she didn't yet know the form they would take, or their ultimate intent, she sensed the tides moving about her and the answering echo in the surges of her own half-human blood.

When Narid-na-Gost arrived, there was, to her surprise, no ceremony and no spectacle. She turned away from the altar to squint at the sun for one brief moment, and when she looked again, he was there, his hunched figure poised between the broken stone slabs. For a few seconds that seemed to slip out of time, they stared at each other. She registered his ugliness, which with the years of familiarity had in her eyes become a perverse kind of beauty; he in turn gazed at her, assessing the creature that she had become.

Ygorla was a woman now. Twenty years old, she had grown to a beauty that many fully mortal females would have killed to possess. Her hair hung almost to her knees in a shimmering cascade like a blue-black waterfall; it glittered and rippled like water, too, as no human hair could have done. Her eyes were cool sapphires in the frame of her delicate face, her body small, full-breasted but slender, the curve of arm and hip achingly lovely. She looked the epitome of mortal perfection and—to anyone who didn't gaze too deeply into those brilliant blue eyes—mortal innocence, and the sight of her gave Narid-na-Gost great pleasure. Men would willingly die for his daughter if they could but see her. That thought amused him deeply.

He stepped forward and took her hand, raising it to his lips in an old chivalrous gesture as he bowed to her.

"My child. You are the incarnation of beauty. You are, truly, an empress!"

Ygorla's eyes widened with surprise. "Father?" She didn't comprehend this, it wasn't like him. "What's happened?"

The demon's crimson eyes narrowed with approval. "Ah. Then you sense it?"

"I sense something. But I can't give it a name."

Narid-na-Gost released her hand and turned slowly about, regarding the crater's bleak vista with a blend of distaste and detached interest. At last, he said:

"You have been alone in this place for a long time, Ygorla. I know that your life here has been far from easy." He looked back at her and his lips twisted in a quick, conspiratorial smile. "You have been patient and you have been obedient. And it won't be long now before you will reap the rewards that I promised you long ago."

Ygorla's heart missed with a painful jolt. She opened her mouth to ask an eager question, but the demon held up a hand, silencing her before she could speak.

"No," he said, "I'm not ready to explain what I mean; not yet. Not *quite* yet. There is one phase of my plan still to be completed, the most crucial and the most perilous of all. When it is done, then there will be great changes, Ygorla. Then it will be time for you to leave this miserable place for a new home more suited to your destiny."

Ygorla's eyes were avid; her heart pounded so hard and so painfully that she felt sick. "What is this crucial phase, Father?" she begged. "What do you mean to do? What part can *I* play in it?"

"Your part, child, is the simplest and yet most taxing of all," the demon told her. "I want you to retire to your cavern and wait there for me. Nothing more than that. Strictly and emphatically, *nothing* more."

She frowned, not liking this. "But—"

"No." She knew that tone of old, and it silenced her instantly. Narid-na-Gost regarded her for a few moments, and in those moments she felt a sensation in her gut like fire and ice together as his eyes, blood-dark now and glittering like garnets, stared into her own. At last he spoke again.

"I will say this to you only once, Ygorla, and I will stress only once that, if all that I have worked for is not to be thrown away, you must obey me utterly and not dare to question me." A pause. "I will not see my work wasted, daughter. If you fail me in this, your soul will have millennia in which to regret your folly. Do I make my meaning clear?"

Her face whitened; even her lips were drained of color. She nodded.

"Good. Then listen and heed. You will retire to your cavern and you will stay there, no matter what may befall, until I return. You will not set foot in the crater bowl, indeed you will not so much as venture into the tunnels. Above all, you will not practice your art. Cast no spells, summon no companions or playthings. Do *nothing*. Only wait for me to come to you again."

There was a long tense silence. Ygorla felt that her mind was on the point of bursting: furious questions were welling like a spring tide and she railed against the stricture he had set on her, cursing herself for fearing him, at this moment almost hating him for the power he had over her. Then suddenly Narid-na-Gost smiled.

"Don't think I don't know your thoughts. Your anger and your frustration are like flames devouring the air around you; you ask *why?* and the fact that you have no answer to your question maddens you. Well, I will give you an answer. I demand this of you for one reason alone— because while I am away it is vital that even the smallest hint of your presence here should not be detected."

Ygorla was nonplussed. "Why should it be detected? I've dwelt on this island for near on seven years, and in all that time—"

"In all that time no one has had cause to search for you or even to suspect that you are still alive. But in the days to come, that may change. And if something should come seeking, I want there to be nothing here that might draw its attention."

He spoke carelessly enough, but something underlying his words—and in particular the phrase *if something should come seeking*—sent a steel-cold sensation thrusting down Ygorla's spine. She was on the verge of asking the demon what he meant, but at the last moment held her tongue, suddenly not sure that she wanted to hear the answer to such a question.

"So," Narid-na-Gost said softly, "now that you understand, can I trust you?"

She hesitated, but only for a few seconds. It was, after all, a small price to pay.

"Yes, Father," she said. "I will do exactly as you say."

"Good." Then the demon's harsh expression relented. "It will be only for a short while, child. A few days perhaps, as this dimension measures time. When I return I will bring you a gift. A great gift, greater than anything I've yet bestowed on you."

The hungry light began to creep back into Ygorla's eyes. "What manner of gift, Father?"

Narid-na-Gost laughed quietly, lazily. "Oh, just a pretty bauble to delight you. A very, *very* pretty bauble." The smile, which had continued to hover, abruptly broadened into a feral grin. "And when I place it in your hand, you will know that all the years of waiting have been worthwhile!"

She had dwelt here in this cavern, in dark and anomalous stability beneath the shifting, glittering surface of the Chaos realm, for as long as she could remember—for as long, in fact, as she had existed—and in all that time her duties had neither changed nor varied. Oblivious of the constantly shifting tides of the world she had never seen, ignored by the other inhabitants of Chaos, she crouched constantly at her post, guarding the gateway to another level of Yandros's kingdom, obeying the single rule that was her only purpose for living. She was the sentry, she was the keeper of the portal. None but the gods themselves might pass her and go down by this route to the deeper world. Why this should be so, and what lay below that she must protect so assiduously, she didn't know, and even if it had occurred to her to wonder, there was no one to whom she could have put such a question, for her masters never troubled to visit her or even to glance down from their lofty heights to see that she still fulfilled what was required of her. Her loyalty and diligence was taken for granted; they had been, after all, deliberately instilled into her nature. She was trusted and therefore dismissed as irrelevant.

But though she was aware of her drab limitations and never railed against them, she was nevertheless not entirely immune to something that, had she known the word, she might have called emotion. She knew that she was female and she knew what that meant, not because she had ever been told but because she felt and instinctively recognized the essence of female nature within her. Sometimes, too, she felt the innate desires of a female, too innocent to be lust yet too ill-formed and vague to be love, and at those times she thought she understood what sadness was, because she had no means to fulfill those desires and no hope that her situation might ever change. Her creation had been the work of a careless moment by the great lords who ruled her world. She was the lowliest of the low, and she suspected that even by the idiosyncratic and often bizarre standards of Chaos she was too misformed and unprepossessing to be of any interest to a potential mate.

Still, she had her place in the scheme of things and, considering what she was, it was a good place. She was content enough with it and had looked for no more.

That is, until *he* had entered the sphere of her existence.

Though she knew he was one of the low demons, he was nonetheless of a far higher order than herself, and the idea that such a one should find her pleasing was like a draft of clear water to her parched soul. He brought her gifts—tiny things, but she was simple and they were enough to delight her—and he talked to her of places beyond the reach of her imagination, worlds outside the closed and murky confines where she dwelt and carried out her duties. And he touched her. Since her creation, no being had ever done such a thing, and it thrilled her.

She was waiting for him, for he had promised her that he would come with a new gift for her, finer and more delightful than any he had brought before. Crouching on the stubby stalagmite of black rock which she had chosen for her guard post, she swung her blue, reptilian head with its long jaws and rows of needle teeth this way and that, torn between obligation and more personal preoccupations. To her left, its surface reflecting from the rock walls in shivering and unstable rainbows, was a water-filled shaft surrounded by a low wall. This was the portal that she was constrained to guard, the gateway to the deeper level of the Chaos realm. As the appointed guardian, she knew that the portal wasn't barred to her as it was to others, but she'd never had the courage to explore it. To her right was the narrow tunnel that led from her cave through twisting, turning ways that changed treacherously and capriciously with every moment, and finally out into the whole breathtaking spectrum of those *other* places of which he'd told her so much. Nothing would ever persuade her to venture in that direction, but it was from there that he would come to her. She waited, gnawed by eager impatience, eaten by longing, two of her clawed little hands drumming on the rock and setting up a muttering vibration.

At last she heard him approaching. Her tail with its hard ridge of fin lashed excitedly and her tongue flickered as she used her remaining four hands to lever herself down from her perch and crouch on the cave floor. She saw his shadow first, distorted by the peculiar phosphorescent light into something strange and wonderful, and she crooned the welcoming song that in her long hours of solitude she'd devised to please him.

Narid-na-Gost stopped on the threshold of the cave and his twisted face broke into a smile. The creature hadn't the wit to see that the smile didn't extend to his eyes, and he felt a familiar surge of contempt for her gullibility, swiftly followed by an equally familiar sense of revulsion. Gods, but she was a hideous thing. Grotesque, malformed: their masters must indeed have been exercising their sense of humor to the full when they created her, and that thought conjured afresh the seething resentment that had been his watchword and his goad for so long. The ugly and the misshapen, careless by-blows of a moment's imagination, given life and then tossed aside to fend as best they could while those who considered themselves higher and greater ignored them and denied to them any chance of advancement. Narid-na-Gost knew the sting of being such a creature, and under other circumstances he might from his relatively exalted position have pitied this ugly little drudge. But any such patronage was eclipsed by the twin hungers that drove him: the goal of ambition and the desire for revenge. In that she would find her fulfillment— and her nemesis.

"Ah, little one. How beautiful your song sounds to me." He bent to touch her gently between her small over-bright eyes, the lie gliding easily from his tongue. "I have longed for this moment, little sweeting. I have yearned and I have barely been able to contain my eagerness." He planted a kiss on her scaled brow; she was unaware of his inward flinching. "I have brought you the gift I promised. A gift worthy of my lovely one, a gift to please and delight her. Look."

She hissed when she saw it, an involuntary expression of a thrill she couldn't contain. It was so *beautiful.* It shone and it shimmered and it danced, and when she took it in her malformed hands it turned to a thousand exquisite colors and it showed her scenes of such beauty that her eyes filled with tears.

"Thank you!" Even her voice, he thought, was repellent, a wet-throated, guttural croak. *"Thank you, my lord!"*

She was entranced with the bauble, and Narid-na-Gost smiled contemptuously down at her. Choosing his moment carefully, he suddenly plucked the gift from her and held it out of her reach. She made a frightened, pleading sound, holding up imploring arms, but the demon only allowed his smile to broaden a fraction.

"Ah, no, my little one," he said in a honeyed tone. "You *shall* have your gift, of course you shall. But there is something I want from you in return."

Her hands, still stretched out in supplication, clasped

together. "Anything!" she breathed. "Anything, beloved lord!"

He found the sheer naiveté of her promise faintly amusing but let it pass. She could perform the task he required of her well enough; in fact, she was almost uniquely qualified to perform it, however inadequate she might be in other ways.

"Well, then, sweeting." He dropped to a crouch so that their faces were on a level, and his hot crimson eyes looked into her small watery ones. "Listen to me now and listen carefully. This is what I wish you to do."

———————————⟩ ⟨———————————

She didn't want to agree to it. It wasn't that she feared the consequences of discovery, for there were no strictures on her, and besides, her feeble intellect didn't allow her to consider any possible implications. What she feared was the well itself. She had never found the courage to do any more than dabble a hand in the dark waters; she didn't know what lay below the well's mysterious surface, and she had an illogical dread of finding out. What if the shaft should be bottomless? What if she should swim and swim and never reach the place he wanted her to find? What if she lost her way and couldn't return?

Skillfully and ruthlessly Narid-na-Gost broke down her arguments, and with them her defenses. Could she not swim as well as any fish ever hatched from spawn? Could she not breathe water as easily as she breathed air? And was she not his clever sweeting, who knew no fear and who had sworn that she would fight through fire and storm and gale and flood to please him? He had been so proud of her and so honored by her love. Would she break his heart now by telling him that he had misjudged her?

It was this last sting, barely hidden in the honey of his persuasions, that finally undid her. He had twisted her pledges of love and made rhetoric of them, but she didn't know it, she couldn't remember the fine details of all she had ever said to him. All she knew was that she had disappointed him, failed him, hurt him. She was wicked. She was cruel. She wanted only to make amends, so that he would shake off the sadness she had caused and be proud of her again.

When she capitulated, bowing her monstrous head while her tears splashed on the veined rock floor, Narid-na-Gost stroked her brow and smiled a triumphant smile that she couldn't see. He had her precisely where he wanted her; she would succeed in the mission he had set her, or destroy herself trying. If she succeeded, then by the time her masters learned what she had done, he would be far away and beyond their retribution. If she failed, there would be no one to tell them the tale. Yes, he thought, a most satisfactory position. At this stage he could not have asked for more.

Before he left, he kissed her mouth. He'd never done such a thing before, and it left her giddy with awe and adoration. She watched him go, watched until even his shadow had vanished from the tunnel, and silently she repeated the instructions he had given, over and over in her mind. She *would* achieve it. She would make the journey and find the gift, and bring the gift back and put it in his hands. He would love her for that, as she loved him. A whole new future was opening for her, as brilliant as the Chaos-light that shone, so he had told her, when the gods came from their sanctuaries to walk the realm. She would know joy. She would know passion. She would be *fulfilled*.

―――――――◇――――◁――――

Narid-na-Gost emerged from the tunnel mouth and took a deep, grateful breath of the cleaner atmosphere outside. The seven lords of this world had chosen, for the present, to create a colossal vista of vast green and amber plains above which thin, smoky tatters of cloud raced across a purple sky. A single black star hung pulsing on the horizon, framed by erupting geysers of steam which, with perspective made a mockery by the land's numbing scale, might have been one or a thousand miles away from the demon's vantage point. He heard energy crackle somewhere, followed by a thin and bone-shakingly eerie wailing as something sang a reply, and he glanced reflexively over his shoulder. But there was nothing interesting to be seen, and after a few moments he began to move down the slope of the hill from which he had emerged.

Interesting that amid the ever-shifting, ever-changing panorama of the world they had created for themselves, the gods were unimaginative enough to have given stability to just a small number of precise locations. Seven landmarks which never altered their form—it was as clear an indication as anyone could have wished that those locations had some special significance. Did the Chaos lords truly have so much faith in their invulnerability that they had never considered the possibility that other minds might recognize and probe their secret? Had it never occurred to them that an enemy might lurk within their walls as well as without them? Narid-na-Gost touched a finger to his lips to suppress laughter as he wondered what Aeoris of Order might have said had he known of his old adversaries' carelessness. Yandros and his brothers, who called themselves gods, who called themselves masters of Narid-na-Gost and all his kind, were fools. Sightless, complacent fools.

He was making his way toward the mirage of a many-towered castle that shimmered some way off when he heard a rush of air behind him, the herald of something approaching. Turning, he saw a flying carriage sweeping toward him, drawn by five massive black horses with snakelike necks and flaming manes. The carriage had only one occupant, who held a silver hawk on her wrist; for an instant her riveting amber gaze met Narid-na-Gost's eyes and he recognized her immediately. He made a knee, abasing himself, and felt the intensity of her stare as the carriage swept by. Tarod's paramour, the human woman whom Yandros had elevated from mortality to a seat of greatness to which she had no just claim. The demon felt again the inner knife-twist of jealous contempt. She was away no doubt to indulge her pleasure by hunting the creatures of her own mind's creation. Another worthless pastime, while the mortal world went its own unfettered way and forgot how to fear the power of Chaos. Disgust filled him, and he turned his head to spit upon the ground. A crimson-and-yellow toad took brief form where the spittle landed, tried to crawl away, then disintegrated as the demon brought his momentary ire under control. Patience, he counseled himself, patience. He'd learned the lesson well over the years; he could apply it for just a little while longer. Just a little while. And then not only Chaos but all the worlds of gods and men would see a change that was long overdue.

16

She crouched on the lip of the shaft for a long time before she was at last able to quiet her fluttering nerves and slip into the well. The water felt cold, and it moved over her like dark silk as she let herself sink, covering her legs, her body, her arms, and finally closing over her head and submerging her in buoyant, shifting darkness.

She took a few moments to adjust to the strangeness below the surface, finding unexpected pleasure in the sudden change from an earthbound existence to this three-dimensional water world where she could move in whatever direction she chose with a languid ease that, for her, was almost graceful. Contrary to her fears, it wasn't entirely dark in the well. A little light filtered down from the cave above the surface, and there was another glow, faint but reassuring, a phosphorescent glimmer which seemed to reach up to her from somewhere far, far below.

For a while she waited, and then, when nothing came to investigate her presence or to challenge her and tell her she had no right to venture here, her confidence began to grow. Experimenting with her new freedom, she twisted about and kicked strongly downward. Her tail flicked instinctively, surprising and delighting her with the impetus it gave to her body, and she swam deeper, letting the distant glow be her guide and rapidly learning the wriggling fishlike movements that propelled her down with the minimum of effort.

Despite her initial terrors, she was beginning to enjoy herself. Though Narid-na-Gost's instructions were fixed firmly in her mind, she was for the moment able to set these aside and concentrate solely on the pleasure of this new and fascinating experience. Deeper still, and now the glow was stronger and taking on a hint of a wonderful blue, like the first glimmer of a priceless sapphire seen shining from a crevice in an obsidian wall. Gentle currents touched her, thrilled her and passed on, and the initial coldness was beginning to turn to warmth that livened her blood and her bones. On further, on down. Why had she never dared to venture here before? There was nothing to fear. There were no guardians to bar her way, no masters to punish her for presumption. She had been such a silly, cowed, and fearful fool. This was a part of her own world and it was beautiful.

Then a new current from below swept up and hit her without any warning, and it tumbled her over in a welter of churning water, its iciness shocking her out of her happy daydream and jerking her mind back to the reality of her situation. She floundered, suddenly and frighteningly losing her sense of direction—but then, as the first shock passed, she realized instinctively that this was no threat but merely a sign that she had almost reached her destination.

Excitement shot adrenaline through her. She had almost reached the place where she would find the gift to take to her beloved lord! She twisted in the water, drawing on all her newly discovered skill and strength to turn toward the current and forge against it. Silver turbulence streamed from her as she made her body into an arrow, and her lashing tail powered her downward with new and awesome vigor, further, further, defeating the pressure that tried to force her back from her goal. The blue light strengthened suddenly, flaring into a blinding glare that pulsed like a seven-rayed star—

She burst out of water into air, and fell heavily onto a solid surface.

She yelped in pain as she struck and her spine jarred agonizingly, and for some moments lay still on her back, too afraid to move lest she should discover some damage to her body that she couldn't repair. Above her she could see the shaft of the well set into a low black ceiling, the water in it glimmering and creating patterns that made her feel dizzy. Her back and her tail hurt and her head was pounding, but after a while—she couldn't judge how long—the pain began to fade and she risked moving her limbs.

It seemed she was unhurt. Slowly and awkwardly she clambered upright, staggering a little at first as her limbs struggled to adjust to the abrupt change back to leaden weightiness. She had arrived. This was the place Narid-na-Gost had told her to seek; the world at the bottom of the well. And irrationally, foolishly, she felt disappointed. She had anticipated something wonderful and arcane; instead it seemed she had arrived in a dark, dank, and all-but-featureless cavern that was no better than a reflection of her own murky domain at the top of the well.

Except, she realized suddenly, for the light.

That lovely sapphire glow permeated the cavern, and when she turned in a slow, questing circle, she realized that it shone out from a slit in the rock wall some ten paces away to her left. Her pulse quickened eagerly. The fissure was narrow, but she could squeeze through it, she *knew* she could. And the sapphire light was the sign her beloved lord had told her to seek; it was the way, the path that would lead her to the gift.

She stumbled across the uneven floor and thrust her body into the narrow gap. It was crushingly tight, but she could just force herself through, and as she went, as she pushed on between the claustrophobic walls, the light grew brighter and brighter, until she was forced to shut her eyes against its brilliance. Then she burst out into free space and, on hands and knees, stared in astonishment at the scene confronting her.

She could hear singing. That was the first conscious thought to strike her, though it was a tiny and trivial irrelevance amid the greater, awesome whole. The sound was beautiful and yet dreadfully discordant, and it took her some moments to realize that it was conjured by the movement of air through a network of passages and chambers that honeycombed the rock of the spherical chamber into which she had emerged. The entire chamber shone with a deep, pulsing blue light that played across the curving walls and rippled like water. Huge columns of the same light moved with slow majesty across the cavern, as though following the movements of some arcane dance; as they passed, dazzling silver reflections sparked from striations in the rock, flashing and flickering like chained lightning.

She was hypnotized. For what seemed liked half a lifetime she could only stare and stare at the sheer loveliness of the place while the eerie singing shimmered about her. So she might have stayed, entranced and unmoving, but for the imperative that suddenly reasserted its presence in her consciousness, striking a discord with the cave's music and reminding her guiltily of her mission. Ashamed of herself, she forced her mind to break the spell that held her, and realized immediately that she was presented with a new dilemma. *Dared* she enter this incredible place? Dared she step forward into the ripples of light, among the misty columns, and sully them with her presence? *Yes,* a voice inside her said emphatically. *For your beloved, you will dare anything. You promised him this. Will you betray his faith now?*

Memories of Narid-na-Gost's pained and poignant words on the subject of fidelity stung her, and she hung her head. She couldn't fail him. She *must* not, or she would show herself unworthy of him. More than anything else in her world, she dreaded that stigma.

Raising her head again, she stepped forward.

She wasn't sure what she had expected, but every fiber of her being was unconsciously tensed against some unidentifiable horror that might strike her down for her dire presumption. Instinctively she had shut her eyes, and when after three tentative paces she stopped and waited for retribution to fall, it took some while before she realized that there *was* no retribution, no violent change in the atmosphere, no voice booming out of the blue light to accuse her, no awesome power roaring from above to cut her down. The strange rock voices still sang their languid song, and when at last she ventured to open her eyes once more, she found herself standing amid the currents of light with the tall pillars continuing their graceful minuet around her.

She let out a pent breath and heard it echo incongruously through the chamber. Another pace forward. She had courage now; fear was slipping from her like an outworn and discarded skin. Another pace. Was the music changing? It sounded sweeter and more beautiful than ever, but there seemed to be a new, underlying urgency in its tones. The blue light flowed around her, tendrils of it caressing her body. It was warm; so *warm*. And the pillars . . . they were altering their pattern, some moving to her right, others to her left, until they formed an avenue—a guard of honor, she thought, and wanted to laugh at the foolish idea—stretching ahead of her to the far side of the cavern.

At the end of the avenue, something awaited her.

Blue. In that moment the word, the concept, took on an entirely new meaning, and the lovely colors of the light which suffused the chamber faded to utter insignificance. There had never been such a blue as this: it burned, it radiated, it *lived*. It called her with a power she couldn't hope to resist. She started forward between the ranks of shining columns, and all her six hands reached out, clawing at the air before her, clawing at the light as though it were a physical barrier, clawing with a longing to touch and hold and possess. She broke into a run, stumbling the last few steps, and fell to her knees, grazing her rough skin but oblivious of the pain as she reached her goal and came face-to-face with what she had sought.

She had found the gift! Dizzy elation surged through her, making her want to lift her head and shriek with the sheer joy of her triumph. She had succeeded! And the gift —oh, but the gift was all he had promised, and far more. It was beautiful, it was wonderful; it was . . . Her clawed, misshapen hands hovered over it, quivering. It *was*. She knew no words that could describe it. It simply *was*.

The giant gem hung unsupported within a column of velvet darkness. It had a thousand facets and each facet seemed to shine with a subtly different shade of blue, from the near-black of an ocean under starlight to the ethereal icy paleness of a glacier. In its depths the shades merged and swirled into a central core of color of such intensity that she could hardly bear to look at it. This was her salvation. This was the jewel that would buy her Narid-na-Gost's love.

She didn't think to ask herself what the gemstone

might be or why it had been placed here. In the moment of discovery, of success, all fear and all doubt had been swept from her mind: nothing mattered to her but that her mission was complete. Crooning with delight, her heart soaring, she closed two hands tightly around the jewel and plucked it from the darkness.

The pulse of sheer brilliance lasted only a fraction of a second, but it blinded her, sending her reeling back as her crooning song changed to an ugly cry of protest. An image flashed before her inner eye—a seven-rayed star—but then in an instant the brilliance and the image were gone and she crouched on the rock with the huge sapphire still safely clutched in her fingers.

Something had changed. The singing . . . yes, the strange and lovely singing had suddenly and inexplicably stopped. Slowly, nervously, she turned her head, and her breath rattled sharply in her throat.

The rippling blue light and the gravely dancing columns had vanished. Stunned as her eyes were by the nacreous flash from the stone, their disappearance hadn't registered at first. Now, though, as if obeying some command which her senses couldn't discern, the light had gone and the cavern was dark.

A peculiar sound broke from her throat as the fear that she'd believed conquered came crawling back. What had she done? What had happened? Fearfully she raised her two clenched hands and opened the fingers a crack, terrified yet compelled to look. Deep blue light spilled out over her fingers and she felt the stone's hard contours pressing against her skin. It was still there, it hadn't vanished with the currents and columns. But something had happened. *Something.*

Unsteadily she rose to her feet. Where was the fissure through which she'd entered the cave? For a moment panic threatened to overtake her, but then with what was for her extraordinary presence of mind she thought to open her hands again and let the gem's light illuminate her surroundings. The effect was eerie; the great sapphire gave off a dark, ominous glow that cast menacing shadows across the walls. But unnerving or not, it was enough, and like a frightened animal scurrying from a predator, she hastened across the floor until the curve of the far wall loomed, coldly blue-lit, and she saw the narrow mouth of the fissure. She flung herself at it, squirmed through with such force that she tore more of her skin, and burst out to the second cave at the bottom of the well. In the low roof the shaft of water glinted and shifted; she scrabbled across the uneven floor until she was under the shaft, then stretched up with all the power she could wring from her muscles, her body arching to reach the surface.

Her fingers touched the water. Abruptly the cavern seemed to tilt; she felt herself tipping over and her mind lurched with disorientation. Then she was falling upward —no, *downward,* she was diving, plunging headlong into the well. Instinctively her tail lashed, propelling her forward, and she surged through the water, thrusting aside the current that tried to push her back, kicking out, swimming with all the strength she possessed toward the sanctuary of her own territory.

Her head broke surface in a rush and swirl of bubbles, and as her streaming eyes cleared, she saw the familiar outlines of the well's edge and her cave home beyond. Gasping with relief, she swam to the rock side and clambered out, then scurried to her favorite perch and squatted down behind it. Here, hidden from the prying or accusing eyes which haunted every cranny of her imagination, she hunched over her clasped hands and slowly, slowly, opened them.

The jewel was still there. Its inner light seemed duller here, but it still glowed darkly, casting a strange bloom over her fingers. She clamped her palms tightly over it once more, fearing that it might escape by some arcane means if she relaxed her vigilance even for a moment, and sought in her mind for the instruction that her beloved Narid-na-Gost had given her.

Wait for me, he had said. *Bring the gift back to your cavern, and wait. I will know when you have it, and I will come.* So, she would wait as he had told her. How long it would be before he arrived, she didn't know, but she would be patient.

She settled her ungainly body into a more comfortable position and, with the sapphire held tightly in her hands and her gaze fixed unwaveringly on the tunnel entrance at the far side of the cave, she composed herself for her vigil.

As always, she saw his shadow before she heard his steps, and she started to her feet, eagerness thrilling through her. As the demon appeared, she crooned her customary welcome, trying at the same time to convey her excitement, her pride, and her pleasure in her success.

Narid-na-Gost stopped, and his crimson stare bored ferociously into her. "Well? Have you found it? Did you bring it back?"

She was too involved in her own feelings to notice that he spoke to her in a tone he'd never used before. She scrambled upright, and four of her hands pawed the air while the third pair, still clenched, held the precious gem out toward him.

"I found it, beloved lord! I found it and brought it back!"

He was across the cave floor in three strides. "Show me!"

She unfolded her fingers, and the sapphire's dark brilliance splashed over her arms and over Narid-na-Gost's face as he bent to see. Breath escaped the demon's throat in a hissing rush.

"Oh, yes . . ." he said softly as he plucked the gem from her and laid it on his palm. "Oh, *yes!*"

"I brought it back to give to you, beloved lord," she told him eagerly. "Are you pleased with me? Have I made you happy, and have I proved that I'm worthy of your love? I did what you asked. I was afraid, but I did it! Have I pleased you?"

"What?" He looked at her and she realized to her dismay that he hadn't heard a word she'd said.

"Beloved one—"

"Ah, stop prattling! I've better things to do than listen to you."

"But—"

"I said, *be silent!*" His voice cut across her plea like a whiplash, and as she reached bewilderedly out to him, he

236

struck her aside with his free hand. She wailed—an ugly but piteous sound—and flailed upright once more. Four hands stretched toward him imploringly.

"Beloved one, what is wrong? What have I done?"

"Done?" Narid-na-Gost looked up from his scrutiny of the stone. He seemed surprised. "You've done what you were told. Isn't that enough?"

"But you promised me . . ." Then she paused. What had he promised her? There had been so many sweet words and so many sad words, and yet . . . What *had* he promised?

"My gift!" She remembered, and her mind latched instantly on to it. "You said I should have my gift! Dear one, I thought—"

He didn't let her finish, but sighed sharply and angrily. "Ah, that. Very well, have your gift. And much joy may it bring you."

He had brought the lovely, shimmering thing: the token, she believed, of his love; and he tossed it carelessly toward her. Taken unawares, she grabbed for it but missed, and her precious prize shattered to a thousand pieces on the rock. She moaned, her head swaying from side to side, and scrabbled after the fragments, trying fruitlessly to gather them together, as though she could mend them and make her treasure whole again.

"Gods!" Narid-na-Gost watched her efforts contemptuously. "A creature so stupid that it hasn't even the wit to catch a crumb when I throw it from my table!"

Her head jerked up. What did he mean? Misery and fear blossomed in her eyes, and the demon sneered.

"Yes, *you*, you misshapen cretin!" He had no need to hurt her and he knew it, but his pent fury and driving resentment at having had to demean himself and consort with such a low thing to achieve his ends were clamoring for an outlet, and he wasn't about to stem them for the sake of sparing her finer feelings. "You've had all from me that you'll ever wheedle, you daughter of slime. No, don't dare to come near me!" as she started to grovel across the floor toward him. "You have the *temerity* to try to touch me? You're nothing! Do you understand? *Nothing!*"

She moaned again and clawed at her own face with

two hands, while two more stretched toward him in supplication. "No, beloved lord! I am yours, *yours!* You want me —you said that—you *love* me! I'm not unworthy! I have been good, I have been brave—oh, dearest master, I love you!"

Narid-na-Gost stepped back and stared down at her with eyes like cold, dead fires.

"You," he said with icy deliberation, "know nothing of love and deserve nothing of love, for you are less than a worm. No intelligent being could ever love you. What have you to offer? Your ugliness? Your stupidity? Your hideous voice?" He smiled cruelly. "You are offal, my sweeting, and you're not fit to lick filth from my path. Crawl back to your dismal hole and do your pointless duty. Sing your dreadful songs and play with your toys. You have completed the one and only worthwhile act of your life: be content with that!"

And before her stunned, tear-blurred, and pitifully uncomprehending gaze, he turned his back on her and strode away from the cave for the last time.

She didn't cry out. She didn't wail or shriek or howl, she didn't move so much as a muscle. The grief inside her was too huge for any reaction to break free; it froze her and held her both physically and mentally motionless. She might have been nothing more than a grotesque carving on the cavern floor, and there she stayed, with only the gloom and the silence and the cage of her own inexpressible misery for company.

By the time he reached the brighter, cleaner air outside the cavern, Narid-na-Gost had utterly forgotten the pitiful creature he had discarded and left behind. The land hereabouts was wreathed now in mist shot through with a spectrum of pastel colors; somewhere overhead he heard the beat of huge wings, but otherwise all was quiet. Well and good. With none to see him depart, it would be a while before his absence was noticed.

He calculated that on the White Isle it was almost midnight now. A special and precious midnight, for the new day would dawn on the twenty-first anniversary of Ygorla's birth. By any account, this was a milestone in a human life, but for Ygorla—though she didn't yet know it —its significance was to be far greater than anything in the sphere of mortal experience.

Narid-na-Gost looked down at the jewel in his hands. This was their safeguard, their ransom, the key that would open the door onto their new world and their new power. A gift fit for a Margravine of Margravines, for a queen among demons. It was time for the gift to be given and for the celebration to begin.

At a gesture, the shimmering supernatural door appeared in midair before him. He touched the latch, the door swung silently open, and he stepped up onto the threshold between Chaos and the mortal realm. Balanced between worlds, Narid-na-Gost turned his face up to the occluded sky one last time, and smiled a cruel, secretive smile.

"I bid you all farewell," he said softly. "At least, for a while."

The door swung shut behind him and faded into the mist.

A vast gold river tumbled and crashed through a canyon walled by titanic crags, its noise echoing shatteringly from the peaks. Huge creatures, momentary creations of the random energies of Chaos, leapt and played in the current, their forms changing and changing with every moment as they were swept downstream. Overhead the sky pulsed sulfurous yellow, as though reflecting the river's molten brilliance, and high above the crags on a blinding horizon, the seven giant incandescent prisms that signified the presence of the Chaos lords in their realm turned unceasingly in slow, stately majesty.

The first warning that something was awry came in the form of a short-lived but violent fluctuation, a pulse of unstable energy from the sky that set crosscurrents shouting in the river and shook the peaks in an ominous answering rumble. The scene darkened momentarily, then settled. But the hiatus didn't last. Something was wrong with one of the prisms. Its steady rhythm was faltering as though some contradictory force had thrown it off kilter; its outline blurred, swelled, shrank, lost harmony with its fellows—

A colossal flash of blue light ripped through the dimension, hurling the canyon and the tumbling river into ghastly negative, and a sound that had never been heard in the realm of Chaos erupted from the heavens. Screaming, bellowing, drowning all other sound, it was the voice of pain and shock and rage incarnate, roaring out over the gargantuan landscape. The crags howled in response; chunks of rock split from the canyon faces and smashed down into the river, hurling spray hundreds of feet into the air and scattering the water beasts into new and hideous metamorphoses. The ground humped, rising like an awakening monster, and a network of fissures ripped through the cliffs, tearing them apart and hurling the river onto a new course that sent torrents flooding over the land and sweeping away everything in their path. Appalling colors began to wheel across the heavens—then black lightning cracked the sky and thunder roared through the Chaos realm as a gargantuan supernatural storm, the monstrous progenitor of the Warps that scourged the world of mortals, exploded into being. The tortured land shrieked and roiled, the river and the peaks melted and collapsed into a single mad tide that crawled with striations of spitting, flickering light. And above the mayhem, grim ghosts in the torn and raging sky, six titanic prisms turned in their dark, pulsing, inexorable rhythm, where before there had been seven.

17

The force hit Karuth like a sledgehammer and brought her shrieking out of her dreams with a gigantic spasm that flung her from her bed and onto the floor. Arms flailing, she rolled like a madwoman in the throes of a fit, completely out of control as dream and reality collided headlong and hurled her mind and body into chaos. A table crashed over, a rug skidded under her, propelling her forward—and she fetched up hard against the stone wall under her window with her teeth clamped on her tongue and breath rattling into her lungs in a violent gasp.

Light. There wasn't any light, she couldn't *see*, she had to have *light*. She was whimpering with fear and didn't know why, but she couldn't make the awful sound stop. Blood ran down her chin from her bitten tongue; she groped for the window ledge, found it, dragged herself to her knees, and beat feebly at the curtains, trying to force them apart so that moonlight—*light, blessed light!*— could stream into the room. At last the heavy draperies parted a fraction and a chilly silver-gray shaft speared across Karuth's face. Her whimpering disintegrated into a groan of relief and thankfulness, and as the groan died away into silence, reason began to take over from panic.

A nightmare. Surely that was all it could have been. Just a very, very bad dream which she couldn't now recall. Her knees and elbows were grazed from her wild flailing across the floor, and she licked blood from her lower lip, wincing as her tongue throbbed with the pain her teeth had inflicted. Gods, but it must have been a monstrous dream to have caused such a reaction, and for a moment which set her heart lurching, she wondered if she truly was awake or if this was another level of the nightmare. The sill under her hands felt solid enough, and the room, dimly lit now by the second moon, looked normal and in proportion. But at the same time she felt . . . unnatural. That was the only word she could find for the sensation. Unnatural. As though she were still in the throes of sleep and at any moment this reality would twist into something mad and uncontrollable, and plunge her into the depths of a new and worse nightmare.

She hauled herself to her feet and pushed the curtains fully back. Part of her didn't want to look out at the courtyard, fearing that she might see something which would confirm her doubts, and she had to force herself to gaze through the glass, down to the empty vista of unlit windows and rustling creeper and the dry, silent central fountain. There was nothing untoward, only the familiar sight of the sleeping castle. But still something felt *wrong*.

Hugging herself, Karuth turned to face her bedroom door. She felt an overwhelming urge to run from the room —but to where? What was it that called to her? A summoning, or a warning to flee? That thought sent a shot of discomfort through her nerves and she was halfway to the door before she was consciously aware of it—then stopped. *No*, she told herself sternly. *This is ridiculous! You're a high adept and a skilled sorceress, not a novitiate first-ranker frightened of a shadow in the night!* But reason wasn't enough of a weapon. She had to get out of this room. She *had* to.

Snatching up her woolen robe from where she'd draped it over the bed foot, Karuth flung the door open and strode out into the passage. The last torches had been extinguished and the corridor was a black maw opening onto the unknown. She didn't fear the dark, but she did fear something else, something to which she couldn't yet give a name or an identity. The castle seemed to breathe in its sleep like an old but powerful animal which it might be better not to disturb. She took a tentative step beyond the door—then bit her tongue again to stop herself from screaming as light flared out of nowhere to her left.

"Karuth!" A figure with a white, shocked face, made

more ghastly by the unsteady glow from the single candle he carried, emerged wide-eyed from the side passage, and Calvi Alacar let out a sigh of relief that set the small flame guttering. "Sweet gods, I thought my last mortal moment had come!"

They stared at each other, both feeling a little foolish, neither willing to be first to confess their reasons for prowling the castle at such an hour. The calling sensation was still tugging at Karuth's mind, and now it was starting to take shape, but she ignored it.

"Calvi . . . you're abroad late." A fatuous and obvious statement, but in the throes of relief, she could think of nothing better.

"Yes." She thought Calvi reddened, though it was hard to tell in the gloom. "I . . ." Suddenly his bravado crumbled. "Oh, Karuth, I had such a *nightmare!* I thought I must have roused the entire castle with the yell I let out when I woke!" He hesitated, then shrugged helplessly. "I had to find someone. I couldn't stay there alone, I just *couldn't.* I'm so sorry. I didn't mean to wake you."

Karuth shook her head. "You didn't wake me, Calvi. I had a nightmare too. Or at least I think I did." Again the sense of being called set ice-cold claws into her. This time she couldn't banish it, and it was accompanied by a darker imperative. *Something is wrong.*

"Something's wrong." Calvi's words, so closely echoing her thought, shocked her, and her face showed her dismay. The young man nodded. "I know it, Karuth. The gods alone know why I do. I'm no psychic, but I can feel it like a disease in my bones."

"Yes," she said. "I feel it too." And abruptly she understood the imperative, understood what she had to do, and the words came out before she could stop them. "It's in the Marble Hall."

"*Aeoris!*" Calvi's eyes widened and he made the sign of the fourteen gods with his free hand. "That was my dream! You've brought it back! I knew that something was wrong in the Marble Hall but I couldn't enter it because I'm not an adept, and so I was running through the castle trying to find someone to help me, and there was no one. Then suddenly I knew that something was following me,

243

and I turned round, and—" He stopped abruptly and shivered. "I don't want to remember that. It was too real."

Karuth needed no more confirmation. Swiftly she thrust her arms into the sleeves of her robe and belted it around her. When she spoke, her voice was terse and authoritative.

"I'm going to investigate. You'd best go back to your room, Calvi. There's no danger here; you'll be quite safe."

"No, Karuth. I'm coming with you."

"You can't. As you just pointed out, the Marble Hall is closed to all but the higher adepts. Obey me and go to your room. *Please.*"

"No." His tone was suddenly reminiscent of his brother the High Margrave, and it startled her. "I'm not the child I used to be," he said. "And—with all due respect —I'm not under your tutelage. If you mean to find out what's afoot, then I'm coming with you, and I honestly don't see any way in which you can stop me."

In a purely pragmatic sense he was wrong: Karuth could have stopped him, for she knew a sorcerous trick or two that would send him running back to hide behind a locked door until morning. But to resort to such methods would waste time and energy. Besides, she had no right to do it—and she had to admit, if only to herself, that she would be thankful for his company.

"Very well," she said. "I won't argue with you. But you may come only as far as the library. I can't break the Circle's rules."

He nodded quickly, "I understand."

Shadows jerked and loomed among the banisters as they made their way down the main staircase, and by unspoken agreement they both kept close within the small circle of candlelight as they crossed the flagged floor and eased the great castle door open. Cold air and cold moonlight flooded in together as the door creaked back on its vast hinges; outside, the courtyard was a mosaic of black and silver.

"Can you hear the sea?" Calvi's voice was an uneasy whisper as they started down the stone steps.

"No." Karuth was irrationally angry with him for drawing her attention to the peculiar silence. She could count on the fingers of one hand the days in her lifetime when the roar of the tide below the castle stack had been inaudible, and didn't want to think of the possible portents. "There's no wind tonight, though, and it's a neap tide." A rational explanation, but it didn't quite ring true, and she thrust it forcibly from her mind. "Come on. Don't let the candle go out."

They moved like ghosts along the colonnaded walk to the library door. As Calvi pulled the door open, Karuth's nostrils caught the scent wafting from below, of dust and mildew and old parchment. She'd always liked that odd but comfortingly familiar smell. Tonight, though, something within her recoiled at it.

"I'll go first," Calvi said.

"No." She mustn't let this ridiculous, unfounded fear get the better of her. "I'll lead. Hold the candle high—and don't let it go out!"

Calvi forced an amusement into his voice that he didn't feel. "Don't worry, I heard you the first time."

They began to descend the spiral staircase. Cold struck up from the stone through Karuth's bare feet; once her toes touched something small that scuttled out of the way, and her stomach turned over. She sucked in a sharp breath of the stale air, continued on. It was so *quiet*. Quiet as a tomb, and that wasn't normal, for down here among the castle's foundations the sound of the sea usually echoed and rang up from the caves at the stack's foot. Tonight, though, as in the courtyard, there was nothing.

At last the unstable glimmer of Calvi's candle illuminated the dim outlines of a door ahead of them. They hastened down the last few steps and Karuth pushed the door open to reveal the castle library.

Calvi slowly let out a pent breath. "There are some brands in the sconces. Shall I light a few?"

"Yes, do that." Karuth felt a fool for being unnerved by the darkness, but primal disquiet had a hold on her and light would help to keep it at bay. Slowly the vaulted chamber lifted into quiet yellow illumination as Calvi touched the candle to three torches, and the atmosphere also seemed to lighten a little as the shadows retreated.

Karuth looked toward the ancient, unassuming door, barely visible behind its shield of bookshelves, that led to the Marble Hall. As though the physical contact were some form of talisman, she reached out and touched Calvi's hand.

"Wait for me here," she said. "I hope I won't be long."

She expected—hoped, perhaps?—that he might argue that she should break the rules after all and let him go with her, but he didn't. Some laws were sacrosanct and Calvi knew the strength of the proscription that barred him from the Marble Hall. Whatever awaited her, Karuth must face it alone.

He stood by the open door, holding the candle high and watching her as she started along the narrow and peculiarly symmetrical passage that would bring her to the silver door. Cool light spilled toward her; as Calvi's feeble flame fell behind and the nacreous brightness strengthened, Karuth began to gain a little confidence. This was familiar territory, the adepts' inner sanctum. She had nothing to fear here.

Or had she? Tonight, had she?

She thrust the insidious thought away. She was an adept of the Circle. She had nothing to fear, she told herself again. There *was* nothing to fear, and she repeated the assertion in her mind like a litany as at last she approached the silver door and stopped before it. She reached out to touch the coldly glowing surface—and almost laughed aloud as she realized that one vital thing had entirely slipped her mind in the urgency of the moment. She had no key to the door. The one and only key was in Tirand's care, and without it no one could enter the Marble Hall. Fool, Karuth castigated herself, and she didn't know whether she was angry or desperately relieved. *Fool!*

Suppressing the self-deprecating mirth that was trying to overtake her, she pressed her hand against the door's surface to steady herself.

The lock clicked, and the door swung open.

The sound that escaped from Karuth's throat was

sharp, ugly, and abruptly truncated as shock hit her. This wasn't possible. But vision didn't lie: the door, securely locked by the High Initiate, untouched since the last performance of a Higher Rite, had defied logic and opened the way to her.

"Sweet gods . . ." Karuth's hands started to shake as instinct swept logic aside, and her soft words were as much a plea for protection as for enlightenment. The door stood wide now, revealing the hall's interior, and she could see that the pastel mists shifting among the pillars were twisting into distorted patterns, as though a gusting wind had strayed in and was agitating them. She thought, though she tried to tell herself it was imagination, that she could hear distant ethereal and alien voices whispering in troubled tones.

She couldn't stand here on the threshold like a mouse afraid of a prowling cat. She had to decide—go in, or admit herself a coward and return to the library and Calvi's comforting presence. Resolutely Karuth reminded herself that as an adept of the Circle it was her duty to see this through. If a sign was coming from the realm of the gods, then she, as their servant, must be ready and willing to receive it.

She closed her eyes and ran through a swift but effective mental exercise to calm her racing nerves. Then, making the splay-fingered sign of reverence, she forced herself to walk forward into the hall. The mists enfolded her and the pillars swam into focus all around her like the trunks of a petrified forest; she half-expected to hear the sound of the door shutting of its own accord at her back, but it didn't move. There was a faintly acrid taste to the air, which she recognized but couldn't place at first, until she recalled the experiments with elemental forces which she sometimes conducted in the privacy of her chambers. This was akin to the atmosphere that often followed those rituals, a sense that something had been and gone and had left its mark. But she detected no such forces here, and the whispering, whatever its source, was not the whispering of elementals.

Now she could dimly make out the seven statues of the gods looming through the mist ahead. No detail was discernible; as yet, they were merely dark, blurred outlines

breaking the random patterns of color, and she averted
her eyes from them, aware of how easily in her present
state she could start to imagine that the statues weren't
inert blocks of stone but living things, ready at any moment to move their carved limbs and step down from their
pedestals. Her gaze roamed over the complex mosaic of
the floor; without knowing why, she was searching for the
black circular design that as far as anyone knew marked
the Marble Hall's precise center. At last she saw it, standing out in stark contrast to the delicate patterns of its
surroundings, and she quickened her steps toward it.

Then stopped.

Something's wrong. The words came back into her
head with shocking suddenness, and this time they weren't
speculation but utter certainty. The mosaic circle—it was
far too black, it didn't look like marble at all, but like a
gaping vortex of nothing, a mouth opening into another
dimension. It was drawing her eyes, disorienting her, and
she swayed back dizzily as her sense of perspective
warped.

Suddenly the agitated whispering swelled in her
mind, and through the jumble of sibilance she heard one
word, repeated over and over again in a mad litany—NO
NO NO NO NO NO . . .

Karuth gasped, looked up to where the seven statues
loomed out of the mist—and her gorge rose in shock and
disbelief.

The seven statues stood in their places, towering
above her head. But while the faces of the seven lords of
Order were as serene and remote as ever, the carved features of Yandros and five of his brothers had changed.
Their mouths were open, drawn back in a terrible rictus
that stretched and twisted each countenance; their eyes
were wild and mad. Silently, captured in an eternal frozen
moment, the statues of the Chaos gods were screaming.

And on one carved figure, a grotesque and grisly contrast to the impassive face of its counterpart in the realm of
Order, the face of the seventh lord of Chaos had shattered,
leaving nothing but a jagged stump of broken stone.

Calvi had withdrawn from the doorway, but it made little difference, and now he couldn't pretend to himself any longer. He was frightened. Foolish, stupid: the library was one of his most frequent haunts and he'd spent more hours than he cared to count here among the books and parchments. However, those visits had been under happier circumstances, and even with three torches ablaze, there was a vast gulf between being in this shadowed vault in the cheerful company of his peers and waiting alone in the dead of night while Karuth pursued her solitary mission to the Marble Hall.

He wondered how long she had been gone. The passage of time was subjective; a minute or an hour might have passed since he'd watched her walk away along the dimly glowing corridor. Calvi wondered if he should run back up the stairs to see how far the second moon had progressed across the sky, but dismissed the idea. Not yet. It couldn't be more than a matter of minutes since she had gone. Better to wait: she'd return soon enough. It was too early to start worrying.

His gaze roamed the library shelves in search of something to occupy his mind and drive out unhealthy speculations. The books and manuscripts looked too intimidating; he knew he wouldn't be able to concentrate on reading, and instead began to pace the floor, adjusting his steps to the rhythm of a fatuous little tune he'd heard at the last Quarter-Day celebrations. Some group of itinerant players had come to try their luck at the castle, and Tirand, in an unusually expansive mood, had hired them to put on a short performance in honor of the dawning summer. He couldn't remember the words of the song, but the melody had lodged in some recess of his brain and he dredged it up now in an effort to distract himself. But even that didn't work—it was, he recalled, a drinking song, and it only served to remind him that he'd feel a good deal happier with something to drink, preferably something very strong. Or better still, some human company.

As the heartfelt thought took form, he heard a footstep on the stairs beyond the library door.

Calvi's stomach rebelled violently at the shock, and

for one awful moment he thought he might vomit with sheer fright. He'd merely *thought* the words, and—

The wild, rising panic was abruptly curtailed as a familiar voice called from the stairwell.

"Who's there? Who is it?"

"Tirand?" Calvi's own voice cracked and squeaked on the second syllable as tension rushed from him. "Tirand, it's me, Calvi!"

The door opened and the High Initiate, in crumpled clothes and with his hair uncombed, stood on the threshold. "*Calvi?* What in the name of Aeoris are you doing here?"

Calvi fought down an irrational urge to start laughing, and put the back of one hand to his mouth to quell the spasm. "I could ask you the same, Tirand! I woke after a nightmare, and I felt a compulsion—"

"A compulsion?" Tirand frowned quickly, and the frown, together with an abrupt change in his tone, made Calvi realize what he was implying.

"Gods," he said. "You too?"

Tirand's gaze raked the library. "Yes," he replied tersely. "And I don't think we're the only ones. I've been looking for Karuth. She isn't in her room."

"No. She's here, Tirand. I came with her, but this was as far as she'd permit me to go." He nodded toward the small black door. "She's in the Marble Hall now. She said that was the center of it. Whatever it is."

The High Initiate's frown deepened. "How long has she been there?"

"I don't know." Calvi shrugged helplessly. "It seems like an age, but you know how time can deceive you when you're waiting. Probably no more than a few minutes."

"I'd better follow her." Tirand started toward the door, then paused. "I'd go back to bed if I were you. There's nothing you can do here."

The young man forced a pallid smile. "I'll wait, Tirand. I'd rather, if it's all the same to you."

He thought for a moment that Tirand might object, but the High Initiate only shrugged. "As you wish."

He ducked under the door's low lintel and started along the dimly glowing passage. Calvi hovered, hand on the latch, watching after him, and Tirand made a mental note to thank the young man later. Good of him to escort Karuth here, though he wondered why Calvi of all the unlikely people should have been affected by whatever was in the wind tonight. Karuth and he were one matter, but Calvi? It didn't make sense.

The passage curved around ahead of him, the light from the silver door reflecting at an angle on the wall. Tirand had almost reached the curve when a shadow dipped across the light—and an instant later Karuth, her robe hitched up around her knees and all dignity abandoned, ran around the curve and cannoned into him.

"Karuth!" They both reeled back against the corridor wall, and Tirand caught hold of his sister's arms. "Karuth, what is it? What's happened?"

"Tirand?" Karuth's eyes were wide and wild and for a moment she looked utterly bewildered. Then, like a shutter opening on a dark room, recognition and lucidity returned. "Oh, thank the gods! Quickly—come with me! You've got to see it, you've got to see for yourself!"

She took hold of his hands, and before he could protest, started to pull him toward the Marble Hall. He had no chance to voice the questions that roiled through his mind, and her feverish urgency was lighting an answering spark in his own mind, though he couldn't even begin to guess at the reason for her agitation. They ran into the hall and across the floor. Karuth swerved to avoid the black mosaic, then slid to a halt before the seven great statues.

"There!" Her voice rang harshly through the hall and set echoes clashing among the pillars. *"Look!"*

Tirand looked. There was a tense pause. Then:

"What am I supposed to be looking at?"

"Wh—" The word died unfinished in Karuth's throat as she saw for herself.

The carved figures loomed huge and silent in the slowly shifting mist. Yandros was smiling his knowing private smile, while his brothers—all six of his brothers— gazed serenely into the shimmering mist. The statues were unchanged and unscathed.

Tirand turned to face his sister.

"Karuth, what's this all about?" His voice was gently puzzled.

She swallowed. Her throat seemed to have closed, and she couldn't tear her gaze from the statues. This was impossible. She'd seen the changes. She'd *seen* them, and they'd sent her fleeing from the hall, running to find Tirand and the other adepts.

"They were screaming . . ." Her voice sounded as though it belonged to someone twice her age.

Tirand frowned. "*Screaming?* Karuth, what in Aeoris's name do you mean?"

She drew two deep breaths to calm herself, and told him. Tirand listened in silence to the terse account, and as she finished, Karuth saw his gaze shift from her face to the floor. His expression was taut and wary.

"Karuth." She knew the tone; it combined sweet reason with utter implacability. "You were dreaming. You must have been."

"*Dreaming?* You mean I met Calvi and came down to the library and then on to the Marble Hall, all in my *sleep?*"

"No, of course I don't mean that. But it's the middle of the night, your mind isn't likely to be at its clearest. You might have slipped between dream and reality without realizing it after you came in here—"

Karuth shook her head emphatically. "I was fully awake, Tirand. I'm in no doubt about it."

He raised both hands in a placatory gesture. "All right, if you say so, I'm not about to argue the point. So there must be another explanation."

His uncertainty, which in her fevered state she took as skepticism and mistrust, made Karuth suddenly angry. "Of course there's another explanation!" she said sharply. "Dammit, Tirand, I'm not blind, I know what I saw! Those statues were *tormented!* Something's happened—something terrible, something we don't yet comprehend—"

Tirand interrupted, swinging around to face her. "You can't say that with any certainty! Where's the evidence now? Where are the signs now? There's nothing amiss here!" He swung one arm to indicate the entire hall. "Do you feel any astral disturbance? Do you feel anything out of kilter? Because I don't."

"But I *did!*"

"That isn't good enough, Karuth. It isn't enough to convince me that you weren't either dreaming or hallucinating."

An indrawn breath hissed violently between Karuth's teeth. "Are you calling me a liar?"

"No, of course not! For the gods' sakes, be rational! I'm not questioning what you *thought* you saw, I'm merely saying that it must have been some form of illusion!"

"*Gods!*" Karuth exploded. "You *fool!* What form would you *expect* a sign from the gods to take?"

Tirand shook his head, his expression weary. "Karuth, an illusion isn't necessarily a sign from the gods. You're a fifth-rank adept; you of all people must surely acknowledge that we can't assume every momentary aberration to have some deeper significance. As High Initiate it's my duty to keep some sense of proportion—"

"Oh, your *duty*." Karuth spat the words; then rage rose again and she couldn't check it. "Your duty is to the gods—*all* the gods, not just Aeoris and his weakling brothers!" And she stopped, appalled, as she realized what she had said.

For a few moments there was dead silence. Then, very quietly, Tirand spoke.

"Karuth. I don't believe that you're wholly in control of yourself and so I'll overlook that blasphemy and the fact that it was uttered in this sacred place. But I'll hear no more. You're tired and you're overwrought; go back to the castle and go to bed. If there's anything more to say, it'll be said in the morning."

She couldn't answer him. If she allowed herself to speak, she'd say something that she might regret for the rest of her life. She flung a last look at the statues, then turned on her heel and walked toward the door. Fury and bitterness were clawing at her with their talons, and bleakly she realized that at this moment she despised Tirand almost to the point of hating him. He was so blind, so pompous and stiff-necked—gods, she thought, couldn't he *see?* Didn't he *feel* something hideously wrong? What manner of High Initiate had he become, to stand by and allow his adept's skills to drown in the pettifogging obsessions of form and propriety? What had happened to the brother she loved and admired?

She heard footsteps behind her as she approached the silver door, and Tirand called her name. There might have been a conciliatory, almost pleading note in his voice, but she didn't pause to analyze it. In her present mood she didn't want to know what he thought or felt, for she didn't care. On the door's threshold she paused and looked back, and her eyes were stone-hard.

"Years ago," she said. "you told me that you didn't consider yourself as fit for the role of High Initiate as I could have been had the honor been open to me." A pause; she could see Tirand dimly in the mist, and he was hesitating. Part of her didn't want to say it, but another, darker part goaded her, and the words came, bitter and savage. "I'm beginning to think that perhaps you were right."

She strode away along the softly shining corridor.

Calvi sprang up from his chair at one of the library tables as Karuth appeared in the doorway. "Karuth!" Relief and concern mingled in his tone. "Are you all right? What happened?"

"I'm well and fine." She brushed past him, not meeting his eyes, and headed for the stairs. Calvi started after her, but before he could follow, Tirand appeared.

"Ah. Calvi." The High Initiate's face was flushed and he clipped his words as though he were exerting tremendous self-control. "We're all returning to the castle. There's nothing to worry about."

"What about—"

"*Will you stop asking questions!*" Then Tirand got a grip on himself. "I'm sorry." He turned and pulled the black door shut, then began methodically to extinguish the torches. "I'm overtired: forgive me. Nothing's amiss."

Calvi picked up his candle and allowed himself to be shepherded toward the stairs. "Karuth looked—" he began.

"Karuth's simply a little upset." An unconvincing smile curved Tirand's lips. "Probably her dream. Forget about it, Calvi. I assure you, there's nothing wrong."

Calvi wasn't satisfied, but he didn't have the confidence to press Tirand. Nor, he felt, would it be prudent at this moment to ask the High Initiate's opinion about his own nightmare and its possible implications, and so he stayed silent, though inwardly seething with questions, as they left the library and climbed the stairs. When they emerged into the courtyard, Karuth was nowhere to be seen, and Tirand led the way along the colonnaded walk and up the steps to the main door. As they entered, Calvi thought he heard faint footsteps on the landing at the top of the stairs; he glanced up quickly, but there was no one in sight.

"I'll say good night to you." Tirand turned to face Calvi, and the look in his eyes forestalled any comment the younger man might have made. Then, as though something hitherto suppressed had struggled to the surface despite himself, his expression relaxed a little and became, Calvi thought, almost sad. "There's no need to worry, Calvi, and no need to dwell on tonight's events. All's well."

With the candle guttering in his hand, Calvi watched the High Initiate walk away, not toward the stairs but in the direction of his study, and it seemed to him that Tirand's upright stance was a mask, a defense hiding something that he neither could nor wished to share. His assurances that all was well had been baldly and painfully obvious lies, but Calvi felt that perhaps the lies had been repeated as much for the High Initiate's own benefit as for his. Tirand looked careworn. More than that, he looked *old*. He might be only ten years Calvi's senior, but the gulf that separated them was far greater than mere physical years. They were worlds apart, Calvi thought. And with an insight that had never before been granted to him, he suddenly and deeply pitied Tirand.

18

Two winged horrors came for her, arrowing through the passage into her cave and falling upon her as she cowered in terror by the side of the well. The molten fire that scattered from their jaws burned her skin and made her scream, and her screams redoubled when, carried in talons that tore her flesh, swept at breakneck speed from her sanctuary, she and her captors burst into the blinding light of the outside, alien world.

They carried her high into a sky that roared and spat lightning of a hundred livid colors. Buffeted by gales, seared by the howling elements, incapable of understanding what was happening to her or why, she writhed helplessly in the grip of the two chimeras as they bore her implacably onward. And at last, cowed by the sheer magnitude of her terror and no longer able to struggle, she saw a wall of solid black rock looming ahead of her and towering a thousand feet above her head. Beyond the cliff face, hideous amid the mayhem of the shrieking storm and almost unraveling the last vestiges of her sanity, six monstrous, ghostly prisms turned slowly in the sky, pulsing with their own grim light.

The chimeras suddenly and violently changed trajectory, powering steeply upward as the cliff sped toward them at a terrifying velocity. Through eyes blurred by tears of fear and pain, she saw the black wall streaking past, seemingly mere inches from her face. Then they broke above it to soar high over the summit, and when she looked down, all hope died.

The great peak was truncated, forming a black, featureless plateau like a broken finger. On the plateau two figures were waiting. In all her simple subterranean life she had never seen them before this moment, but she knew them. Though she meant nothing to them, though she was so low as to have no significance in their titanic minds, she belonged utterly to them, for they and their brethren were her creators.

One figure slowly raised his head and looked up at the chimeras, which were now circling slowly. He had assumed the form and proportion of a human man, but even from this distance she felt the awful power that radiated from him, a power that spanned dimensions and made a mockery of mere physical stature. Eyes like burning white stars flared in his gaunt skull, and his long gold hair flowed and streamed in the gale. At his breast, as he raised one commanding hand to beckon the chimeras down, she saw a deadly, pulsing light that hurled seven spears of brilliance out into the night. The seven-rayed star—the highest symbol of Chaos's absolute authority.

She started to plead incoherently, the words bubbling in her throat, and her limbs threshed feebly in a last effort to escape her captors. It would be better to fall, to plummet shrieking into the depths below and be shattered to a thousand fragments as the last precious and coveted gift from her treacherous lord had been shattered, than to suffer this horror and the fate it would surely bring. But she could do nothing. Gently now, horribly gently, the chimeras were spiraling downward. Then the talons suddenly released their hold and she dropped like a stone onto the plateau's surface as her tormentors beat their great wings and sheered away into the darkness.

She couldn't move. She had struck the ground with tremendous force, and agony consumed her as she lay with her broken face pressed against the rock. Four of her hands groped feebly at nothing; the other two were twisted and crushed beneath her body. A great rushing dinned in her ears like the pulse of a ghastly heart, and pale thin fluid trickled from the corners of her eyes.

She felt the presence before her. It compelled her, breaking down her terror and tossing it aside, reaching through consciousness into the most fundamental depths of her being. Battered and bleeding and hurting though she was, she could only obey the compulsion to raise her damaged head, inch by painful inch, and look up.

They were gazing down on her, and as Yandros's eyes changed from white to gold to green and finally to utter black, she saw wrath and loathing and a thirst—a vast, unslakable thirst—for vengeance. Beside him the second figure, his eyes like dark, deadly emeralds and his hair as black as the smoke of a funeral pyre, watched with a dispassion that to her seemed as dreadful as Yandros's rage. She opened her mouth and tried to make a sound, but no sound would come. She was dumb, hope was cold ashes inside her, and in her mind she repeated over and over again a piteous, futile, but desperate mental plea. *Beloved one, don't forsake me now! Come back! Help me! Please, oh, please . . .*

The thought shattered as Yandros raised his graceful hand once more. A long finger pointed at her, sending a racking spasm through her body and firing the agony afresh. And the greatest Chaos lord spoke in a voice sibilant with all the pent power of the storm raging overhead.

"Traitorous spawn, what have you done?"

———————⟩ ⟨————————

The earthly thunderstorm began with a colossal lightning-flash that hurled the volcano's peak into blinding brilliance and with a clap of thunder that seemed to shake the White Isle to its foundations. From her vantage point on the ledge overlooking the crater bowl, Ygorla felt the surge of anticipation that made her want to challenge the storm's racket with a scream of sheer joy. This was the day. She had known it, she had longed for it, she had waited for it with all the self-control her formidable mind could muster. Now at last the dawn was coming and the herald was sounding its blast. Her birth anniversary, seven times three. The moment of greatest significance since the night she had been brought from her dead mother's womb far away in that grim castle on the Star Peninsula. She had come of age. And her emergence from the chrysalis of adolescence into full adulthood would place the world at her feet!

She heard the first hiss of the downpour and sprang upright, lifting her face to the circle of black sky high above her. A gigantic triple flash illuminated the bowl, and Ygorla laughed wildly as the thunder spoke its echoing answer. He was coming to her. She knew it, *knew* it. The long years of waiting were over, and this day she would claim her heritage.

Lightning and thunder bawled again, and on the crater floor where the broken remains of the old votive altar stood, a hot light began to glow like the fierce, disembodied eye of a furnace. She held her breath, staring fixedly through the rain and struggling to contain her excitement as the door between this world and the world of Chaos slowly took form and solidified within the light. She saw the latch lift, saw the door begin to swing open. Smiling with new and triumphant confidence, Narid-na-Gost stepped through the portal and entered the mortal realm.

"Father!" Her cry was shrill and all but lost as the thunder roared out once more, and she started to run down the steep path toward him. The demon saw her and a long-nailed hand shot out in a violent, repelling gesture.

"Wait, daughter! Stay back!"

Nonplussed, Ygorla slithered to a halt on rock already slippery from the rain. The demon swung around and faced the door again, then raised both arms and spoke an alien word that, though she didn't comprehend it, sent a shaft of violent excitement through her.

The furnace light and the gateway within it imploded. The flash was ten times more brilliant than the lightning; Ygorla was momentarily blinded, and reeled back with a shocked oath. When her vision cleared and she was able to look down to the bowl again, she saw that not the smallest trace of the portal remained. There was only the empty crater—and the still-smiling figure of her sire.

Narid-na-Gost looked up at her, and his eyes burned like live coals.

"It is done," he said. "The path between this world and Chaos is closed. I have come to you at last, daughter, and I shall not leave you again."

Ygorla stared back at him, then began to laugh. It was

259

a peal of delight, of triumph; laughing, she raced on down the path and over the crater floor, and flung herself into the demon's welcoming arms. Narid-na-Gost was laughing too, unhumanly, maniacally; he swung her around, kissed her fiercely, and finally released her so that she spun away and stopped, still gripping his hands at arm's length.

"My daughter." Suddenly all mirth vanished from his voice, though pleasure and a chilling pride still remained. "Ah, my own sweet daughter. I bring you felicitation on this happiest of days. And I bring you the gift that I promised you so many years ago." He smiled, a slow, feral curving of his lips. "I bring you the power that you have craved to wield since the night when you took your first faltering step into the mysteries of sorcery."

Ygorla's heart began to pound so hard that she thought the force of it might snap the bones of her rib cage, and her brilliant blue eyes took on an avid light. This day was what she had waited for through all the long frustrating years, and now that the moment approached, she could barely contain her excitement.

Narid-na-Gost, though, was savoring his pleasure and not about to be hurried. "Do you remember that night, Ygorla?" he asked softly. "Do you remember how you felt when the stone column burned at your command? Do you remember the flames of Chaos that obeyed your will?"

She did, just as she remembered the screaming women and the panicking men. Remembered, too, the last appalled look on the face of her great-aunt the old Matriarch, in the moment before the Chaos fire incinerated her. She began to smile a smile that matched the demon's own.

"You have come a long, long way since that time," Narid-na-Gost continued, ignoring another deafening bawl of thunder. "Such minor sorceries are child's play to you now. But the hunger is still there, isn't it? The hunger for power. For more of it, and more—as much as your soul can contain."

"Yes!" she breathed. "Oh, yes!"

"Then, my demon daughter, you shall have that power. Or rather, *we* shall have it. For I, too, have my ambitions. While you shall come to greatness in the world of mortals, I mean to take power of another kind in an-other realm."

He began to pace across the crater floor, and above the hunched and deformed shoulders his face turned up to stare balefully at the sky. Lightning flashed, scouring his features into stark relief, and when he spoke again, his voice was laced with sweet venom.

"There is a storm of another kind in Chaos today," he said. "And that storm is only just beginning. A new age is about to dawn, Ygorla, for the gods as well as for human-kind."

Ygorla watched him with feverish eyes. She didn't comprehend his meaning, yet she felt an answering surge of eagerness in her own soul.

"My masters," Narid-na-Gost continued at last, sav-agely, "have grown complacent. They have forgotten their purpose and forgotten the heritage that once gave them the will and the strength to break Order's grip on the mortal world. Since Aeoris and his anemic minions were overthrown, there has been peace." His face grew ugly with contempt. *"Peace!* Where is the pleasure for Chaos in that? Where is the glory, where is the pandemonium, where is the *terror* that Chaos once commanded? Yandros has failed us! He stands by, content to let balance prevail and to allow men to worship or not as they choose—and by that he has proved himself a weakling and a fool!"

Ygorla looked uneasily up to the sky. Did the gods hear such blasphemy? Surely, if they did, then—

"There will be no reprisal." Narid-na-Gost swung around sharply to face her, and she realized that he had read the fearful thought in her mind. His eyes were angry, but there was a ferocious smile on his lips. "There *can* be no reprisal, Ygorla, not now, for you and I are beyond Yandros's reach and he cannot control or threaten us." He paused. "The time for secrecy is over. We are about to reveal ourselves to an unsuspecting world, and we are about to embark on our ultimate purpose—to rule not only the realm of mortals but also the realm of Chaos!"

Ygorla's eyes widened, starting in their sockets. *"What?"*

The demon laughed softly. "Ah, so I surprise you.

Hadn't you guessed my true purpose, daughter? Hadn't you realized what my ultimate goal must be?"

She struggled to speak, but all she could muster was an incoherent denial. "I . . . I didn't . . . I thought . . ."

"You thought that my ambitions were earthly ones? Oh, no. I am not of mortal flesh, I am of *Chaos*. And though Yandros and his highborn kind might despise such as me, I am closer to the heart of true Chaos than they are. *True* Chaos is madness, Ygorla. It is the wild and glorious wielding of power for power's sake, for the sheer and magnificent joy of it! That is our heritage, the heritage that those who style themselves gods have abandoned and allowed to be forgotten. Now it is time for that neglect to be remedied. It is time for the full might of Chaos to rise once more and to take an iron grip on the world, as it should rightly have done at the time of Change."

He had begun to pace again: suddenly he stopped and turned, shaking a gnarled finger at Ygorla. "Yandros is no longer fit to rule Chaos! He has betrayed everything that Chaos stands for and he no longer deserves the power that he wields. It is time that he was cast down from the throne." He paused, sucked in breath. "*I* mean to be the one to take his place as Chaos's new lord!"

His words hit Ygorla like a hammer blow. She couldn't utter a sound; all she could do was stare at him, her jaw working, her body shaking as her brain took in the full meaning of what he had said.

"Ygorla." Narid-na-Gost darted to her side in one quick, fluid movement. "Ygorla, think of it. Think of what it could mean for us. You might be a Margravine of Margravines in this world, but what use would such mortal glory be to you if you were set about by the inane restrictions of a pallid and feeble human society?" He touched her face, caressing her, sending shudders through her spine. "You are my daughter, and your soul was born of Chaos. What would you have for your heritage? A Margravate exalted in nothing but name, with advisers to direct you and sages to confine you and arrogant mortals to call themselves your equals? Or *true* power—power with the entire might of Chaos at your back, to bring the world to your heel and to quaking obedience of your every desire?"

Oh, but it was such a vision! Such a vision of glory and of greatness, that dwarfed all mortal pretension—she could *see* it, see herself robed in majesty, feared and adored by an awestruck world, while her demon father ascended the throne of Chaos itself to channel its pandemonium through her and join with her in a reign of unassailable might that would span dimensions. She wanted it. She craved it with a ravenous, all-consuming hunger that smashed reason to shards.

But reason wouldn't entirely loose its hold, and suddenly it thrust its icy knife into her brain, splitting the vision apart.

"No!" she cried out in despair and swung around, covering her face with her hands, as her dream of dominion crumbled. "It isn't *possible!*"

"Ygorla—"

"It isn't, it *isn't!*" Tears blinded her as she turned on him again, torn between desperate appeal and furious railing. "Father, I want that power! I *want* it! But it's out of our reach!"

Narid-na-Gost's hand shot out and gripped her wrist. "No, daughter. It is in our hands."

She froze. Detachedly and amusedly, the demon thought that her face was a study in melodramatic shock. No matter; she was young yet and still tainted by human qualities. She would learn.

"I said," he repeated softly, "that it is in our hands." His fingers tightened on her wrist. "Be calm, and cast your mind back. Do you remember my telling you that I would bring you a pretty bauble to delight you?"

She frowned. "I remember. Surely, though—"

"Hush. The bauble I have brought is more than a plaything, Ygorla. It is a key. And with it we can unlock the door to everything we desire."

As Ygorla continued to stare at him, uncomprehending, he touched his free hand to his own breast. For a moment it seemed the movement was merely a gesture, but then Ygorla saw the dark, hard glitter of something in his closed fist. She drew in a sharply eager breath, not knowing what he held but sensing a sudden and acute change in the atmosphere.

The demon's hand uncurled and the gemstone was revealed. A soft sound that was part gasp and part sigh whispered from Ygorla's lips as she stared at it. It was beautiful; perhaps the most beautiful single object that she had ever seen. In this world few of its true Chaos-born hues were visible, but even so it seemed to refract and reflect a hundred different subtle shades of blue. And at its core, like a tiny heart, was a darkness that radiated power of an order beyond imagining.

She could barely tear her gaze away from the stone, but at last with a tremendous effort she looked up at Narid-na-Gost once more.

"What is it, Father? I've never seen anything so . . ." Her voice trailed off as words failed her, and she shook her head helplessly.

Narid-na-Gost smiled. "This," he said, "is the key to our goals, and our surety and safeguard against any who might attempt to stand in our way. Touch it, Ygorla. Feel something of its nature."

She reached forward. Her outstretched fingers made contact with the jewel, and for one stunning instant a vision flashed before her inner eye. Roiling darkness, a titanic storm that dwarfed any earthly cataclysm—and power—immense and immeasurable power.

Narid-na-Gost's crimson eyes met her gaze slyly. "The lords of Chaos have grown a little careless in the years since they snatched the reins of power from Aeoris. They still keep vigilant watch on the machinations of Order, but it has never once occurred to them to look over their shoulders at what might be afoot in their own realm." Briefly his fingers closed over the stone once more, gripping it tightly. "This is no mere bauble, Ygorla. I have stolen something from Yandros which he and his brothers value beyond price—for this pretty gem contains nothing less than the soul of a lord of Chaos!"

An extraordinary, inchoate sound broke from Ygorla's throat as every human part of her rebelled against this insane revelation. *The soul of a god*—no, it was mad, it was *crazed!*

Yet even as the terrified rejection surged in her, another inner voice rose up to clash with it like a powerful crosscurrent in a tide. She didn't know how such a thing could be possible, but a dreadful, unshakable instinct convinced her that Narid-na-Gost was speaking the truth.

But a god's soul—

The demon's voice cut across her turmoil. "There are many things that you still must learn to understand, my daughter. One is that Yandros and his brothers are neither omnipotent nor entirely indestructible. We of Chaos possess souls, though our souls are of a different order to those of mortals. And the souls of our erstwhile masters take the form of gems, which they have kept safe within an elaborate system of caverns at the heart of our realm." He paused, then chuckled. "Until now."

Ygorla was still too stunned to speak. She reached out toward the jewel, driven by a compulsion to touch it again; then her hand stayed inches from the shimmering thing as awe overcame desire.

"I hadn't dreamed it would be so easy," Narid-na-Gost said with soft satisfaction. "But the theft was as simple and as facile as taking the nipple from a newborn child; yet another sign of Yandros's decaying prudence. The stone had only a single guardian of an order so low as to be all but mindless, and one small piece of trickery was enough to snatch it from its sanctum and secure it. Now, Ygorla, we hold the life of a god at ransom!"

Ygorla had been so fascinated by the gem that she hadn't yet paused to consider its deeper implications. Now, though, she began to understand its true value to them.

"It would be the work of a moment to destroy this stone," the demon said. "Another little secret that our masters neglected to guard carefully enough. Just one word, and the gem would shatter and the soul within it be snuffed out. That is our safeguard against any attempts Yandros might make at retribution. He won't dare to intervene against us; the dangers are too great. While this gem remains in our possession, he is impotent, and we are free to stamp our mark upon this world and to make our plans for domination of Chaos itself!"

The vision that had struck such joy into Ygorla's heart was taking form once more. Might and glory, power and acclaim, life and death themselves slaves to her will. She had the means to achieve those things. Thanks to this crimson-eyed demon who had sired her and who, seven years ago, had returned to reveal his legacy to her, the future was in her grasp.

She couldn't express what she felt in words, but it was there in her eyes, a clear and fearsome message. Narid-na-Gost saw it and read it, and he smiled.

"Come, my sweet daughter." He took her hand. "It is time for you to leave this place at last."

The breaking dawn was as cold and miserable as Karuth's churning thoughts as she stared out across the sea from the giddying height of the castle's northernmost spire.

Inasmuch as she felt capable of being glad about anything at this moment, she was glad that she had forced herself to make the exhausting climb up the thousands of stairs that wound through the spire's core to this eyrie at the summit. Without something to challenge her mind and her body, her self-control might well have snapped in the wake of what had happened an hour ago. This self-imposed ordeal—and the climb *was* an ordeal, she believed that now even if she'd thought it an exaggeration before—had channeled the furious energy building like a storm within her, and now she was, at least, calm.

This cramped room, one of three at the top of the spire, was savagely cold and smelled strongly of damp. Probably no one had set foot in it for thirty years or more; looking about her, Karuth could see the detritus of old and forgotten times heaped everywhere and left to decay. Candle stubs, a tinderbox, a pile of books underneath the small worm-eaten table. Two glasses, one of them broken. A discarded piece of cloth, unrecognizable under layers of dust. Other days, other lives, reduced now to ghosts. Perhaps, she thought with uncharacteristic bitterness, she should move her own possessions into this bleak place and make it her sanctuary, for she was beginning to feel as anachronistic and out of place in the main body of the castle as any restless revenant from the past.

The interview with Tirand which had taken place as dawn broke had been one of the most painful moments of Karuth's life. Guessing, rightly, that she wouldn't be sleeping, in the light of earlier events, Tirand had sent a servant to her room with a message asking her to attend him in his study. The message's formal tone had hinted at what was to come, and when his sister walked into the study and sat down, the High Initiate wasted no time on pleasantries but said what he had to say bluntly and without embellishment.

Like Karuth, Tirand had had no thoughts of sleep, and after their acrimonious parting in the Marble Hall he had decided that certain steps must be taken without delay. He wanted, he said, only to be fair, and so he had done what any reasonable man would do in the circumstances. He had woken four of the senior adepts and they had all returned to the Marble Hall to perform a Higher Rite which would confirm or disprove Karuth's claim.

"We tested the astral planes, and we tested all levels of the ethers," he told her solemnly. "I have to inform you, Karuth, that we found nothing. No disturbance in the occult realms, higher or lower. No sign from the gods. Nothing that we could interpret, however tenuously, as corroboration of your experience." He looked up, his eyes wary and sad and a little—just a little—resentful. "So I have to say I can only conclude that your vision was a delusion."

"I see." Karuth stared at her hands, which were clenched tightly in her lap, then met his gaze challengingly. "Did you call me here now simply to tell me that?"

There was a pause. Then: "No," Tirand replied. "Not entirely. There is more."

She waited. He was clearly very uncomfortable but she didn't want to give ground by helping him. At last he spoke again.

"Karuth, I want your promise that you'll consider this matter closed."

It was what she had anticipated, and she had a ready answer. Quietly but firmly she said, "No, Tirand. I will not."

"Why not?"

"Because I *can't!* I've told you before, now it seems I must tell you again—what I saw was *not* a hallucination or delusion!"

Tirand ran his hands distractedly through his hair. "Karuth, you're wrong! Our ritual *proved* it—"

"It proved nothing other than that you and a few other adepts failed to see what I saw! Rituals aren't infallible, Tirand, and it's shortsighted and dangerous to rely on them to the degree that you do!"

"And far more dangerous to rely on a momentary psychism with no evidence to back it!" Tirand retorted angrily. "Gods, Karuth, what's the *matter* with you? This is utterly unreasonable—"

"It is *not!*" she shouted back. "Something has happened, and I was a witness to it!" She was on her feet now and turned away from him in sharp, angry frustration. "But my word isn't good enough, is it? The word of a high-ranking elemental sorceress who also happens to be one of the most sensitive psychics in the entire Circle—that isn't good enough!"

"It's not a question of your word, dammit! I'm not calling into question what you saw, only the circumstances under which you saw it."

"*Ohhh . . .*" She faced him again, staring down coldly. "Do you know, you're beginning to sound exactly like Father! All those years ago, do you remember, when the old Matriarch was killed and her ward disappeared? Father said just what you're saying now; close the book, forget about it, we've found nothing and so we'll do nothing."

"Father was right."

She stared at him, incredulous. "*Right?* Gods, you hypocrite! You've forgotten, have you, coming to my room after the meeting with Lias Barnack and the sisters from Southern Chaun and virtually begging me to conduct a private investigation on the elemental planes? Or is that memory just another of my delusions?"

Tirand flushed, angered by the fact that, until she reminded him of it, he had indeed forgotten that old incident. "That was a very different matter."

"Was it? Why?"

"Because at the time no Higher Rite had been performed. Father only closed the book later, after we'd conducted the proper rituals and found nothing untoward!"

"Oh, I *see*." Karuth began to pace like a caged lioness. "So the fact that the Matriarch of the Sisterhood had been burned to death by an unnatural fire, and that same fire had incinerated a pillar of solid stone, as well as apparently consuming all mortal traces of a fourteen-year-old girl, was nothing untoward?" She swung back toward him, her fists clenched. "That's exactly what I mean about the rituals, Tirand! They're *fallible!* Of *course* there was something afoot, but we couldn't find it. Now, exactly the same paradox has happened again!" She hesitated, then added in a defiant rush, "If you really want me to spell it out for you, I believe that there may be a connection!"

Those words, she knew now, had been her greatest mistake. Until that moment there had been a chance, slender, but a chance nonetheless, that she might persuade Tirand to reconsider his attitude. Instead she had raised an old ghost that no one besides herself wanted to remember, and in doing so she had finally damned her case in his eyes.

Tirand laid his palms flat on the table and stared at them. "Gods," he said hollowly. "Not *that* again."

Karuth made a desperate effort to redeem the situation. "Tirand, I'm not necessarily saying that—"

He interrupted her before she could finish. "I think you are, though. I think that's at the root of it all, isn't it, Karuth? Ria Morys's grandniece. Your favorite old mystery rearing its ugly head again." Suddenly one palm screwed into a fist and he thumped the tabletop. "I have had *enough* of that obsession, and I will hear no more!" He rose, his chair scraping back with a sound that set Karuth's teeth on edge, and his shoulders set in squared determination. "Karuth." His voice was clipped, harshly formal. "I will ask you again. Will you give me your pledge that you will consider this matter closed as of now?"

It had gone too far. She couldn't withdraw from this point, not unless she was willing to compromise herself and be untrue to her deepest convictions. And that was something Karuth could not do.

"No," she said. "I will not."

For perhaps half a minute there was a tense silence. Tirand stood motionless, staring down at the table, and Karuth felt a cold, unpleasant sensation in her stomach as she realized that almost for the first time she didn't know what he was thinking or how he would react. The revelation was a shock, and suddenly she felt adrift.

At last Tirand looked up.

"Very well." He spoke quietly. "You leave me no choice, Karuth, though it grieves me to do this. As High Initiate it is both my duty and my privilege to be the final arbiter in matters of Circle conduct and discipline. In that capacity, I must inform you that as of now I am placing an interdict on this matter."

Karuth drew in a sharp breath and her eyes narrowed. She hadn't expected this. "Officially?" she said.

"Officially." If Tirand noted the dangerous edge in her tone, he showed no sign of it. His gaze met hers. "I take no pleasure in it, but I also see no sensible alternative. No"— as she opened her mouth to protest—"there's nothing more to be said. The necessary document will be drawn up and witnessed this morning and will take immediate effect." He hesitated; then: "I'd be insulting both your rank and your intelligence if I elaborated any further."

That was true; yet at the same time Karuth felt a sense of insult far deeper than any protocol. She knew precisely what the interdict meant: from this moment all adepts of the Circle were expressly forbidden from any investigation of what had happened in the Marble Hall, even to the point of further discussion. Such drastic measures had always been the prerogative of the High Initiate alone, and the penalty for disobedience was the prospect of a full disciplinary hearing before the council. In one move Tirand had chained her, and she couldn't break the chains without jeopardizing her entire future as an adept.

She felt bile in her throat, the bile of anger and rejection and humiliation. He couldn't do such a thing to her— his own sister, his companion, his helpmeet—did loyalty count for nothing in his mind? Somewhere a worm of guilt was writhing, the knowledge that in all justice she couldn't lay the entire blame for this situation at his door, but her fury was too great now for the small voice of reason to be heard. It was then, seething with hurt and betrayal, that she abandoned self-control and said the words that should never have been spoken.

"Very well, brother." She all but spat the title at him. "I have no choice—unless, of course, I should choose to openly defy you and accept the consequences. Though if the Circle is as blind or as psychically inept as its leader seems to have become in these latter days, then perhaps defiance would be no bad thing."

Tirand stared at her, his cheeks flaming.

"Leave this room." His hands clenched and the muscles of his neck stood out like whipcord as he struggled to hold in his temper. "Damn you, *leave!* And don't *dare* to show your face near me again until you're ready to apologize!"

She smiled bitterly. "I think we'll both have a long wait." And she turned on her heel and walked out, slamming the door behind her.

Now, in the undisturbed sanctum of the spire, Karuth mentally relived those last few minutes of their encounter. She was beginning to regret her reckless words; they'd been needlessly cruel, even if—as she believed—there was a grain of truth in them. Knowing herself, she was aware that she would apologize to Tirand eventually, though the apology would have to wait until both their tempers had cooled a little. But the injunction was another question entirely, for where her conscience and her instinct clashed with the rules of the Circle, it simply wasn't in her nature to bend the knee. And in the matter of her vision in the Marble Hall, she knew in her bones that Tirand's judgment was fundamentally, dangerously wrong.

What she had seen had been no hallucination. Rationality might argue that the weight of evidence was against her, but Karuth didn't feel that rationality had much of a part to play in this situation. When she had stood by the central mosaic in the moment before she looked up and saw the seven statues, she had felt insane and terrible power rising in the hall, the sense that some monstrous force was threatening to bludgeon through to the mortal world with the mosaic as its focus. It had been like the sense of deep-rooted dread that often assailed her before the coming of a Warp, but worse, a thousand times worse. Savage, uncontrollable energy. *Chaotic* energy. And as the statues silently screamed, a huge voice had drummed in her head, that one word, NO, NO, NO . . .

A chill, malevolent breath of wind stole in through a broken windowpane and touched her with icy fingers. Out over the sea, a break in the cloud cover threw down a vicious spear of sunlight like a sword thrusting into the ocean. Karuth's unhappy thoughts suddenly crystallized like the light ray into a single sharply honed certainly. It was what her subconscious had been trying to tell her since she woke yelling from her nightmare and its power had called to her, impelled her to the Marble Hall, and set the true vision before her. It defied all reason—but she was certain now, and with certainty came cold, implacable fear.

Something more dreadful than anyone yet knew had happened in the Chaos realm. Though her groping mind couldn't even begin to grasp at its nature or its purpose, Karuth knew that it was inexorably linked with that other, older mystery that had haunted her for so many years. With the eerie wisdom of a dying man, Keridil Toln had known the truth, and though he had taken his knowledge to the grave, Karuth believed with all her heart that, whatever the Circle might dictate, it was vital that the insight which had been granted to the old High Initiate in his last hours should be sought and rediscovered. For now, more than twenty years after lurching into life, the nameless wheel that had been set in motion on the night of Ygorla Morys's birth was, like some dire and dark avatar, finally coming full turn.

19

Yandros looked down at the pathetic figure crumpled at his feet. And Tarod, turning his own smoldering green gaze to watch his brother, knew and shared the feelings behind the mask of his expressionless face.

"There's no point in it, Yandros." He spoke quietly. "To torture her wouldn't bring back what we have lost. She's told us all she can; she hasn't the wit to know anything more. Let her die now."

Yandros sighed. The soft sound quieted the storm that still raged overhead; a single fork of silver lightning flung itself through the heavens, but there was no thunder in its wake. The clouds, tatters now, were beginning to break up and flow away, leaving only silent bands of color turning like the spokes of a titanic wheel across the sky.

"Yes." Yandros nodded at last. His voice was desolate. "I have no quarrel with her. She is only what we made her; she meant no ill, she simply knew no better. The fault was ours, not hers."

Quite gently he held out a hand toward the broken, abject creature on the plateau floor. She was still conscious but her wrecked mind had passed beyond the point where she could even whimper, let alone beg for mercy and a release from torment. She existed, helpless, in a world of pain and terror that her soul couldn't bear.

"It will end now," Yandros said to her.

His fingers moved slightly. The form of the little demon shuddered, faded and vanished.

Yandros looked down for a few moments at the place

273

where she had lain, then hunched his shoulders and turned to stare over the shattered landscape.

"So," he said. "We know how the crime was perpetrated and who is responsible. Unhappily, that changes nothing; in fact, it makes matters worse. We're helpless, Tarod. We have been betrayed by one of our own kind and there's nothing we can do but stand by and wait to see what he means to do with his prize."

Tarod didn't reply. Unwillingly his thoughts were ranging back into the past, and he silently cursed the lapse that, by a terrible irony, had allowed an old error to be repeated. He among all of them should have been vigilant, for he knew from bitter experience what the loss of his soul stone could mean to a Chaos lord. They had been seven; now they were but six, for one of their brethren had been snatched to a limbo existence from which they had no power to restore him. And if the soul stone should be destroyed, then their helpless brother would be destroyed with it.

He felt rage beginning to boil within him, a white-hot fire at the core of his heart. Yandros, sensing it, turned to look at him with eyes that were suddenly dark and dangerous.

"No, my brother. We must control our fury, however deeply it galls us to do so." Tarod started to protest and Yandros held up a hand, forestalling him. "I said, *no*. It would be all too easy for us, Tarod. We know that Narid-na-Gost has fled to the mortal realm, and we could find him and bring him back and have the pleasure of putting his soul to an eternity of suffering for what he has done. But to strike against him now would risk bringing death to one of our number, and I will *not* take that risk under any circumstances."

"And if he begins to wreak havoc in the mortal world? What then?"

"My answer will be the same. Besides"—Yandros's eyes glittered with sudden venom—"you forget the pledge that we made when we overthrew Aeoris's rule. We can't concern ourselves with events in the mortal world unless we're called upon to do so."

Tarod hissed through clenched teeth. "Damn the pledge! What's more important?"

"Believe me, I agree with you—and if it were merely a question of principle, our promise would count for nothing. However, there's another complication." His eyes became harsher still. "The small matter of our old friend Aeoris. If we break our bargain, then we also free the lords of Order from the stricture we imposed on them. That would give Aeoris the chance he has been waiting for, to try to snatch back control of human affairs and strike a crippling blow to us at the same time. He *will* try, Tarod, be assured of it. If he learns of our predicament, he'll exploit it in any way he can."

Yandros turned back to the tormented land shifting far, far below the crag where they stood, and as he stared out across the awesome vista, a cold, harsh glow appeared in the sky, hanging low on the numbingly distant horizon. Out of the gloom a gigantic seven-rayed star took shape and began to pulse in a slow, implacable rhythm, sending spears of nacreous light throbbing out across the night.

"I would destroy the mortal world and all in it, if that alone would restore our brother's soul," Yandros said contemplatively. His voice was old and savage and lethal. "Yet it would gain us nothing. We're at stalemate, Tarod, and until and unless we are called into the mortal world, there's nothing we can do." He glanced obliquely at the other Chaos lord, and his eyes changed suddenly to hot scarlet. "Nothing but wait and watch. But in time we'll find a way to break this deadlock. And when we do . . ." The fluctuating light of the great star suddenly pulsed more strongly, highlighting his face in unhuman relief, and for one moment everything that he was, everything that he represented—the pure, insane incarnation of Chaos—radiated from his gaunt frame to dwarf the power of the distant star.

"And when we do," Yandros said softly, "there will be a reckoning."

They stood together at the top of the giant staircase that swept down the White Isle's steep flank. The storm was passing, only a few echoes of distant thunder were audible now, and in the southeast a slash of livid sunlight broke the dark overcast near the horizon as the clouds began to clear.

From here the grim, narrow inlet of the old harbor looked no larger than a vein on Ygorla's own hand. She gazed down at it for a few moments; then a light hand came to rest on her shoulder and Narid-na-Gost, at her side, said:

"Are you ready, daughter?"

"Yes." Her eyes shone almost as richly as the sapphire light of the soul stone. "I am ready!"

She extended an imperious hand toward the staircase and felt power rise in her. They began to move, gliding over the great steps without once touching them, traveling steadily, graciously, effortlessly down the huge flight. Ygorla's black hair streamed behind her, though there was no wind now, and Narid-na-Gost watched her face with pride and satisfaction. Such changes he had wrought in her since the night of her first stumbling and uncontrolled attempts to explore her latent talents. Now she used her skills with a consummate and careless ease that made mockery of this world's precious Circle, whose members were deluded enough to call themselves adepts of the occult arts. Beside Ygorla they were as dim candles to the midday sun. As a sorceress she had no equal, as a beauty she was matchless; and Narid-na-Gost was reminded of an old, sardonic curse, thinly disguised as a blessing.

May your lives be deeply interesting. Though they didn't yet know it, the lives of many, many people were about to become more deeply interesting than their worst nightmares could predict. From his vantage point at the background of Ygorla's stage in the theater of the mortal world, Narid-na-Gost would greatly enjoy the spectacle.

He came out of his reverie and realized that they were approaching the foot of the vast staircase. Rock walls towered to either side of them, masking the brightening sky as the stairs cut through the island's protecting cliff ramparts.

They turned in one final sweeping curve and the harbor lay before them.

Ygorla released her hold on the small magic that had carried them down the flight, and they came to rest on the pavement of the harbor quay. Dank and moss-grown, eternally shadowed from the sun by the vertiginous cliffs, the harbor reeked of desolation. Forty feet or more below the quayside, the sea looked stagnant and oily as it shifted listlessly against the eroded stone.

Narid-na-Gost gazed around him and his lip curled with distaste and with a hint of contempt.

"Many years ago one very particular ship was moored here," he said. The cliff walls threw back cold echoes of his voice. "They called it the White Bark—Aeoris's own ship, it was said, a relic from the centuries of Order's rule."

Ygorla looked obliquely at him. "What became of it?"

"Who knows?" The demon shrugged. "Perhaps it sailed away to another harbor beyond this dimension, or perhaps it simply fell apart as it should have done centuries before, and sank. Either way, it's long gone and forgotten, and of no more moment than the self-styled pilgrims who came after it. *Pilgrims.*" He enunciated the word with heavy sarcasm. "The pious and the curious, and the greedy who hoped to find treasure or relics and scurry home with a fortune hidden in their coats." He leaned toward the quay edge and spat deliberately into the water. The sea hissed briefly as though a burning ember had struck its surface.

Ygorla stared thoughtfully at the scene, her eyes narrowed as she pictured how the harbor might have looked with the pilgrim vessels tied to the giant capstans, dwarfed by the awesome scenery about them. It must have been many, many years since the last such boat had visited these shores.

"Many years indeed." Occasionally Narid-na-Gost's ability to know her thoughts still gave her a quick, startled frisson. She turned her head and saw the demon smiling at her.

"But today," he said, "the White Isle is to be graced by a new vessel." Turning to face the grim inlet, he tilted his head back and uttered the most terrible sound that Ygorla had ever heard. It was like the voice of a ghastly, supernatural hunting horn, harsh and clear and ominous; it rang starkly out over the water, shouting between the lowering cliffs and echoing chillingly to the sky. A thousand cold needles pricked Ygorla's skin as she heard it—and then around a curve in the inlet something appeared. It was huge, black and shapeless and as yet indistinct in the gloom, and it moved slowly, ponderously toward them. She heard the groan and creak of timber, the snap and rattle of canvas moving sluggishly in the thick air, the sullen rumble of the tide beneath the thrust of a keel.

And the towering ship emerged into the harbor, gliding with dreadful grace to dock gently at the quayside.

"Lady," Narid-na-Gost said, and lifted Ygorla's fingers to his lips to kiss them in affectionate parody, "your bark awaits your pleasure!"

It was utterly black. Black sails like the wings of some bird of ill omen. Black masts, spearing the sky. Black hull, high and proud and awesome, the forecastle looming over her and casting its own black shadow. At the prow a single lamp burned with a black radiance that gave no illumination but seemed rather to suck in and devour the pallid daylight from the air around it.

On the main deck the ship's crew stood at their posts among the shrouds. A few—a very few—were still clothed in flesh, but their flesh was the dismal gray-green of the seabed, their hair transmuted into rank, straggling tendrils of weed. The others, those who had no flesh and no hair, could only smile the ghastly rictus of the long dead from leprous skulls of brown, decaying bone. Weed and seashells clothed them in the place of fabrics that had rotted away to nothing years ago. And, feral pinpoints amid the ship's all-embracing darkness, white embers burned in the empty sockets where their eyes had once been.

Ygorla gazed at the ship and its grisly crew, and began to smile. *Hers.* Hers to command, hers to order as she pleased. A fit vessel to take her from this island on which she had been incarcerated for so long and to carry her back to the world of humanity. Now she knew what her destination was to be. The throne of thrones; the Margravate of Margravates. The seat of this world's highest ruler. A triumphal progress and a triumphal entry, in a ship of Chaos crewed by dead men who had been called by sorcery from their sea graves, with her banners of terror flying at the masthead.

She turned to look at her demon father, and something that transcended mortal understanding passed emphatically between them. Narid-na-Gost, too, was smiling now, and he held out one hand toward the ship in a gracious gesture.

Ygorla laughed, a short, sharp bark of a laugh that ricocheted discordantly between the cliffs. She glanced down at herself, made a careless, sweeping move with her fingers, and stood robed in a silver gown that flowed about her body as though it were a living symbiote. Black fur cloaked her, and in her hair, strung across her brow like a constellation, seven gems of blinding brilliance shone out to challenge the grim day.

She took her father's hand at last and faced the black ship. From the deck, a wave of intense darkness emerged, flowing toward them until it spanned the yawing gap between the quay and the now silent vessel. Not hesitating, Ygorla set foot on it and walked with regal grace to the deck. Shapes moved to greet her; a skeleton hand to which a few decaying strands of sinew still clung reached out to assist her. She scorned it and stepped onto the black planking with Narid-na-Gost behind her. As she turned to survey her new domain, eerie sounds broke the stillness—the soft slither of seaweed, the slide and click of bone on bone as her dead crew bowed low and gave her homage.

Overhead the giant black sails moaned as an unnatural wind sprang up to fill them. Dead hands, imbued still with the skills of the long-vanished minds which had once controlled them, fell to the ropes, and the grim cliff walls shifted, gliding into new perspective as slowly the vessel turned about to face the inlet and the Bay of Illusions beyond.

Like a demonic queen among her abominable legions, Ygorla stood in the prow, a shimmering, ethereal figure.

She gazed fixedly ahead, her eyes as hard and as brilliant as the jewels at her brow. And her wild, joyous laughter echoed into the brightening morning as the ship set sail for the open sea.

Here is a preview from

THE PRETENDER
by Louise Cooper
Book 2 of *The Chaos Gate Trilogy*

Hidden for seven years on the White Isle, Ygorla comes of age in *The Pretender*—and into the full, awesome power of her demonic heritage. Her ambition is clear-cut. She means to rule. Under her aegis a new reign of terror will dawn on the world, and no mortal power, not even the full might of the Circle itself, can stand in her way.

The High Initiate's only hope is to appeal directly to the gods of Order and Chaos, to break the pact they established at the time of Equilibrium and take a hand in mortal affairs once more. . . .

Though he'd always been a good sailor Strann firmly believed in the wisdom of not tempting providence, and so an hour after dawn he was making his way toward Shu-Nhadek's harbor with two small offerings to cast on the sea in hope of securing a calm voyage. He was also nursing the grandfather of all headaches, but that was something he'd long been accustomed to, and the vile-tasting herbal draught he'd forced himself to drink before leaving the Full Moons would chase away the miasms soon enough.

There would be no ceremony to mark his departure. Those guests who hadn't managed to stagger to their homes after the night's revels were still snoring under Koord's roof, and even Yya had been dead to the world when he slipped out of bed and gathered his belongings together in the early light. It was a pleasant enough morning, fresh and bright after the squalls of the last two days, and the brisk westerly wind smelled bracingly of salt. A fair day to be putting out to sea, and by the time he arrived at the quayside where the cargo ship *Cloudfisher* waited for its quota of passengers Strann's stomach and spirits felt considerably improved.

He made his offerings, throwing the two flower garlands on the tide's oily surface with due solemnity. One tribute to the gods of Chaos and one to the gods of Order; it was prudent, he believed, to show no preferences. Some of the *Cloudfisher*'s crew watched him from the deck but made no comment, and at last, shouldering the bags containing his precious manzon and a few changes of clothes—Koord would take care of the rest of his possessions until he returned—Strann walked up the gently flexing gangplank.

In addition to the twenty or so passengers who had business on Summer Isle, *Cloudfisher* was carrying a fair tonnage of food and wine from Shu, Prospect, and Southern Chaun provinces to the High Margrave's court, and the smells of her cargo mingled headily in the cramped quarters below decks. Even though the herbal draught had settled his queasy stomach Strann decided to find himself a place up by the forward rail where he could enjoy the fresher scents of the sea, and as the ship dipped out into the Bay of Illusions, seeming to curtsy an acknowledgment to her home harbor as she met the stronger currents, he settled down to enjoy the voyage. For some hours he sat comfortably propped against a pile of coiled ropes, alternately dozing and gazing at the steadily moving seascape ahead, until eventually he was woken from a half-formed dream by a shadow falling across his face.

"Good day to you, Master Strann. How are you enjoying the voyage?"

Strann opened his eyes and squinted up at the silhouette which towered over him.

"Captain Fyne." He struggled into a more upright position and took off his hat in a courteous salute. "I'm enjoying the voyage greatly, and counting my luck in having a calm day for it."

Fyne Cais Haslo, *Cloudfisher*'s master, grunted agreement and hunkered down beside him. "We've been lucky, I'll say that. All the soothsayers predicted more rain."

"Which only goes to show that you shouldn't listen to soothsayers. I should know; I saw enough of their chicanery in my fairground days."

"I don't doubt it." Fyne smiled drily. "Though that must be a good few years ago now, eh? From huckster to court favorite's a long road."

Strann wondered for a moment if there was a sour note lurking behind the captain's words, then saw the mischief in his eyes and relaxed as he realized what this was leading up to.

"True," he said, "but I don't forget my origins. And to save you the trouble of asking, yes, I'd be glad to help the ship's company pass the voyage with a song or two. I've a few new stories of events in Han and Wishet that may not have reached your ears yet."

Fyne reddened, but only briefly before his expression cleared and he laughed, a deep, chesty sound. "Well, you don't waste time tacking about. How did you know that I meant to approach you?"

"It's a hazard of my profession." Strann grinned. "When we landlubbers meet you seagoing men in a tavern, don't we invariably start talking to you about winds and tides and shiplore? Well, by the same rule, wherever I go I'm asked to sing songs and pass on the latest gossip. And I'm always glad to oblige. Mind"—he looked about him—"I'll need to find a more sheltered place than this if I'm to play any music. Salt spray and my manzon don't make a happy combination."

Fyne nodded toward the stern. "There's plenty of space under the aft bulkheads, and they're well protected from whatever the sea throws at us."

"Well then, Captain, I'm at your disposal." Strann got to his feet. "How long, do you think, before we sight Summer Isle?"

"Oh . . . an hour, perhaps a little more if the wind teases

us. Then probably the best part of another hour to reach harbor."

Two hours to harbor: say, then, an hour of entertainment. He could put on a fair enough performance in that time, Strann thought, and if he gave the crew good value Fyne might see his way to refunding at least part of his passage fee at the end of the voyage. Even if he didn't—and it was unlikely, for Strann knew the captain to be a generous man—it would give him the opportunity to try out one or two of the new songs he'd prepared for the High Margrave's celebration.

He heaved his packs onto his shoulders and would have started along the deck, but a disembodied voice suddenly drifted down from above.

"*Captain!*" The lookout, high in the crow's nest at the top of the mainmast, was an indistinguishable black smudge against the brilliant sky, but his cry was clear enough. "*Storm!*"

Fyne's head jerked up. "What?"

"*Storm ahead, sir!*"

The captain said something that made even Strann raise his eyebrows, and swung round to scan the horizon. There was nothing to be seen but the calm ocean, the bright sun, a few placid and isolated white clouds.

Fyne raised his head again, and his voice bellowed up like a bull-roarer. "What are you raving about, you bloody idiot? There's no storm, within a hundred miles of here!"

The lookout's voice floated back despairingly: "But sir—"

"Sir be damned! Get down from your perch at the double, and don't—" And he stopped abruptly as a sudden gust of wind scudded across the deck, ruffling his hair and lifting the brim of Strann's hat.

Strann hastily clamped a hand to his hat to stop it from blowing away. The precaution was needless; the gust had vanished as swiftly and suddenly as it had sprung up. But Fyne's angry expression had changed to one of puzzlement.

"That gust came from the east." He spoke softly, glancing up to where the ratlines quivered as the lookout began his agile descent. "Odd. . . ."

Strann frowned. "Pardon my ignorance, but why odd?"

"What?" Fyne looked at him in some surprise, as though he'd momentarily forgotten Strann's existence. Then abruptly his eyes focused. "Why? Because it was in direct opposition to the prevailing wind, and that's not natural."

"It was just one gust," Strann said, hoping he sounded

more nonchalant than he felt and surreptitiously touching the iron band on a nearby belaying pin for luck. "Probably means nothing."

Fyne grunted noncommittally. "Maybe. Nonetheless—"

This time the sudden cold slap came from the south, and it snatched Strann's hat off his head before he could react. He opened his mouth to shout an indignant protest, but the wind whipped his voice away too, and both he and Fyne staggered under its onslaught. They heard a yell from the frightened lookout, still suspended in the rigging; *Cloudfisher* heeled sharply and the sails roared as the squall filled them and beat them against the masts. For a few seconds there was nothing but shouting, buffeting confusion—and then, just as before, the wind vanished in the space of a moment.

"Gods . . ." Strann's ears rang in the sudden quiet; he found himself clinging to the rail as though it were a long-lost lover, and slowly slackened his grip. "What in the name of the seven hells was *that*?"

Fyne didn't answer, and Strann walked unsteadily along the deck to retrieve his hat, which lay forlornly some twenty paces away. As he returned, the lookout, who by a combination of instinct and grim determination had managed to keep his hold on the ratlines, came scrambling and slithering down to the deck, jumping the last ten feet. His face was the color of bilge water.

"Captain, I—"

"All right, all right." Fyne silenced him with a sharp gesture; this wasn't the time for superfluous words. "What did you see out there?"

"L-lightning, sir." The sailor's teeth were chattering and he had difficulty forcing the words out. "Dead ahead. Southeasterly."

A sensation like a kitten's claws at the base of his spine made Strann's flesh shrink abruptly as memories stirred and mingled with an unpleasant sense of premonition. Fyne, unaware of his disquiet, glared at the lookout. "*Lightning?* In a clear sky?"

"It's what I saw, sir. It couldn't have been anything else." A pause. "But . . ."

"But *what*? Spit it out, for the gods' sakes!"

The sailor met his furious stare unhappily. "It was *red* lightning, sir. Crimson, like blood." He shivered. "And not a cloud anywhere. I've never seen anything like it before!"

Oh gods, Strann thought, *but I have. . . .*

Fyne swore softly. "Unnatural squalls, unnatural lightning—if I'm not drunk or deluded, then there's something uncanny afoot." He swung about, staring hard at the sea as though challenging the elements to play some new trick, but nothing happened. Fyne paused for a moment, considering his next move, then abruptly turned back to face the lookout.

"Right. I want every man at his station and the ship made ready for storm conditions." His voice was suddenly crisp and decisive as his mind moved on to familiar territory. "Send the first mate to me here—but don't do anything that might disquiet our passengers without my order. This may be a false alarm, and there's no point in creating needless worry."

The sailor saluted and sprinted away along the deck. When he was out of earshot, Strann said drily, "I fear, Captain Fyne, that one of your passengers is already very disquieted indeed."

Fyne looked at him, and was surprised by what he saw. Strann's face was sickly pale under its tan, and beads of sweat were banded across his forehead despite the wind's briskness. His studied nonchalance was slipping, and the effort he made to sound and seem lighthearted failed badly. Unaware of the underlying cause of his agitation, Fyne grinned sympathetically.

"Don't worry, Strann. The gods have never yet sent us a storm that *Cloudfisher* couldn't ride out, so you've little to fear apart from maybe a dose of seasickness." He hesitated. "All the same, I'd go below if I were you, and take your gear with you. At least that way you'll keep dry, and your talents might help to take the other passengers' minds off their predicament if we do get a rough blow."

Strann was tempted to say that the other passengers could rot or riot for all the difference it would make to him in his present state, but held the words back. He was beginning to feel sick with the peculiar and unmistakable queasiness of apprehension; his legs were growing less willing to support him with every moment, and he was suffering the first sensations of vertigo: all a warning that if he didn't get a grip on himself quickly he was in danger of losing control and panicking.

Red lightning, out of a clear sky. . . . An ugly, involuntary sound bubbled at the back of his throat, and Fyne said, "What?"

"Nn." Strann shook his head, dismissing the captain's

query with a hasty gesture. "Nothing; nothing. I'll . . . ah . . . take your advice, I think."

Fyne peered at him uncertainly. "You're sure you're all right? You're as white as a dead fish."

Strann wanted to be truthful and say, No, I'm not all right, there's something very unpleasant in the wind and because I'm a craven coward, I am at this moment terrified half out of my mind. But he wouldn't say it, firstly because he didn't want to make a fool of himself in Fyne's eyes and secondly because he didn't want to give the embryonic panic any fuel on which to feed by admitting the truth aloud.

"I'm fine, Fyne." He tried to grin at the unintended joke, but failed, and started to move along the deck, resisting an urge to grip the rail to steady himself. "I'll just go below, and— *Oh, Yandros!*"

The appalled yell startled Fyne, and for a moment he didn't see it; he knew only that Strann was staring out to sea and that his eyes were bulging in their sockets, his mouth working, gasping like a newly landed fish. Then, belatedly understanding, the captain looked toward the horizon.

The cloud was purplish black, the color of a fearsome bruise. It towered into the otherwise empty sky, and it was boiling into the shape of a vast anvil, the flattened, tapering head rising two miles or more above the sea. And it was moving—no, Fyne thought; this wasn't possible, it wasn't *possible*! No cloud could move at such a speed: seconds ago there had been nothing on the horizon, and now the entire southeasterly sky was filling with darkness as the monstrous thunderhead rolled toward them. This was no natural storm—it was something from a hell beyond imagining!

Suddenly the suffocating quiet was ripped apart by a stentorian voice from the ship's bows. *"Storm ahead! Storm ahead!"* To Strann it was like a physical blow, breaking the hypnosis that gripped him. He reeled back from the rail with a cry of horror and despair, and cannoned into Fyne as the captain started toward the source of the shout.

"Get below!" Fyne took Strann by the shoulders, spun him violently around, and shoved him in the direction of the companion steps. "Don't stand there gibbering, you fool—*get below*!"

Intelligence snapped back into Strann's eyes, and with it a renewal of his fear. He didn't speak—he couldn't, words were beyond him—but lurched away, hampered by his packs, staggering along the deck. He vanished through the hatch with a stumbling clatter, and Fyne swung round to face the approaching horror again. Now he could see what the lookout had seen: the lightning, the flickering, crimson tongues spitting like demonic fire in the heart of the darkness. Minutes—minutes, no more—and it would be on them. And for the first time in his life, Fyne knew what true terror was.

His hand went to his belt and he snatched from it a short brass horn. In all his days of seafaring he'd never used it, for the signal it sounded was a warning of the direst emergency and danger, and until now Fyne had been a lucky man. Now though, his luck, and the luck of his ship, had run out.

He put the horn to his lips, and blew. As the sharp, clear, and urgent note rang out, bringing the crew racing to their stations, the first bawl of thunder rolled across the sea to swamp *Cloudfisher* in a deafening wall of sound.

Even from the vantage point of this highest of all the palace towers, the horror unfolding in the Bay of Illusions was far beyond the scope of human vision. But the eyes that gazed down from the tower and across the well-tended acres of grounds to the distant harbor and the sea were not entirely human, and the mind behind the lovely face in its frame of jet-black hair was capable of reaching beyond ordinary dimensions to see and hear things that no ordinary mortal senses could discern.

She hadn't moved for upwards of half an hour. She had an uncanny ability to remain so still for so long that any observer could easily have taken her for a bizarrely lifelike statue, and only the slow, controlled rhythm of her breathing betrayed her and intruded on the silence.

Outside, the heavy overcast was almost complete and sunlight only broke through in a narrow, brazen scar to the south. In the tower room's deeper shadows, away from the window, a second figure sat hunched and watching the woman with an unwavering gaze. He was naked, and his red hair gleamed like embers in the semidarkness, hanging in ropes about his stunted and distorted frame. One hand rested on a nearby table; now and then the taloned fingers moved idly over the polished surface as though caressing it. He waited; and at last there was a long, gentle expulsion of breath, the woman's shoulders relaxed, and she turned to face him.

"We will have guests before too long, Father," she said. "I must make myself ready to receive them." A smile parted her lips, voluptuous but feral. "Our very first visitors from the mainland."

The red-haired demon returned a smile that more than matched hers. "Go then, child. And make sure they see you at your most magnificent."

"Oh, I will." She glanced back toward the window. The sliver of sunlight had vanished, swallowed by cloud, but at a gesture from her hand another light began to creep in from the world outside. It was dull, copper-colored, and as it grew stronger it began to fluctuate like the pulse of a slow and massive heart. The woman smiled again, and when she turned back to face her father the light flung her figure into silhouette and throbbed behind her like an ominous aura.

"What will you do with them?" the demon asked softly.

"I haven't yet decided. But I'll find a use for them. One way or another, I'll find a use." Silk rustled as she began to move across the room, then she paused by the table and looked down at a small, ornate casket that rested on the surface. It was a deliberate mockery of another and far older box which she'd never seen, but which all the history tracts described in detail, and it amused her to think of the use to which this virtual twin was now being put. Her fingers hovered near the catch; the demon looked obliquely up at her and she held his gaze for a moment, then withdrew her hand.

"No," she said. "I don't need to see it again. I know it's there: that's enough." She looked into a small, oval mirror that hung on the wall behind the demon, and pushed her hair back from her face, turning her head to study her reflection from a variety of angles. Then she threw a last glance over her shoulder.

"Watch the audience room in the scrying glass, Father. I plan to entertain our guests in ways that I suspect you'll find quite amusing."

The demon listened to the sound of her light footsteps skimming away down the tower stairs. For a few moments after they had faded there was silence, then a thin, silver-tongued bell sang somewhere below and he heard his daughter's voice calling sharply for her servants. He smiled once more, indulgently and yet with faint cynicism, and ran his hand fondly, possessively over the lid of the casket before rising and moving toward the window, from where, unseen, he could observe the outside world and await the guests' arrival.

* * *

The hoarsely shouted words "Land ho!" were, Strann thought, the sweetest he had ever heard in his eventful life, and more precious to him than the truest promises of love or money or acclaim. With a great creaking of damaged timbers and groaning of torn canvas, *Cloudfisher* lurched through the choppy water, and the grimly determined chants of the rowers at their benches below decks vied with the noises of the elements as what was left of the sails bellied to the sudden thrust of a strong following wind.

Strann picked himself up from the floor of the big communal cabin, trying to ignore the stinks of sweat and vomit that were threatening to make his stomach rebel afresh. He'd long ago lost his breakfast, not from seasickness but through blind and shaming fear; and even when the danger and the horror were over it had been a long time before he could force his muscles to move. He didn't know how long the storm had lasted or even how bad it had been. Throughout its duration—minutes? hours? days?—he had been in the grip of a terror that had reduced him to a piece of physical and mental flotsam curled amongst his hapless fellow passengers on the cabin floor with his eyes tight shut and his fingers jammed into his ears. Only when he had forced himself to believe that the scream of the gale and the crack and thunder of the lightning bolts had finally ceased had he regained any self-control, and even now his grip on himself was precarious. He didn't want to think about the storm. He didn't want to think about what the *Cloudfisher*'s crew, battling in the midst of black mayhem to save their ship and passengers, might have seen and faced up on deck, and he certainly didn't want to think about his own cowardice. All he wanted was to feel solid ground beneath his feet, dry land where he could crawl away and nurse himself back to something like sanity. And—if his stomach would only tolerate it—a very, very large quantity of liquor to send him into blissful and dreamless sleep.

He realized, as he found his feet and began to move slowly toward the companion steps, that he was alone in the cabin. He must have been the last to recover his wits, and the knowledge made him feel ashamed of his weakness in giving way to the terror and the panic. Damn it, he was a Master of the Musical Arts, a true bard and not some posturing amateur! He of all people should have been ready to distract his companions and soothe their fears, but instead he'd shivered like a rat in a trap and proved himself worse than useless. He was disgusted with himself—the more so as terror receded and his confidence started to crawl back—and for a moment he saw in his mind's eye the face of his old master at the Guild Academy of Musicians; the same man who had subsequently, and successfully, pressed for his removal from the guild's roll of honor for disreputable behavior. The old vulture would have liked to see him now, Strann thought. He would have nodded his head sagely and smiled the smile of triumphant vindication. At this moment Strann couldn't in all conscience have argued with him.

He reached the steps and started to climb unsteadily toward the deck. Daylight was slanting down from above. Cold air laden with the tang of salt slapped against his face and he paused to take several deep and grateful breaths before completing the climb. As his head emerged through the hatch and he instinctively looked up, he had a sharp shock, for where the sails should have towered in their full glory only a few tattered remnants clung to the masts and struggled to hold and take advantage of the wind. Beyond them the sky was washed to a clean and hard blue: all traces of the storm had vanished, but it had taken its toll on the ship. The top third of the mainmast itself had snapped off, leaving a jagged spear pointing toward the sky, and broken spars and torn rigging were tangled like monstrous seaweed in the sails' remains. *Cloudfisher* was listing sharply to port, and over the noises of sea and wind, shouts, running feet, and, from somewhere below, a rhythmic thumping as men frantically worked the bilge pumps, the voice of the first mate roared orders and encouragement in equal measure.

Strann shook his head in an effort to clear his mazed mind, then looked about for Fyne Cais Haslo. At last he saw the captain in the forecastle, surrounded by a knot of anxious-looking passengers. Fyne was holding a spyglass to one eye, and Strann hauled himself out of the hatch and made his way along the wet and slippery deck to join the group. As he reached them, Fyne lowered the spyglass, saw him and nodded brief acknowledgment. His expression was tense and uncertain.

Strann swallowed back the sickness, which the lurching of the ship had brought welling up again. "Is something wrong?"

"No. No, I don't think so." But Fyne's eyes belied his words. A painfully thin woman beside him suddenly reached out and clutched at his arm.

"We're going to sink, aren't we?" Her voice was shrill, on

the edge of hysteria. "The ship's holed! We're going to be drowned!"

"Madam, I tell you again, the ship is *not* holed." Fyne turned wearily toward her, trying to pry her fingers from his sleeve. "She's battered and bruised, but she's still perfectly seaworthy—I assure you, you're in no danger!"

For the first time Strann saw clearly just how exhausted the captain was, and it shamed him afresh. It was almost impossible to imagine the sheer skill and seamanship that Fyne and his crew must have displayed in bringing the ship through the storm: he and the other passengers owed these men their lives, and that was a sobering realization. Yet he had a disquieting feeling that all was not entirely well. Not the ship herself: Strann had no reason to doubt Fyne's assurances to the frightened woman that *Cloudfisher* was in no danger of sinking. But something else. Something else. . . .

He said, "We're in sight of land?"

"Yes." Fyne couldn't quite suppress the small frown that appeared on his face. "Summer Isle's in sight. We should put in to harbor within half an hour." The frown deepened. "That in itself's a miracle from the gods. I'd thought we'd been blown miles off course by that—that *thing*." He shuddered.

Strann couldn't help it; his curiosity was stronger than his prudence, and goaded by the uneasy instinct. "That . . . *is* Summer Isle ahead?" he ventured.

Fyne shot him a filthy look. "Of course it's Summer Isle. What do you take me for?"

"No, no; forgive me, I didn't mean to imply any slight. But you seem a little . . ." Strann paused, then reasoned that he'd already cast tact overboard and caution might as well follow. "You don't look entirely happy at the prospect of making landfall."

Fyne turned fully to face him. *"Happy?"* he repeated incredulously. "After what my crew and my ship have been through, you don't think I'm *happy* to see land ahead of me? Aeoris's eyes, man, you must be either jesting or mad!"

Several of the other passengers laughed at this, releasing nervous tension, and even the thin woman managed to smile. But as Fyne made his excuses and left the forecastle, Strann stared thoughtfully after him, then on impulse followed him down the steps and along the deck toward *Cloudfisher*'s stern.

"Captain Fyne."

Fyne stopped and turned round. They were out of earshot of the other passengers now, and Strann looked the other man directly in the eye. Gently, he said, "I don't believe you."

Fyne stared back, and for a moment Strann thought he might have overstepped the bounds. But then with an abrupt gesture the captain held out his spyglass.

"Summer Isle lies thirty degrees off our starboard bow," he said brusquely. "Take a look through this, and tell me what you see."

Strann took the glass and put it to his eye. At first he could see nothing but the blurred images of the torn sails; then Fyne guided his arm until the glass was focusing on the sea. A coastline slid into view—Strann was impressed by the glass's power, for the image was clear and sharp—and then he saw the familiar curve of harbor walls, like two arms reaching out to embrace the ocean.

"I see Summer Isle harbor," he said.

"Yes. And what else?"

Strann was nonplussed. "What else should I look for?"

A pause. Then Fyne said, "Try looking for ships."

Realization dawned. Slowly, Strann lowered the glass, and his hazel eyes narrowed as he turned to stare at the captain.

"The harbor's empty."

"Precisely."

"But—"

"But with guests coming from all over the provinces for the High Margrave's celebrations there should be vessels of every size, shape, and color you can think of at anchor in that harbor today." Fyne took the glass from him; Strann released it as though all the strength had suddenly gone from his fingers. "Why, Strann? You're the storyteller: what manner of story is this?"

"I . . ." Strann's voice caught; he tried again. "I don't know."

"Neither do I. But there's something peculiar afoot, and now that the passengers can't hear me I'm prepared to admit that I don't like the look of it." Suddenly he scowled. "I don't want anyone starting an alarm, do you understand? If you say one word to anyone—"

"No," Strann assured him hastily. "You have my promise. And I apologize"—he nodded back toward the forecastle—"for speaking out of turn." He paused. "Though I don't know how much difference my silence or yours will make. They'll see the truth for themselves soon enough."

"Maybe so. But by then we'll be dropping anchor and there'll be no question of turning back. The men are exhausted, and I won't sanction a return voyage to Shu-Nhadek in our present state. I intend to put in to harbor and I don't want any arguments about it. Whatever's waiting for us can't pose a greater risk than trying to get this ship back to the mainland without repairs."

Strann nodded. "I understand. And, self-preserving coward that I am, I agree that it's the only sensible course."

"Sensible?" Fyne eyed him sharply. " 'Sane' would be a better word with the damage we've suffered; and that's something else that I don't want you babbling to all and sundry."

"Depend on it."

The captain continued to look at him for a few seconds more, as though trying to decide whether or not Strann could be trusted to keep silent. Then, abruptly, he nodded.

"Well, then. There's work to be done and I'm not about to leave it all to my subordinates. We'll reach harbor in about half an hour, as I said: then we'll see what's what."

He strode away, leaving Strann alone and distinctly unhappy.

Despite Fyne's hopes, the realization that something was amiss on Summer Isle couldn't be avoided as *Cloudfisher* approached harbor. A chance word from a thoughtless crewman, sharp eyes and sharp minds among the passengers, and the heightened state of tension that already existed on board all played their part, and as the ship yawed toward the twin arms of the harbor wall her bows were crowded with people staring anxiously shoreward. Strann was among them, though he wasn't overanxious to shoulder his way through to the rail for a better view. And when the murmuring began, and rapidly swelled into cries first of chagrin and then of alarm, he felt the sinking crawl of horror in the pit of his stomach.

"What in the gods' names—?"

"I've never seen anything like—"

"What is it?"

"Aeoris! Look there—look!"

"There! There's more of them!"

"They're all—"

"Back now, ladies and gentlemen." Fyne strode into the midst of the crowd. "Stand back now, please." His voice was steady but his eyes gave away the feelings and the fear that he wouldn't allow himself to show. Three crewmen followed behind him, gently but firmly shepherding people away from the rail, and slowly the press began to clear. Fyne flashed a quick look at one of the sailors and spoke quietly.

"Take them below, and persuade them to stay there in their own best interests."

"Sir." The passengers began to move away, and for the first time Strann had a clear view of the scene beyond *Cloudfisher*'s bow.

The harbor wasn't entirely empty. A solitary ship was moored to the main pier, rocking gently on the water's surface. The vessel—of a design like nothing else Strann had ever seen—was entirely black from stem to stern: black hull, black masts, black sails hanging unnaturally still like crows' wings at rest. Her prow bore no figurehead and she boasted no name. She looked utterly deserted.

And then Strann saw that, contrary to first impressions, there were people on the quayside. Or at least, men. With the momentary appalling clarity that shock brought to his senses he realized that there must have been a hundred or more of them, some in sailors' or stevedores' or harbor officials' garb, others in the distinctive uniform of the High Margrave's personal guard. A hundred or more, littering the docks and the harbor front beyond in a bloody carnage of broken, twisted corpses, and without a single survivor to be glimpsed among them.

The Chaos Gate Trilogy is an epic story of struggle among gods, demons, and men. In *The Pretender* the High Initiate is faced with a terrible and potentially deadly dilemma, for if the two ancient adversaries Order and Chaos are summoned back to the world, humanity must face the awesome prospect of being trapped again between the warring factions and becoming pawns in a lethal game.

The High Initiate must somehow choose between the two age-old enemies. But in making his choice he is unaware that, on Summer Isle, a new and unlikely player is about to take his place upon the stage. . . .

Watch for *The Pretender*, Book 2 of *The Chaos Gate Trilogy*, on sale from Bantam Books in April 1991.

ABOUT THE AUTHOR

Born in Hertfordshire, England, in 1952, LOUISE COOPER says she "hated school" as a child; she completed her formal education at the age of fifteen. She had already begun to write stories by then, and continued to do so while working at what she describes as "a succession of thoroughly detested office jobs." She married in 1970 and in 1973 published her first novel, *The Book of Paradox*. In 1975 she and her husband, Gary, moved to London, where she worked at two leading paperback publishing houses and continued to write novels, finally turning to writing full time in 1977. Her first major success was the *Time Master* trilogy (to which the *Chaos Gate* trilogy is a sequel). Among her other novels are *Nemesis, Mirage*, and *The Thorn Key*. She enjoys cats, cooking, gardening, steam locomotives, and music.